Praise for *The Good Thief's Guide* series

'Chris Ewan [is] at the vanguard of a new wave of young writers kicking against the clichés and producing ambitious, challenging, genre-bending works [and] adding some wit and balls to [the] genre' Bateman

'With a nimble touch and effortless charm, *The Good Thief's Guide to Vegas* carries us along on an utterly irresistible sin-city caper filled with high-stakes gambling, cunning stagecraft and a dizzying series of twists Ewan pulls off with the skills of a master illusionist' Megan Abbott, Edgar Award-winning author of *Queenpin* and *Bury Me Deep*

'In Charlie Howard, Chris Ewan has created one of contemporary fiction's most unlikely yet likeable heroes – a razor-sharp Raffles for the 21st century, whose easy expertise in the dubious arts of breaking and entering intrigues as much as it entertains. Wacky, witty and above all great fun, The Good Thief's guide to Vegas moves at a blistering pace through the sleazy backrooms of Las Vegas's casinos, and – with more plot twists than a corkscrew – delivers a satisfying but unexpected denouement, and happily leaves the door open to Charlie's next adventure' Anne Zouroudi, author of the *Mysteries of the Greek Detective* series

'A stylish and assured debut that introduces the fascinating Charlie Howard. Let's hope Charlie's as much of a recidivist as Highsmith's Ripley, cause he's a character you'll definitely want to see more of' Allan Guthrie, author of Two-Way Split, winner of the Theakston's Crime Novel

Chris Ewan's acclaimed debut, *The Good Thief's Guide to Amsterdam*, won the Long Barn Books First Novel Award. Both *Amsterdam* and *The Good Thief's Guide to Paris* were shortlisted for CrimeFest's Last Laugh Award for the best humorous crime novel of the year.

Chris lives in a small village in the Isle of Man with his wife, Jo, and their labrador, Maisie, where he spends his days planning imaginary burglaries and learning how to pick locks. His neighbours are thrilled.

Find out more at: www.thegoodthief.co.uk

THE GOOD THIEF'S GUIDE TO VENICE

CHRIS EWAN

SIMON &
SCHUSTER

London · New York · Sydney · Toronto

A CBS COMPANY

First published in Great Britain by Simon & Schuster UK Ltd, 2011
A CBS COMPANY

1 3 5 7 9 10 8 6 4 2

Simon & Schuster UK Ltd
1st Floor
222 Gray's Inn Road
London WC1X 8HB

www.simonandschuster.co.uk

Simon & Schuster Australia
Sydney

A CIP catalogue record for this book
is available from the British Library

ISBN 978-1-84739-959-5

Typeset by M Rules
Printed in the UK by CPI Cox & Wyman, Reading, Berkshire RG1 8EX

For Vivien Green and Susan Hill,
who gave this writer his break.

ONE

There was a burglar in my apartment, and for once it wasn't me.

I knew it wasn't me because my intruder was stomping round my living room, bumping into furniture, and I'm a stealthy kind of thief. Added to that, I hadn't picked a lock or cracked a crib or been anywhere unbidden since I'd first set foot in Venice, almost a year ago. What's more – and this really closed the case for me – I was tucked up in bed, scribbling a few notes at just after 2 a.m.

Actually, you can scratch that last bit. I don't want to be accused of being anything but straight with you, so perhaps I should say that I wasn't simply jotting down frivolous ideas. In truth, I was thinking of ways to transform my latest Michael Faulks novel into something that might turn my life around for good – my breakout book. Except now my attention had been snatched away by what appeared to be a *break-in*.

Hmm.

I hopped out of bed in my boxer shorts and crept to the door of my room. Peering along the darkened hallway, I could see the glow of torchlight.

Now, as a general rule – and perhaps this is just me being terribly old-fashioned – I've always preferred to burgle places that are empty. In my experience, it makes the whole enterprise a lot more enjoyable and the chances of being caught a good deal less likely. Sadly, my unexpected visitor appeared to disagree. Either that, or he hadn't done his homework, and whichever it was, I wasn't altogether keen to point out his error. Then again, I wasn't altogether keen to stand idly by as he ripped me off.

But what could I do? I didn't own a gun, or anything that could be mistaken for one. There were knives in the kitchen, just off the living room, but I didn't relish the idea of waving a blade around. Sure, it'd be dandy if my intruder went all weak at the knees, held up his palms and sat nice and quiet while the boys in *azzurro* found their way to my home, but suppose he came at me and got hold of the knife and plunged it somewhere soft and fleshy that I'd rather it didn't go?

The torch swept the living room slowly, as if the person holding the flashlight believed they had all the time in the world. When the beam hit a certain angle, I could almost make out the shape of Mr Curious through the internal glass doors. He didn't strike me as an ogre, but neither was he a waif. He seemed broadly average, except that the average Venetian resident doesn't make a habit of breaking into people's homes –

least of all when the front door of the home in question has been fitted with quality locks by an experienced thief.

I smiled in the darkness. Thinking of my door had given me an idea. No, I wasn't about to run outside and rouse a vigilante mob – I'd simply remembered the coat hooks in my hallway. And I'd also remembered the umbrella hanging from one of them.

The umbrella was as long as my leg, with a black fabric canopy and a sturdy wooden handle. If I could get to it, I could swing it like a club, or jab it like a sword. Hell, if push came to shove, I could ram the thing in the bugger's mouth and open it inside his oesophagus.

I edged into the hallway and skulked through the dark on my toes, but I needn't have worried. My visitor was making so much noise striding around the living room that I could have bumbled into a drum kit without being heard. Funny, I'd always favoured baseball trainers when I was on the prowl, but this clown appeared to be wearing tap shoes.

I lifted the umbrella down from its hook. It felt heavy enough to do some serious damage, assuming I was really prepared to use it. I didn't know about that. Speaking as a thief, it was all too easy to put myself in his (very noisy) shoes, and I was reluctant to barge in and land a series of blows without waiting to gauge his reaction.

I rolled my shoulders and circled my neck, trying to loosen the tension from my muscles. Nope, didn't work. Wiping my brow with my forearm, I glanced down at my bare feet. I was naked aside from my boxer shorts and the umbrella. It didn't make me feel any better.

The light from the torch had settled on the wall at the end of the living room, exactly where my desk was positioned. My laptop was there. It contained the working draft of my novel. The *only* version.

I lifted my foot in the air and kicked the double doors hard. They spread like a split log and I burst through with the umbrella high above my head. The light from the torch hit me square in the eyes and I squinted and reeled, thumping into the wall and fumbling for the light switch. The room lit up brightly. I spread my feet and prepared to swing hard with the umbrella.

Nobody was coming for me.

My eyes were stinging and watering from the stark electric light. I squinted towards my desk. My laptop was still there. I swivelled left and finally I saw him.

Her.

She was blonde. Very blonde. A platinum wonder with a red painted smile on her full, plush lips. The teeth were white and dazzling, the eyes sparkling and alert. Her pose was provocative, taunting even. Shoulders back, chin up, she had one leg through my window and the other in my living room, straddling the sill. Long leather boots with high heels. Blue skinny jeans and a zipped leather jacket. A climbing harness around her waist.

All too slowly, I remembered the situation I was in.

'Who the hell are you?' I asked.

4

The smile grew wider. The head barely shook.

'What are you doing here?'

The plump lips puckered up and she raised a gloved finger to them. I gaped at her, unsure how to react, and before I was able to resolve the puzzle, her long lashes fluttered, her left eye closed in a wink and she leaned right back in a graceful curve and fell plumb from the window.

'Wait!'

Rushing across the room, I braced my hands on the crumbling ledge and thrust my head out into the foggy night air. I caught a flash of her torch, close to the shrouded canal water below. She had one hand gripping the rope she was lowering herself on and the other wedged behind her bottom. She glanced down just once before letting the rope slip free and dropped with a thud onto the flagstone pavement, the noise muffled by the soggy air.

'Hey!' I yelled. 'What the hell? Come back.'

Ignoring me, she freed the rope from her climbing harness, then stepped aboard a white speedboat, kicked off from the moss-clad canal bank with a grunt and reached for the starter cord. The engine fired with a throaty splutter and a blue diesel puff.

I tugged at the rope hanging beside my window. She'd secured it to the roof, which suggested she'd targeted my apartment from above. I gave some thought to lowering myself down to her – the kind of thought that's destined to go precisely nowhere – and meanwhile she cranked the throttle and sped off beneath a low, arched bridge in the direction of the lagoon, her blonde hair flickering in the misty darkness like a guttering flame. Within seconds she was gone, and all that remained was the slap of disturbed water, the stench of diesel in the dank air and the fading note of her engine rebounding from the walls of the crooked buildings that surrounded me.

I dragged my head back inside and shook it groggily, then turned to find my friend and literary agent, Victoria, emerging from her guest bedroom to do much the same thing. She stumbled towards me in spotted pyjamas and fluffy slippers, her hair like an Eighties revival night gone wrong and a slick of drool glistening on her chin.

'Charlie?' She yawned without covering her mouth. 'What's all the fuss?'

'Break-in,' I mumbled, cupping my hand to the back of my neck.

'My God. Anything gone?'

I looked again at my laptop, untouched on my desk. My notebooks and papers were there too.

'Nothing,' I told her.

But then my eyes drifted up to an empty space on the wall and my heart clenched with the sudden realisation of what I'd overlooked. Something was very much missing, and something else had been put in its place.

TWO

It's fair to say that most writers are superstitious. I've heard of authors who have to write with a favourite pen on a particular brand of writing paper, and others who can't begin a novel until they've completed some familiar ritual – like running a half-marathon, or clipping their toenails, or getting divorced. Me, I have two quirks that I'm aware of. I like to move to a new city when I'm about to start a book, and I always write with my framed first edition of *The Maltese Falcon* hanging above my desk.

The Maltese Falcon is my most valuable possession. It's worth a tidy sum – somewhere approaching six figures based on the last time a first edition came up at auction – which explains why I store it in an airtight picture frame. But more importantly, I've never succeeded in writing anything publishable without it watching over me. I've tried once or twice, just to see if the spell could be broken, but I've always found it impossible to get one of my burglar novels moving without the spirit of Sam Spade along for the ride. So, crazy as it might seem, *The Maltese Falcon* had become a kind of talisman for me.

And now it was gone, replaced by a square of red card.

'What is it?' Victoria asked. 'Charlie?'

I couldn't answer her. The best I could manage was to let go of a despairing wail and stagger towards the space on the wall where Hammett's novel used to be.

'For God's sake, speak to me.' Victoria clicked her fingers. 'What on earth is the matter?'

I passed my hand over the floral wallpaper, as if something of the book's magic still lingered. I wailed some more. I'm pretty sure my bottom lip trembled.

'Oh, Charlie,' Victoria said. 'Tell me they haven't taken your copy of *The Maltese Falcon*.'

I swallowed something the size and consistency of a cricket ball, then found my voice.

'Gone,' I croaked.

'Gone?'

I nodded.

'You bloody idiot. I said you should have kept it somewhere safe.'

Now, I firmly believe that if anyone else had uttered those words, I would have felt compelled to toss them out of the window into the shallow waters below. But since it was Victoria, I chose to let my shoulders sag instead.

'In fact,' she went on, in the manner of a dentist drilling two extra fillings for no particular reason, 'I distinctly remember warning you that something like this could happen. I believe I even mentioned that you, of all people, should have been aware of the risks.'

At this point, I confess that my patience began to fade just a smidgen, and I may have mumbled something a touch uncharitable.

'Excuse me?' she asked.

'I said, "Would you mind closing the window?"'

Victoria placed her hands on her hips and squinted at me. She tapped the toe of her slipper on the floor.

'It's getting cold,' I added, shivering for effect.

'You don't need to tell *me* that.'

She gave my torso a dubious once-over and I remembered how little I was wearing. The boxer shorts and umbrella didn't do a great deal to cover my modesty. I folded my arms across my chest. My arms didn't do a great deal to cover my modesty, either.

'I'll go and find some clothes.'

'You do that.' Victoria slammed the window closed against the dismal fog. 'And I'll put the kettle on. It appears we have some thinking to do.'

We had plenty of thinking to do, as it happens. First, we thought about who could have known about my Hammett novel. Then we thought about how we might set about identifying and tracking down a female cat burglar. But more than anything else, we thought about the square of red card she'd left behind.

It was about half the size of a paperback novel and it featured an image of an open book on one side. Printed in black ink on the pages of the book was a good deal of Italian text. My Italian was terrible, but we managed to make some sense of it with the help of a battered language dictionary.

From what we could decipher, the card was a flyer for a business that specialised in bookbinding and restoration, located in the district of San Marco. The intricate craft of bookbinding, and the stores that promote it, are very much a Venetian speciality. But for the life of me, I couldn't recall asking for any assistance with the preservation of my Hammett novel, and it was more than a little perverse to suppose that a shop might send a burglar to collect my book for restoration in the dead of night.

'This is weird,' Victoria told me, her hands wrapped around a steaming mug of English tea.

'You're telling me. I've heard of burglars leaving calling cards, but never anything like this.'

'Perhaps it's a guerrilla marketing campaign.'

'For a Venetian bookbinder?'

'Hmm, I suppose it is a touch aggressive.'

'You think?'

I slapped the language dictionary onto the wooden steamer trunk that functioned as my coffee table and placed the card on top. I was perched on the rickety dining chair I used when I was writing. Victoria was sitting on the leather chesterfield across from me, her legs and feet folded beneath her and hidden by the pink dressing gown she'd put on.

There wasn't a lot of furniture in my apartment, and much of what there was hailed from England. The building I lived in was owned by the retired couple in the maisonette below – a former GP from Cambridge and his Italian wife – who'd furnished each floor with the belongings they'd brought with them to Venice more than a decade before. The apartment above me was currently unoccupied, as it was likely to remain for another few weeks until the tourist season picked up for *Carnevale* in February.

Victoria had been in my apartment for three days so far. She'd come to visit me for a fortnight with the intention of reading my new novel. I suppose I should have felt relieved that she could still do that, given that my laptop hadn't been swiped. But for the moment, I was struggling to focus on the bright side of my situation.

'And you say the burglar was female?' Victoria asked me.

'Very.'

She scowled. 'Attractive?'

'It was dark, Vic. And she was in something of a hurry to leave. And to be honest, I had other things on my mind.'

Victoria rolled her eyes and slurped her tea. She clenched her dressing gown across her chest, then reached for the flyer and subjected it to another assessment. 'Any theories about this card?'

'Maybe she's goading me – telling me where I might buy a replacement for my book.'

'Is that likely?'

'If she's a complete bitch.'

'No, you idiot, I meant about there being a replacement. How many first editions of *The Maltese Falcon* are there?'

I gave her question some thought. 'Few enough for them to be worth an awful lot of money. And let's not forget that my copy was signed.'

'It's funny.' Victoria swallowed more tea. 'You never did tell me how you came to own it. Where did you find the money?'

I treated her to a level gaze.

'My God,' she said. 'You stole it.'

I threw up my hands, as if that much should have been obvious.

'Who from?'

'Does it matter?'

'It might. If they decided to steal it back.'

'Oh. I hadn't considered that.'

'Is it possible?'

I drummed my fingers on my chin. On balance, it struck me as highly unlikely. It was more than eight years since I'd acquired the book and I hadn't been back to England since. So far as I was aware, the person I'd liberated it from had no idea who I was, and I'd never felt the need to contact a dealer to establish its worth because I had no intention of selling. To me, the book was priceless.

I'd first read *The Maltese Falcon* when I was at boarding school. It hadn't been on the curriculum. Nothing that *was* on the curriculum could possibly have swept me away with the same force. I fell hard for the wise-cracking private eye, the overblown villains, the tawdry San Francisco backdrop and the switchback plot (the cross, the double-cross, the triple-cross – I could go on). Anything I ever learned about writing I learned from Hammett. So perhaps you can imagine how much it had meant to me when, years later, I found myself in a position to pinch a first edition, signed by my own personal hero.

'I don't think it's possible at all,' I told Victoria, in what I hoped was a conclusive tone. 'In fact, I'm sure of it.'

'Well, somebody must have known it was here.' She raised an eyebrow. 'Have you entertained many guests since you've been in Venice?'

I did my best to navigate a safe response. 'One or two, perhaps. Though I wouldn't have drawn their attention to the book.'

'If you say so.'

'I do.'

Victoria plonked the flyer down on the steamer trunk and peered into the depths of her cup. The dregs of her tea seemed to fascinate her. 'How about your landlords?'

'Martin and Antea? They're scrupulously honest. The rent I pay them is evidence of that. Antea's a real sweetheart. She's always fussing over me – bringing me a treat from the market, or forcing jars of home-made pasta sauce onto me. Besides which, they have a key. If they wanted to steal my things, they'd have no need to hire a cat burglar.'

'Could anyone else have been in here?'

I scratched my head. 'I have a cleaner who comes on Tuesdays.'

'Well, there you go.'

'She's not the type.'

'But what does that even mean, Charlie? It's not as if *you* look like a thief.'

'Maybe that's because I haven't been for the past nine months.'

It was perfectly true. In fact, it was 279 days (and counting) since I'd stolen anything at all. Now, that may not sound like a big deal to you, but to me it was mighty significant. I'd always made a fairly decent – if not entirely respectable – living as a burglar, and changing my habits had been a genuine challenge.

It didn't help that I enjoyed it. Reprehensible, I know, but I get an undeniable buzz from snooping through a person's belongings. There's satisfaction, too, in setting about a theft in the right way. It takes brains, as well as guts, to exploit a property's weaknesses and get out without leaving any evidence behind. Oh, and of course, there's always the chance, however remote, of finding something, someday, that might just turn my entire world on its axis.

In short, it had been tough to go straight, and if I'm honest, I'd only succeeded in abstaining because I'd focussed all my energies on my new book. Mind you, I couldn't have done it without cigarettes. Speaking of which, now seemed a good time to reach for the packet on the steamer trunk and fire one up.

'You know,' Victoria told me, 'I really think your cleaner could be a suspect.'

'Forget it.' I exhaled smoke into the room, shielding myself from the tight expression that had gripped Victoria's features. 'She looks nothing like the woman who was here tonight.'

'Not what I'm suggesting.' She wafted my smoke aside in a deliberate fashion. 'Very few people hang books on their walls, agreed? And an Englishman in Venice, doing something like that – she might have found it curious enough to mention to someone.'

'Maybe.'

'So will you speak to her?'

'Maybe.'

I rubbed my eyes with the heels of my palms, the smoke from my cigarette wreathing my forehead. It was closing in on three in the morning according to the grandfather clock in the corner of the room and I was beginning to feel it. I'd been up making notes far later than I'd intended, and now that the adrenaline of the break-in was leaving my system, I was struggling to stay alert. Perhaps I'd been fortunate. If I'd gone to sleep at my usual hour, I might never have heard my intruder blundering around in the first place.

I frowned and gave my last thought a little more air. Wasn't that a bit odd? On reflection, she was clearly experienced, because her getaway had been seamless. *Audacious*, some might say. Speaking personally, I'd never abseiled away from a building, or used a climbing rope to access a property. And all right, my window hadn't been locked – largely because there wasn't a lock on the thing – but it would have been tricky to open the catch from the outside. All of which suggested she was something of an expert. So why the heavy footsteps and the bumping into furniture? Had she wanted to wake me? Had she wanted me to *see* her?

It seemed like a crazy notion at first, but the more I thought about it the more I began to believe there could be something to it. Your average thief would be ecstatic if you failed to notice that anything had been stolen from your home until long after they'd gone. But she'd drawn my attention to what she'd taken by leaving the flyer behind.

I reached for the card and read the text once more, coaxing another jolt of nicotine from my cigarette.

'What are you thinking?' Victoria asked.

'I'm thinking that we should get some sleep,' I told her. 'Because I have the strangest feeling we'll be visiting this book-shop in the morning.'

THREE

My apartment was located on the Fondamenta Venier, about halfway between the Accademia di Belle Arti and the Peggy Guggenheim Collection, in the district of Dorsoduro. Traditionally, the area had been popular with artists and writers, and considering how expensive Venice could be, I knew that I was fortunate to live anywhere close. The downside, at least this morning, was that I was on the opposite side of the Grand Canal from where I needed to be, and there was only one nearby crossing point – the wooden Accademia Bridge.

The mid-morning air was brittle with a lingering frost that had coated the railings and plank treads in a glitter of crystal slush. I had on a knitted hat, scarf, and mittens, as well as a thick woollen coat. The mittens were a necessity – it was freezing outside, and I couldn't wear conventional gloves because the middle and fourth fingers of my right hand are slightly crooked and bent over one another. I suffer from localised arthritis in my finger joints and the damp Venetian weather hadn't done anything to improve my condition. Neither had the constant typing I engaged in when I was writing. But hey, I get by, and Victoria had even commented on how fetching my mittens happened to look – although she had been disappointed that they weren't stitched to my coat sleeves.

Speaking of Victoria, she was pacing across the wooden bridge struts beside me in suede boots, dark jeans and a red padded jacket, the lower half of her face hidden behind the zipped collar of her coat.

'Do you know where we're going?' she asked me.

'Of course. I know Venice pretty well by now.'

'You don't want to borrow my map then?'

'Please, Vic. I'm hardly a tourist.'

Below us a water bus, loaded down with an army of passengers, churned the grey-green waters into froth at the Accademia *vaporetto* station, while a pristine water taxi cruised by a grocery barge carrying boxed vegetables to market. Further along the canal, beyond a scattering of timber mooring posts, a string of gondolas had been roped together and covered in blue tarpaulin, their curved black bows nodding ponderously in the tides like a line of oil derricks.

'I need coffee,' I told Victoria, fighting to stifle a yawn.

'Good idea. Where's your nearest Starbucks?'

'Philistine. Don't let the locals hear you say that.'

The locals, every last one of them, were crammed inside a warm and steamy bar just beyond Campo San Maurizio.

Leaving Victoria by the door, I pushed my way to the counter and ordered two espressos, then slipped my map out of my pocket and snuck a look at it under cover of the people around me.

My map had all but disintegrated from heavy use. The wax paper was torn and gaping where once it had been neatly folded, the corners were curled and badly frayed, and I was missing an entire quadrant of the Giudecca. Even so, I had a curious affection for the thing and I was reluctant to replace it. I'd learned to my cost during my first weeks in Venice how easy it was to become hopelessly lost among the mazelike alleys and waterways of the city, and it had come to my rescue more times than I could count.

Happily enough, it worked the same trick again, and I plotted a route through a series of backstreets that I felt confident I could remember. Then I necked my coffee and delivered Victoria's. Once she'd sipped it down, and wafted her hand in front of her mouth as if she'd just swallowed a shot of firewater, I led her on as far as the gloomy fissure of Calle Fiubera without a single wrong turn.

The bookbinding business was double-fronted, with two large windows on either side of a recessed glass door. The left-hand window featured a display of leather-bound volumes embellished with contrasting leather patches in the shape of stars, moons, cats and witches' hats. A small cardboard sign beside each book, in English only, noted which volume in the Harry

Potter series was for sale as a bound and signed edition, along with a price in euros that was frankly insane. The right-hand window was devoted to quality pens, paper supplies and stationery. We entered the shop and discovered that the interior was laid out in the same fashion.

The place smelled strongly of tobacco smoke. A ragged-looking chap with unruly grey hair and wire-rim glasses was sitting behind a leather-inlaid desk among the book shelves, a scratched and dented pipe resting in the corner of his mouth. He was peering through an illuminated, table-fixed magnifying glass at a supple piece of tan leather. On the corner of his desk was a stack of red flyers just like the one that had been left in my apartment.

He glanced up when we entered, eyes rheumy and networked with fine red lines, then returned his attention to his stitching and smoking.

I approached the shelved books and scanned the titles that had been hand-embroidered on their spines. They were arranged in alphabetical order and I crouched down until I was facing the shelf given over to authors with a surname beginning with the letter *H*. I read from left to right, then raised a mitten in the air and repeated myself to be sure I hadn't missed anything. I hadn't. There were no books by Dashiell Hammett.

I straightened, knees cracking, and led Victoria towards the stationery supplies on the opposite side of the shop. I pretended to give some consideration to a notebook with a black leather cover that was affordable enough to have been manufactured in the Far East. Victoria smoothed her fingers over a sheet of wrapping paper with a marbled effect that had probably originated from the same factory.

'Well?' she whispered.

'Nothing,' I told her.

She inclined her head towards the owner of the shop. 'Are you going to say something?'

I set the notebook down and reached for a gift set containing a strip of red wax and a letter seal. 'I'm not sure it's going to get us very far.'

'Even so.'

'Even so?'

She nodded and freed the gift box from my grip. 'No time like the present.'

The shopkeeper appeared to disagree. I shuffled across and hovered before his desk, but it wasn't until I'd removed my mittens, clapped my hands, cleared my throat and conjured up a hesitant, *'Scusi?'* that he finally muttered a dubious, *'Si.'*

'I'm looking for a book.'

'Si.' His beaten-down eyes didn't seem the least bit interested in anything I might have to say. A sprig of silvery hair was growing out of a mole on his right cheek, and the collarless brown shirt and green cardigan he had on looked sorely in need of a wash.

'A particular book,' I went on. *'The Maltese Falcon.* I was led to believe you might have a first edition. Signed.'

The shopkeeper looked me up and down very carefully,

without the least embarrassment, and then he set aside the piece of leather he'd been stitching and cupped the bowl of his pipe. He wore a pitted rubber thimble on his thumb, and he knocked it against the pipe as he watched me some more.

'I've already checked your shelf,' I told him. 'I couldn't find a copy.'

He grunted, as if that much was obvious, then leaned backwards in his chair and tugged at a drawer in the middle of his desk, showering tobacco from his pipe along the sleeve of his cardigan. He removed a green ledger that he parted before him. The handwritten entries were slanted and compressed – and impossible for me to read upside down.

'No,' he said, and shut the ledger with a definitive, and quite dusty, thud.

'No?'

He shook his head and cupped the pipe.

'You're quite sure?' I pressed.

This time, he remained silent. If I hadn't heard myself speak with my own ears, I could have believed that I hadn't actually said anything.

'Okay then,' I said. *'Grazie mille.'*

'Prego.'

I turned to Victoria. 'Let's go.'

'That's it?'

'He doesn't have a copy.' I shrugged. 'I don't know what more we can do.'

I followed Victoria out of the shop, determined not to look

back as we walked away, even though I had the distinct feeling that we were being watched. Victoria waited until we were crossing a humped bridge over a brackish canal before delivering her verdict.

'Well, he was grumpy. And not exactly helpful.'

'Welcome to Venice.'

She glanced up at me, a pensiveness in her eyes. 'Do you think he was hiding something?'

I gave the matter some thought. 'No,' I said, eventually.

'Really?'

I wrapped my arm around her and gave her a friendly squeeze. 'I know we weren't in there very long, but I didn't spot any really unique editions. It's just not that kind of place.'

'I don't know, Charlie.'

'Always so suspicious.' I bumped her with my hip. 'You ever wonder if perhaps it's time you stopped searching for the plot twist behind everyone you meet?'

Victoria made a noise that suggested she wasn't entirely amused by my observation, and meanwhile I raised my head to discover that we were entering Piazza San Marco, through the archway that ran beneath the ornate clock tower. The brick Campanile loomed ahead of us, and to our left a group of children clambered over a pair of lion statues that appeared resigned to their fate. The greasy flagstones were clotted with pigeons and tourists. I craned my neck up towards the mosaics on the front of the domed Basilica. The golds and yellows seemed to lack something in the dreary grey light. I knew just how they felt.

'So what's next?' Victoria asked. 'Should we go to the police?'

I frowned. 'What would be the point of that?'

'Well, I know you're not exactly a fan ...'

'Because they're usually trying to arrest me, Vic. And more often than not, for the wrong crime.'

'But think about it, Charlie. A female burglar. There can't be too many of those around. Perhaps they'll know who she is.'

'I wouldn't bet on it. And I dread to think how long we'd have to wait to speak to someone. All day, probably.'

She prodded me in the chest. 'That book was worth a bloody fortune.'

'Still is,' I told her. 'Just not my fortune, regrettably.'

Victoria squealed in frustration and stamped her heel into the ground. It wasn't her smartest move ever. A cluster of pigeons scattered in a burst of wings, charting a course for her hair. She yelped, flailing her arms like she'd stumbled into a bat cave.

Once the last of the winged rodents had cleared the air space in the vicinity of her head, she cursed me under her breath and bit down on her lip. 'You don't fool me, Charlie. You've told me before what that book means to you. What it means for your writing.'

The joke was Victoria didn't know the half of it. Stealing the *Falcon* had involved one of the biggest gambles I'd ever taken. As a professional thief-for-hire, ripping off one's employer is a dumb move. The chances of being caught are high, because you're an obvious suspect, and even if nothing can be proven against you, you still risk causing irreparable damage to your reputation. So rule one of the burglary game is never to bite the hand that feeds you. It's a good rule. A fine one, even. And that's why I've seldom broken it.

But I broke it for Hammett.

At the time in question, my client was a bloated old Etonian – a boastful lush who'd inherited a vast and sprawling family estate that happened to include a renowned library of rare volumes. The library was of scant interest to him – in fact, I was reliably informed that the only thing he read for pleasure was the *Wisden Cricketers' Almanack*. His passion, you see, was cricket, and I'd been hired by a go-between to acquire a piece of memorabilia for his private collection – a bat that had been used by a particular player in a particular Test that I'm not at liberty to mention just now. Needless to say, I stole the bat and I was paid handsomely for my toils, but from the moment I'd heard talk of my client's library of books, I'd had a hankering to break in and peruse it.

Several weeks later, when I happened to know that he was in Yorkshire for a County Championship match, I did precisely that, and it's fair to say the quality of the collection was far beyond anything I could have anticipated. But the greatest surprise was on a shelf high up to my right, where I happened to notice a familiar yellow dust jacket winking out at me. Somewhat breathlessly, I wheeled across a stepladder and took the book down, turning it in my hands and gently opening it to the first printed page where, to my life-long surprise, I found that my hero had signed his name, in his very own hand.

I wanted to take the book, right there and then, but I reminded myself what a hazardous thing it would be to do, and I reluctantly slipped it back in its place. But from that night on, through the days and weeks that followed, I could think of little else. Ideas of snatching the book plagued me during the day and haunted me in my dreams. I'd swiped plenty of things by then – some for myself, others for clients – and nearly everything had been worth an awful lot of money. But with *The Maltese Falcon*, it was the first and only time I'd truly known what it meant to covet something. I was obsessed by the book, I couldn't rest without taking it, and gradually I convinced myself that there was a good chance its theft wouldn't be noticed by the library's cricket-obsessed owner. So I broke in, and I nabbed the *Falcon*, but I also left England for the Continent the very next day, at the start of what was destined to become my roving lifestyle throughout Europe and beyond.

'Oh, I'll get by,' I told Victoria, doing my best to rid my mind of the memories I'd just conjured.

'Will you, though?'

I reached for her chin, lifting it with my thumb. 'Well, you tell me,' I said, in what I hoped passed for a carefree tone. 'How about we head home and you can start reading my new manuscript?'

A sad smile flirted with her lips. 'Oh, terrific. No pressure there, then.'

Reaching for her hand, I swung her arm and led her on through the square towards the steely waters of the lagoon. The main expanse of the piazza was away to our right and the pink-on-white fancy of the Doge's Palace was off to our left. But I wasn't interested in either of them. My attention was focussed on the two granite columns ahead of us, at the entrance to the Piazetta. The columns framed a view across the lagoon to the cathedral of San Giorgio Maggiore, and in times gone by, thieves and criminals had been strung up from them, as a warning to others not to follow their example. And there I was, ignoring the lesson, already planning in my own mind how I might set about breaking into the bookshop after dark and, more to the point, asking myself how best to access the antique floor-safe I'd spotted behind the shopkeeper's desk.

FOUR

If there's one thing I try to focus on when I'm writing my Michael Faulks burglar novels, it's *barriers*. By tossing as many obstacles as possible into the path of my hero, and making life fiendishly challenging for him, I hope my readers will feel compelled to read on to find out what happens next. It's a handy technique, and it's served me pretty well over the years. The part that troubled me, however, was that someone seemed to be pulling the exact same trick with yours truly.

Take, for example, my decision to break into the bookshop. It was by no means easy. I'd made a promise to myself to focus on my writing while I was in Venice – to see what kind of crime novel I could produce when I really committed to the *novel* rather than the *crime* side of the equation – and I felt guilty turning away from that pact.

Just to make things more awkward, I'd given Victoria the same pledge, and I could well remember how pleased she'd been when I'd told her the news. Yes, she enjoyed hearing about the stunts I'd pulled over the years, and I'd long suspected that she found the roguish side of my personality somewhat endearing, but the thing that had originally brought us together had been my writing. She was the first person to truly believe in my work, and she had absolute faith that one day my stories would reach a wider audience. It was because of her that I'd decided to attempt the kind of ambitious thriller I might never have tried otherwise – and it was for her, as much as for me, that I'd been prepared to knuckle down to my career in writing and draw a line under my career in theft.

So it was for this reason, above all others, that I found myself not long after midnight, in the somewhat curious position of having to sneak around my own home (very much like a burglar in the night) with the intention of letting myself *out* undetected.

Fortunately, Victoria was snoring, and being a keen student of human behaviour, I took this to mean that she was asleep. I nudged her door open a fraction to peer inside. Sure enough, she was out cold, eyes shut and jaw slackened, with the duvet pulled up to her chin. I suppose I should have been relieved to see it, because it made leaving my apartment a good deal simpler, but the truth is I felt stung.

Why? Well, it was only a few hours since I'd passed her a copy of my new manuscript. And granted, I'd been nervous because I'd invested time and energy into the novel, and there was a lot riding on her verdict. But one thing I'd felt confident about was the opening third. I thought it was gripping. *Unputdownable*, in fact. And yet Victoria had happily abandoned the script on her bedside cabinet before plunging into a deep and tranquil sleep.

I backed away and returned to my bedroom, trying not to let it get to me. Too late. It already had. What could I have overlooked, I wondered? More to the point, what had *she* missed? And just how far had she got before tossing my work aside?

Now, if I were a normal person, I imagine that I would have been able to give the matter some sensible consideration, and that I might have concluded that I was being unreasonable. It was only the previous night that her sleep had been interrupted by the break-in. On top of that, she was due to stay with me for at least another week, so perhaps she was hoping to read my novel at a leisurely pace, to enjoy it all the more.

But alas, I'm not normal – I'm a paranoid writer – and by the time I'd dressed in dark clothes, freed my trusty burglary tools from inside the lining of my suitcase and stuffed my faithful map into my pocket, I'd convinced myself that there was only one thing to do.

Sneaking back across the hallway, I crawled on my hands and knees over the thin carpet towards her bed. Her snoring had become fainter, and there appeared to be a longer pause between breaths. I cautiously raised my head, freed the top page of the manuscript from the pile and lowered it to the floor. I checked on Victoria, and once I was certain that she hadn't stirred, I flashed the beam of my penlight.

Now, speaking as a thief, I can tell you that there are some things you simply don't lose, no matter how rusty you might be, and it's a testament to my composure that I didn't gasp loudly or swear and give myself away. Because the sad discovery I'd made, and the troubling fact that stuck with me as I slipped out of my apartment and trudged through the sombre alleys and abandoned *campi* to Calle Fiubera, was that Victoria had stopped reading my book midway through chapter four.

Even when I'm on my game, this burglary lark is a risky business, and it had been a long time since I'd last applied my skills. Talk about barriers. I could have sworn I had enough to be going on with, and that was before I clocked the metal grilles that had been pulled down in front of the darkened exterior of the bookbinding business.

I paused and pretended to tie my shoe. I couldn't see anyone in the darkness surrounding me. Further up the alley was an *osteria* that had long since been closed for the night, as well as a number of shops protected by metal shutters and several layers of graffiti. The only nearby light came from the safety lamps that had been fixed to scaffolding poles outside a boarded-up building undergoing renovation. In short, the coast appeared to be clear, and so I gave the grille a good shake. It creaked and rattled, but it was securely fastened to the ground with three industrial padlocks.

I considered the other obstacles in my way. There didn't appear to be an alarm, thank goodness, because although I knew how to bypass all but the most complex of systems, I wouldn't have relished the prospect of poking around in any of the dodgy Italian wiring snaking across the exterior of the shop. Aside from the padlocks, I could spy a modest collection of locks and bolts on the front door itself. And that, so far as I could tell, appeared to be it.

Satisfied with my assessment, I took a stroll to the end of the alley and stuck my head out into Calledei Fabbri, just to make sure that nobody was likely to interrupt me. It was just as well I did. The tunnel-like space had appeared empty at first glance, but as I turned, I glimpsed a hunched figure leaning against the doorway of an unlit restaurant.

I couldn't remember seeing the man when I'd approached the shop, and I doubted very much that I would have forgotten him if I had. He was very large, almost bear-shaped, and he was dressed in a scruffy camel-hair coat that must have made quite a dent in some unfortunate herd, and that fitted him the way a mess tent fits an army unit. A pair of black suit trousers extended below the hem of his coat to hover disconcertingly above his polished black brogues, revealing a slither of white ankle sock. A tatty black fedora was plonked on top of his sizeable head, among a mass of knotted black curls, shading his eyes. What I could see of the face was mostly beard – a thick, tangled number that obscured his jawline and ringed his open mouth. Coiled about his feet was a mangy-looking cat.

For a moment, I was too stunned to say anything, and then I remembered that my Italian wasn't up to the task in any event.

I wasn't sure what I planned to do next, so it was kind of him to save me the trouble. With a nasal grunt and a sudden swing of his foot, he sent the cat yowling across the alley, then lowered the brim of his hat, turned on his heel and limped awkwardly away in the direction of the Rialto.

I suppose if I was a lesser thief, the encounter might have unsettled me, but the truth is that it takes more than a shambling, overweight chap with a disregard for animal welfare to put me off my stride. Evidently, the same was true of the stray cat, because it stalked along behind its bashful companion until I was all on my lonesome once more.

Never one to be shy about seizing the moment, I returned to the shop, reached inside my jacket for the spectacles case that contained my torch and my picks, removed my mittens and exposed my hands to the cold. Yes, I had on a pair of plastic disposable gloves, but they provided my arthritic joints with barely any protection. It didn't help that I'd had to snip away two of the fingers on my right-hand glove to accommodate my gnarled fingers. They were wrapped in surgical tape to prevent my leaving any prints, but my knuckles still had a tendency to seize up all too fast, and that was something I couldn't readily afford. Speed was of the essence, so I crouched and addressed the first padlock.

Even though I do say so myself, I was mighty pleased with the way things turned out. Yes, in my pomp I might have been a touch quicker, and perhaps my approach might have been a shade more elegant, but there was no denying that I still had the knack. And heck, when I pulled a can of lubricant from my pocket and squirted it into the shutter mechanism, then hauled up the weighty grille and ducked beneath it with barely a sound, I couldn't ignore the wave of satisfaction that washed over me.

Easing the grille back down, I cupped my hands around my eyes and pressed my face against the blackened glass until I was certain that I couldn't see the infrared blink of any sensors. Then I went down on one knee and offered a heartfelt proposal to the pin and tumbler lock in the middle of the door. At first it played coy, but after a spell of prodding and tickling, it came around to my advances. The bolt down by my feet was of a more stubborn disposition, and for a while it had me debating whether I should break the glass. I've never favoured that approach – there's the risk of cutting oneself, as well as making too much noise – and it has always struck me as the last resort of any self-respecting thief. Eventually, it turned out that a little breathless fumbling was all that was needed before the bolt was putty in my hands, and as soon as I'd withdrawn the thing, the door swung open on its hinges.

I surprised myself by hesitating. Yes, I might have just picked some locks, but the moment I entered the shop, I really would have reverted to my bad old ways. And granted, I could console myself with the thought that all I was doing was trying to reclaim my own property, rather than stealing some-one else's, but if I were to get caught, I doubted the owner of the shop, or more to the point, the Italian police, would see it that way.

But despite what I'd said to Victoria, I didn't trust the shop-keeper. Anyone with a genuine knowledge of books would know the value of a first edition of *The Maltese Falcon*. If he'd had a copy available to him, he would have been aware of it without needing to consult any records. That made me think that the routine with the ledger had been a way of stalling me while he tried to figure out what my angle might be. And that, in turn, led me to suspect that he knew about my copy of the book.

I headed for the safe. Now admittedly, there was no reason to think that my book would be inside. He could be keeping it anywhere he pleased. It might be that he lived in a nearby apartment stuffed with priceless volumes, or it might be that he had a safe storage box in a local bank where my book was temporarily hidden, awaiting shipment to a collector somewhere else in the world. But my only lead was the shop, and the only secure place I'd spied inside the shop was the safe.

Well, I say secure, but really it was vulnerable. In the light from my torch, I could see that it was a squat, heavy-looking brute, dating from the 1940s or '50s. It had been finished in a dark-blue enamel, and it wouldn't have surprised me to learn that the paint was thicker than the metal it covered. If I'd had a decent drill with me, I dare say I could have attacked it quite productively from the side. But, as it happened, I was content to focus my attentions on the very basic locking mechanism.

There was no combination dial, and certainly no electronic keypad. A brass keyhole and a multi-pin lock was all that stood between me and the interior of the thing, and after sorting through my burglary equipment for a likely looking pick and a sturdy torsion wrench, I gripped my torch between my teeth and got down to business. Moments later, the weighty tumblers turned with a deathly echo, the brass handle rotated and a gust of stale air wafted out.

I covered my mouth with my hand and flashed my torch inside. There was a shelf in the middle and the space beneath it contained four cloth bags. The bags were heavy, and when I lifted them from the safe I discovered that they contained euro coins in various denominations. I put the petty cash back inside. I was after my book, not a profit.

On top of the shelf were two books with blue cloth covers, frayed around the edges. The pages were yellowed and the text was in a language I didn't recognise – Russian, perhaps. Disappointed, I reached for a set of keys that had been hidden beneath the books. They were attached to a Fiat key fob. The car they fitted was most likely parked at the Piazzale Roma – unlikely to be used on a daily basis but ready to be driven across the bridge to mainland Italy whenever convenient. I returned them to the safe and removed the final item.

A mobile telephone.

The handset looked cheap, with large rubber buttons and a dim-lit monochrome screen upon which a telephone number had been entered. If I was ever to buy a mobile myself, it was just the kind of thing I'd go for – the base model in a manufac-turer's range, with the ability to make and receive calls and, on a good day with a following breeze, perhaps even send a text message or two. Ordinarily, I might have said that there was nothing the least bit remarkable about it. But that would be to ignore the yellow Post-it note that had been stuck to the keypad, and the arrow on the note that pointed upwards to the button with the little green handset on it. And it would also require me to overlook the writing beneath the arrow, where someone had scrawled the words: *Ring Me, Englishman*.

FIVE

Funny, I really didn't want to. And not just because I can be a stubborn fellow who doesn't take kindly to being told what to do, but also because I can recognise danger when I see it. Like any self-respecting burglar who'd prefer not to be caught, I have a well-developed instinct for self-preservation. And if ever there was a time to walk away from something, my every faculty told me that this was it.

Two things struck me as highly likely.

One: The phone had been placed in the safe for my attention. After all, the flyer that had been left in my apartment had led here, and the note on the phone had been written in English and addressed to one of my countrymen.

Two: If I made the call, I almost certainly wouldn't like what I heard.

Problem was, if I *didn't* place the call, I felt sure that I'd never again see my copy of *The Maltese Falcon*. And while it was hardly comforting to think that whoever had planted the phone had already decided that my need for the book would outweigh any reservations I might have, I couldn't escape the feeling that if this *was* a trap, it was one I had to at least dip my toe into.

Pressing the little green button with my gloved thumb, I raised the handset to my ear and listened to the tinny bleat of the Italian ringtone. I heard it only once before my call was answered.

'You are late.'

The voice was female.

'Who is this?' I asked.

Stupid question. In my mind's eye, I was picturing the shapely blonde who'd broken into my apartment. Even as I spoke, my brain was reassembling her image and trying it alongside the voice I'd heard. The two seemed to fit. Her English was good, if studied, marked with a strong Italian accent and a notable flourish.

'You know who I am,' she told me, in a hurried tone. 'We have met. You have pretty underwear, I think.'

I covered my face with my hand and did my best not to groan. 'I don't know your name,' I told her. 'And I have no idea what you want from me.'

'My name is not important.'

Strange, it seemed mighty important to me.

'You would like your book back, yes?' she asked.

'That would be nice,' I agreed.

39

'*Perfetto,*' she purred. 'Then you will do as I say.'

Didn't I tell you it was a bad idea to make the phone call? I already didn't like the way the conversation was going, and I was pretty sure it had the potential to get an awful lot worse.

'How about I don't?' I said. 'How about I hang up and walk away right now?'

'Then, I am sorry, but you will never see your book again.'

'And?'

She paused for a moment, and I could sense doubt building on the other end of the line. 'And I think that is enough.' Her tone suggested she wasn't as confident as she'd like to be. 'I know this book. I know its value. To you, especially, yes?'

I didn't respond. It would have been nice to think that I could have stayed in the darkened shop in silence and never said anything more. It would have been even nicer to think that I could have gone home, climbed into bed and forgotten that any of this had ever happened. In fact, it wouldn't have been at all hard for me to invent a whole other life for myself – one where I didn't have to listen to my short-tempered new friend on the other end of the line.

'You will follow my instructions?' she asked.

'That really depends on what your instructions are.'

She tutted, and made a huffing noise, then proceeded to outline what she expected from me. '*Allora* ... You will go to Calle Cavalli. It is in San Polo, near Campo di San Polo. There is a building there – number 1952. Let yourself in. The locks are not so hard – even for someone slow, like you.'

'Hey!'

'There is an apartment on the first floor. The door, it will be open. You will meet me there. *Capito?*'

'Then what?'

She hesitated. 'Then we will talk about what I need you to do.'

Boy, didn't this sound like a golden opportunity? If I did as she said, I had absolutely no control over what might happen to me, and no idea of what I might find inside the apartment she wanted me to access. There could be a group of thugs awaiting my arrival, with detailed plans about the specific pain and discomfort they wished to cause me. Or the place could have been ransacked, and my tormentor might have designs on setting me up for the crime. Or ... Hell, what was the point in torturing myself with worse-case scenarios?

'This is crazy,' I told her. 'I'd have to be an idiot to do what you're asking. I can't think of one good reason why I should.'

'There is your book ...'

'That's a half-reason, at best.'

'I do not believe it.'

'Believe what you like. I'm beginning to think we've chatted enough for one night.' I stood from my hiding place and moved to the door. Craning my neck, I peered up at the decrepit buildings, trying to identify where she was watching me from. I supposed it was possible that she had some kind of camera equipment rigged up inside the shop, but I thought it unlikely. 'Tell you what,' I said, surveying the unlit windows of the property across the way, most of them obscured behind wonky shutters, 'I'll keep this phone. You have my number. Call me if you want to talk about returning my book in some other way.'

'No,' she blurted. 'You must wait.' And for some murky reason best known to the most witless part of my psyche, I did just that. 'I will tell you something now. Something important. Please. You will trust me because of this.'

'Well, make it quick. I have a pressing appointment with my duvet.'

'There is a door at the back of the shop. Do you see it? It is not locked. You must leave that way.'

I turned and gazed over my shoulder towards a plain internal door that was positioned close to the stationery supplies. It gave no indication of what lay behind it.

'Thanks all the same, but I think I'll go out the front.'

'But this is what I must tell you. The *polizia* are coming. I cannot stop it. They will be at the shop in less than a minute.'

'Oh, please.'

'It is the truth. I give you this, and you trust me, yes? Please, I think so.'

'Well, I don't.' I frowned. 'And besides, how could you possibly know the police are on their way?'

She drew a breath, and when she spoke again, I could detect a note of desperation in her voice. 'Because I called them. Yes, I see them now. They will be with you very soon.'

I gripped the phone tight to my ear. 'Are you serious?'

Oh, she was serious all right. Quite suddenly, the sound of

footsteps reached me from further along the *calle*. Pressing my cheek against the door, I strained my eyes in the direction of the noise until I caught the blurred reflection of two figures in a slither of window glass. Then the figures themselves came hurtling into view – two men in blue police uniforms skidding to a halt outside. They were young. White-faced. Tense.

They flinched when they saw me, and I did much the same thing. Fortunately, I also had the presence of mind to hook my toe around the door bolt and slide it home before either of them could think to lift the metal shutter. They thought of it soon enough, but by then all I heard was the clank and shuffle of the grille from behind me as I darted for the rear of the shop.

The space behind the internal door was pitch-black and damp-smelling. I stretched my hand out in front of my face and the wall I found was wet and cold to the touch, even through the plastic of my gloves. Fumbling for my torch, I pointed the thin beam at my surroundings, but it barely tickled the darkness.

'Which way?' I yelled into the phone.

'To your right. You should not waste time. They are close.'

No kidding. A thumping sound came from the shop – the noise of the policemen using their shoulders for a key. They shouted in frenzied Italian.

I aimed the torch beam down at the ground. The floor seemed to have been carpeted with drenched sponge – water was seeping through and bubbling up around my shoes. To my right, sodden cardboard boxes were stacked one on top of another, covered over with plastic sheeting. Drips splattered the plastic from above.

A loud bang from behind me was followed by the crack and splinter of wood, the yammer of voices. The dark, slippery corridor beckoned, and I set off along it with my feet slapping through the wetness and my torch arcing dizzyingly from side to side.

I found myself at another wall. The corridor swung left and I swung after it, stomping along the sodden carpet with the mysterious black liquid seeping through my canvas baseball shoes to my socks. It was as if the building was suffering from some kind of localised exposure to the *acqua alta* – the high waters that periodically flood the city.

'Where are you?' panted the voice on the phone. Touching. She almost sounded concerned for my welfare.

'I can see another door,' I hissed. 'Is it safe?'

'*Si*. I have told you this.'

'Excuse me if I take a little convincing.'

'But you have no choice, Charlie. The *polizia*, they are inside now.'

I thought it best to ignore the way she'd just used my name. 'If you're lying,' I whispered, 'I'll find you. You won't get away with this.'

'Do as I say and you will find me for sure. Take the door. Hurry to San Polo. Be there before two o'clock or I will destroy your book. I will do it. Understand?'

I didn't understand, not even close, but the phone line went dead before I had a chance to tell her so. I cursed under my breath, then reached out tentatively and prodded the door. It wouldn't budge. I put my shoulder to it. It snagged on the frame, then began to give way. I barged it once more and it banged open against the external wall. I was afraid another police officer might be waiting for me there, but I found nobody at all – the dingy, cheerless alley was deserted – and so I kicked the water from my shoes and lurched into a squelching run.

SIX

By the time I reached the address I'd been given, my feet were itching from the cold and the damp, and I badly wished that I could whip off my shoes and socks to scratch my toes for a couple of days. I would have settled for a change of footwear. Unfortunately, I couldn't indulge either fancy, and my feet were destined to remain as miserable as my mood.

Stuffing my map into the pocket of my overcoat, I tucked my gloved hands under my armpits and rocked from side to side, shivering. I was lurking beyond a squat fire hydrant in a dog-legged alley blighted by graffiti. The neighbourhood was dark and deathly quiet. Every window that surrounded me was shuttered and unlit. The silence was so complete that it felt like a form of deafness, and if someone had told me that the entire city had been evacuated, I could have quite readily believed it.

The ramshackle building I was concerned with should have looked no more suspicious than any of the others, but it seemed to tower above me and vibrate with menace. The front wall bulged in the middle, where a rusted metal brace had been used to stitch it together, and ornate metal fretwork filled the arched space above the door, like a prison with ideas above its station. The door itself had been sanded back for a fresh coat of paint that had yet to be applied. The exposed wood was scarred and gnarled, and a corroded lion's head knocker sneered out at anyone fool enough to approach.

There was no sign of a tangible threat, but I felt uneasy all the same. Digging my hand into my coat, I felt around for the mobile and redialled the number of my new Italian gal pal, hoping that I'd be able to hear the ringing of her phone from inside the property. I couldn't. I supposed it was possible that her handset was set to silent, or that I'd made it across the city before her, but the fear that I was being set-up was hard to ignore. I would have loved for her to ease my concerns, but since my call went unanswered, so did my doubts.

I pocketed the phone and gave myself a quick pep talk. It didn't help a great deal. Until tonight, it had been a long time since I'd performed my burglar routine, and I was being forced into a rushed encore. Perhaps it wouldn't have been so bad if the first show had been a resounding success, but my undignified escape from the police had hardly merited a bow, and I really would have preferred some kind of rehearsal before tackling a strange building I hadn't had an opportunity to case.

Looking at my watch, I saw that 2 o'clock was fast approaching. Part of me was tempted to stay where I was and see if she called. But I was worried about what the consequences might be – most especially, if she was serious about destroying my copy of Hammett's novel. Life is all about risks, I suppose. Some I'm prepared to take, and others I simply can't contemplate. And this time around, flexing my burglary skills against my better judgement seemed like the easier decision to live with. True, I was being manipulated, but at least I'd have some control (however small) over what happened next. If I turned my back on the scary building and walked clean away, I'd never know if I might have saved my book.

I suppose if I'm honest, it did occur to me that my decision might have been somewhat different if the person doing the manipulating hadn't been a quite mesmerising blonde. I'd never met a female burglar before, let alone one with the credentials to model lingerie, and I confess that I was more than a little intrigued. Whether my curiosity would bring me anything other than trouble I wasn't yet able to say, but one thing I couldn't ignore was the hum of excitement in my veins. If my past attempts to quit smoking had taught me anything, it was that abstinence can be hellish, and the truth was that I'd badly missed my life of crime. There had been times during the last few months when I'd found myself gazing blindly at the wall above my writing desk, pining for the danger of the unknown, the flutter in my heart that came from creeping through a stranger's home. Sure, writing had its appeal, but I was a completely different person when I was planning a burglary. A rule breaker. An outsider. Someone who made things happen.

Talking of making things happen, my drenched feet seemed to be clomping towards the unpainted door ahead of me, and my stiffened fingers appeared to be reaching for my spectacles case. Training my eye on the lock, I selected a medium rake and a standard torsion wrench from my collection.

I slipped the raking tool inside the keyhole, used the wrench to apply sideways tension to the locking cylinder, leaned my shoulder on the door and agitated the pins inside the lock. The pins skittered into position, the lock turned, the bolt withdrew and the door opened all in one fluid movement. Why, it was almost as if I knew what I was doing.

I closed the door behind me, then traded my spectacles case for my torch. I was standing in a communal hallway, with a flight of stone steps to my right and a collection of mail boxes fixed to the wall on my left. Ahead of me was a blank door with a coconut mat on the floor outside. Next to the door was a push-button light switch.

Somehow, I didn't think I'd be using it. Halfway up the first flight of stairs, I craned my neck out over the banister to shine my torch upwards. Nobody was looking down at me, which was something of a relief. In fact, I might go so far as to say that I'd started to relax when I swung the torch beam back around and a dark fuzziness sprang out of the black towards my throat. It scratched my chin and clawed at my chest and then dropped in a twirling mass before haring off down the stairs.

I followed it with my penlight. Two yellow eyes glinted back from a distant corner. *Bloody cat.* It must have been sleeping on the window ledge above me. I dislike cats at the best of times – not least because I'm allergic to them – but when my nerves are on edge, having one jump out at me doesn't rate very high on my list of favourite things.

This particular feline arched its back and hissed, and I decided that aiming my torch into its face wasn't perhaps the best way to make friends. Instead, I wiped my coat sleeve across my nostrils to ward off any sniffling and sneezing, then turned my torch back to the stairs and climbed on, hoping that before long my heart rate might drop out of the zone where a cardiac arrest seemed imminent.

As soon as I reached the first floor, I could see that the door to apartment 2 was slightly ajar. Switching the torch to my left hand, I felt inside my coat and armed myself with one of my screwdrivers, holding it up by my shoulder.

The door appeared innocuous enough, and when I put my face as close to it as I dared, I couldn't hear a sound from the other side. I checked my grip on the screwdriver, gritted my teeth, and eased the door open with my toe.

No resistance. No noise.

Now for the tricky part. Did I lead with my hand, my foot, or my face? Difficult to tell. I switched the torch for the screwdriver, then switched them back again. Flattening myself against the wall, I drew a breath and starting counting to ten. I quit at seven and gave the door a solid shove. Before the handle had struck the wall, I moved round and paced swiftly into the apartment.

The place was unlit and very cold, with a strong smell of mould and decay. Instinct took me to my right, where the cone of light from my torch revealed two modest rooms, both empty. I turned and retraced my steps as far as a bathroom with a white porcelain sink, squat toilet and grimy cubicle shower. Next to the bathroom was a cramped kitchen with a stand-alone cooker, an unplugged fridge and bare cupboards. No signs of habitation whatsoever. I tried the light switch – nothing.

That left one room at the front of the apartment, which was almost as big as the rest of the place put together. The floor was linoleum, laid in a geometric pattern and covered in a fine layer of dirt and grit. A low, empty bookcase had been fitted along one wall and a time-worn sofa abutted it. There was nobody on the sofa or anywhere else for that matter. Across from me, a pair of full-length doors had been flung wide open. Discoloured net curtains billowed inwards in the faint night breeze.

The open doors explained the wintry temperature in the apartment, but they didn't explain much else. I cut the light from my torch and waited in the darkness for a short while, watching the curtains gust and sway, feeling the chill breeze against my face. It was possible this was just another sign of an abandoned apartment, but somehow I didn't think so. Lifting the screwdriver up by my ear, I moved slowly forward, then parted the curtains and stepped onto a cramped stone balcony ringed by iron railings.

The balcony looked down over a stagnant canal and a small

humped bridge away to the right, beyond a cat's cradle of plastic washing lines. Across the canal, one floor above me on the opposite building, was another balcony. And standing upon it, glancing up from her watch and venting a relieved sigh, was the agile blonde who'd lately burgled my home.

SEVEN

She wasn't blonde any more. Gone were the flowing platinum locks, replaced with a severe black bob-cut. The hairstyle gave her a harsher, more steely appearance. Still striking, undoubtedly, and without question the same woman, but quite different all the same. Her features looked sharper, especially the cheek bones, though I guess that could have had something to do with the cold.

Her balcony was far grander than my own, adorned with carved stone heads that had the appearance of Greek gods. She was leaning her elbows on a discoloured stone plinth, her chin balanced on her clenched fists, dark hair grazing her knuckles.

'*Ciao*, Charlie. You are late again,' she said, with an elaborate wink.

I didn't answer. I was too busy closing the French doors so that I couldn't be sneaked up on from behind. She might have wanted me to believe that she was working alone, but I had to balance the risks.

I leaned out over the edge of my balcony and considered the drop. It was perhaps fifteen feet to the inky waters below, and there was no pavement or walkway where a muscle-bound accomplice could lurk – the scummy liquid pressed right up against the walls of the buildings.

I looked again at the property my late-night caller had chosen to access for our rendezvous. On closer inspection, I could see that it was little more than a construction site. Large sheets of thick plastic had been draped inside the unglazed windows on the upper floors, and scaffolding filled the alleyway to the side, just beyond the bridge. The scaffolding would have made it easy for her to climb up and get in through one of the unsecured windows, and part of me was a little disappointed by that. The other part was disappointed by the fact that her blonde locks were no more.

'What happened to your hair?' I asked.

She raised a hand to her head, as if surprised and delighted by my question. 'Last night, I wear a wig.'

'And tonight?'

She lowered her face and peered up at me from beneath long, curling lashes. 'You like?'

'It's very becoming.'

She laughed quickly and covered her mouth with her hand. Then she shook her head and released a faltering breath. 'This is fun, don't you think?' She chewed on her lip and rocked to and fro like a child with an abundance of energy. There was a strange glint in her eyes and a nervous twitch at the corner of her mouth – as if she couldn't quite believe she was winning a private wager she'd made with herself.

I tried my best to hold her eyes, but her body was making itself known to me. It would have been kinder if she'd dressed in baggy clothes and a heavy overcoat but she'd opted for a tight black, roll-neck jumper over black leggings and knee-length leather boots. A grey fabric satchel rested on her hip, suspended from a strap that ran crossways from her shoulder, bisecting her ample chest.

'You have a strange definition of fun,' I told her. 'It's freezing out here. Why don't you come over and we can talk inside? Better still, we can find somewhere with heating.'

She frowned. 'But it is safe like this. You cannot reach me, yes? The gap, it is too big.'

She was right about that. We were close enough to talk, but even on my best day, with a good run up and a pair of industrial springs for shoes, there was no way I could leap across the canal that separated us. I glanced at the spiderweb of washing lines, telephone wires and electricity cables stretching between the two buildings, but none of them were capable of bearing my weight.

'Aren't you afraid we'll be heard?' I asked. 'I'm assuming this isn't your apartment. What if the neighbours become suspicious?'

'*Oohh*, you are right.' Her eyes widened, as though she was thrilled by the idea. 'Perhaps we should whisper? Like spies.'

'Or we could SHOUT,' I said, surprising us both by doing just that.

My voice hurled itself along the canyon formed by the high buildings backing onto the canal, echoing off the water, like some panicked creature bolting through a tunnel.

'Quiet!' Her fingers tightened on the hard stone plinth. When nobody stuck their head out of a window to yell at us, she shook her head ruefully and fixed me with a flinty glare. 'There will be no shouting,' she said, in a low, controlled voice.

'Oh?' I lifted my shoulders. 'Why ever not?'

'Because you do not want to be arrested, yes?'

'Maybe I'm reckless. I must be to have come here.'

'Perhaps,' she said, straightening her back and puffing out her chest, 'but there is also your book.' And with that, she unzipped her satchel, and a moment later I caught sight of a familiar yellow dust jacket clutched in her hand. Any relief I felt at seeing my copy of The Maltese Falcon was dashed as soon as I noticed that she'd dispensed with the airtight picture frame. I was painfully aware of the three tiny tears on the spine that were in danger of becoming worse if the book was handled carelessly. And she wasn't wearing gloves, which made me dread how the grease from her fingertips might affect the jet-black falcon illustration. I was no expert, but I knew that one small crease could wipe several thousand pounds from its value.

Before I could begin to point out the terrible risks she was taking, she thrust her hand out over the balcony and held my book over the murky waters below. 'Now will you shout?' she taunted me.

'You wouldn't dare.'

'Oops.' She released her fingers, then closed them again before the book had dropped entirely. She licked her lips, knitting her brow in mock concentration. 'Ooh, it is heavy. Almost *too* heavy. It could fall *so* easily.'

'All right,' I snapped. 'You've made your point. That's enough.'

She waved the book in the air. 'Then you will listen to me?'

'I'll listen.'

'And you will not shout?'

'If that's what you want.'

'*Buono.*' She hoisted her nose in the air and cradled the book close to her chest, swaying from side to side, as if it was a baby she planned to soothe with a lullaby. I tried not to think how badly she might be crushing the dust jacket. 'So, you are a thief, yes?'

I shifted uncomfortably. 'Used to be, perhaps. Now I'm just a writer.'

She pouted. 'But I watched you at the bookshop. You did not have a key, I am thinking. And you ran from the police, also.'

'Because you set me up,' I said. 'You made it seem like my book was there.'

'But I do not think the police will believe this. I know your name, Charlie Howard, and your address. Do you think the *polizia* would recognise you? Did they get a good look at you?'

I couldn't see much sense in answering her. She'd made her point.

'Oh,' she added, patting the cover of Hammett's book, 'and I have this.'

'It's quite a collection,' I managed.

'And you do not know me at all.' She plucked absently at her bottom lip. 'Poor Charlie.'

'Yeah, you're a real criminal mastermind.'

She batted her eyelids and pretended to blush. 'But do not worry. I am no friend of the police. And the owner of the shop. *Pff.*' She waved a hand. 'A rude man. So, you are safe. And I will give you my name, if you wish.'

'Your real name?'

'So suspicious.' She wagged a finger, then stabbed her nail down onto my book. Hell, why didn't she just chew on it too? 'My name is Graziella. And you will have your book back.' She paused, smoothing the jacket with her fingers. 'If you do *exactly* as I say.'

Funny thing – years ago, when I'd been starting out as a writer and struggling to get published, I'd penned the odd short story for erotic magazines that had tended to begin in a not too dissimilar fashion. Alas, despite the plentiful curves and playful demeanour of my crooked Juliet on the opposite balcony, I didn't think she was about to demand that I strip to my underpants and nibble her thigh. For one thing, she'd already had the misfortune to see me in a state of undress, and for another, I just wasn't that lucky.

'What is it you want me to do?' I asked.

She watched me for a moment, eyes narrowing, pupils flickering, as if debating something with herself. 'At your feet, there is a case.' I looked down to the area in question. Tucked into a shadowed corner of the balcony, I could see a metal attaché briefcase. It was of the type featured in blockbuster movies, usually handcuffed to the wrist of a wealthy crook in a double-breasted suit, with two oversized bodyguards for company. 'You will take it to the Palazzo Borelli on the Grand Canal. The security, it is not so difficult.' She raised a finger. 'But you must be careful. Very careful. You cannot be seen – this is the most important thing. There is a strongroom on the *piano nobile* – the main floor of the palace.'

'Whoa,' I said, waving my hands. 'You're getting ahead of yourself. I told you – I *used* to be a burglar. I don't know where you got your information, but I don't steal things any more.'

'But this is perfect,' she told me, eyes bright and glistening.

'I fail to see how.'

'Because I do not want you to steal anything. All I want is for you to return this case.'

Great, more semantics. First I'd broken into the bookshop to *reclaim* my book. Now I was expected to break into a grand Venetian home to *return* a briefcase.

'Are you telling me it belongs to the owner of this palazzo?'

'Count Frederico Borelli.' She shuddered. 'The palazzo belongs to him. The case too.'

'*Okay,*' I said, thinking how this had to be one of the craziest assignments I'd ever had the misfortune to hear. 'But why not return it to him yourself?'

She flinched at the suggestion. 'Because he does not know that it is missing. That I took it.'

'*You* took it?'

Glaring at me, she thumped her fist onto the stone plinth. 'You have too many questions. Please. It is simple. You return the case for me, and I will return your stupid book.'

'Hey! That novel is important. It means something. And not just to me.'

She shrugged, not the least bit impressed.

'Let me think a moment.' I rested my chin on my knuckles, as though consumed by a number of terribly complicated matters. 'Now, here's the thing. You're a burglar, and I'm aware that you have some ability – the way you got into and out of my apartment was beyond anything I can do. Plus, you have local knowledge. So why have me return the case? There must be something you're not telling me. Something dangerous. A risk you're not willing to take.'

'It is not so.' She shook her head resolutely. Implored me with her eyes. 'It is simply this. The Count knows me. We are friends, yes? He knows what I can do.'

'You mean your cat-burglar routine?'

'Exactly so.'

'And?'

'And I do not want him to suspect that I took this case. So I will be with him when you return it.'

'With him?'

'In the Casinò di Venezia. I watch him play.'

Oh good grief. Why did she have to go and mention the blasted 'c' word? As if her proposal didn't sound perilous enough already, now she'd managed to make it even less enticing. A recent escapade in Las Vegas had contributed to my decision to swear off burglary, so I was hardly ecstatic to think that there might be a gambling connection.

She bit her lip and rolled it between her teeth, watching me closely. There was a tension in her. Something hidden. I guessed she had a lot riding on this, that she badly needed my help. But at the same time she was loath to trust me – perhaps scared by what the consequences would be if I screwed up. 'Will you do it?'

'Maybe. I don't know just yet.'

And I really didn't. It seemed plain odd to me. All the effort she'd gone to, all the planning and the preparation, just to have me return a briefcase on her behalf. Was she really so concerned about offending this Count, or was I right to suspect that there was more to it? More risk, more danger. Less chance of me getting away unscathed with *The Maltese Falcon* hanging neatly on my wall again and just a pleasing anecdote for my troubles.

The situation needed a good deal more thought, and the most natural way for me to think was to smoke. Fetching my cigarettes from the back pocket of my jeans, I jabbed one into my mouth and sparked my lighter. To my surprise, when I raised my eyes with my first dizzying inhalation, I found Graziella beckoning at me with curled fingers, a look of calculated innocence on her face.

'You want one?' I asked.

'It would be nice.'

Huh. No doubt it would be. My petty streak told me to refuse, but that would have meant turning my back on a fellow member of the Smoker's Union. Our numbers are low enough already, and it wasn't a step I was prepared to take. So, after slipping my lighter inside the carton, I tossed the package across the canal to her and watched as she pushed a cigarette between her plump lips and coaxed the most wondrous fumes out of the little fellow.

'Good?' I asked.

'Mmm,' she replied, exhaling in an appreciative fashion, then appearing to shiver.

I took a long hit, closing one eye in thought. 'So, how did you find me?'

She smiled, as if embarrassed. Inhaled some more. 'Your novels, yes? About the amazing Michael Faulks.' She looked puzzled for a moment. Blew smoke from the corner of her mouth. 'They are, I suppose, quite good.' *Terrific*, another critic. 'But the details are too much. It is *so* obvious you have done these things.'

'It's fiction,' I told her.

'Some of it, perhaps. But I decide I will test you. To see if I am right.' She shrugged. 'I was.'

'It still doesn't explain how you found out about *that*.' I pointed with my cigarette at Hammett's book, nestled in the crook of her left arm.

She screwed up her nose and tapped some ash into the sluggish waters below, watching after it, the black strands of her wig tickling her cheeks.

'I don't know,' I said, mostly to myself. 'I get the impression you're not being entirely straight with me. And I'm out of practice. If this palazzo is well secured, I'm really not sure if I could do it.'

She glanced up, a pleading in her eyes. 'The security is not so good. And I have the code for the strongroom.' She smiled tentatively. 'Please. It is simple.'

Simple? I squished my face with my gloved palm. Flicked my cigarette away into the dark. Was I really about to do this, I wondered? And at what cost?

EIGHT

'You'd better tell me what's in the case,' I said to Graziella, and kicked it with my foot.

She stiffened, then ground her cigarette into the stone plinth. 'This does not concern you.'

'Wrong answer. You could have drugs in there. Or counterfeit notes.' *Or even a severed hand*, I thought, recalling the troublesome plot of a Michael Faulks novel I'd had difficulties with in Amsterdam some years ago.

'No, it is nothing like this. You may trust me.'

'Ha! Right now, you're about the last person I'd trust.'

Her fulsome lips pressed into a thin line and she gave me a haughty, uncompromising look. I got the impression she wasn't used to people saying no to her, and I don't think she liked it when they did. There was something of the princess about Graziella. A fairy tale gone awry.

I lifted the briefcase from the ground. It was surprisingly

heavy and I experienced a stabbing pain in my bad fingers as I heaved it up, then dropped it with a *clang* on the iron handrail. Two brass combination locks were on the front of the case – the kind that can be tough to open, assuming you don't happen to have the knack, or better still the code.

'How about this for an idea?' I said. 'I'll pop the case open, see what's inside it, and if I'm comfortable with the contents, I might return it for you.'

'No.' She stamped her foot. 'The case must stay closed.'

'It's really important to you that I don't see what's inside?'

'Nobody must look.'

'Huh.' I tipped my head onto my shoulder. 'Quite the predicament. And it absolutely must be returned?'

'*Merda!* I already told you so.'

'Wonderful.' And with that I grabbed hold of the sculpted rubber handle, straightened my arm and held the case out over the edge of the balcony. The damn thing was so weighty that I tottered forward on my toes. 'Now, give me my book back,' I grunted.

Anger flared in her eyes, but panic attacked her features. Her jaw dropped and her throat pulsed. For just a moment, her lips moved soundlessly, as if she couldn't decide whether to shout another curse or issue a command, then she settled for an odd kind of distressed mewling.

'Be very careful,' she said, in a strained voice.

'Return my book and I will be.'

She glanced down at the novel in her hands, and I swear I

could almost see the thought process her brain was running through. It didn't take long for her to settle on a response, and to my dismay, she matched my gesture with the case by holding the book out above the darkly brooding canal water. She seemed pleased with the move. It showed in the way she threw back her shoulders and nodded to herself, as if confirming that it had been the right thing to do.

'If you drop the briefcase, I will drop your book. This is not what I want. But if you make me, I will do it.'

Kind of stupid that I hadn't thought of that.

'Well, this is interesting,' I told her, doing my best to sound composed.

'Do not drop the case.'

'Then don't drop my book.'

She transferred her gaze from the novel in her hand, to the case at the end of my wobbling arm, to the grimace I was wearing. My fingers were beginning to numb in the chill, in spite of my plastic gloves and the surgical tape, and I wasn't sure how long I'd be able to maintain my grip.

'I make you a promise,' she said. 'If you return the case, you will have your book back. I swear it. But if you drop it now, you will never see your book again.'

'Then at least tell me what you have in here. It's damn heavy. My arm's getting tired.'

'But I cannot tell you.'

'Not sure ... how much longer ... I can hold on.'

She gauged me for a crucial few seconds and then, to my

considerable relief, she returned my book to safety. Or rather, she returned my book to what I'd mistakenly imagined to be safety. Because mere seconds after having it in both hands again, she opened the thing up and gripped the top corner of a single page between her finger and thumb. She tugged at the paper, testing its hold. She held my eye, seemed to wince slightly, and then to my everlasting horror, I heard the faintest tear.

'All right,' I yelled, hauling the case back onto the balcony and holding up a hand. The impasse had left me at a real disadvantage. We both knew how important the book was to me, but I had no idea how significant the contents of the case really were to her. 'I give in.'

Her shoulders sagged. 'You will do as I say?'

'I'll return the case.'

'And you will not look inside?' Her voice was small now. Pining.

'If you insist. But just so there's no misunderstanding, how will you know if I do look? Granted, I might not have the combination, but with a little time I think I could crack this sucker. You must realise that.'

'I will know if you try,' she said, steeling herself.

Hmm. Was that really possible? It could be she'd done something simple, like pasted a hair to the lip of the case, or something more complicated, involving a sensor of some sort. Either that, or she was bluffing. All of which was something I could turn my mind to when I had a little more time (and a little less weight) on my hands.

'When is it you want me to do this thing?' I asked, not bothering to conceal my resentment.

'Tomorrow night. I will call you when it is time. You still have the phone, yes?'

I felt for the device in my coat pocket, then nodded at her. 'You'd better give me some details. Tell me what to expect.'

She assessed me warily, as if my sudden compliance was more troublesome than the resistance I'd previously offered. While she looked me over, I plonked the case down by my feet and consulted my watch. Way past my bedtime.

'Details?' I pressed.

Turning her back on me, she reached for her satchel, slipping Hammett's book inside and removing a small white envelope. The envelope bulged in the middle, the paper crinkled, as if overstuffed. She lifted the flap to her mouth, ran her pink and very appealing tongue across the gum, and stuck it down. Then she crossed to the side of her balcony and stood on her toes to peg the envelope to one of the washing lines that stretched between us. I tried not to ogle her bottom, failing miserably.

The line was wrapped around a pulley wheel at both ends, and after checking on me for a final time, as though afraid I was planning an elaborate trick, she tugged hard, sending the envelope over to me with a few determined jerks on the squeaking mechanism.

I waited until the envelope was quivering beside my head, then plucked it out of the frigid air and turned it in my hands. Prising open the soggy flap, I removed a folded bundle of paper.

The sheets had been torn from a spiral-bound pad and they were covered in detailed notes and haphazard sketches. The package would take some studying, but at first glance, it looked like a comprehensive breakdown of everything I was likely to come up against.

Stuffing the pages back inside the envelope, I bent down for the briefcase, then stood in my winter coat, the case in one hand and the envelope in the other, looking, I imagine, a lot like a businessman about to set out for a day at the office. 'Be sure and look after my book,' I told her, turning to open the doors to the empty apartment.

'Then do not look inside the case.'

'Wouldn't dream of it,' I called over my shoulder.

But not for the first time that night, I turned out to be wrong.

NINE

I slept like a man in a coma – assuming, that is, that men in comas don't just find themselves in the very deepest of slumbers, but that they also experience the most vivid and disturbing dreams imaginable. The terrors that visited me were all connected to the briefcase. In some, I mislaid it or had it stolen from me. In others, I returned the case, just as I was supposed to, only to find myself arrested and locked up in some dismal Italian prison. But mostly, I opened the briefcase inside my dreams, and each time I flipped back the lid the contents became ever more sickening: snakes and spiders; eyeballs and body parts; photographs of Victoria being subjected to the most appalling torture imaginable. You name it, I saw it, and when at last I woke with a pitiful groan, drenched in cold sweat, I stumbled to the bathroom wishing that I could rinse clean my brain in the same way that I was able to swill the gummy muck from my teeth with mouthwash.

Peeling off my pyjamas and stepping into my shower, I didn't just feel drained and groggy – I also felt ashamed, and not a little embarrassed. Truth was, mixed in with the looped nightmares, I'd had one or two dreams of an altogether different nature – torrid, erotic numbers, if you really must know. And since I'm nothing if not predictable, it probably won't surprise you to learn that the star of these segments was none other than the curvy Venetian who'd taken to meeting me on strange balconies. I suppose, if we're to indulge in a spot of pop psychology for a moment, that my attraction might have had something to do with the way Graziella was ordering me around. I've heard it said that men with female bosses often find the scenario quite intoxicating, and apparently I was susceptible to the same weakness. Mind you, I also didn't think it hurt that she had a figure capable of leading a magazine artist to lay down his airbrush for good, or a way of looking out from beneath half-lidded eyes, lips parted just so, that made me feel like a man standing on a very high ledge who was oddly tempted to jump off.

The spit of water coming from my shower was enough to wash by, but it achieved little else. So I still felt uncomfortable in my own skin, let alone my own mind, as I wrapped a towel about my waist and ambled into the kitchen, where I found a note stuck to the kettle.

Morning Sleepyhead. I'm off to explore. Speak later.

Now, since I'm a crime writer by profession, I was able to deduce that far from having two mysterious individuals leaving clues about my apartment, the note in question had been written by Victoria. On any other morning, I suppose I might have been content to bask in the warmth of my mental faculties and steaming kettle for a pleasant few minutes, but rather than make things simple for myself, I hurried along the hallway to Victoria's room and invaded her privacy.

It didn't take long to find my manuscript. In fact, it didn't take any time at all. To my not-inconsiderable disappointment, the printed bundle hadn't moved in the slightest – the middle page of chapter four was still on top.

From what I could see, she hadn't felt the need to read any further during the morning, or even to take the script with her to some friendly café. She'd simply preferred to go outside in the biting cold to wander aimlessly around, leaving my book as far behind her as she possibly could.

No doubt that was unfair, but I was feeling grumpy and irritable, and it helped to blame someone other than me for my foul mood. In fact, it helped so much that I blamed Victoria for the rest of the afternoon, nurturing my huff with care and attention by turning my focus to the notes Graziella had passed me about the security at Palazzo Borelli. There were pages and pages of information, ranging from detailed reports on the type of locks fitted throughout the property, to haphazard schematics of the electricity circuits and rushed sketches of the different floors, to a list of potential entry and exit points (including the benefits and risks associated with each one), and a run-down of the palazzo staff and their hours of employment. She'd flagged wonky floorboards and creaking door hinges, inserted approximate timings for moving between rooms, and even included a short essay on how she wanted me to exploit the surveillance cameras. In short, Graziella had gone far beyond casing the joint – she'd practically autopsied the place – and I suppose I should have been grateful for the heads-up. But I wasn't thankful. Not in the least.

Frankly, I found her notes insulting. As a fellow pro, it would have been nice if she could have trusted me a bit more. And yes, maybe to her mind I'd been winging it all these years, or perhaps her exhaustive planning was just a sign of how serious the situation was for her, but it seemed to me that a little spontaneity was key to a truly satisfying theft. A good burglary takes skill and ability. But a great burglary involves flair. The best thieves are known as break-in *artists* for a reason. And Graziella's more scientific approach left me cold.

I tucked the notes away and fed my bad temper with uncharitable thoughts while I rocked backwards on the hind legs of my writing chair, waiting for my new mobile phone to ring. I spent the long minutes balancing an unlit cigarette on my bottom lip, staring mawkishly at the space on the wall where Hammett's novel used to hang. And I gave my sulk a useful shot in the arm every time I sneaked into my bedroom to slide the heavy aluminium briefcase out from under my bed and asked myself if I should tease the locks open. I was pretty good at being peeved, I must say, and truth be told, I'd got myself in quite the fug by the time I heard Victoria climb the stairs to my apartment, fit her key in the lock and call out a singsong, 'Hello!' as she stepped through my door.

I was on the floor of my bedroom at the time, subjecting the briefcase to a gruelling examination. I still hadn't found anything to indicate that Graziella really could tell if I tricked my way through the combination dials, and it was beginning to kill me not to do just that. As a natural-born burglar, a sense of curiosity is a given, and I'm proud to say that my snooping gene is very highly developed. If I'd stumbled upon the case by pure chance, my first instinct would have been to flip back the lid and see if it contained anything I desired, and being forbidden from doing exactly that simply made me want to do it even more. The only thing stopping me was the enormous value I placed on my copy of *The Maltese Falcon* and my reluctance to take any kind or risk – no matter how small – that might wreck my chances of having it returned to me. Oh, and Victoria's inconvenient return.

Sliding the case beneath my bed and peeling off my plastic gloves, I moved into the hall to find her wiping her feet. Of course, by the time she'd treated me to a blazing grin and gushed about what a fabulous day she'd had, all while climbing out of her coat and insisting that I simply *must* touch her cheeks to see how *freezing* it was outside, my healthy dose of righteous indignation had rather begun to escape me. And once she'd announced that she was taking me out for an evening meal in a charming little restaurant she'd found down by the Rialto markets, I'd almost reached the stage where I could have forgotten what I'd been upset with her for in the first place.

Almost.

We'd cleaned our plates and were waiting for dessert before it all got too much for me. The restaurant was located on a mezzanine level above a popular bar, and it featured rustic furniture, vaulted brick ceilings, a good deal of candlelight, and three arched windows that looked out onto the Grand Canal. It was a small place, filled to the gills with Venetians, and mostly serving gills, as it happens – on account of it being a fish restaurant. Not far from our table was an ice tray stocked with a colourful selection of molluscs and crustaceans, eels and octopuses, dead-eyed red mullet, gawping skate, cod-sized sharks, and an ugly-looking fellow I couldn't readily identify. Across the room, beside the door to the bustling kitchen, a gang of brownish lobsters stalked a murky fish tank, their pincers secured with yellow elastic bands.

'Isn't this fabulous?' Victoria said, leaning back in her chair and spreading her fingers on her belly.

'It's certainly something.'

'You could go to a hundred restaurants in London and you'd never find fish this fresh.'

'Uh huh.'

'And I absolutely love prosecco.' She took a swig from her tall wine glass as if to confirm the revelation.

'Why wouldn't you?'

Victoria hesitated, then did something clever with her face, so that one eyebrow dropped much lower than the other, taking on a diagonal slant. 'Charlie, is there something you want to say to me?'

'Say? I don't think so.'

'Are you sure?'

'Believe me, if there was something I wanted to say, I'd say it.'

'Okay.' She leaned across the table and grabbed the empty bottle of prosecco by the neck, tilting it by way of invitation. 'Shall we order more bubbly?'

I gritted my teeth. 'If you like.'

'Super.' She lifted a finger in the air, signalling our waiter.

'After all,' I told her, 'if it fits in with *your* plans, why shouldn't we order another bottle?'

'O-*kay*.' She showed the label to the waiter, together with a hopeful thumbs up.

'I mean, *your* schedule is important. If *you* want to get blotto and go back to my flat and pass out on your bed, *I* shouldn't have a problem with that, should I?'

Victoria dabbed her lips with her napkin and backed away from me with a palms-up gesture, like I was a stack of playing cards she'd carefully balanced and was loath to upset.

I scowled at the table and snatched up my wine glass. I could have done without the bubbles. Sparkling wine isn't the best accompaniment to a bad temper. Then again, neither is it the most suitable preparation for a night of pilfering. I could feel the weight of the mobile phone in my trouser pocket, and I had no idea when it might begin to vibrate.

Perhaps I'd have felt less grouchy if I hadn't been facing the windows. Somewhere out there, beyond the reflections of twinkling candles and our fellow diners, was Palazzo Borelli. I wasn't sure I needed the reminder. I was even less sure that I wanted it.

'Is this about your manuscript?' Victoria asked me.

I glanced down, straightening my dessert spoon on the tablecloth. 'What if it is?'

'Then I think we should talk about it, don't you? I am your agent, after all.'

'Oh, so you've remembered, then.'

'*Charlie.*'

'Forgive me.' I kept my eyes down. It seemed my pastry fork needed rearranging too. 'It's just with all the sightseeing you've been doing, one might be forgiven for thinking you'd forgotten about my novel altogether.'

Victoria drew an audible breath. I got the impression she was counting numbers in her head. I wondered how far she might get before letting me have it with both barrels.

'Charlie, I'm going to be honest with you.'

Oh boy. Nothing that starts out with those words is ever destined to be good. I was beginning to wish I hadn't pushed things – maybe it would have been better to let Victoria leave Venice with both of us pretending I'd never handed her a new script at all.

'Look,' she said, 'I've only read the beginning. Barely got

into it. But it's very ...' she raised her eyes to the ceiling, searching for the right word, 'different.'

Christ, stab me in the gut, why didn't she? *Different*. That was just wonderful. Next thing she'd be delivering the old 'taste is subjective' line.

'Listen, everything is subjective, you know that.' *Told you*. 'What one person likes, another might not. Agreed?'

'Ah, I see,' I said. 'And what you're saying is – you don't like it.'

Victoria winced, as if I'd kicked her under the table. I was pretty sure I *hadn't* kicked her under the table. Although, now I thought of it, maybe it wasn't such a bad idea.

'It's not that I don't *like* it per se. It's just that it's ...'

'Different?'

'Exactly.'

We reached for our wine, monitoring each other closely, as if neither one of us was entirely sure which glass contained the deadly poison. We swallowed dryly and set our drinks to one side. Victoria circled the rim of her glass with her fingertip and I switched the salt and pepper pots around.

'It seems very commercial,' Victoria told me, in an apologetic tone. 'Almost overtly so.'

'That's what I was aiming for,' I mumbled, moving the pepper behind the salt pot, like a magician working the three-cups routine. 'You do want to sell it, don't you?'

'Yes, but as a Faulks book, I'm just not sure how it sits alongside the rest of the titles in the series.'

'Maybe it won't sit beside them. Maybe it'll sit on one of those shelves where the books that actually sell end up.'

Victoria reached across and stilled the salt and pepper pots. She was about to say more when our waiter reappeared. He popped the cork on our new bottle and poured the frothing alcohol into our glasses.

I met Victoria's eyes. She smirked and covered her mouth with her hand. I couldn't help smiling too.

'Listen, if you hate it, just tell me,' I said. 'It's not the end of the world, right?'

'I don't hate it ... yet. The truth is I don't know how I feel about it. I've only read the opening chapters, so I'm really not in a position to comment.' She shrugged. 'I suppose the truth is I'm scared.'

'Scared? I'm the one who just spent months planning and writing the damn thing.'

'But that's exactly it. I know how significant this book is to you, Charlie. I know what you hope might come from it.' She lowered her voice and leaned across the table to cover my hand with her own. 'I know the things you gave up to write it, okay?'

Ah, hell. 'And?'

'And I'm afraid I won't like it. And I'm afraid of having to be the one to tell you that.'

Hmm. Would it make her feel any better if I told her I hadn't given up my larcenous lifestyle, after all? That I was, in fact, destined to break into a luxurious home at a moment's notice?

'That's my problem,' I told her, freeing my hand. 'The important thing is that you're straight with me – that you tell me if it's no good.'

'Okay.' She swallowed, eyeing her wine glass.

'Go ahead,' I told her. 'Drink.'

'I will. In a minute. But there's something I want you to promise me first.'

I looked at her blankly. She hesitated, then seemed to resolve herself to pressing on.

'If I don't like the book – this one particular story you've given me – I don't want you to give up on this new lifestyle of yours. You're good, Charlie – really good – and one day the world is going to wake up to that fact. But if it takes a little longer to get there than you were hoping for, will you promise me that you won't fall back into your bad old ways?'

'Eh?'

'The stealing,' she whispered. 'I wouldn't want to be responsible for you getting yourself into trouble again.'

'Oh *that*,' I told her, and took a healthy pull on my wine. 'Christ, the very idea couldn't be further from my mind.'

TEN

One of the things I'd tried to do in my new novel was to create a compelling villain for Michael Faulks to go up against. To this end, I'd spent many hours at the planning stage, breaking down Faulks' strengths and then using those components to build an adversary who was more powerful in every department. I ended up with the character of Don Giovanni, a seven-foot-tall, six-teen-stone Mafia godfather with a network of enforcers and crooks throughout Italy and beyond. Don Giovanni lived in a heavily guarded villa on the shores of the Lido, from where he oversaw his extensive criminal enterprises. A chess grand master, a dab hand at Shaolin Kung Fu and a champion breeder of Argentine Dogo fighting dogs, he was the most complete enemy Faulks had ever had the misfortune to come up against.

In short, I knew everything I could care to know about The Godfather of the Veneto, and the threat he represented. So, on reflection, it was hard for me to ignore the fact that I knew next to nothing about my own aggressor. Most importantly, I had no idea what was in the attaché briefcase Graziella had given me, or whether anything she'd told me about returning it happened to be true. I was aware that she had a talent for burglary, I got the impression she was in some kind of bind, and I could hazard an educated guess at her cup size, but beyond that, I was clueless.

And yet, somehow, I still found myself trudging through a sleety drizzle and the musty, sinuous alleys of San Marco, heading for the district of Cannaregio at a quarter past eleven that night.

Graziella's call had reached me less than an hour before, shortly after I'd escorted Victoria back to my apartment and watched her climb into bed with my manuscript for company. I'd been in the kitchen making Victoria a cup of tea at the time, and the noise of the kettle had masked my half of the conversation.

'It is time,' Graziella had announced, in a breathless voice. 'We will be at the casino in thirty minutes. You have the briefcase?'

'Yes, I have it,' I told her. 'And I'm assuming you still have my book.'

'Then you have read my instructions? You are ready?'

That was hardly answering my question, but I decided to let it go. 'As ready as I can be. Are you sure there'll be staff on the property?'

'*Si*. But just two, I think.'

'Anything else you want to tell me?'

'Be very careful. Do not make a mistake. And when you put the case in the strongroom, make sure it is somewhere he will see it.'

'Would you like me to open it for him too?'

'Do not joke about this. Please. The case must stay closed.'

Touchy, touchy. 'Or?'

'Or you will be killed.'

She cut the connection just as the kettle came to the boil. Talk about raising the stakes. I'd gone from having my favourite book confiscated to having my life threatened in one short phone call. I suppose it was the sort of thing that a mind more reasoned than my own might have spent a good deal of time considering. In fact, it was exactly the kind of plot development I'd normally have discussed with Victoria.

Hmm. Was now the time to bring her on board, I wondered? Somehow, I didn't think so. If I told her what I'd become involved in, there was no way she'd see things from my point of view. There'd be a lot of talk about calling the police, for starters, and even if I got her past that, she'd never be comfortable with the prospect of my breaking into the palazzo. Too many risks, she'd say. Too much unknown. And you know what? She'd be right.

I carried the tea through to her, along with two biscuits. I dare say you can put the chocolate digestives down to my guilty conscience.

'This section works well,' she told me, with a strained smile that reminded me of the look my old art teacher would give me when I'd produced something dazzling with a set of poster paints and a potato stamp.

'Oh? Which one?'

She angled the manuscript towards me. The passage she was referring to happened to describe Faulks' third break-in – the one that went horribly wrong and turned everything on its head. Lucky I don't believe in bad omens, I guess.

'Listen, I'm sorry about tonight, my mood and everything,' I told her.

'It's okay, Charlie. I know what you writer types are like. I should have been more sensitive.'

'Are you planning to read for long?'

'A few hours, probably.' A series of frown lines appeared between her eyes. 'Should I wake you when I stop? Give you some feedback?'

I shook my head and waved my hands. 'Not what I had in mind. Look, I realise this may sound crazy, but I'm going to head out for a while.'

'Out?' She pushed herself up in bed. 'But it's started to rain. And it's late.'

'It'll help me to relax,' I said. 'Take my mind off things.'

Victoria flattened her hands on the manuscript and scrutinised me. 'Is this going to be a law-abiding walk?'

Christ, she really did know me a little too well.

'Absolutely.'

She studied me for a long moment, as if she expected me to

slip up and confess what I was really planning. 'All right then,' she said, at last. 'Knock on my door when you get back. *Lightly*. If I'm still up, I'll tell you how I've got on.'

'Perfect.'

'Yes, I am rather. Now, skedaddle.'

And so skedaddle I did. And while I was at it, I gathered together my spectacles case, my plastic gloves and the rest of my burglary equipment, and then I stuffed the envelope of information about Palazzo Borelli into my overcoat pocket, eased the attaché case out from beneath my bed and sneaked past Victoria's room to embark upon my foolhardy assignment.

The palazzo was a statement in crumbling Veneto-Byzantine splendour, overlooking a sweeping curve in the Grand Canal to the front, and sandwiched between the Palazzo Mangilli-Valmerama on one side and a constricted passageway known as Ramo Dragan on the other. Four storeys in height, the buff-coloured façade was adorned with marble lion statues and several imprints of the Borelli family's coat of arms, and it was dominated by a prominent stone balcony that stretched for the entire width of the building, interrupted only by a series of sculpted columns and stilted arches.

The balcony could be reached through the glass French doors of the *piano nobile*, and it extended outwards above three metal watergates that formed the canal-side entrance to the palazzo. The water entrance didn't appear to be used very often. There was no floating wooden jetty, ringed by candy-striped mooring posts, although a nearby pontoon did stretch out into the rain-pocked canal from the shadowed alley running alongside the building. Since the front was far too visible, not to mention too wet, I was planning to gain access from the pedestrian entrance around the back.

The rear of the palazzo featured a high-walled garden, fringed with sodden, overhanging shrubs. Even supposing I had a rope with me – which I didn't – there was no way I could scale the damp brickwork with the heavy briefcase for company. It was fortunate, then, that a tall iron gate had been fitted at the rear of the garden, where only a sizeable cylinder lock, an alarm sensor, a security light and a closed-circuit camera stood in my way.

Before getting too close, I rested the briefcase on the slick ground at my feet, flexed my good fingers and turned to scan the murky pathway behind me. There was nobody nearby, which came as little surprise. The confined passage ended abruptly at the timber pontoon and the icy waters beyond, and the only property it offered access to was the very one I was interested in.

It felt strange standing in the blackened alley on my own, with the misty rain beading in my hair, only a short hop and a skip away from the bustling Strada Nova, with its tacky restaurants and English-language bars and souvenir outlets. This was a private Venice, unknown to all but the wealthiest residents, the odd disorientated soul and the occasional reluctant thief.

Reaching upwards, I grasped the edge of my woollen hat and rolled the material down over my face until the eye holes were in place. As a general rule, I don't like to wear a balaclava. Too many terrorists and career criminals have given the garment a bad name, and I've never relished the idea of being spotted wearing a ski mask and having someone assume that I'm an armed robber. Tonight, I was willing to change my approach. There were the security cameras for one thing, but since this wasn't a job I'd gone looking for, or cased by myself, it made sense to be as cautious as possible. And besides, the balaclava would keep my face warm and dry.

I hefted the weighty briefcase and made directly for the gate, triggering the security light and embarking upon my patented Step Programme for Recovering Law-Abiding Citizens.

Step one: I planted the briefcase down, jumped onto it and scrambled up the slippery fretwork of the gate until I was level with the security camera. The lens was pointed directly at me, but it didn't see me for long. Removing my mittens, I stuck one of them on the end as a makeshift lens cap. According to my instructions, this wasn't the type of situation where a watchful security guard would be glued to a bank of security monitors at all hours of the day. Instead, the camera footage was simply recorded. That suited me, and it also suited my Italian pen friend. Her plan involved me returning the case without being caught, all while leaving enough evidence to pinpoint the exact time at which the dastardly deed was done – thus keeping her in the clear, if it ever became relevant, by virtue of the fact that she was currently enjoying the company of Count Borelli at the oldest, and some would say, finest casino in all of Europe.

Step two: I jumped down from the gate and inspected the magnetic sensor alarm. *Jeez*. I was starting to think that maybe I should set up a company selling modern security systems in the city, because at this rate I'd make an absolute killing. The alarm was about as basic as it gets – short of tying a string of tin cans to your door – and after pulling the necessary tools from my spectacles case, I had the thing neutralised in less time than it takes to tell it.

Step three: I armed myself with the heftiest pick I carried and tinkered with the lock. It was trickier than it had any right to be. The temperature didn't help. Yes, it was getting to my fingers through my plastic gloves, but it seemed like the mechanism had frozen up just a touch. I dug around in my pocket for my cigarette packet and fished out my lighter. I worked the flame and held it to the keyhole and counted to ten. I stopped at eight when I realised the tip of my glove was melting, then I poked at the lock a second time round. Lucky for me, the thing yielded and clunked open, and I was finally able to grab for the briefcase and scurry away from the glare of the lamp.

The garden was carpeted in sodden lawn, with no discernible path. I took my time crossing it, wary of any sudden dips or concealed fish ponds. The footprints I was leaving in the muddy grass didn't make me spectacularly happy, but they didn't bother me all that much, either. It was too dark for them to be seen from the house, and even if they were still visible in the morning and some wily detective decided to record my tread imprints, I didn't see what harm it could cause. After all, there had to be more than one or two people residing in Venice with size-ten feet.

Halfway through the garden, I caught sight of a gap in the wall and made my way to a courtyard area, where the cobble-stones were greasy with rain. A nude male statue was coated in water droplets over to my left, and an ornate well-head plugged an old drinking well in the very centre of the space. The main entrance to the living quarters was on the floor above, reached by an external stone staircase supported by a vaulted red-brick structure. Above the large wooden door were a number of lighted windows. Directly ahead of me was a darkened arch-way.

I scurried beneath the arch and clicked on my penlight. There was a strong smell of brine and decay, and I could hear the slap of waves. The flagstones beneath my feet were clogged with moss and algae, and when I pointed my torch ahead into the darkness I could pick out the shimmer of blackened water beyond the scroll-work of the entrance gates.

I backed off and went in search of the door I was looking for. It was constructed from green, riveted metal, edged in rubber, and a white-on-blue sign had been screwed to the front of it reading: *Cabina Elettrica*. It was also unlocked. I heaved it open and sprayed the light from my flash over the fuse boards and hazard warning signs I found there. Now true, I don't go in for a lot of that hi-tech twaddle you see in most caper movies, but even without my handwritten instructions, I like to think that I could have cast my eyes over the mess of wiring and panels and switches, and still figured out that the giant lever with the bright red handle was sort of important. I tightened my fingers around it and checked my watch: 11.40 p.m.

'Okay Charlie,' I whispered in the darkness, 'you have ten minutes to complete this exam. Starting *now*.'

I threw the switch, and to my genuine disappointment, there was no pleasing sound effect of the entire residence powering down. Back out in the courtyard, however, I could see that the lights were no longer shining in the windows above, and in less than a minute, the sound of voices – a grumbling man and a nagging woman – could be heard from the direction of the internal stairs leading down to the ground-floor area I'd just vacated. I hurried up the external staircase to the huge front door with the briefcase in my hand, dropped to my knees in the wetness and assessed the lock.

It was an old-fashioned warded lock with a keyhole that was almost large enough for me to crawl through, if only I hadn't gorged myself at dinner. I fumbled inside my spectacles case for my ring of skeleton pass keys, peeled my balaclava up as far as my nose, popped my penlight into my mouth and set to work. Modesty aside, I honestly don't believe that I could have been any faster. The third key I tried fitted the bill and the lock turned every bit as easily as I imagine it had done for the hundreds of years since the place had been built. So easily, in fact, that I was back on my feet almost before the cold and moisture had penetrated to my kneecaps.

I turned and glanced over my shoulder, but all that was behind me was rain and darkness and silence. Strange. Things had been going pretty well so far, but I couldn't shake an odd sense of foreboding. I wanted to tell myself that it was just Venice – the peculiar way the city had of lending menace to an unlit canal, a deserted street or the echo of your own footsteps. But for all my efforts, I was afraid it was something more than that, and as I pulled my balaclava down, eased the mighty door open and stepped inside, I couldn't help but wonder if I was making a horrible mistake.

ELEVEN

The interior was striking, even by torchlight. I knew from Graziella's handwritten directions that the door opened directly onto the *portego* – a formal hallway that ended in a T-shaped space overlooking the balcony and the Grand Canal beyond. What her instructions had failed to prepare me for was just how imposing and elaborate this 'hallway' would be.

Put simply, the space was immense. The terrazzo floor was a stunning mixture of coloured stone, mother of pearl and cut glass that glimmered in the light from my flash in a most appealing way. One entire wall appeared to be draped in heavy red silk and gold brocade, and the opposing wall featured a number of large oil paintings of bearded, Godlike figures. In between the paintings, lavish stucco work drew my eye up towards the biggest treat of all.

The coved and frescoed ceiling wouldn't have looked out of place in the Sistine Chapel. It was a riot of pudgy cherubs, raven-haired nudes and prancing stallions tussling with noble lions. Naturally, I shouldn't have been pointing my torch up at it, and I certainly shouldn't have been wasting time, but I honestly couldn't help myself. Never in my life had I been anywhere quite like it, and on that basis alone, I thought I should cut myself a little slack.

A little, but not too much, and after no more than a minute, I picked my jaw up off the floor along with the attaché case and headed into the heart of the galleried room. I passed a narrow flight of wooden stairs that led to the upper floors of the palace and a wider stone staircase that connected with the basement area below. I listened carefully for any indication that the man and woman who'd decided to investigate the electricity failure might be about to return, but I couldn't hear anything at all. True, the ski mask was muffling my senses to a degree, but not enough to cause me to miss something like that.

Up ahead, beyond a pair of banquette-settees and a richly lacquered side unit, the picture windows were draped with simple net curtains that had been tied back to leave the view unobstructed. I crept as close as I dared, killed my penlight and allowed myself a quick peek at the expanse of lamp-lit water below. A lonely *vaporetto* was churning through the drizzle, bleeding milky light from its sides as it charted a diagonal course towards the Rialto Mercato stop, just along from the *traghetto* station. To the left, I could see the darkened exterior of the empty fish market and the recessed windows of the restaurant where Victoria and I had eaten.

Peeling myself away, I located a stately door fashioned from lush walnut to my right and was brazen enough to pass right through. It opened onto a small room lined with dark wooden panelling. The beam from my torch revealed a ladder-backed chair, an ornamental rug and a marble fireplace decorated with Murano glass tiles. A pair of French doors opened onto the balcony.

I set the briefcase down on the chair and started to feel my way along the panelling on the back wall. Around a third of the way along, I sensed the outline of a crack, and I followed it down to waist level before reaching across to the panel to the right. I flattened my hand against the wood and pressed firmly. It eased back, I heard a pleasing clunk, and a concealed door swung open to my left.

I hauled the door aside until I was faced with a large slab of glistening steel with a metal wheel in its centre. Above the wheel was an electronic keypad. I lifted the balaclava on one side of my face and pressed my ear against the cold metal, shaped my left hand into a fist and knocked twice. I couldn't hear even the vaguest echo. That made it solid – six inches, at least. It wasn't something I needed to know, since I hadn't planned on attacking it with a laser, but I was intrigued all the same.

Reaching for my envelope of instructions, I flipped through the handwritten pages under the light from my torch until I found the section I was looking for. The code consisted of nine digits, and it had been printed down the left-hand margin of a sheet of notepaper. I was a tad miffed by the way it had been laid out, as if I was prone to making basic errors, but since cracking the code for myself would have been seriously time-consuming, I decided to set my grievances to one side.

Facing up to the keypad, I rolled my neck around on my shoulders, extended a finger and began to carefully input the code. I was halfway through when I was interrupted by a sudden buzz and crackle in the walls, followed by a bright light being flung around the room. My heart jitterbugged in my chest and I jumped like I'd been prodded with a stick, until it dawned on me that the electricity had been turned back on and that the light was coming from the giant glass chandelier above me. I spun round and checked the corners of the ceiling. Sure enough, a camera was pointing down at me from an area above the window. There was no point covering it now – it had done the job it was designed for. Luckily, so had my balaclava, so I turned my back to the camera without even a wave and resumed my work with the code.

Not long afterwards, the keypad emitted a friendly melody that prompted me to place my hands on the metal wheel and steer the palazzo to the left. The locking mechanism clanked and clunked, much like a nuclear sub taken way too deep beneath the ocean, and then it fell quite silent. I hooked a finger around the wheel and the door surprised me by swinging out very fast and striking my shin.

I yelped and hopped and cursed, and then I raised my head, peered inside the lighted vault and fell into a mournful silence.

The strongroom was larger than the kitchen in my apartment. It had a thick concrete floor and the walls and ceiling were clad in shiny steel plating. It was lined with an extensive selection of metal shelving, and the greenish light from the twitching fluorescent bulbs gave it the appearance of a top-secret science lab.

Mouth open, I stepped inside to a world of high-denomination bank notes wrapped in neat plastic bundles, jewellery boxes from all the right stores containing all the right stones, and a selection of oil paintings and sketch works from a number of artists I'd very definitely heard of. I ran my gloved fingers over stacks of bond certificates and formal-looking deeds, display cases of gold coins, a shelf of Rolex watches and a stack of locked metal security boxes that teetered alarmingly at my approach. A pair of antique pistols were hanging on the far wall, barrels crossed, and beneath them was a very fine porcelain jug of Oriental origin. In short, it was a veritable Aladdin's cave – by far the most extensive bounty I'd ever stumbled upon – and sadly for me, I'd been expressly forbidden to take anything at all.

I turned and raised a quizzical eyebrow to the camera above me, which was somewhat pointless, on account of my balaclava. Then I lowered my head and offered the briefcase a similar assessment. Well, at least it wouldn't be lonely once I'd returned it to the vault. I could set it down on the floor, right in the very centre, where it could wait undisturbed for its lucky owner to discover it.

Yeah, right.

Looking back, it amazes me that I'd managed to resist temptation for so long. Almost twenty-four hours with the case in my possession, and I hadn't opened it. Yes, I'd thought about it. And sure, it had been hard to see what harm could possibly befall me. Graziella had claimed that she'd know; that I'd lose my Hammett novel for good; that I'd be killed. Well, phooey to all that. I'd taken a long, hard look at the case. *Several* looks. It was nice. It was expensive. But it wasn't magic. It wasn't wildly futuristic. And I simply didn't believe there was any way she'd be able to tell if I took a swift peep at exactly what I was depositing on her behalf.

More to the point, it seemed reasonable to assume that the case contained something truly special, bearing in mind how Graziella had chosen to swipe it ahead of all the other riches on offer in the vault. Hell, it could be that I was about to find something that would dwarf the value of Hammett's book, and buy me a small Caribbean island besides.

I cracked my knuckles – the good ones at least – and knelt down in front of the case. The combination dials that secured it were about as good as they come. High quality, no flex, which made it difficult to feel any stiffness when I hit upon a correct number. Difficult, but not impossible, and I was determined to do the job right. Two minutes in, and I had the sequence for the three rotary dials on the left. Five seconds later, and my thumb had rolled the same code into the dials on the right. I checked the room for prying eyes, glanced up at the prying camera lens, let go of a sharp breath and sprang the catches.

The lid bounced up. I levered it fully open, and right then, I heard a two-tone electronic note, as if the case had received a text message. *Crap*, I thought. Perhaps Graziella had been telling the truth and the case had dispatched some kind of alert straight to her. Ah well, no sense in going back now ...

Glancing down, I readied myself for my first glimpse of the precious bounty I'd been lugging around Venice for the best part of a day, and it took me precisely three seconds to understand what I was seeing.

I know it took me three seconds because the display on the digital watch in the middle of the egg-box interior told me as much. The watch had been set to *10* and now it was at *7*. It was flashing and beeping. Oh, and it was wired to two packages of dun-coloured putty.

6, 5 ...

The case was steaming, and it was starting to hiss, like a ready meal left in a microwave for too long. And there I was, mindlessly gawping at it, waiting like an idiot until my brain finally caught up with the plummeting sensation in my gut and the frantic thump in my temples to dispatch a message with the letters *B. O. M. B.* to the parts of my body that were able to react.

4 ...

I slammed the lid closed and pushed up from the floor.

3 ...

Hands around the case, I threw it like a rugby ball into the back of the strongroom.

2 ...

I slammed the door closed, spun the locking wheel to the right and dived for cover.

1 ...

But there was no cover. There was just the rug and the chair.

Flattening myself on the ground, covering my head with my hands, I braced myself for the long duration of that one terrible second.

And then a jump jet took off from inside the vault.

TWELVE

You have no idea how precious life is until a tonne of steel door flies past your head at close quarters. I felt the breeze as it went by, and I pressed myself so hard into the ground that I probably left an imprint of my bellybutton on the floorboards.

The door was followed by a tornado of hot air that singed the back of my neck and almost prised me from the floor to throw me against the wall in a heap. Debris showered over me – chunks of plaster and metal and itty bitty pieces of jewellery and expensive artwork. A thick, acrid fog of smoke and dust filled the room. It draped my body, clogging my throat and lungs with the first breath I took. Gasping for air, I cracked my eyes open and squinted out at my surroundings. I was half-blinded by the grit and the smoke, and blinking only made it worse.

I had no idea how big the blast had been. It had seemed mighty substantial to me, but I didn't appear to be fatally wounded, and so far as I could tell, the palazzo hadn't begun to lurch and sink into the waters of the lagoon. Probably the vault had contained it. Almost certainly the vault was destroyed.

Turning my head, I found that the strongroom was a scorching furnace of flame and smoke. The remains of the door were hanging at an absurd angle from the buckled frame, and there was no sign whatsoever of the damn briefcase that had triggered it all.

Very carefully, I pushed my chest up from the floor, and by some minor miracle my arms came with me. I patted myself down, probing for injuries. I seemed remarkably unscathed. There were cuts and abrasions to my hands and the back of my legs, and I was fairly sure I'd taken a hefty knock on the head, but aside from the difficulty I was having breathing and seeing, everything seemed to be roughly in order.

Of course, it took me a few seconds more before I discovered that I was experiencing the aftermath of the bomb blast in absolute silence. I'd like to be able to tell you that my ears were ringing, at the very least, but the truth is they were doing nothing of the sort. There was an odd sensation of pressure, like I was in the middle of some hellish aeroplane journey with a severe dose of flu, but the only thing I could come close to hearing were my own thoughts, and sadly enough, they weren't altogether lucid.

For far too long, I rested on my skinned elbow, gaping at the destruction and the flames with an odd kind of detachment, as if I was viewing everything on a television with the volume set to mute. Then, gradually, what was left of my senses began to take hold of me and I realised there was no way I could stay where I was. The fire might spread, or I might suffocate on the smoke. And I could hardly wait to be rescued, since I was the one who'd ignited the bomb in the first place – and granted, I may not have known about the explosives I was carrying, but I somehow doubted that explanation would be good enough for the Italian authorities.

But where to go? Not back through the palazzo, surely. The house staff might be fleeing the building, but they might be on their way to investigate, and I was in no shape to fight my way past them, or to engage in an impromptu game of hide and seek. It wouldn't be long before the place would be crawling with firemen and police, and considering my injuries, not to mention the dust and rubble I appeared to have showered in, it wouldn't take Giuseppe Columbo to figure out that I might have been involved in the explosion.

I made it to my knees, then tottered gamely for a while before struggling to my feet. Swaying woozily, I stooped beneath the reeking smoke billowing across the underside of the ceiling and staggered in the direction of the French doors. The doors were gone, along with most of the wall surrounding them. I rested my hand against the ragged hole in the brickwork and laboured over a mound of plaster until I slipped and toppled onto the balcony.

Broken glass gave out beneath my feet. I raised my foot in a daze and stamped it back down. The sound didn't carry – I couldn't hear a thing.

Across the canal and through the hazy drizzle, a group of people at the lighted *vaporetto* stop seemed to be pointing at me. One woman was waving her arms with her mouth wide open in a noiseless shout.

Wiping the dirt and crud from my lips, I tested the wet air. It whistled through to my lungs – the finest thing I'd ever inhaled. My panic eased by a fraction, and I reached for the damp stone balustrade to steady myself. I almost missed. The balustrade was cracked and buckled, drooping over the edge of the balcony as if it was melting. Off to my right, a water taxi was turning at speed, its driver gazing back over his shoulder to log my position.

I looked groggily down at the water of the Grand Canal. The curdlike surface was pricked with rain and alight with the reflection of the flames escaping the gap in the wall behind me. I didn't know how deep it was, but it looked very cold – ice had formed around the timber stilts that supported the wooden pontoon and the tarred pilings close by.

I turned and glanced back. The room was fully ablaze now – no way through.

I leaned more weight on the balustrade, and almost before I'd made the decision for myself, the thing shuddered and flexed, then hung suspended for a fleeting moment, before shearing loose and tipping me down towards the freezing waters like a vending machine dispatching a dinged can of fizzy pop.

*

It was almost dawn by the time I'd limped back to the Dorsoduro. I was soaked right through, and I was so blue with cold that I could have passed for a Smurf. I couldn't feel my feet, let alone my fingers, and it took me an age to shunt my key into the lock on the front door to my building and turn the damn thing with my teeth.

The stairs to my apartment took on the proportions of the Dolomites, and I scaled them by leaning against the wall and pausing between steps to catch my breath, as if each riser delivered me to a higher and altogether more demanding altitude. The treads whirled and dipped before me like a staircase in a fairground funhouse, and I teetered in the manner of a concussed drunk. I would have called for help if it had been an option, but the last thing I needed was for Martin and Antea to see me in this state. So long as I kept moving and I focussed on the door to my apartment, I thought I could make it.

Of course, when I eventually did reach my door I faced the challenge of the three substantial locks I'd fitted. The challenge was too much. With my keys gripped uselessly in my swollen hands, I laughed a faint, wheezing laugh at the damn stupid irony of it all – and then I slumped against the door, tried to shape my hand into a fist, gave up, and slapped my open palm on the wood.

I had no way of telling how hard I was knocking. I couldn't feel the impact and I certainly couldn't hear it. I laughed my silly, dazed laugh again. I couldn't hear my laugh, either. I laughed some more, feeling like a comedian in an old silent movie.

My eyes slid sideways. I watched my hand pat the door. I was a man tapping a pillow – a guy punching foam. I blew bubbles from my lips and twirled round onto my back and slid down the door until my soggy buttocks struck the ground. My useless hands rested in my lap, curled and bloated and hooked like those of an old crone. I let my keys drop to the floor and a long, ragged breath escaped my lips.

Then the door opened and I tumbled backwards.

Victoria was standing above me with her pink dressing gown open over her spotty pyjamas and my umbrella raised in her hand like a spear. She frowned at me, then bared her teeth and yelled words that I couldn't hear in the slightest. I would have liked to have replied – come to mention it, I would have loved to have engaged in a long and detailed conversation. Only I couldn't, so I did the next best thing and voiced my most pressing concern.

'Don't call for an ambulance,' I told her.

She winced, as if I'd yelled savagely in her face. Perhaps I had.

'Or the police,' I went on, my volume a mystery to my ears. 'In fact, don't call anyone. Promise me.'

She planted her fists on her hips and glared at me. Tight-jawed, she offered me some carefully selected words, but even though I did my best to lip-read, somewhere in the middle of her inaudible monologue, my eyelids fluttered closed, my mind became as limp as my body, and I finally gave in to the overwhelming shock of it all.

It must have been the friction that brought me round – the rubbing of the parquet floor on my lower back. My arms were stretched far above me and the living room was sliding away in a jerking fashion. I rolled my eyes in my head and discovered that Victoria had a hold of my wrists. She was dragging me along the hall, and making hard work of it. Legs spread wide, with her slippers planted either side of my shoulders and the hem of her dressing gown skimming the floor, I could see from her flushed face and the way her eyes were squeezed tight shut that I was carrying a shade more weight than I might have preferred.

'What are you doing?' I asked.

She grimaced and heaved some more. My wet jeans bunched up around my bottom.

'Let go,' I told her. 'I can move myself. You don't have to drag me.'

She paused and scowled at me. Her lips started moving again. Spittle flew from them and I was pretty sure I could see sparks coming out of her ears. She reminded me of a mime – a particularly irate one.

'Just let go of my arms.'

And blow me, she did. I hadn't been ready for it. The back of my head struck the floor hard. I moaned and clutched at my temples as the blurred ceiling dropped down from above and bounced back up, like a yoyo on a string. I covered my eyes with my hands and peered out through my puffy fingers. The ceiling plunged down again, growing darker all the while, and then I passed right through it until I was lost altogether.

THIRTEEN

I woke to find myself in bed. Naked.

I couldn't remember how I'd ended up between my sheets and I had no recollection whatsoever of undressing myself. I felt sickly cold, despite the heavy covers pressing down on me, and I was aware of an odd whistling in my ears, like the static from a badly tuned radio.

I cupped a hand over my left ear, but the whistling grew more intense, which suggested it was coming from inside my head. Not a good sign. Even worse, my palm came away spotted with blood.

I rubbed my fingers beneath my nose. Disinfectant. The scent was unmistakable, conjuring memories of playground accidents. I sniffed some more, and discovered that the skin on my face and arms was coated in the stuff, like an unwanted cologne. Raising my forearms, I considered the network of fine cuts and abrasions I found there, each of them weeping as I flexed my skin.

'Do you think you might stay conscious this time?'

I recognised Victoria's voice before I saw her. She was sitting in the chair in the corner of my room, huddled up inside her dressing gown, reading my manuscript in the light from a standing lamp with a fringed shade. I squinted against the pain the light was causing me. Squinting didn't help – it just seemed to increase the pressure in my head and make my ears pop and crackle in a most disturbing manner.

'I used the first-aid kit in your bathroom,' she told me. 'Dressed your wounds as best I could.'

'I'm naked,' I croaked, and the sound of my own voice was like fingernails running down a blackboard inside my head. 'Completely . . . naked.'

She lowered my manuscript. 'Staggering, isn't it?'

I cradled my forehead and braced myself to speak again. 'Where are my clothes?' I asked, and while I did so, I tried very hard to recall climbing out of them.

'In the washing machine. I didn't think you'd thank me for putting you to bed sopping wet.'

Oh, boy.

'*You* put me to bed?'

'I'm afraid you were in no fit state to do it yourself. But don't worry, I didn't spend my time feasting my eyes on your body – what's left of it, that is. Are you going to tell me what on earth happened to you?'

'Maybe once Radio Italia stops broadcasting from inside my skull.'

Very carefully, I propped myself up on my elbows until my back was resting against the headboard. I pulled the blankets over my chest. It wasn't simply out of modesty – I was still chilled to the core by my unexpected dip in the Grand Canal. Lord Byron would have been hugely disappointed in me – he'd viewed swimming in the lagoon as a major test of one's manhood.

Speaking of manhood, I really would have preferred it if Victoria hadn't seen me in the nude when I'd been flirting with the prospect of hypothermia. True enough, it was only a minor quibble in the context of the near-death experience I'd recently endured, but it was a concern all the same.

'You'll be glad to hear I didn't call the police or an ambulance,' she said, interrupting my thoughts. 'God only knows why I listened to you. You were practically raving when you got back here, shouting at the top of your voice. For the past hour, you've been looking worse than a corpse.'

'Charming.'

'Want to know why I didn't call anyone?'

I didn't say anything to that. I couldn't imagine there was anything fruitful to be said.

'It's because I'm assuming you've been up to no good. The balaclava and burglary tools I found in your coat gave it away somewhat.'

I didn't say anything to that, either. I'm not quite as stupid as I might seem, and I was aware that our conversation had the potential to be almost as dangerous as the bomb blast I'd inadvertently triggered.

'Look, you must realise that you're going to have to offer me some kind of explanation, at least.'

I squirmed beneath my sheets. 'It's complicated, Vic.'

'I had a feeling it might be.'

'Maybe it's best left until morning.'

'It practically *is* morning. And knowing my luck, you'll be unconscious again soon. Come on, spill.'

'You really want me to?'

'Oh, like you wouldn't believe.'

And so I told Victoria everything. Well, not *absolutely* everything – I skipped over the details of my torrid, erotic dream, for instance – but other than that I was completely honest. I spoke in a halting, breathless voice for close to thirty minutes, without interruption, without questioning. If only I'd been in a church, it could have passed for a confession. Maybe it was, of sorts – a confession as to exactly how brainless I'd been.

And what happened? Well, Victoria walked straight out of my room. She did it without speaking and without even looking at me. I called after her, but to be perfectly frank, I couldn't give it the gusto it deserved. I tried, naturally, but my throat wasn't up to it yet – it still felt like it was lined with the dry ingredients for a cement mix.

Sliding down beneath my bedcovers, groaning pitifully to myself, I listened, where I could, to the sounds of Victoria moving about in her room. They weren't the most encouraging noises imaginable. There was a lot of pacing, and a good deal of huffing, and the unmistakable sound of a suitcase zipper. It didn't take a genius to deduce that she was packing her things – even I was capable of it.

'Victoria,' I called, my voice sounding faint and hopeless. 'Don't go. Stay with me. I'm sorry.' I didn't think she could hear me – I could barely hear myself. 'Please don't go,' I added, but I might as well have tried communicating through the wall in sign language.

What on earth would I do if she did leave? I had no idea how long I'd be suffering from the after-effects of the explosion, and I really didn't like the idea of being on my own. At the moment, a simple trip to the bathroom would mean crawling on my hands and knees, and the only thing I was capable of rustling up in the kitchen was a dramatic faint. More to the point, I was vulnerable.

The way I saw things, Graziella had been telling the truth – she really could tell if I opened the briefcase. Hell, come to mention it, most of Venice could tell. If she returned to the palazzo with Count Borelli, the gaping, smoking hole in the front of the building would give the game away somewhat, but even if she didn't, the explosion would soon be the talk of the city. I supposed there was a chance that she might assume I'd been killed – which was a fate I couldn't quite believe I'd avoided – but it wouldn't take long until the witnesses who'd seen me tumble into the canal spoke to the press. And all right, I'd managed to swim to an unlit area and haul myself out of the freezing waters without being spotted (or so I hoped), but I really couldn't imagine Graziella taking a chance on my having drowned.

Yes, there was a possibility that the police might interpret the bomb as a warning of some sort, or perhaps even a random act of terrorism. But I knew better. The idea must have been for the Count to find the case and open it. I'd been lucky, but I doubted he'd have been as fortunate. So I thought it fair to assume that there'd been a somewhat backward plot to kill the man – and at the very least, I could offer a good description of the woman behind it.

Three things struck me about all this:

1. Graziella knew where I lived.
2. She was capable of getting in without being heard.
3. I was incapable of defending myself.

Hardly a reassuring combination.

Then there was the fact I'd lied to Victoria. I didn't relish thinking about how badly I'd let her down. She meant more to me than I could begin to express, though now seemed like a good time to try.

And so, with a reluctant grunt, I swung my legs out over the edge of the bed, clinched a sheet around my waist and dropped to my knees, then shuffled towards the doorway to my room in a most undignified manner.

The door seemed to tilt and pivot to the right. I leaned my head in the opposite direction but all I succeeded in doing was upsetting my balance. I fell onto my side with a thud, aggravating the cuts on my arm, and my yelp was enough to bring Victoria back to check on me.

'What on earth are you doing?' she demanded.

'I was coming to see you,' I said, cradling my forearm. 'To apologise. I'm sorry, Vic. For everything. I've been an idiot and I want to make it up to you. Please don't leave.'

I pursed my lips and tried my best to look endearing. Judging by Victoria's reaction, it had the opposite effect.

'Leave? I'm not leaving.' She planted her hands on her hips. 'Whatever gave you that idea?'

She looked genuinely cross with me. I felt genuinely bemused.

'But I could hear you packing your things,' I said.

She clucked her tongue and hooked a hand under my armpit, hoisting me upright like a nurse who'd been trained by the army – the enemy army. 'No, Charlie, you could hear me *un*packing.'

'Eh?'

'Honestly,' she said, 'you didn't think I'd come unprepared, did you?'

'Huh?'

'Charlie, I've spent time with you in two cities now, and each time you've involved me in mayhem and murder. So let's just say that while I can't pretend I'm not disappointed by your behaviour, I'm not entirely surprised by it, either. In fact, I'm really rather pleased that I anticipated that something like this might happen.'

'You anticipated that I'd become involved in a bomb plot?'

She sighed and shepherded me back to my bed, pushing me firmly down onto the mattress with her hands on my shoulders.

'Wait here,' she said.

'Where else am I going to go?'

She made for the door, then glanced backwards over her shoulder. 'Oh, and do cover yourself up. I can see far more than either of us would prefer.'

Ah, hell. I rearranged the covers and did my best not to blush while I waited for her return. I didn't succeed. My cheeks were flushed by the time she came back to my room with a pigskin document wallet in her hand. She fixed me in the eye and flipped the wallet open.

'What the bloody hell is that?' I asked.

Victoria grinned. 'Thought you'd be impressed.'

FOURTEEN

'It's a little something I picked up back home,' Victoria told me, walking her fingers over the contents of the document wallet. 'There's this wonderful boutique near London Bridge. They deal in all kinds of spy gear, and they also do a nifty line in self-defence. The gentleman in the shop told me it's called "weaponising oneself".'

She wasn't kidding. The range of equipment strapped into the case was quite astonishing. A folding knife, a telescopic baton, a snub-nosed gun with the word *Taser* along the barrel, a collection of cuffs for hands and ankles and thumbs, plus much more besides. Each tool had its own particular nook in the case, and each was neatly strapped into position – like an executive washbag gone rogue.

'Christ, Vic, you've got yourself a mini bloody armoury. How on earth did you get it through airport security?'

'Ah, yes.' She held up a finger. 'I had to pay a little extra, but the shopkeeper was able to use a local contact as a courier. This was waiting for me at Marco Polo when I arrived.'

'*I* was waiting for you when you arrived.'

She tapped her nose. 'But I went to powder this, remember?'

I did remember, now that she mentioned it. I'd been a tad irritated at the time, not least because she'd insisted on wheeling her suitcase into the ladies' washroom with her – almost as if I couldn't be trusted with her bag.

'I can see it rings a bell,' she said, smiling at my expression. 'It just so happens that a young woman approached me in one of the cubicles. All most clandestine.'

'Bloody hell. Must have cost you a fortune.'

'Quite. But it struck me as a sound investment. And I was right, wouldn't you say?'

I would say. Victoria's ordnance cache was enough to give Batman weapon envy.

'What's that?' I asked, pointing at a rectangular slab of matt-black plastic.

'Stun gun.'

'Huh,' I said. 'Quick question for you. What's the difference between a stun gun and a Taser?'

Her mouth twitched into a crooked grin. 'Want me to show you?'

No, I didn't think that'd be strictly necessary. 'Why don't you tell me about the lipstick instead?'

'Ah, one of my favourites.' She set the document wallet

117

down on my bed and freed the lipstick from its Velcro fastening, then yanked off the top to reveal what looked like a mini aerosol. 'Pepper spray.'

'Ingenious.'

'I think so. And the lid conceals a tiny listening device.' She tapped it with her nail, as if she was aiming to deafen a team of MI6 spooks in a safe house across the street. 'It transmits wirelessly to this digital data recorder,' she told me, pointing to a small chrome object that had the appearance of a miniature Dictaphone. 'The signal's good for a distance of 500 metres.'

'And the thing that looks like a pen?'

'It's just a pen.'

I felt my eyebrows knit together as I gave her my best don't-mess-me-around look.

'Oh all right,' she said, with a wave of her hand. 'The nib contains a powerful sedative.'

'Holy crap. And the cigarettes?'

There were three of them, strapped into position in a perfect line. The filters were pale-white in colour, ringed with two gold bands, but in all other respects they looked remarkably normal.

Victoria winced. 'Would you believe me if I told you I really don't know what they do?'

'Seriously?'

'Yes, though I wouldn't recommend that you smoke them. They were my one extravagance. I just saw them in the display case and felt like I had to have them.'

'Didn't you ask?'

'By that stage I was like a kid in a sweet shop. Point and grab.'

'Christ, the owner must have loved you.'

'I suppose he did do rather well.' She shrugged. 'But then, so have you, wouldn't you agree?'

I crossed my arms over my chest. 'How do you mean?'

Victoria replaced the lid of the lipstick and set about returning it to its little sculpted hollow in the wallet. 'Well come now, don't tell me you haven't given some thought to the predicament you're in. This Graziella character, the cat burglar – if we believe that's all she is – she'll know you opened the briefcase.'

'Possibly.'

'No possibly about it. Of course she'll know – a bloody big bomb went off. And she also knows where you live.'

I gulped. Thinking the same thoughts myself had been troubling enough, but having Victoria voice them aloud was even more disturbing.

'It seems to me quite obvious,' Victoria went on, 'that she may come looking for you. And that this time, she could do something much worse than steal a book.'

'You think she may threaten me?'

'I think she may kill you.'

I felt myself blanch. I supposed it made a change from blushing.

'Well, attempt to, anyway,' Victoria said, patting my knee through the bedcovers. 'But thanks to me, you have the means to protect yourself. Here.' She removed the stun gun

119

from her arsenal. It was no bigger than an electric razor, with a lid that flipped back to reveal a pair of metal prongs. 'Click this switch,' she said, meanwhile sliding a locking device to one side with her thumb, 'and then depress this button. And Hey Presto!' Blue sparks arced between the red-hot prongs at the head of the device. Victoria grinned toothily in the glow. 'Fifty thousand volts. Quite disabling. Like to try for yourself?'

'Not just now, thanks,' I said, raising my hand. 'And stop waving the damn thing about, will you?'

'Killjoy.' She released her finger and the current fizzed away to nothing, leaving a smell of burned carbon in the room. She threw the contraption at me. 'You can keep it under your pillow.'

The plastic casing was toasty-warm, and I wasn't all that happy to conceal it close to where I planned to lay my head, but Victoria clearly wasn't in a mood to take no for an answer. She watched me until the device was safely stowed, then nodded as if it was perfectly conventional behaviour.

'There's more,' she told me.

'I feared there might be.'

'Nonsense. I expect you'll recognise this little fellow.'

She was right about that – I did have more than a passing familiarity with the piece of equipment in the vacuum-packed case she removed from the pocket of her dressing gown. It was a small, battery-operated sensor alarm, a very basic model, capable of casting an infrared beam into a room and sounding an alarm if anything happened to disrupt it. I didn't mean to dent Victoria's enthusiasm, but I couldn't see it helping us a great deal.

'Listen, Vic, I think I can see where you're going with this, but if Graziella is even half as good as I believe she is, she'll be able to disarm it no problem.'

'Ah, but you're forgetting the element of surprise. Last time she broke in there were no alarms. Why would she think you'd have one now?'

Hmm, I supposed there could be something to her theory, and perhaps it wouldn't do any harm to rig the thing up. Not that I was the man for the task – I could hardly keep my head straight on my shoulders. I yawned, then wriggled down between my sheets, cringing at the stab of pain in my inner ear.

'You're not getting up?' Victoria asked me.

'I can't,' I groaned. 'It's a wonder I'm still conscious.'

Victoria tucked the intruder alarm back inside her pocket, then ran the zip around her modified document wallet. She smoothed her hand lovingly over the pigskin, and I got the impression she was every bit as pleased with the case as she was with its contents. Standing there in her pyjamas and dressing gown, a contented smile on her lips, she looked like a child who'd just received the perfect birthday gift.

'By the way, I read some more of your manuscript,' she told me, clutching the case to her bosom. 'It's beginning to grow on me.'

'Like a fungus?'

'No, in a good way.' She hitched her shoulders. 'I can see the potential now, but I do think it needs toning down. There's too much action, too many explosions and gun fights and chase scenes.'

'Really?'

A line of furrows appeared on her forehead. 'Of course. And you've gone rather overboard with the new complications you introduce for poor Faulks at the end of each chapter. Once or twice, maybe, but not all the time. It's too much.'

I hummed, then I hawed. 'Doesn't that make you read on, though?'

'Yes, but it doesn't always have to be such a big thing. It could just be a matter of having one character ask a question that hasn't been posed before. Or even better, a simple knock at the door.'

Now, you may very well not believe me, but I swear that just as Victoria said those self-same words, there was a *tap-tap-tap* on the front door. She tensed and exchanged a look with me. It wasn't the most complacent expression I'd ever seen. In fact, it was downright accusing.

'Was that you?' she whispered.

'Nope.'

The knock sounded again, a jaunty little rap, the kind a friend might make – or a burglar-cum-killer in a deceptively good mood. I showed Victoria my palms, as if to prove I'd had nothing to do with it.

She looked from me, to the hallway, and back again. 'What do we do?' she hissed.

'Well, I know what Faulks would say. If you want to find out what happens next, he'd tell you to go and answer the door.'

FIFTEEN

Victoria took her pepper spray with her, concealed in the sleeve of her dressing gown, and I kept watch from my bed with her Taser for company. The Taser was fitted with a laser to assist my aim. I closed one eye and circled the red dot menacingly over the wall at the end of my bed, straining to hear what was happening.

Naturally, it would have been a lot easier if my ears hadn't been buzzing like a couple of horse flies were trapped in them. The interference wasn't quite as bad as it had been, but it was enough to cloak Victoria's words. Luckily, I could at least make out her tone, and she didn't sound alarmed or threatened. Perhaps more reassuringly, there was no howling or wailing or, in fact, any other indication that she'd opted to discharge a dose of chemicals in our visitor's face.

A few moments later, footsteps approached. I hooked my finger around the trigger on the Taser, depressed it slightly and edged the red dot towards the back of my bedroom door. The handle turned, the door opened, and Victoria poked her head through the gap, then recoiled as the laser hit her square in the eye. She glared at me and I cringed an apology before lowering the gun.

'Charlie,' she said, in her most polite society voice, 'your landlords are here. They'd like to check that you're okay.'

As she finished speaking, Victoria jabbed an accusing finger towards her weapons cache. I shoved the case beneath my bed covers, along with the Taser.

'Er, okay,' I said, rearranging my blanket.

'*Ciao*, Charlie,' Antea called, in a cheery, sing-song voice, from somewhere out of sight behind Victoria's shoulder. 'We are just a little worried about you.'

'I'm fine,' I replied, my throat still hoarse. 'But you can come in.'

Victoria stepped inside, followed by Antea and Martin, and I watched with some embarrassment as Antea's jaw dropped and she made the sign of the cross over her generous bosom. She had a round, pudgy face, and an equally round and pudgy body. Her customary outfit, which she'd favoured again this morning, was some variety of floral house dress with a plunging neckline, usually set-off with a chunky Murano glass necklace. She wore plenty of make-up, and her raven-black hair was permanently fixed into a tight bun. Flighty and emotional, she was the polar opposite of her husband.

'Bastards really roughed you up,' Martin said. 'Best let me see.'

He advanced towards me and swung an old-fashioned medical bag onto the foot of my bed, close to where I'd concealed the Taser. He removed a pair of disposable surgical gloves that he stretched over his hands and snapped against his wrists. The gloves were something to bear in mind – a convenient future supply, perhaps.

Martin was dressed in brown corduroy trousers and a plum-coloured V-neck jumper over a plain white shirt, yellowing at the collar. He was rake-thin, with a full head of silver-grey hair that he liked to comb into a floppy, slanted fringe. The fringe was Martin's pride and joy. He was constantly smoothing it down or throwing it back over his head with a foppish waft of his hand. He might have retired as a doctor many years ago, but I'd long-since formed the impression that he'd never fully abandon his medical persona.

Placing his hands on either side of my head, he probed my skull with his fingers and thumbs. I could smell the rubber of his gloves, and the musty scent of his forearms.

'I explained about the mugging,' Victoria said, finally bringing me up to speed on the tale she'd weaved.

'We hear you last night.' Antea rubbed her hands together in an anxious fashion. 'And when we hear talk of the *polizia*.' She gasped and clapped a palm to her cheek. 'I tell Martin to come check on you, but he say we must wait until morning.'

'No fractures,' Martin announced, as if there was a nurse in the room to take notes. 'I understand you took a blow to the head.'

I locked eyes with Victoria. She nodded minutely.

'I think so.'

'No sign of any serious trauma. What about these cuts on your arms?' He raised my limbs for closer inspection, then turned up his nose as if underwhelmed.

'I was pushed into a wall. I used my arms to protect myself.'

'Hmm. They'll heal.' He dropped my wrists and flicked his head back, clearing his fringe from his eyes. 'Anything else?'

'My hearing,' I told him. 'There was a loud noise when they first attacked me. I think they may have used some kind of banger to disorient me.'

'*Mamma Mia!*' Antea cried, and covered her mouth with her hands.

Martin ignored her outburst and returned to his medical bag for an otoscope. He clicked the little light on, poked the pointy end into my ear and crouched down to take a peek at my deepest, darkest thoughts. 'Hmm. Looks like you may have sustained some damage. There's a small amount of blood, and the area looks inflamed. Check the other side.' I tilted my head as much as I dared. 'Same thing,' Martin said. 'They must have fired this banger bloody close.'

He backed up and looked at me with a stern expression that suggested he didn't entirely believe me.

'I don't remember too much about it, to be honest.'

'Mmm.' That got a scowl. 'Any dizziness?'

'A bit.'

'Well, you're doing the right thing by staying in bed. Hearing should improve with rest, but I'll check up on you tomorrow. Get much sleep?'

'Not a lot.'

'He lost consciousness for a while,' Victoria put in. 'I'm not sure you'd call it sleep.'

'Should he go to *l'ospedale*, Martin?' Antea asked, worrying her hands in such a complex manner that I was amazed she didn't break a finger.

'The hospital *and* the police.' He smoothed back his fringe, then fixed on me. 'Going to do it?'

I shook my head. Cautiously.

'Didn't think so. Can't blame you, either – lot of red tape over here. I'll give you something for the pain, help you sleep.' He dropped the otoscope into his bag and searched around until he removed a disposable syringe and a tiny vial containing a clear plastic liquid. He passed the vial to Antea. 'Read the date will you? Didn't bring my glasses.'

Antea held the little glass bottle up to the light of the standing lamp and peered at the label. 'It go out of date last year, Martin.'

'That'll do.'

'Er, will it?' I asked.

'Absolutely, old man. Not licensed to get fresh supplies these days, understand? But the dates are just flimflam. Drug *might* be a little less potent. I'll up the dosage to compensate.'

Taking the vial back from Antea, he upended it and pierced the seal with the needle, then eased back the plunger, peering myopically at the measurements along the side. Once he was satisfied, he squirted a little of the liquid into the air, flicked the syringe with his nail, swabbed a spot on my bicep and stabbed me.

'Nothing to it,' he said. And he was right – when you compared the sensation to being in the middle of an explosive inferno. 'You'll begin to feel drowsy. But it may help with the hearing.'

'I appreciate it.'

'Poor *bambino*,' Antea said. 'We are sorry, but his is not normal. It's not *Venezia*.'

'Crime wave,' Martin said, removing his gloves and tossing them into his medical bag. He closed the bag with a snap of the clasps and smoothed back his fringe. 'You'll have heard about the explosion at Palazzo Borelli last night?'

He subjected me to a hawkish assessment and I watched his pupils shift left and right as he gauged my response.

'I'm afraid not,' I told him, doing my best to keep my face as blank as possible. 'What happened?'

'Nobody knows for sure. There's talk of a bomb.'

Antea clucked her tongue. 'No Martin. It will be gas. Or electricity. Something like this.'

'The radio said that a masked man was seen falling from the balcony at the front of the palazzo just after the blast,' Martin told her.

'But this is too much,' Antea said. 'It is like something out of one of your books, Charlie, yes?'

I didn't know what to say to that, but fortunately Victoria had a contribution. 'My word,' she put in. 'Makes you wonder sometimes, doesn't it?'

'Mmm,' Martin replied, looking no less suspicious of me, or my supposed mugging.

'I will make you soup!' Antea announced, and patted my toes through my bed covers. 'A family recipe. It make you better, no problem.'

Martin shook his head with pained indulgence, as if he was listening to the ravings of a tribal shaman. 'Well, come along Antea.' He lifted his medical bag from my bed. 'Time that we were going.'

Yes, I thought. Time indeed.

I regained consciousness more than six hours later. Whether the dosage Martin had administered was responsible for my slumber, I couldn't say, but one thing I could tell you was that until Victoria informed me that it was almost 3 p.m., I could have quite happily believed that I'd had my eyes shut for half an hour at the very most. Mind you, as I indulged myself with a spot of stretching and yawning, I was at least able to recall that I hadn't passed the time in a state of complete nothingness. No, true to form, my pesky subconscious had bombarded me with yet more striking and undeniably kinky images of Graziella. Forget oysters – if you want to expose yourself to a powerful aphrodisiac, just arrange to have someone break into your home and dupe you into making an assassination attempt.

'Your soup arrived,' Victoria told me. She was dressed in jeans and a lengthy knitted cardigan. 'Plus some fruit from the market. And some fish. And bread. And two jars of fresh pasta sauce, along with some homemade ravioli. Antea spoils you, you know.'

'Told you she was a saint.'

'That, or a sweet old lady whose good nature you're only too happy to exploit.'

'I'll thank her,' I told Victoria. 'Profusely. But right now, I'm going to get up. Could you have a look in my wardrobe and pass me my jogging trousers and a shirt?'

She glanced sceptically at the wardrobe, then back at me. 'Need any help?'

'How about you wait outside the door? If you hear me fall over, you have my permission to come in and pick me up.'

'My, that sounds tempting.'

Victoria fetched the items I'd requested, then moved outside into the hall. I carefully fed my arms through the sleeves of the shirt, wary of my cuts snagging on the material, then squirmed into the elasticised trousers before attempting to stand. To my relief, the room didn't lurch violently to one side. Or the other.

'Hey,' I said. 'I've just realised something. My hearing's better.'

It was true. A small amount of buzzing still lingered – the kind one might get when one's heart rate is up – but compared to before, it was like being gifted a whole new set of ears.

'Say something,' I called.

131

'Like what?'

'That's perfect,' I told her. 'It's bloody perfect.'

I snatched the door open and clapped her on the shoulders. And if only this was a musical, I would have leapt into the air, snapped my heels together and burst into a rousing song.

'Martin's some kind of medical genius,' I told her. 'Let's go out. I mean, obviously, first let me pee and wash – but then let's go for a walk.'

'A walk? Where on earth do you want to walk to?'

'Oh come now,' I said, nudging her with my elbow, 'don't tell me you're not just a tad intrigued to see how the palazzo is looking?'

SIXTEEN

The palazzo wasn't looking good, and Victoria was more than a bit intrigued – she was positively full of questions. We'd already been through a number of them, but apparently there were plenty more still to come.

'And that hole,' she said, 'that huge, gaping, charred hole, is where the strongroom is?'

'Was, I'd guess you'd say.'

'And that's the balcony you fell from?'

'Hush,' I said, 'keep your voice down.'

We weren't alone. Half of Venice seemed to be gathered around us, standing on the opposite bank of the canal from the devastation I'd been responsible for, on the square of land in front of the restaurant where we'd eaten the previous night. Most of the onlookers were a grey-haired bunch talking in the local Venetian dialect, and there was a lot of arm-waving and head-shaking and proclamations of despair – at least, that's what I took them for. There was also a gaggle of tourists – their camera flashes illuminating the gathering dusk, throwing the tarnished exterior of the palazzo into bright relief. Private boats dawdled on the greying, rippled waters of the canal, their passengers marvelling at the destruction that had been visited on a building that had endured hundreds of years without sinking or collapsing and now, it appeared, would survive this too.

The windows of the *piano nobile* that remained intact were brightly lit by a collection of temporary arc lights that had been set up inside, and I could see figures moving around behind the glass. Some were dressed in tan raincoats – standard issue for police detectives, even in Italy. Others were clad entirely in white disposable jumpsuits. Forensics officers. If anything remained of the attaché briefcase, at least I could console myself with the knowledge that I'd worn gloves whenever I'd touched it. And while it was reasonable to suppose that I might have left hairs behind, not to mention the odd layer of skin, it wasn't too outlandish to think the explosion and the fire might have done a good job of destroying any biological evidence. That just left the surveillance footage, and even assuming it hadn't been consumed by the inferno, all it could really reveal was the masked figure that eye-witnesses had already described.

Perhaps that should have been a reassuring thought, but the truth was it didn't make me especially proud to see the devastation I'd been responsible for, or the distress it had caused the locals surrounding us.

Victoria whistled, then spoke in a low voice from the corner of her mouth. 'Charlie, that balcony has to be at least fifteen feet high. You were lucky.'

'Falling from the balcony was the easy part,' I whispered. 'The bomb blast was the tricky bit.'

'Was it very loud?'

'Enough to deafen me.'

Victoria bumped me with her hip and gave me a lopsided smile. 'Point taken.' She turned back to consider the palazzo once more, her face tangled in thought. 'Could anyone else have been hurt?'

I frowned. It was something I'd been trying to avoid thinking about too hard. 'I don't believe so,' I said, letting my words linger. 'The vault was reinforced with steel, and it contained most of the explosion, or else I wouldn't be here. I suppose there might have been some structural damage behind the strongroom – and if so, there's a chance one of the staff could have been caught up in it. But I imagine Martin and Antea would have said if that was the case, because it would have been on the news.'

'I hope you're right.'

'You're not the only one.'

While we'd been speaking, my eyes had started to water. It was partly because of the breeze whipping off the choppy canal water, but it didn't help that bits of debris from the explosion seemed to have worked themselves into the backs of my eyes, and were only now beginning to work themselves out again. I could feel tiny chunks of who-knows-what floating around in there, which wasn't a very appealing sensation.

'Oh, Charlie, this has really shaken you up, hasn't it?'

I peered through my blurred sight to see Victoria offering me a sympathetic smile. She wrapped an arm around my waist and clinched me to her, resting her head on my chest. And all right, I was a fraud, as well as a thief, but being hugged was sort of nice. I *had* been through a nasty experience. And since my winter coat was still drying out after my impromptu dip the night before, I was feeling the cold despite the roll-neck jumper and sports jacket I'd slipped on.

Victoria helped. She was warm and comforting, and she smelled perfectly fragrant too. More pleasant, in any case, than the sweaty odours emanating from the chef who was standing behind us in a tight white T-shirt and chequered trousers, his fatty torso steaming in the chill.

Shuffling to one side, I wrapped my arm around Victoria and hugged her back. We stood there for a few moments, holding one another, my sham tears running down my face. Then I had a thought that really should have occurred to me a good deal sooner.

'Hey,' I said, 'when you, er, helped to undress me last night – you didn't happen to find a mobile phone, did you?'

'As a matter of fact, I did.'

'Well that's a stroke of luck,' I told her. 'That's the phone Graziella has been contacting me on.'

'Not any more.' Victoria grimaced. 'I tried switching it on

and nothing happened. Then I took it apart, dried everything with a towel and left it on your radiator. No joy, I'm afraid.'

'Balls.'

'Quite.'

I felt my shoulders sag. 'She might have been trying to contact me.'

'It's possible.'

'And I can't call her, because my only record of her number was in the phone.' Almost as I said it, a fresh idea struck me. 'Wait a minute,' I said, 'can't you put the SIM card in your mobile?'

'Tried it already. Thing's completely dead.'

'Balls.'

'Quite.'

Victoria gave me a final squeeze and pulled away, shuddering. It seemed our hug was officially over.

'Do you really think Graziella planned for this Count Borelli character to be killed when he opened the case?' she asked me.

I returned my attention to the ragged tear in the fascia of the building, the avalanche of rubble and the decimated balcony. 'Has to be what she had in mind,' I muttered.

'Not necessarily. It could be she just wanted to destroy the items in the vault.'

I stroked my chin for a moment, considering the notion. 'But the bomb was triggered by my opening the case. If she'd just wanted to torch his valuables, she would have used a remote detonator. Or better still, she could have tasked me with opening the vault and lighting a fire.'

'Maybe she was afraid you'd help yourself to one or two of the goodies before burning them.'

'If I'd had my way, I'd have helped myself to the whole lot. But she must have assumed the risk of not getting my book back would stop me. Unless ...' I raised a finger to my lips and let my thoughts stretch their legs for a moment.

'Yes?'

'Well, maybe she thought the Count would open the case elsewhere. And *Boom!* – once he was out of the way, she could empty the vault in her own sweet time.'

'So what does that make Graziella? She has to be more than just a burglar, right? Are we dealing with an assassin here?'

'Possibly.' I made a humming noise in my throat. 'Though it doesn't really fit. I'd have thought a professional killer would want to carry out a hit by themselves. They wouldn't entrust the job to a random thief who might screw it up. And she seemed ... I don't know, put upon when we met. As if she was caught up in something that was bigger than her.'

'But she had the bomb, Charlie. If we assume she was the one who made it ...'

'Hell of an assumption.'

She rolled out her bottom lip. 'Even so, there has to be much more to her than we first thought, right?'

'Maybe.'

'No maybe about it. Listen Charlie, I really think we should—'

'*Hush*,' I said.

'Excuse me?'

I leaned close to her ear. 'Don't look round, but there's a man behind you who seems to be very interested in our conversation.'

There was, too. I'd been watching him for some minutes from the corner of my eye, shuffling gradually towards us. Perhaps his behaviour alone would have been enough to make me suspicious, but what really raised my hackles was the fact we'd met before. And all right, we hadn't shared a long and amorous conversation over a bottle of grappa, but he wasn't the type of chap I could easily overlook.

The heavy camel-hair coat hung loosely from his ample shoulders, spreading like a tepee above his shiny black shoes and fluffy white sport socks, and his fedora was balanced precariously among his curling black locks; the ratty feather poking out from his hat band looking like something he'd swiped from a diseased San Marco pigeon. His knotty beard and wonky gait gave him the appearance of a rabbi on the skids, and although there was no feral cat entwined around his ankles, in every other respect he looked just the same as when I'd spotted him lurking in a restaurant doorway on Calledei Fabbri shortly before I'd broken into the bookshop.

Victoria's eyes had widened with alarm, and I could tell it

was all she could do to stop herself from turning to stare. 'An eavesdropper?' she said, stiff-jawed.

'Something like that,' I told her. 'Come on, let's get out of here.'

SEVENTEEN

I led Victoria through the crowds by her hand, dragging her behind me until we emerged from the group of onlookers to find ourselves beside the entrance to a restaurant. A waiter dressed in smart black trousers and a red jacket was leaning against the wall, a cigarette glowing from behind his cupped hand. He dropped and extinguished it with a twist of his shoe.

'For two, *Signore*, for two?'

I shook my head at him and turned to look behind us. The man in the camel-hair coat was barging folks aside, following. His limp was dragging him down to the left, like a tanker that had been overloaded and was listing to port.

'Keep moving,' I said to Victoria, and yanked her on into Campo San Giacomo.

The lighted bars and trattorias of the square were beginning to fill. Young people had gathered outside with drinks and cigarettes in their hands. Some had dogs on leads – sausage dogs and terriers and miniature dachshunds, all of them dressed in snazzy winter coats or knitted sweaters. I ushered Victoria towards the Rialto Bridge.

Street salt was being cast around the steps at the foot of the bridge by a stooped character in a high-vis jacket. I rounded him and held tightly to the stone balustrade with one hand and to Victoria with the other, then raised myself onto my toes to scan the clutch of jewellery and handbag stalls we'd hurried through.

A feathered black fedora bobbed along past the green canvas shelter of a restaurant targeted at holidaymakers. Half-hearted fairy lights twinkled beside a stand featuring a menu of photographed meals. The man hobbled by without pausing to make a selection.

'Can you see him?' Victoria asked.

'Yup,' I said, pulling her on. 'Hard not to.'

'Who is he?' she asked, in a breathless voice.

'No idea.' And I was far from sure I wanted to find out.

The pale stone bridge was illuminated by powerful floodlights from below and the stark glow made Victoria's face appear worryingly gaunt.

'Where are we going?' she asked.

'Just away.'

'But he's not really following us, is he? Charlie?' She turned to check over her shoulder and lost her footing. 'Crap,' she said.

'You see him?'

'The big beardy one in the funny hat? Looks like a bear?'

'That's our guy.'

We climbed until we reached the middle of the bridge span. I pulled Victoria through the central arch, into the crush of tourists and garishly lit shops, their interiors brimming over with painted carnival masks and yellowing lace, hunks of plastic glass, paper fans, disposable cameras and postcards.

Victoria freed herself from my grip, her lips peeling back over her teeth as she drew a sharp breath. 'Ouch,' she said, shaking her hand.

'Sorry. Didn't realise I was hurting you.'

'Do you think he heard what we were saying?'

'I sincerely hope not.'

As I finished speaking, a tout in a dirty windbreaker approached us with an armful of single red roses wrapped in cellophane. He held one out to me and inclined his head towards Victoria.

'You buy rose for beautiful lady?' he asked.

'No,' I snapped.

'No rose for beautiful lady?'

'Go away.'

He lifted the rose to my face, prodding it beneath my nose. 'Is beautiful rose, yes?'

'Oh for Christ's sake. Here.' I snatched it from him, forcing it on Victoria, and rummaged in my pocket for some money. I slapped a note into his open palm. 'Now, go away.'

I made a shooing gesture with my hand, which perhaps

wasn't my finest moment, and turned to find Victoria gripping the rose in an awkward fashion, a look of bemusement on her face.

'Seemed the easiest way to get rid of him,' I said with a shrug.

'Such a romantic.' She craned her neck to peer over the heads and shoulders surrounding us. 'This man with the beard. Why would he want to follow us?'

'Your guess is as good as mine. The worrying thing is I've seen him before.'

Her eyes bulged. 'You have? When?'

'When I broke into the bookshop. He was nearby.'

She clasped a hand to her forehead. 'Why didn't you tell me?'

Beyond her shoulder, I caught sight of his sizeable reflection in the tinted glass of a shop window. 'We have to move again.'

We did just that, leaving the bridge behind and taking random alleys and even more random turns, doing a good job of thoroughly disorientating ourselves until I happened to spy Campo Manin up ahead. We caught our breath beneath the oxidised and pigeon-pooped statue of Daniele Manin in the middle of the square. By virtue of Manin's large overcoat, crumpled clothes and flowing locks, the statue bore a striking resemblance to our pursuer.

'Do you think we're being paranoid?' Victoria asked me, doubled over with her hands on her hips.

'I'd like to be able to say yes,' I told her, arching my back and exhaling a long plume of vapour into the evening sky.

'Well, why don't you then?'

'Because,' I groaned, 'I can see him again.'

'*No.*'

We set off at speed once more, ploughing through tangled lanes, swerving around tourists and darting into ever thinner and more contorted channels. Past blackened walls, shuttered windows and barred doors. Past neglected bars and vacant businesses covered in peeling fly-posters. Past torn bags of litter and beneath lines of tattered laundry. On into the gnarled and twisted labyrinth, until I no longer had the faintest idea which direction we were heading in.

'Wait!' I called out, stopping abruptly, and Victoria thumped into me from behind, her rose tickling the back of my neck with a rustle of cellophane.

We'd passed through a low *sotoportego* – the gloomy underpass running beneath a terrace of buildings – and were halfway along a rambling, unlit *calle* that I couldn't recall having visited before. The walls were so close that there wasn't room for us to stand alongside one another. Up ahead, the street ended in the dull, dark-green glimmer of slow-moving water. The putrescent stench of wet mud was overwhelming. There was no bridge and nowhere to turn. Just the dilapidated buildings leaning precariously towards one another above our heads and the silence between.

In other words, a dead end.

Hmm. I looked back to where we'd come from. The entrance to the alley was a considerable distance away, beneath the flat overhang of the buildings that lined the adjoining street. There was nothing to suggest we were here. No reason at all for him to find us.

And yet he did. Lurching into the twilit passage, his bulging shoulders skimmed the sooty brickwork on either side of him until he twisted with a grunt and limped forward at an angle. I began to wonder if he might get wedged between the tilting walls, and if he did, whether he'd be incapable of moving backwards – like a shark.

Victoria cursed, then fumbled in her handbag.

'What are you doing?' I asked.

'Pepper spray,' she told me. Her hand emerged gripping the lipstick-shaped canister she'd shown me back at my apartment. She must have taken it from her weapons stash when I wasn't looking.

'Whoa.' I steadied her wrist and prised the canister out of her fingers. The last thing we needed was for her to assault a complete stranger.

No, it seemed to me the situation required a little more finesse. Something to dissuade the brute from lingering, but that avoided confrontation. I'd heard that grizzly bears could be warded off by a high-pitched whistle, though I somehow doubted that would work. I titled Victoria's face up by the chin.

'Kiss me,' I said.

'Eh?'

'Kiss me,' I whispered.

'You what?'

I swooped. Her lips were still framing her words, and they squirmed awkwardly beneath my own. She made a noise of protest in the back of her throat and shaped as if to step away but I used her momentum to push her back into the grimy wall behind her, as if overcome with passion.

Her lips were rigidly still. I nuzzled a little on the bottom one, then sneaked a look at her. Victoria's eyes were squeezed closed, face pinched, as if a dreaded aunty was planting a sloppy one right on her.

I lifted my hand to conceal the side of her face and kissed my way around to her ear. She seemed to quiver and relax just a fraction. By the time I approached the lobe, a rogue hand had slipped down to my buttocks with an undeniable clench.

'That's right,' I told her, and cupped her waist. She groaned and pressed herself against me. 'Make it look good for the bastard.'

It may have been my imagination, but Victoria seemed to hesitate for a moment.

'Sorry?' she panted.

'If we make him think we came down here for some privacy, he may leave us alone.'

I returned my attentions to her mouth. Raising my eyes, I caught sight of an odd expression on her face – a look of consternation mixed in with something else. What was that – Terror? Disgust? Nausea? Her pupils slid sideways.

'He still there?' I asked.

'Uh huh.'

'Best take it up a notch.'

I lifted her arms above her head, pressing her wrists flat against the powdery brickwork. I scanned her body for a moment, as if consumed by lust, and then I lunged for her mouth. This time, she dropped the rose and reciprocated, tickling my lips with little darting movements of her tongue. Chest heaving, she pressed into me some more, and then to my surprise, she leapt clean off the floor, wrapped her thighs around my hips and braced her feet flat against the wall behind me.

Snatching her mouth away, she whipped her head to one side. 'Pervert,' she yelled, and her voice seemed to amplify as it carried off along the alley. 'Why don't you take a picture, you sicko?'

I turned too, my cheek pressed against Victoria's. His bearded face was shadowed by the walls that sandwiched him, not to mention the low, angled brim of his fedora. His too-short trousers hung comically above the bands of white sock. Breath misted on his swollen lips and I saw his fingers flex and tighten. If this was a Western, I could have believed he was about to go for his gun – not that he could have reached his holster without some serious contortion.

'Get out of here,' I shouted. 'Go find a girl of your own.'

In the silence that followed my words, I heard a hollow bumping noise from behind us followed by a gentle splash. I turned to see a sleek, black prow ease by, followed by two red-velvet love seats, a glimmer of brass and a sprig of fake carnations. A gondolier appeared, dressed in a blue water-proof tunic over a striped jumper and a straw hat with a blue ribbon. He wedged the tip of his oar against the wall at the end of the alley.

'Gondola, gondola, gondola?'

Normally, whenever I'd heard those words, uttered like a chant by the scavengers who loiter on bridge spans all across the city, it was all I could do not to yell at them to leave me in peace. Now, though, I'd rarely heard anything sweeter.

'Come on,' I said, lifting Victoria down from my hips and pushing her ahead of me.

'You're not serious?'

'You have a better idea?' I asked, gathering her rose from the floor.

'Pepper spray!'

'Nuh uh. Not this time.'

The gondolier extended his hand and I lifted Victoria's arm by the elbow until she was forced to accept. Using his oar as leverage, he walked along the backwards-gliding gondola until the love seats appeared, and then he helped Victoria aboard.

Behind us, our shabby friend with the out-of-control facial hair was simply watching me. He didn't speak. He didn't gesture. He didn't attempt to move closer or back away. He just stood there, a tubby, forlorn figure badly in need of a good shave and a better tailor. And for some reason, I found his stillness the most disturbing thing of all.

'*Signore?*'

The gondolier was beckoning to me. He gripped my wrist as I stepped aboard, then waited until I was seated and the craft had stopped rocking before kicking away from the wall and steering us towards the gloopy blackness ahead.

'Well,' I said, offering Victoria the rose, 'you can't say I'm not spontaneous.'

She conjured a wavering smile and rested her head on my shoulder, lifting the rose until I sniffed the petals. There didn't appear to be any scent, at least nothing capable of overcoming the dank smell of the muddy canal.

'God, that felt so *weird*,' she said, and shivered for effect. 'Didn't that kiss feel weird to you?'

I swallowed. 'Uh huh. Weird, all right.'

She wiped her lips with the back of her hand, then seemed to become aware of how it might look. 'Sorry,' she whispered.

'Not to worry.' I wrapped a companionable arm around her shoulders. 'Once we manage to get off this thing, I'll buy you a drink. I hear alcohol is good for killing germs.'

EIGHTEEN

I wonder how best to describe our gondola trip. Magical? Evocative? Enchanting?

Nope, I think painful should just about cover it. Painful and awkward. Oh, and tense too. So tense, in fact, that by the time we'd finally disembarked, I was clenching my jaw so fiercely that I must have looked as if I'd just survived a rollercoaster ride.

Of course, no theme park in the world would dare charge nearly so much as I was obliged to pay. Still, I guess it takes a born thief to recognise one, and as I emptied my wallet into the palm of our gondolier and held his shameless gaze, I couldn't help but think that his stripy jumper was strangely apt. Add an eye mask and a bag of swag, and we could have been cousins.

And yet, I can't say I felt unduly cheated. His timely arrival had saved us from a situation that had made me feel uncomfortable, at the very least, and back in that dead-end alley, I reckon I would have agreed to pay twice as much just to get away.

The gondola had delivered us to Ramo del Selvadego, in the shadow of the Planet Hollywood restaurant just behind Piazza San Marco. There was a cash machine close by, and I had a sudden need to frequent it.

'I'm sorry that was so expensive,' Victoria told me. 'Here, let me pay you half.'

'Don't be daft,' I said. 'It was so much fun, we'll call it my treat.'

Before Victoria could argue the point, I took her by the elbow and led her to Campo Santo Stefano. The large, wedge-shaped square was one of my favourite spots in the city. During the day, I often walked to it to buy an English newspaper from the magazine stall and spend time reading over a cappuccino at one of the pavement cafés. Children might play football against the wall of the domed church, where the faded chalk outline of a goal was just visible, or trail a kite behind them as they ran circles around the bronze well-head in the middle of the square. Neighbourhood dogs would stroll unaccompanied, sniffing for a rare unfamiliar scent, while tourists pondered the menu cards of the restaurants that ringed the campo.

The night was quite different. The magazine stall was closed and boarded up, the outside café tables and chairs had been stacked away, and there was not a child to be seen.

Leaving the square by a side alley at the far end, I ushered Victoria on as far as a cramped neighbourhood *bacàro* I'd visited a few times before. The walls were lined with shelves of dusty wine bottles, rising from the floor to the low, beamed ceiling, and a mismatch of rough-hewn tables were located at the far end of the marble-topped counter, where three gnarled old men were perched on high stools. A television screened a *Serie A* football match in a high corner above the bar, the voiceover so fast and enthusiastic that it sounded as if the commentator might hyperventilate. One of the men had a pink *La Gazetta dello Sport* folded in front of him, his hands reaching absently for the varied dishes of *cichèti* spread along the counter. The small plates of spicy sausage, pork rissoles, calamari, langoustines, and thinly sliced ham looked mouth-wateringly good.

The barman was barrel-chested and balding. He was watching the football too, leaning against the cash register with a cigarette in his hand, his white shirtsleeves rolled up to expose the hairs on his lower arms.

None of the men offered a friendly *'ciao'* or paid any attention as I guided Victoria to one of the tables, or when I approached the counter and ordered us two *Spritz con Campari*, a Venetian speciality. The orange-red drinks were prepared without a word of greeting or of comment, and the barman didn't so much as raise an eyebrow as he plonked an olive and a slice of lemon in each glass before reaching below the counter and passing me a plate of sandwiches wrapped in cling film.

I carried the tumblers over to Victoria, ice cubes rattling, then returned for the sandwiches.

'What's this?' Victoria asked, pointing at her drink.

'Just try it. You'll like it.'

She gave me a suspicious look, then raised the glass to her mouth and sipped cautiously. 'Tastes pretty good.' She smacked her lips together, running her tongue around.

'Better than me?'

She coloured, and looked down into her glass, prodding at her olive with her nail. 'Can we just pretend that whole thing never happened?' she said, her voice tight.

'If you like.'

'Wipe it from our memory banks?'

'Wipe what? I don't know what you're talking about.'

I wiggled my eyebrows and took a mouthful of *Spritz*. The first time I'd tried the concoction, I'd imagined it would taste like orangeade. Lately, I'd begun to think it was reminiscent of diluted cough medicine. Not necessarily a bad thing – it might even protect me from any bugs I'd picked up during my dip in the Grand Canal.

'Sandwich?' I asked, removing the cling film and tilting the plate of little, white bread squares towards her. 'These are called *francobollo*,' I explained. 'It means "postage stamp".'

Victoria prised up the corner of one of the snacks. 'Is this aubergine?'

'Roasted vegetables. I think there are some with meat too.'

Victoria shrugged and nibbled the corner. My own selection had some variety of dried salami in it. I chewed it thoughtfully, trying not to pine after the chilli prawns the barman was presenting to his wordless friends at the bar.

'So do you have any idea who the big guy with the beard is?' Victoria asked me, covering her mouth with her hand as she swallowed.

'No more than you, I'm afraid.'

'He seemed very keen to follow us.'

'But reluctant to speak. Maybe he's a mute.'

I rummaged in my pocket for my cigarette packet. Holding the box in the air, I shook it until I caught the barman's attention. He gave his consent with a reserved nod. It would have been hard for him to say no, considering he was puffing merrily away.

'Perhaps he followed us on a whim,' I said to Victoria, meanwhile selecting one of my cigarettes and firing it up. 'He could have heard some of our conversation, I suppose.'

'But didn't you say you'd bumped into him before?'

I took a long drag, shaking my head. 'I'm beginning to regret having told you that.'

'Why?'

'Because I can't explain it. The first time I saw him, I thought he was some kind of tramp. Maybe even a drunk.'

'And now?'

'Now, he's another part of the mystery.'

Victoria's eyes seemed transfixed by the glowing tip of my cigarette. I got the impression that if I circled it in the air, her head would move with it. Perhaps I could even swing it from left to right, luring her into a deep trance.

'Want one?' I asked.

'Excuse me?'

'Cigarette,' I said, lifting the guilty exhibit between my finger and thumb.

'Oh, sorry. I was miles away, wondering if this man with the beard could be linked to our cat burglar in some way.'

'Almost certainly.'

She backed off from me. 'You think?'

'Sure.' I selected another mini-sandwich and popped it into my mouth.

'You sound very confident.'

'Tissue of connections,' I told her, speaking with my mouth full.

'Come again?'

I swallowed. 'A pet theory of mine. In any half-decent mystery novel, all the characters should be connected in some way. Keeps the story tight. Ensures every character serves a purpose.'

She rolled her eyes in mock despair. 'I can see we're going to have to run through that dreary fantasy-versus-reality thing again.'

I smiled and took another pull on my cigarette. 'Seriously, though. He must have had a good reason to track us as far as he did – especially with that nasty limp of his.' I vented the smoke through my nostrils, for variety if nothing else. 'The interesting part will be whether he's waiting for us when we get home.'

'That's the *interesting* part?'

'Well, it occurred to me that perhaps he didn't try to stop us getting away on the gondola because he knows where I live. And if that's the case, it increases the likelihood that he's working with Graziella in some capacity. It could even be that he followed us from my apartment in the first place.'

'You sound oddly relaxed about the possibility, I must say,' Victoria told me, pausing to take a sip from her *Spritz*.

'Listen, if he'd wanted to cause us harm, he could have done it in that alley.'

'Maybe he just wanted to scare us.'

'And are you scared?'

Victoria pouted as she considered her response. 'I suppose unnerved might be a better way of putting it. I wonder if we should have spoken to him.'

'Funny. I wonder the same thing myself.'

'And?'

I shrugged. 'Who knows? If it's important, I expect we'll see him again.'

'Because none of this is over yet, is it?'

'Not even close. Too many loose ends. And from Graziella's perspective, I'm afraid I'm one of them.'

'Then maybe you should leave Venice, Charlie. Go somewhere else for a while.'

I turned my cigarette in my hand, watching the ash develop.

'Problem is, Vic, I'd really like to get my book back. And I enjoy living here,' I added, delicately sprinkling ash on the edge of the plate, away from the remaining sandwiches.

157

'I got that impression. But there's every chance she'll come for you, Charlie.'

'She might.'

'And?'

I winked at her. 'And I've been thinking there's someone I should call about that.'

I borrowed Victoria's mobile and dialled a number I knew off by heart. There aren't too many people in my phone book. To be perfectly blunt, there are so few that I don't own a phone book at all. I tend to think of myself as a personable chap, someone who can hold his own at a dinner party and contribute a winning anecdote or two, but one consequence of my chosen lifestyle is that it's tough to maintain friendships. Oh, there are a couple of fellow writers I know, and one or two acquaintances of a shadier nature, but I rarely speak with them. I call my parents occasionally, and Victoria much more often than that, and then, every once in a while, I contact Pierre.

Pierre is my fence, as well as a patron of sorts. Before my self-imposed career break, he'd pass work my way from his base in Paris and I'd pass goods his, and over the years our relationship had proved beneficial enough that we'd survived the odd bump in the road. During my time in Venice, we hadn't spoken so frequently – partly because he couldn't understand why I'd decided to go straight in a city fairly brimming over with wealth and opportunities, and partly because I hadn't wanted him to put temptation in my way. But, like all solid friendships, he was someone I could call out of the blue without the least sense of awkwardness, which was something I elected to do right now.

'*Allo?*' His voice was warm and relaxed, the way it gets when he has a glass of wine on the go. I could hear a classical track playing on a stereo in the background – either that, or he had the French National Orchestra in his living room.

'Pierre, it's Charlie,' I told him. 'How's tricks?'

'Charlie! It is good to hear from you. *Ça va?*'

'*Oui,*' I told him. 'And you?'

'Not so bad, my friend. But, it is quiet, yes? A slow time of year.'

'Oh?'

'The cold. The rain. Nobody will work for me. I tell them it is dark, this is good, but they do not care. They are lazy. Not like you, Charlie. You are my best.'

'*Was,*' I corrected him. 'And you can save the flattery. I'm not scouting for work.'

He made a snorting noise. It wasn't the most pleasant of sounds. 'You write still?' he asked, and he couldn't have sounded more dismissive if he'd tried.

'That's the general idea,' I replied, and shot a guilty look towards Victoria. She had an eager expression on her face, as if she wanted to snatch the phone away from me. 'Victoria says hello.'

'Ah, *très bien*. She is with you?'

'I'm on her mobile right now. She's waving.'

'Then I blow her kisses.'

I covered the mouthpiece and shared the happy news with Victoria. 'She's blowing them back,' I told Pierre. And she was, too.

'You know, Charlie, she has asked me to write a book myself. The little stories from my life. I tell her I am too young for this – that I still have work to do. But she is persuasive, no?'

'Oh, she's that, all right.' Victoria frowned at me, suspicious all of a sudden. I tried my best to look entirely innocent. 'Listen, Pierre,' I went on, swirling the orange liquid in my glass. 'I have something to ask you. I've bumped into someone here in Venice. A female someone – in my old line of work. I wondered if she might be on your books?'

'A woman?'

'Precisely.'

'Then *non*.' He whistled. 'I am sorry Charlie, but this is unusual, yes?'

'I have a name – Graziella – but it may be a fake.'

'She is Italian?'

'Almost certainly. In fact, I think she may be from Venice originally. Does that ring any bells?'

'I am sorry, Charlie. There was a German. *Mais*, she is retired now. It is a shame – she was good.'

Victoria tapped me on the arm. 'Ask him if he has any men on his books here. They may know something about Graziella. Perhaps Pierre can speak to them and see if they have any information about her.'

160

'Good idea,' I said, and then I told Pierre just what the idea happened to be.

'I will try,' he said. 'For sure, there are people I can speak with.'

'That's great Pierre. I appreciate it. But listen, there is one more thing you could do for me.'

'Name it. Please.'

'Would you keep an ear out for anybody trying to sell a signed first edition of *The Maltese Falcon*?'

Pierre hesitated. 'Charlie, *no*. Your book, it has been stolen? Tell me it is not so.'

But alas, it was so. And as much as losing the book had pained me, I was afraid that there was a lot worse still to come.

NINETEEN

Later that night, back in my apartment, I tried to make some sense of the situation I'd found myself in. It was easier said than done. I knew I'd been tricked, no question, but I didn't know why. Yes, it was fair to assume that the bomb had been intended to kill Count Borelli, but aside from the fact he was worth a bob or two, and that he happened to live at a desirable address, I didn't know a single reason why anyone would want him dead.

A trawl through the internet hadn't shed much light on matters. It seemed he conducted his life with a reasonable degree of discretion. I'd found a few hits in the Italian papers, all of them captions to some variety of society photograph. From what I could gather, he was active in supporting the *Carnevale* festivities, and he was a leading benefactor of an American-based charity that preserved some of the city's endangered buildings (which was somewhat ironic, considering what I'd done to his home).

The figure in the photographs was pretty much what I might have expected for a European Count. A tanned and wealthy-looking, middle-aged gent, with a prominent hooked nose, flawless teeth and thick grey hair set in waves, he was accompanied by a different glamorous woman in each image. In some of the pictures he wore a tux, and other times a bespoke jacket over a silk shirt and V-neck sweater. He sported no jewellery (aside from a pricey timepiece), and most assuredly no wedding ring – the Count was a bachelor, and judging by the daring necklines and fawning poses of the beautiful creatures who clung to his arm, he made the very most of his status.

None of the women in the photographs happened to be Graziella – that would have been much too simple – but she shared certain features with all of them. An attractive figure, a striking face, the ability to turn heads and keep them turned. So it wasn't hard to believe that she really had accompanied the Count to the casino while I was breaking into his home, nor that they might have been more than just friends. Could that mean that I'd become caught up in a lover's tiff? Somehow, I didn't think so. Yes, I'd heard of jilted women carrying out vendettas, but never something this extreme.

Still, if they'd attended the casino together, there was a chance that some of the staff would remember them and might be able to identify Graziella for me. It was certainly something to ponder and in all probability something to act upon, too. In fact, I was a little surprised I hadn't thought of it before, and that only made me wonder what else I might have overlooked.

There had to be other angles to work, more avenues to explore.

One thought that did occur to me was that Martin and Antea might be able to tell me something useful about the Count, but I wasn't sure how to ask without rousing their suspicions. Martin had obviously harboured reservations about my mugging story, and even if I sent Victoria down to speak with them on my behalf, it was an obvious risk, and one I wasn't prepared to run just yet.

Another avenue to explore was the heavyset character with the pronounced limp who'd followed Victoria and me into the dead-end alley. I didn't know whether his involvement went anywhere beyond an overdeveloped sense of curiosity, but the way he'd tracked us had suggested he was interested in my movements at the very least. If he approached me a second time, I made a promise to myself that I'd talk to him and try to find out what was behind his snooping.

Then, of course, there was Count Borelli himself. Perhaps I could call at his home – legally this time – and ask him very politely why Graziella wanted him dead, before going on to enquire if he knew where she might be storing my book? Unfortunately, it didn't strike me as a very credible option. A slightly more appealing alternative was to break back into his palazzo to see if I could find the answers to those questions for myself. Problem was, the place was crawling with police, and even if I went in the dead of night, I'd be taking a huge gamble. The Count and his live-in staff would be on edge right now, their senses heightened, and that made the chances of my being caught infinitely higher.

More to the point, why did I care? True enough, I was a touch miffed by the way Graziella had hoodwinked me, but it could be I was overcomplicating things. So far as I was aware, she was the only person who could link me to the bombing, and I had a funny feeling she wouldn't be giving my name to the police anytime soon, since I could put them onto her in turn.

Hmm. So okay, maybe now I was simplifying things a little too much. The happy scenario I'd just outlined ignored one or two salient points. Like, for instance, it hadn't escaped me that Graziella might not be altogether satisfied by the way the Count had evaded her dastardly plan, and it wasn't too extreme to suppose she might decide to make another attempt on his life. And while, on the one hand, I supposed I could run with the notion that it was no concern of mine, if I did nothing to stop her, I'd have a man's death on my conscience. Worse still, if she was caught, I didn't imagine she'd hesitate to lead the authorities straight to me in the hope that her punishment might be reduced.

Oh, and then there was that other trifling detail – Graziella still had my copy of *The Maltese Falcon* and I still wanted it back. Yes, I'd put on a brave face with Victoria, but superstitions are the damnedest things. They get deep inside you, work on you, until you trust them instinctively no matter what your head might say. I could tell myself that I was capable of penning a good story without Hammett's novel for company, but in my heart, I didn't really *believe* it.

And to some extent, I didn't *want* to believe it, either. The book had always been there for me, watching over me when I was writing, and I missed it badly – not just because it was a handsome object, but also because of what it represented to me. Writing a novel even half as good as the *Falcon* was something to aspire to – perhaps even something worth dedicating one's life to – and it couldn't hurt to be reminded of that whenever I found myself stuck writing a particular passage, or griping about a set of edits.

What's more, I couldn't deny that I was experiencing the desire for some kind of revenge. Graziella hadn't simply stolen something precious from me and duped me into doing her bidding – she'd also hurt my pride. As a thief, it went against the grain to be burgled, but what really rankled was the way Graziella had questioned my professionalism. True enough, I'd taken a sabbatical from my larcenous ways, but while I'd been plagued over the years by doubts about my ability as a writer, I'd never had any concerns about my talent as a housebreaker. I knew I was good at accessing other people's homes, and even better at swiping their things, but Graziella had treated me like a bumbling amateur. She'd insulted me, but worse than that, she'd underestimated me, and I had an undeniable urge to make her pay for it.

So, in conclusion, when I broke everything down, I had plenty to ponder. And, to be perfectly frank, I wasn't altogether sorry to find myself preoccupied. Why? Well, it was far more preferable than thinking about Victoria.

Right now, she was in her bedroom across the hall from me – perhaps reading my manuscript, perhaps fast asleep. Earlier on, we'd worked together to position the two intruder alarms in the hall and the living room, and then I'd made sure that she had her pepper spray and the Taser gun close at hand before going to my own room for the night. I'd offered to book her into the Hotel American just along from my apartment, which she'd point-blank refused to let me do, but for the time being she was as safe as I could possibly make her, short of sleeping on the floor of her room. On a different day, in other circumstances, I dare say I would have done just that. It was very probably the noble thing to do, and I can tell you without any hesitation that if I'd been writing the scene myself, it's undoubtedly what my lead character Michael Faulks would have insisted upon. Mind you, Faulks has something of a runaway libido, and there's no doubt in my mind that he'd have ended up seducing the woman he'd tasked himself with protecting.

Now, I'm not suggesting for one moment that I'd have attempted the same thing with Victoria. In fact, the very idea petrified me. But, no matter how hard I tried to block it from my mind, there was no denying that something had passed between us in that alley (and I don't just mean saliva).

The kiss, that was the problem. I was a fool for having pulled the move and, in hindsight, I didn't doubt that a squirt of Victoria's pepper spray would have been a lot less toxic. I wasn't at all sure how things stood between us now, and from the way Victoria had avoided eye contact with me during the evening, and taken herself to bed at shortly before nine o'clock, I couldn't escape the fact that she was very likely as confused as me.

She was a work colleague, yes, but she was also my confidante and the closest friend I'd ever known. Given the choice, I'd rather have shut myself inside the palazzo strongroom with a hundred briefcase bombs than jeopardise our relationship. And yet, because I was a moron who'd acted on impulse, I might have done precisely that.

Listen, I can't pretend that I'd never noticed Victoria was attractive. She was slim but curvy, smart and funny, and she was more than my equal in just about any department you could care to mention. We liked the same things, shared the same passions, and there was no denying that we'd flirted a little over the years. But the kiss had taken things to another level – one that felt so precariously high I was a little surprised my nose wasn't bleeding.

Was it my imagination, or had she reciprocated? Did that mean it was something she'd secretly wanted to have happen between us, or had she been trying to save me from embarrassment? Was she experiencing the same conflicting emotions as me, or was it all a lot simpler for her? Was she upset?

Questions. I had far too many, and very few that were welcome. Victoria had said that we should erase the entire episode from our minds and I wished to hell I could do just that. In fact, if a little genie had appeared at the foot of my bed and granted me three wishes right then, my first would have been to go back in time and stop the entire episode from happening. Oh, and if you're wondering what my other two wishes would have been, that's easy. Number two, to get my book back safe and sound. And three? Well, that would have been to make it through the entire night without waking to find someone pressing a gun into my stomach.

TWENTY

Damn genies – they never materialise when you need them to. Sadly for me, other people had a habit of doing just that, and one of those pesky individuals happened to be jabbing a gun into my gut.

She had red hair this time. A bright punk-red. The strands, which fell to her shoulders from a centre parting and curled outwards, looked to have been made from the cheapest of plastics. Realistic, it wasn't. Striking, it most certainly was.

Her outfit was just as memorable. Black leather gloves and a zipped leather biker jacket, black commando pants with multiple pockets, black training shoes and, of course, the jet-black pistol.

The gun was large and mean-looking and it was fitted with a silencer. The silencer wasn't a detail I was especially pleased by, but then again, neither was the gun, and to be honest, I didn't like the way her finger was curled around the trigger all that much either.

One of my guilty little secrets is that I don't know a great deal about firearms, which is something of a no-no for a mystery writer. In the past, I've had readers email me to say that I've got the details all wrong in one of my books – that such-and-such a weapon doesn't have a safety, or that Faulks has fired one more bullet than a Glock could possibly hold. But there were certain pieces of information I'd picked up over the years, and one of them was that it was never a good thing to have an automatic pistol aimed at you. Oh, and if you were unfortunate enough to find yourself in such a scenario, one of the least pleasant places to be shot was in your intestine. It hurt like merry hell, by all accounts, but left untreated, it also had a nasty habit of causing your demise.

I'd had characters use suppressors in my books before and there was only ever one reason for it. They wanted to kill quickly and efficiently and escape undetected. So all things considered, my situation didn't look all that encouraging.

'Don't shoot me,' I said. I understand it's de rigueur to utter those words when you find yourself likely to be fired upon. 'Please,' I added, which was an embellishment I'd devised for myself. Good manners cost nothing, right?

'Sit up,' she said, and motioned with her gun for me to do just that.

I could see that she was gesturing with her gun and, come to think of it, I was able to describe her wig, her outfit and her weapon with such clarity because she'd taken it upon herself to switch on the lamp in the corner of my room. Strange. Sudden light was usually capable of waking me, but tonight it seemed that only a pistol pressed to my belly button could hit the spot (and boy, how I wished *that* wasn't so).

'Put your hands behind your back.'

Ah, now that was a command I was perfectly happy to obey. Shuffling towards my headboard, I slid my fingers beneath my pillow. Somewhere underneath was the stun gun Victoria had given me. Fifty thousand volts. If only Graziella moved a little closer, I might have a chance. Flip back the lid, slide the switch to one side and plunge the fizzing prongs deep into her neck. With any luck, she'd be completely disabled, unable to get a shot off.

It was a fine plan, and without question the best one I had at my disposal. Just one problem. I couldn't find the damn stun gun.

'You are looking for this?' she asked, removing the very weapon from the bulky pocket on her thigh.

Oh, good grief. So that was just the bright light and the fact she'd fumbled around beneath my head that had failed to wake me. Typical. The one night when I knew I might have to be on my guard, I'd slept as if Victoria had slipped Rohypnol into my cocoa. Maybe it was the after-effects of the drug Martin had pumped into my system. I was beginning to wonder if he truly had been a doctor – it would have made a lot more sense if he'd treated me to a dose of horse tranquilliser.

Graziella turned the stun gun in her hand and smiled at me the way a cat might smile at a mouse before removing its entrails. Or, more accurately, the way a cat burglar might smirk at an out-of-practice thief before shooting him in the tummy.

'You would use this on me?' she asked, and pouted as if she was terribly upset by the notion.

'The thought had crossed my mind,' I said. 'Given you're holding a gun on me.'

She thumbed back the lid on the stun gun, exposing the prongs, then flicked the switch until the bluish current buzzed in her hand. She rolled down her lower lip, intrigued, before passing an appraising eye over my body. I drew back my legs, folding them at the knees until there was as much distance between us as possible. The move seemed to amuse her. She smiled and cut the charge, returning the device to her pocket.

'You opened the briefcase.' She rolled her eyes and shook her head. The toxic-red wig shimmied like a hula skirt, the vibrant colour making her skin appear paler than normal – as if she was suffering a bout of anaemia.

'You think? What gave it away?'

There was a glimmer in her eye, but it failed to reach her lips. 'You are a fool,' she said, in a voice leaden with fatigue. 'You should be dead.'

'I was lucky. The vault contained the blast.'

She winced, as if she'd feared I might say that. 'The coins? The paintings?'

'Gone. Everything's toast.'

She released a long breath and raised the gun to scratch her temple with the muzzle. Shame my reflexes weren't unbeliev-ably fast. If only I could whip my hands out from behind my back and get to the trigger before she caught up with the move, I could decorate my bedroom wall with her brains. Then again, maybe she'd slip and do it for me.

Nope, sadly not. She lowered the gun, casually resting her elbow in the palm of her hand. I glanced down at her shapely waist. No climbing harness.

'How'd you get in?' I asked.

'Your door,' she said simply.

Huh, so she really was as good as I'd feared. Opening the locks I'd selected would have been tricky, and then there was the alarm sensor in the hallway. Part of me wanted to ask her how she'd managed to sneak in so easily. Only my ego, and a little professional dignity, stopped me from doing just that.

'Can I ask you a question?' I said.

She inclined her head to one side, red locks hanging unnatu-rally straight. Apparently, she wasn't in a hurry to execute me.

'Why me?'

She blinked. Looked almost dazed. 'There is no reason.'

'None?'

'I hoped maybe you would be better. If you listened to me, and did as I told you, I did not think it was so bad for you. You could have taken something from the vault, yes?'

'But you told me not to.'

She raised her eyebrows. Okay, it was a stupid point. She'd told me not to open the case, too.

'I'd still have been involved in killing a man,' I told her. 'I mean, that had to be the idea, right?'

She barely nodded, but it was enough that she didn't deny it. I suppose that should have come as no surprise, but it still shocked me to know that I'd almost carried out all the steps of an assassination. God knows how I would have reacted if my greed and curiosity hadn't got the better of me.

'So what made you think I wouldn't go to the police?' I asked. 'Were you always planning on coming back here to kill me?'

Her face tangled. I didn't know if I should trust my eyes, but she appeared perplexed. Saddened, too.

'Kill you?' she said, as though testing the words on her tongue. 'But this is not so.'

'It isn't? Then how do you explain *that*.' I jutted my chin at her gun.

'Ah,' she said, as if we'd finally broken through a stubborn language barrier. 'But this is for you, yes?'

'Excuse me?'

'When I am gone.' She nodded. 'I leave it for you.'

'Why? Are you expecting me to shoot myself?' Now true, I was feeling a touch sheepish about what I'd done to Count Borelli's home, but it was something I thought I could live with.

'Idiot. It is so you can kill him.'

My eyes widened and my skin began to tingle. I was starting to feel uncommonly warm. Obviously, it was just me, because Graziella appeared ice-cool and unruffled.

'Who's *him*?' I asked, although I really would have preferred not to know.

'The Count.'

My voice had become small all of a sudden. 'But why would I do that?'

She began to smile, coyly at first. 'There is your book for one thing. But also,' she said, the grin breaking for good and revealing perfect teeth beneath innocent eyes, 'there is your friend. Across the hall from you, yes? If you do not do this . . . well.'

'Well?' I gulped.

She shrugged, as if helpless, then lifted the gun to her temple and faked pulling the trigger. 'Poof,' she said, meanwhile unfurling her hand on the opposite side of her head, as if her brain had just exploded from her skull. Something fell from her grip. A light, brownish substance floated down to my bedcovers like a feather. I peered at it. A clump of hair. Nutty, with the odd blondish fibre. It looked very much like Victoria's shade.

Oh boy. So I wasn't the only one who'd slept far too deeply. Apparently, Victoria had dozed through an impromptu trim.

I was beginning to suspect Graziella was a little unstable. It wasn't simply her willingness to turn a loaded gun on herself to emphasise a point, it was also the way she thought it was perfectly acceptable to break into people's homes to cut their hair or demand that they murder someone on her behalf. I was pretty sure that wasn't normal behaviour. Mind you, *normal* was becoming a distant memory to me – it had already been a mighty eventful few days, and I had a funny feeling that wasn't going to change any time soon.

'Don't bring her into this,' I said, pointing at the sample of Victoria's tresses. You'll have to forgive me the line. This wasn't a time for originality – I needed the message to be clear.

'But it will not be necessary,' Graziella announced, sounding like she was completing a basic sum, 'if you kill him.'

'To be perfectly honest, I'd really rather not.' There was a twinge in the muscles around her eyes, like a response to mild pain, and I found myself having to explain my reluctance to commit premeditated murder. 'Look, I've done some bad things in my time, it's true. I used to be a burglar, you know that, and I was pretty good, even if I do say so myself. But I'm no hit man. I'm not in the habit of killing people. It's just not something that I *do*.'

It had seemed like a reasonable argument to me, but judging from Graziella's flustered reaction, it didn't make the slightest bit of sense. She fidgeted on the bed, scratching her neck with her nails, clearly frustrated with me. I just wasn't *getting* it.

'But he is a bad man,' she said.

'What does that even mean?'

'He has done terrible things.'

'Such as?'

She paced to the corner of my room, then turned with her arms folded across her chest, the gun hanging down beneath the crook of her left elbow. Maybe she was slow, I told myself. Maybe she was a terrible shot. If I rushed her I might have a chance.

Before I thought any more of it, she stamped her foot into the ground and made a huffing noise, like a toddler brewing a tantrum. Her fake hair jiggled with a plastic rustle.

'I cannot tell you what he has done,' she whined. 'But you must believe me.'

Believe her. Oh, well sure, I was perfectly prepared to do that. I mean, what possible reason could I have not to trust her?

'Then go to the police,' I said. 'Talk to them. If what you say is true, and the things he's responsible for are so awful, they can arrest him.'

'But this will not work.'

'And why's that?'

She tightened her free hand into a fist. 'Because of who he is. They will not care. They will not help me.'

'Then why should I?'

'Many people want him to die. Powerful people. If you do not do this, they will be angry with you.'

'What people? Do you work for them?'

She chose not to answer me, preferring to bite down on her knuckle instead. She gnawed at her flesh as if she planned to strip it to the bone.

'Because if they hired you,' I went on, 'I imagine they'll be more inclined to be angry with you than me. And if that's the case, I don't see why their feelings should trouble me unduly.'

She stared hard, eyes full of white, nostrils pinched, as though she hoped to convince me by force of will alone. When

I failed to succumb, she raised her chin and closed one eye, then straightened the arm with the gun in it and aimed directly at my head. 'Then I *will* kill you,' she said. 'I have to. You make it so. And afterwards, I will kill your friend. Believe me, I will do it.'

She certainly looked as though she was capable of carrying out her threat. I didn't think there was much she wasn't capable of. Her hand wasn't even trembling. In every mystery novel I'd ever written, when a woman held a gun on Michael Faulks, her arm *definitely* trembled. But Graziella? Not a quiver.

'That's hardly fair,' I told her, which, I confess, was more than a touch weak.

'But what can I do? I cannot allow you to live. You will warn him.'

'Nuh uh.' I pretended to zip my lips closed. 'I won't say a word.' And besides, I thought, the explosion that had ripped through his home had probably given him an inkling that he'd ticked somebody off just a smidgen.

'But I cannot take this risk.' Her face was pinched. Determined. 'You must understand this, yes?'

Actually – much as I didn't want to – I could see what she was driving at. True, she appeared to be quite unhinged, but she made a sound point. If I agreed to shoot the guy, I'd be more than a little reluctant to come clean to anyone. But my hapless involvement in a bombing was a much less powerful motivating factor. There was no way she could rely on me keeping my mouth shut – unless she forcibly shut it for good.

'Wait a minute,' I told her. 'Let me think about what you're asking.'

I didn't need time to think. I needed time to pack, time to get myself and Victoria as far away from Venice as possible, to a place where my beauty sleep wouldn't be interrupted by attractive sociopaths in the dead of night and where demands for me to kill rich, titled Italians were but a distant memory. A couple of hours, nothing more. There would be flights leaving Marco Polo airport from six o'clock or so, and trains departing Santa Lucia station to destinations right across Europe. I could be on any one of them, to any place I cared. Anywhere other than here would do.

'Well.' She gazed hard at me, with an impatient heft of her gun. 'What is your decision?'

'I'll do it,' I said, hastily now. 'I'll kill him.'

'*Grande*,' she said, her face brightening and her finger slipping free of the trigger. 'This makes me very happy. I did not want to shoot you.'

She lowered her weapon and nodded at me, almost as if we were comrades-in-arms and I'd just distinguished myself on the battlefield. Hard to believe I'd indulged myself with fantasies about this woman. Unstable was an understatement. She was more volatile than the plastic explosives inside the attaché case she'd given me.

'You must kill him today,' she told me.

'Not a problem. I'm your man.'

'He must be dead by nine o'clock this evening. No later.'

'Terrific. I'm great at meeting deadlines. Just ask my agent.'

'I will leave you the gun.'

'Wonderful. You want to pass it over now?'

The astounding thing is, she nearly did exactly that. I saw her visibly relax and even take a step towards me before thinking better of it.

'No,' she said, shaking her head, the wig swaying so much that some of the hairs caught in her mouth. 'I will leave it for you. You have a post box, yes? I saw this.' She was right about that. There were three letterboxes built into the wall beside the front door. One for each apartment. 'I will put the gun inside as I go. This too,' she added, patting her trouser pocket with the stun gun in it.

'What if I decide not to shoot him?' She looked at me blankly. Obviously the eventuality hadn't occurred to her. 'I don't know where the gun came from,' I explained. 'Other people may have been shot with it.'

'It is not so.'

'So you say. But what if I use my hands?' I asked, miming strangling someone. 'Or a knife.' This time, I mimed a stabbing action.

She considered the matter, poking her tongue into the side of her cheek. 'As long as he is dead, I do not care.'

'What if he suffers?'

'This does not concern me.'

Wow. She really was something. Either the Count was every bit as evil as she'd claimed, or she was colder than I'd imagined.

She moved for the door, but I wasn't done just yet.

'One last thing. If I do this, are you going to return my book?'

'*Si*,' she told me, her voice clipped. 'It will be my pleasure.'

TWENTY-ONE

Pleasure or not, I wasn't sure that I believed her, and I was quite certain that I didn't trust her. Tossing aside my bedcovers, I threw on a pair of jeans and a T-shirt, yanked on my baseball trainers and hopped through to the hallway. Victoria was sleeping soundly, her duvet rising and falling with her breaths. She didn't appear to be hurt in any way. In fact, she seemed entirely at ease.

Graziella had left the door to my apartment ajar and I could hear footfall on the steps outside. While I waited for her to leave, I glanced up at the alarm sensor in the corner of the ceiling. No sign of it. Turned out the contraption was on the ground, its plastic casing crushed, wires spewed out. Not the most sophisticated way of disarming a sensor, I grant you, but surprisingly effective all the same.

I heard the clang of something heavy being dropped inside one of the metal post boxes downstairs. Reaching for my nylon sports coat, I took the stairs two at a time, feeding my arms through my sleeves as I went.

She was hurrying along the pavement in the direction of the Grand Canal by the time I lurched outside. No boat this time around. It was cold and dark, but visibility was good, the result of a cloudless night and a full moon. Her red wig was impossible to miss, shining like a beacon in the black, and the rapid beat of her footsteps echoed off the stone walls and still waters of the Fondamenta Venier.

I was going to have to take a chance and follow her. Until now, she'd been the one in control, not just anticipating my moves, but planning them for me. Contrary to what you may be thinking, I'm not a complete idiot, and I had one or two moves of my own. By tracking her, I hoped to get some kind of leverage. Perhaps she'd lead me to the people she'd claimed wanted Count Borelli dead. If I could identify them, or gather some kind of evidence on them, it might give me enough ammunition to excuse myself from the role of assassin, or even go to the authorities or the press. Then again, she might be heading home, and if things were really working in my favour, I could find myself with an opportunity to break in to her place and go hunting for my copy of *The Maltese Falcon*.

While I waited to step out from my cover, I asked myself if I should bring the gun along for protection, but then I realised that in my hurry to get out of my apartment I hadn't collected my keys or my picks. Going back for them would take too long, and reaching a hand through the letterbox wasn't possible without a severe mutation. Pursuing Graziella unarmed was certainly a risk, but given the position she'd put me in and the threats she'd made, I feared that losing her altogether could be worse.

I hovered beyond the cone of light from a nearby streetlamp until she turned left at Palazzo Cini, then closed the door to my building on the latch and broke into a half-skip, half-tiptoe affair that transported me to the end of the street as swiftly and as quietly as possible. Flattening myself against the grimy brickwork, I craned my neck around the corner. A flash of red rounded the end of the street and I scurried after it, bent-double, for some reason, as if I was ducking beneath covering fire.

The craft shops and art galleries, sunglass outlets and neighbourhood *tabacchi* that I'd passed countless times during the day were concealed behind shutters and iron bars. Up ahead, the Accademia di Belle Arti loomed before me, the lower half of its stone exterior shrouded in scaffolding and plywood boards that doubled as makeshift advertising hoardings. I used them for shelter as I crept towards the Accademia Bridge.

Graziella was striding across the middle of the span, her shoes thudding rhythmically against the wooden treads, her hands buried deep inside the pockets of her leather jacket. The view of the moonlit canal waters didn't appear to interest her – she wasn't even tempted to glance towards the ghostly dome of the church of Santa Maria della Salute – and her self-absorption was something I was thankful for.

The arched bridge would expose me. It offered no nooks or crannies to crouch behind, and the wooden planking would amplify the sound of my movements. Much as it pained me, I was forced to wait until Graziella's red wig bobbed down the steps on the opposite side before tackling the stairs.

The night breeze whipped up from the tremulous waters of the canal and I turned my collar against the chill, tucking my chin down into my chest. It didn't help that I wasn't wearing any socks. The icy wind swirled around my bare ankles, whistling up my trouser legs.

I saw no sign of Graziella when I reached the far side. There was a chance that she'd taken one of the turnings to the left, following the curve of the Grand Canal and perhaps even passing the *bacàro* that Victoria and I had visited the previous night, but I put my faith in the channel that continued directly ahead.

Smart decision. I caught sight of her red wig approaching the middle of Campo Santo Stefano, the square a wash of darkness around her, aside from the sullen light of some period streetlamps. She moved at speed, not pausing to consider the pensive marble gentleman on the white plinth she was nearing. I hung back, grateful for the construction work at the opening to the square, where an area had been partitioned off with plastic netting.

I couldn't afford to linger for long. Once she reached the far side, there'd be a considerable distance between us, enough for her to lose me in the warren of alleys and zigzagging lanes that lay ahead. I waited until I judged that she was beyond earshot, then moved quickly along the edge of the square, making use of the stacked café tables and chairs for camouflage. My plan was to be level with the statue by the time she exited, but she was faster than I'd anticipated, and I was forced to run.

I reached the corner of the cathedral with blood pulsing in my ears. The red of her hair flared in the dim up ahead, bobbing from side to side with her movements like a lantern swaying in a draught. The flare jolted upwards as she traversed a humped bridge.

I'd been along this route often enough to have a rough notion of where she was heading. Campo Manin was her most likely destination, and from there she could turn right for Piazza San Marco or left for the Rialto. She continued straight on, just as I'd anticipated, but I swung left, then right, jogging along a parallel alleyway in the hope of gaining ground. At one point, the alleys reached a cross-street, and I paused to be sure my way was clear before sprinting ahead and skidding to a halt before the graceful bridge at the outlet of the passageway.

Lurking there, covering my mouth with my hand to stop my breathing from giving me away, I watched her enter the square. Graziella was pacing towards a glass and concrete office block, but instead of veering towards one of the far corners of the *campo*, she surprised me by turning right just beyond the winged lion at the foot of the statue of Daniele Manin, disappearing along a hidden path I hadn't noticed before.

The unknown *calle* had the appearance of the entrance to an army trench. Dingy and chill, it tapered into a clotted blackness without any hint as to where it might lead. Cursing myself for not bringing my penlight, I edged along with my arms crossed in front of my face, passing the barred windows of a gentleman's outfitters and a neighbouring café. Letterboxes, doorbells and utility pipes emerged from the gloom, telling of residential properties hidden behind the walls that towered above me.

I couldn't see her red wig, or hear her footsteps. There was a chance that she'd ducked inside one of the properties, but I felt sure I would have heard the noise of a door closing. There was also the possibility that she was lurking in wait for me, ready to pounce and knock me from my feet. It wouldn't take much. The strange lane and the impenetrable darkness were so unnerving that a child shouting 'boo' would have done the trick.

Inching on, sliding one foot in front of the next, I found myself at a pair of imposing iron gates. The gates were locked and reached as high as the overhang of the building above, offering no way through.

I squinted hard, only just glimpsing the lane swinging away to my left, into a darkness that was blacker and more menacing than anything I'd had to deal with so far. I was sorely tempted to turn back and retrace my steps – it would have been easy enough to convince myself that I'd made a mistake and that Graziella hadn't really come this way. Then I heard a clang of metal, muted but unmistakable, like the ding of a church bell swathed in cloth. I blundered onwards, nearly tripping on a fire hydrant and passing an old doorway covered in layers of fraying posters. To my right was the entrance to another passage, thinner even than the one I was on, the entrance marked by a stone archway above my head. I could just make out the lettering on a small yellow sign. *Scala Contarini del Bòvolo*.

I sneaked forwards, my hands pressed flat against the pulverised masonry on either side of me, my body tensed and ready to flee at a moment's notice. Then, quite unexpectedly, the lane opened up into a hidden courtyard, where the moonlight took the edge off the darkness. To my right, a small lawned area was cordoned off by tall metal railings topped with pointed barbs. The lawn was filled with a collection of well-heads of varying sizes and designs, their white stone shining in the light from the moon with a spectral luminescence. Beyond the well-heads was the façade of an imposing palazzo.

The main building was around six storeys in height, made up of a series of stilted balconies, but it was dominated by a cylindrical tower, which appeared to contain a spiral staircase. The face of the tower was open to the elements, ringed by a concentric series of stone banisters and colonnaded arches, so that anyone who happened to be climbing the stairs could be seen quite easily. The only person climbing them was Graziella. Her red wig and bleached face were ascending the second spiral.

Apparently, the effect worked both ways, and she raised a gloved hand and beckoned to me, smiling ghoulishly. She seemed to find my gormless reaction quite amusing. So much for my skills as a tracker. So much for turning my situation around. I got the distinct impression that she'd led me here deliberately – that she'd been one move ahead of me yet again.

If I'd had the luxury of sulking about it, I dare say I'd have bolted for home. But I felt the need to see this through, to discover exactly how doomed I really was.

A gate was fitted into the barbed railings, but when I pushed on it I found that it was locked near my hip. If I'd had my tools with me, I could have opened it without any trouble, and it occurred to me that Graziella must have done just that and locked it again – the noise of the gate closing against the metal bracket would explain the clanging that I'd heard.

Removing my sports coat, I slung it over the metal prongs, then shimmied up the railings and did my best to climb over without causing myself a mischief. After dropping onto an uneven flagstone path, I reached up for my coat and heard it tear as I snatched it down. Damn. One of my sleeves had almost detached itself, exposing the lining. No matter. I fed my arms through what was left of the material and sprinted to the bottom of the stone steps.

The stairs were kite-shaped and evenly spaced, twisting me around on myself as I climbed. I passed from darkness to sketchy light and back again, moving from the inner recesses of the tower to the moonlit openings until I became so dizzy that I paused and leaned out over the stone balustrade to peer upwards. Graziella was leering down from above, the red hairs of her wig suspended from her face like exotic tendrils. She giggled and covered her mouth, the noise ballooning in the cramped square below us.

'Where are you going?' I called. 'Where are you taking us?'

She giggled some more by way of response, coming dangerously close to a cackle, then snatched her head back inside. Moments later, the patter of her footsteps told me that she was climbing higher still.

I followed, the thin night air slicing into the back of my throat and making my nostrils sting as I inhaled. My thigh muscles burned, itching beneath the material of my trousers, and my bare feet rubbed sorely against the insides of my shoes.

After two more revolutions, I reached the spot where Graziella had been standing, but there was no sign of her. Bowing my head, I gripped my knees and sucked in a couple of painful breaths before bracing my hand against the curved inner wall and staggering on. By the time I reached the top, I was a gasping, sweating, trembling mess.

'*Buono*, Charlie. You make it at last.' She clapped her hands with the boundless energy of a gym instructor.

I let my coat fall from my shoulders with a groan and staggered into the middle of the circular floor. My T-shirt was plastered to my back and my scalp was prickling as if I might pass out. The top of the tower featured a series of arched openings. Graziella was crouching in the middle of one of them, balanced athletically on top of a stone ledge with her hands gripping onto the outside of the arch above her head, like an inwards-looking gargoyle.

'Where are we?' I asked, leaning my head right back to open my lungs and planting my hands on my hips.

'A private place. It is a beautiful view, yes?'

She swayed one arm in an arc behind her and I squinted out through half-closed eyes. Despite the sting of sweat rolling down my brow, I couldn't deny that the scene was breathtaking – something that at least gave me an excuse for wheezing so heavily. Laid out before me was a softly gloaming dreamscape of ramshackle terracotta roofs, concealed garden terraces, wonky television aerials, crooked bell towers and domed cathedrals. In the distance, the black waters of the lagoon were visible only from the dim twinkle of the navigation lamps attached to wooden posts that stretched into the distance.

'And why are we here?' I panted.

'Because you follow me. Not so many people know of this tower. I think, maybe you would like to see it?'

'You knew I was behind you?'

'Of course. I expect it. You wish to know more about me. Where I live, perhaps?' She smiled, full of compassion, and tipped her head onto her shoulder. 'But I am sorry, Charlie, I cannot tell you this. At least, not until you kill Borelli, *capito*?'

Her eyes were smoky with fatigue. With some kind of warped affection, maybe. I tried not to fall into them. Tried very hard.

She reached up with one hand and slapped the brickwork above her, as if testing its integrity. 'You know, Charlie, since I am a young girl, I am always climbing. First a tree. Then a wall.

My parents, they see this, and they send me on adventures far into the Dolomites. To learn how to really climb. On rocks. Up mountains. With ropes.' She grinned. 'Also without them. This is when I learn to abseil. You have seen me do it, yes?'

'What's your point?'

'My point? Only this. I can go anywhere, Charlie. Wherever I like. Up. Down.' She nodded towards the view again. 'Across all of this. But not you, Charlie. You cannot follow me from this place because I do not want for you to do it. And now, I think I will say goodbye.' She raised her hand to her lips. Blew me the softest of kisses. 'This is enough, yes? You are not a climber, I do not think.'

She straightened and reached for a handhold on the lip of the conical roof above. Bending her right leg at the knee, she kicked off the brickwork, grunting with the effort, and I watched her training shoes dangle over the dark abyss far below.

'Wait!'

My shout was followed by a scraping, scratching noise, and then Graziella grunted as a roof tile dropped from above and her left arm swung loosely before me. Her foot searched desperately for support, and for a second I was convinced she would fall. Before I could react, she found her grip, then heaved and groaned until she vanished from view.

Her head appeared a few seconds later, hanging upside down from above the arched window, red hair dangling close to the stone ledge. Just watching her was making my palms sweat.

'Yes? What is it?' she asked, as if nothing the least bit unusual had just happened.

'Police,' I said, glumly. 'I saw them in the palazzo. How do you expect me to kill Borelli with them there?'

'They will be gone,' she told me simply.

'Gone? I don't think so.'

'He told them they must leave. They will do it.'

'The Count did this?'

She nodded, and rolled her eyes in a show of impatience, a confusing gesture now that she was upside down.

'And he's definitely still there?' I asked. 'He hasn't moved to a hotel, say?'

'Do not worry.' She winked. 'He is still there. And now, I go, yes?'

And with that, her head vanished above the roofline, and I listened to the crunch and scrape of the tiles beneath her feet as she scurried away into the night, leaving me to ponder just why I hadn't grabbed for her foot and ended the entire sorry mess when I'd had my chance.

TWENTY-TWO

Victoria was still asleep when I snuck back into my apartment. I left her to snooze for a short while longer, busying myself with stuffing my torn coat into the waste bin and packing my things. Fifteen minutes later, my suitcase and holdall were full to bursting, and I carried them through to the hallway before preparing to wake her.

Calling her name from her doorway didn't work and, apparently, neither did entering her room and switching on her bedside lamp. It was little wonder that Graziella had been able to creep in and snip a lock of her hair. Her slumber was so deep that I was starting to ask myself if Martin had medicated her too.

Reaching out a tentative hand, I tapped the crown of her head. Nothing. Her eyes remained firmly closed, her face turned away from me, jaw hanging loose. I tapped again. Still no joy. She was wearing a skimpy vest top and her bare shoulder was exposed above the duvet covers. I placed my hand on her freckled skin, intending to shake her, but she surged up and around, surprising me with a feral yell just as something fizzed and sparked before my face.

I felt a puff of air close to my ear, followed by a thud and the splinter of wood. Turning, I caught sight of two metal darts embedded in the back of the door. The coiled wires connected to them glowed a quite alarming shade of orange, but that was nothing compared to the determined grimace on Victoria's face as she held tightly to her Taser gun.

'Holy crap,' I said, staggering backwards. 'You nearly bloody got me.'

'Charlie? Oh my God. I'm so sorry. What are you doing in here?'

She was still clenching the trigger, discharging voltage, and her shoulders were quaking, almost as if she'd accidentally electrocuted herself.

These were curious times indeed. It wasn't often I had two women hold a weapon on me in the middle of the night.

'I was trying to wake you.' I raised a hand to the side of my face. 'I felt that thing go right past my ear. You almost shot me in the face.'

'Well what the hell did you expect?' she snapped. 'I thought you were one of the bad guys.'

Semantics aside – I had just agreed to kill a man – I didn't think I'd changed sides just yet. Ducking under the coils of wire, I moved across the room to turn on the main light.

'You might want to let go of the trigger now,' I suggested.

'Oh, Christ.' Victoria did just that, dropping the gun as if it had scalded her. 'I don't know how you get the wires back inside.'

'I'm guessing it helps if you use a pair of pliers to remove the darts from the back of the door.'

'Oops. Sorry, Charlie.'

'That's okay. It's better than having you fish them out of my throat, I suppose.'

Stepping over to the bed, I gingerly picked up the Taser and tossed it away across the floor. I shuddered. For some reason, it seemed less predictable than a conventional pistol.

Victoria rested her hands on her kneecaps. She was wearing sleeping shorts along with the vest. I'd hardly had time to register the information when she caught me looking and covered herself with her duvet. *Not what I'd intended.* I needed her to get out of bed and pack, not tuck herself in. And I definitely didn't want her thinking that her very fine legs, or any other part of her anatomy for that matter, were the reason I was currently in her bedroom at, oh, twenty past four in the morning.

'What time is it?' she asked, blinking and pinching the bridge of her nose.

I told her, then explained why exactly I'd woken her.

I can't say the colour drained from her face because she'd hardly been relaxed before I delivered the news, but she did appear to shiver during a number of points in my tale, and by the end of my account she'd taken to covering her mouth with her hand and shaking her head. I suppose it must have been something of a shock. God knows, it had been unsettling enough for me to go through the experience myself.

'Did Graziella really leave you a gun?' Victoria whispered.

'Wait here,' I said, before making my way downstairs and checking my letterbox. Sure enough, the dirty big pistol and the dinky stun gun were stashed inside. Of course, I hadn't had the foresight to put on my plastic gloves, so I had to return to my bathroom and fetch a towel before heading downstairs a second time to gather the pistol. Graziella had worn leather gloves when she'd handled the gun, so there wasn't much hope of finding her fingerprints (or much I could do about it if I did), but I certainly didn't want to add any of my own.

I popped the stun gun inside my pocket and headed back upstairs, only pausing on my way into my apartment to consider the locks Graziella had defeated. I couldn't see any indication of tampering and there was no sign of any damage. She'd done a clean, thoroughly professional job. The same couldn't be said of the shattered alarm sensor, which had most probably been stomped on, but there was no denying that her invasion of my home had been an unqualified success.

Returning to Victoria's room, I laid the towel out on her bed so that she could inspect the gun. At first, she backed away from it, but soon her curiosity got the better of her and she leaned forwards for a closer look. As she bowed her head, I found myself searching for where Graziella had cut Victoria's hair. There were no obvious bald patches or uneven spots. I guess it helped that she favoured a layered style. Who knew, perhaps she'd even like what Graziella had done? Not that I was stupid enough to tell her about it. But then again, it could be that Graziella had fooled me. Maybe the hair that had fallen from her hand had been a sample from one of her wigs.

'Is that a silencer?' Victoria asked, with some reverence.

'I believe so. That's why I thought she was here to kill me.'

She lowered her face closer still, sniffing the barrel. 'Is it loaded?'

I went up on my toes and craned my neck, but I still couldn't see an obvious gap in her hairline. 'I imagine so,' I said. 'It's certainly heavy.'

'How many bullets does it hold?'

'I've no idea.'

Victoria glanced up to find me teetering above her. 'What the hell are you doing?'

'Nothing,' I replied, trying, and no doubt failing, to appear innocent as I dropped back down to my heels. 'Why do you ask about the number of bullets? Do you think it's important?'

'No,' she said, fixing me with a cool look, then using a corner of the towel to tilt the gun until the muzzle was pointing at my crotch. 'I guess one would be enough.'

'Charming.'

'Although it's not simply idle curiosity.' She waggled the pistol from side to side. 'It occurred to me that she would have to have a lot of faith in you if she didn't provide you with any spares.'

'Eh?'

'Well, it would mean she thought you were a bloody good shot, wouldn't it?'

'Oh,' I said, 'perhaps. But I did say I might not use the gun.'

Victoria offered me a level stare.

'I mentioned a knife, or even strangling him.

She snorted. 'Sounds like you gave it some serious thought.'

'Of course not. I just wanted to make her think that was the case so that she'd go.'

'Which she did. So why did she leave you the gun?'

'Insurance, I suppose.'

Victoria peered at me, then raised a quizzical eyebrow. 'You don't think she's already, you know, used this? I mean, she has tried to set you up for one crime, already.'

'The thought did occur to me. She could have been to the palazzo, say, and shot the Count before coming here.'

'Exactly. Then all she'd have to do is send the police to your door and tell them to look for this.' Victoria's eyebrows made a brave attempt to cosy up to her hairline as she pushed the pistol away from her. I wasn't sure what the expression was meant to tell me, but I didn't imagine it was good. Mind you, there was a flaw in her thinking I couldn't ignore. If this was all an elaborate set-up, Graziella would have had no need to wake me. She could simply have hidden the gun in my apartment and called the police at her leisure. 'Maybe you should toss this in a canal.'

Now that did strike me as a sensible suggestion. Especially as I wasn't planning on hanging around.

'Good idea,' I told Victoria. 'We can ditch it on our way out of here.'

'Out of here? Are we going somewhere?'

I stepped to one side and motioned towards my luggage in the hallway. 'Always best to know when to quit. And now seems like a perfect time to me. It's dark outside. If we hurry, we can probably make it to the train station before dawn. And it would be good if we could get out without Martin and Antea hearing us – I still owe them for last month's rent.'

Victoria leaned backwards, resting on her arms, and stared at me in apparent confusion. I knew it was early, but it had seemed quite straightforward to me.

'Chop chop,' I told her, and snatched at a drawer on the dressing table beside me. It was full of Victoria's underthings. Not the most appropriate items for me to pack. Flustered, I spun round until my eyes settled on the wardrobe. Had to be on surer ground there. 'You fold, I'll fetch,' I said, meanwhile yanking a fistful of blouses from their hangers and tossing them onto the bed.

'*Charlie.*'

'Not a folder? That's okay – me neither.'

Her suitcase was on the floor in the corner of the room. Tipping back the lid with my toe, I dropped the blouses inside and went back for more.

'Charlie, stop. Please.'

I paused, mid-grab, and turned to look at her. 'Problem?'

'Yes there's a bloody problem. What are you doing? We can't just go.'

Uh-oh. I'd been afraid she might say something like that. 'I was only joking about the rent,' I told her. 'I'll leave some cash in an envelope on the sideboard. Okay?'

'No, it's not okay. And that's not the problem.'

Now, there have been times in my life when I've sensed that allowing a particular conversation to develop was the absolute worst thing I could do – that the consequences of not nipping a discussion in the bud would almost certainly be dire. This was one of those occasions. But while I'd matured enough to be able to recognise the danger signs, I still appeared to be powerless to break the pattern.

'Maybe we should chat about this on the way to the train station?' I suggested. 'Or better still when we're actually on a train. I was wondering about Switzerland. It has to be a safe haven, right? You don't hear about murders and bomb plots in the Alps. Peaceful too. I'll bet I could get a lot of writing done. Find a tranquil spot beside a lake. In fact, I suspect—'

'Will you shut up?' Victoria glared at me. 'The point is we can't just leave.'

'Of course we can. I can't for the life of me think of one good reason why we shouldn't.'

'Well, take a seat,' she told me, 'and I'll run through the list.'

TWENTY-THREE

Victoria is a big fan of lists. I don't have the most ordered of minds – which is something of a handicap for a guy who pens mystery novels for a living – but Victoria is my polar opposite. If my brain was an office, it would be one of those cluttered, closet-sized rooms, filled with teetering stacks of paper and a desk that's impossible to access. By contrast, I imagine Victoria's head space would be a spotless glass capsule, smelling of polish and featuring sleek computer equipment, banks of well-organised filing cabinets and perhaps even a whiteboard with a sensible To-Do list written upon it.

Sometimes, I suspect that what she enjoys above all other pleasures in life is pointing out those things that I've over-looked (or preferred to ignore). So, despite the gravity of our situation, the early hour and my distinct lack of patience, I could sense that she was feeling more than a little pleased with herself.

'Tell me,' she began, much like a courtroom lawyer about to embark on an important cross-examination, 'what do you suppose will happen if we *do* leave?'

'I don't know, Vic. I was hoping we might get breakfast at the station and perhaps eat lunch on the train. Our destination might not be somewhere I'll stay for long, but hopefully it'll suit me for a week, at least.'

'That's not what I meant,' she said, in a tone that suggested I'd known very well what she was driving at. Which I had.

I sat down on the end of her bed, a bundle of her clothes resting in my lap. 'Are we really going to do this?'

'Absolutely. So allow me to rephrase my question. What do you suppose will happen to Count Borelli if we leave?'

'Hard to say.'

'Is it really? I'd say it's pretty damn simple. He's going to be killed.'

'Maybe.'

'Charlie, admit it.' Blimey. In a moment, she'd be asking me to place my hand on the Good Book and swear to tell nothing but the truth.

'Listen,' I told her, 'so far as Graziella is concerned, he'll also be killed if we stay. I'm the one who's meant to do the killing, remember?'

Victoria exhaled sharply, threw back her covers and snatched up her dressing gown. She shoved her arms through the sleeves and roughly tied the cord around her waist. I wouldn't have been hugely surprised to learn that she was tempted to tighten the cord around my neck.

'Are you going to take this seriously?' she asked.

'Didn't you see my bags out in the hall?'

Victoria glared at me in frustration, then bolted from her room. No doubt the best thing I could have done would have been to pack her things and deal with her tantrum later. But when I heard her banging cupboard doors in the kitchen as if she was aiming to wake the inhabitants of Mestre, I decided I should try to calm her down.

I sauntered into the kitchen to find her filling the kettle and setting it to boil.

'Victoria,' I tried, but she refused to turn and look at me. Instead, she reached up to the shelf above the cooker for a cup, then hesitated, and finally reached for a second.

'Tea?' she asked, through clenched teeth.

Ah, the traditional British solution for every predicament. Just drink a warm stewed beverage and all your worldly problems will slip away.

'I'm sorry, Vic,' I told her. 'We can talk. I'll be sensible this time.' I stepped towards her and touched her shoulder. 'Go and sit in the lounge,' I said. 'I'll bring the drinks through.'

True to my word, I did just that, and since I was feeling generous, I added my last two biscuits to Victoria's saucer. I found her sitting on the chesterfield. After setting our cups down on the steamer trunk, I turned my writing chair to face her and arranged myself in a slouched position with the heels of my baseball shoes resting on the edge of the trunk. Victoria didn't appear to be bowled over by my biscuit gesture, but despite herself, she was prepared to chomp away all the same.

'All right, here's what I really think,' I said, in something of a heavy voice. 'If we flee Venice, then in all likelihood the Count will be murdered. Graziella might be a touch doolally, but she strikes me as determined. And if we take what she said to me at face value, so are these "powerful" people behind her.' I shaped the speech marks with my fingers, undaunted by how ridiculous it made me look. 'They obviously have resources, not to mention access to guns and explosives. So I'd say it's a fair bet the guy's days are numbered.'

'That's what I think too,' Victoria said, biscuit crumbs tumbling from her lips. 'And if we go without doing anything, we'll have been partly responsible.'

I gave her a dubious look. I hoped the expression was more authentic than the sentiment behind it. 'Listen, we're not responsible for anything. This will happen whether or not we're involved.'

'Not if we do something to prevent it.'

'Like what?' I said. 'I really don't see that there's much we can do. I'm not a trained bodyguard, Vic. And I'm not exactly innocent in this whole scenario, either, so don't even think of suggesting the police.'

'Why not? Charlie, this is a man's life we're talking about.'

'The police already know he's at risk, Vic. We saw teams of

them collecting the evidence from the bomb attack. If they're competent, they'll protect him. And if they're not, nothing I say will change any of that.'

'But you can warn them who to look out for. An anonymous tip describing Graziella.'

'No way.'

'Don't "no way" me,' she said, aping my speech-mark gesture. 'You can do it. You know that you can.' She bit down on her digestive with a triumphant *crunch*, as if she'd just constructed an irrefutable argument. I was beginning to fear she may have done precisely that.

'Say I do call them,' I said, standing from my chair. 'Say I tell them everything I can. We don't know what the people Graziella mentioned are capable of. They might hurt her. I get the impression she's afraid of them. In some kind of fix.'

Victoria gave me a caustic look. 'I don't mean to sound heartless, but I'm not sure I care. She's trouble, Charlie.'

'Then how about this? They may have a mole at the police station. And if they do, it would be simple enough for them to work out that the information came from me.'

'Christ, Charlie,' she said, snapping her biscuit in half and dunking it in her tea. 'That sounds positively paranoid. Who do you think we're dealing with here? The Mafia?'

I pouted. 'They have weapons, Vic. Explosives. Who does that sound like to you?'

'Oh good grief. You have the Mob on the brain.' She shook her biscuit irritably. 'There's far too much of it in your book, by the way. This ridiculous character you created – Don Giovanni – he's totally unbelievable.'

I felt my eyes boggle. 'You really think now's a good time for literary criticism?'

'No. But I *do* think an anonymous tip is feasible.'

'Well, I think it's risible.'

Victoria eyed me for a moment, then eyed her second biscuit. It wasn't long before she picked the little fellow up and acquainted it with her brew. *Dunk, dunk, chomp.*

'You want my opinion?' I asked, then proceeded to give it before she could offer me a tart response. 'If we leave, the Count dies. If we stay, the Count dies. The outcome is exactly the same, except for one thing. If we hang around in Venice beyond 9 o'clock tonight and the Count's not dead, we may very well die too.'

That got her thinking. To be honest, I would have been alarmed if it hadn't. It's not every day you find yourself confronted with your own mortality – at least not by a talented break-in artist with the means and the motivation to put a bullet in your brain.

'What about the chunky guy who followed us?' Victoria asked me. 'Did you mention him to Graziella?'

'Of course not. I didn't want her thinking that I'd compromised her in any way.'

'He could be part of her organisation. One of the people she mentioned.'

'He could be, yes. Or he might have some other connection altogether.'

'It would be helpful if we knew. If we could speak to him, even.'

'Yeah, well,' I said, throwing up my hands, 'I can think of a lot of things that would be helpful. Including a train ticket out of here.'

Victoria raised her teacup to her lips. It seemed it was time for her to sample the wondrous elixir. I still hadn't touched my own. My nerves were jangling, but I wanted them that way. It kept me sharp. God willing, it would keep me alive, too.

'Just for argument's sake,' Victoria said to me, 'let's say we don't flee, but we don't call the police, either. What does that leave us with?'

'An insurmountable problem?'

'But you mustn't think that way, Charlie. There has to be another option. Faulks would certainly find it, so you should be capable of doing the same.'

I smacked my lips and worked a glum smile. 'I don't know what to tell you, Vic. I suppose there are some leads we could consider. The bookbinding business, for instance. Perhaps you could try speaking to the owner.'

'But it doesn't really *feel* right. And I don't see it solving our problem quickly enough. I still reckon we're overlooking something. Some really proactive step we could take, perhaps even a way of extending Graziella's deadline.'

Victoria cupped her chin and pressed her fingertips against her lips, looking away towards her reflection in the window Graziella had escaped from just two days before. I had a feeling she wasn't listening to me any more, that instead of paying attention to what I had to say, she was sorting through that clean, orderly space in her mind, searching for the most elegant solution to the brainteaser she'd composed for us. I didn't think she'd find it – to my mind, the only answer was to run – and I didn't exactly welcome the way she appeared to have tuned me out.

'Perhaps you were right about the beardy guy who followed us,' I said, trying to interest her again. 'I have no idea how to track him down, but I don't suppose it would hurt to go back to where he found us. You know, the view of the palazzo from across the Grand Canal?'

Nothing. Not the slightest reaction. I suppose I should have respected what she was trying to do, but I was feeling pretty miffed. I firmly believed we needed to be on our way. But if we *were* going to waste time brainstorming, the very least she could do was listen to my input.

'Damn it, Victoria, did you hear what I said?'

I kicked the steamer trunk with my toe. Not hard, but loud enough to snap her out of her reverie. Her head whirled around and she peered at my foot. Her eyes narrowed and then widened. A smile crept across her lips. I'd seen her look that way before and experience told me it wasn't a good sign.

'That's it,' she said. 'Charlie, I've got it! I know what we should do!'

And that's when Victoria told me her big idea. And even though her scheme was audacious and moronic in equal measure, somehow, in that particular moment, whether due to some inexplicable weakness on my part, or some spellbinding powers of persuasion on hers, it seemed against all odds to make complete and irresistible sense.

TWENTY-FOUR

Returning to Palazzo Borelli hadn't been at the top of my list of things to do that day. Then again, I hadn't made plans to loiter around the backstreets of the San Polo region, waiting for a delivery man to abandon an empty handcart so that I could nab it, and neither had I intended to take a *vaporetto* as far as the Arsenale and wander the canals of the Castello until I found an unattended boat that happened to have the characteristics I required. If I'm honest, car theft has never been my bag, but I can't pretend I'm ignorant of the principles behind the vocation, and I'd been willing enough to apply them on water. As it happens, the Venetians are a trusting lot, and the flat-bottomed motor launch that caught my eye and transported me home had been moored with a key in the ignition. It had plenty of diesel too – or rather, it had enough to cover a quick boating lesson for Victoria and a trip along the Grand Canal as far as the Rio del Santi Apostoli, just a short stroll from my destination.

It was approaching 8 p.m. by the time Victoria scraped the hull alongside the brick canal wall and I fed a rope through a metal mooring ring. That was the easy part. My sea legs were still shaky, at best, and hauling the handcart onto the canal bank without toppling into the water was a real challenge. So was acting inconspicuous while I heaved at the steamer trunk we'd transported from my living room and fixed it to the cart with bungee cords.

The handcart had a metal frame fitted with large rubber wheels at the rear and small plastic wheels on the front, a design that enabled delivery men to lever the carts up over the stepped bridges of the city. Fortunately for me, there were no bridges on my route, and I had only to roll through a residential square before rounding the nearby church and joining the main tourist thoroughfare that linked to the forgotten channel of Ramo Dragan.

Abandoning my cart just shy of the garden gate and the intruder light fitted above it, I removed my winter coat and mittens, then slipped a pair of my customised plastic gloves on over my bare hands and taped fingers before poking my head inside my balaclava. My balaclava smelled of the washing detergent Victoria had cleaned it with. Once I had the eyeholes positioned just right, I checked the contents of my bumbag.

Well, I say *my* bumbag, but in truth it was an item Victoria had purchased for me from a market stall. I have to admit that I was wearing it with some reluctance. Not only was it bright blue and branded with the word *Italia* in a memorable red, white and green script, it also ruined the lines of my outfit. Still, I'd been forced to concede that my trusty spectacles case couldn't possibly contain all the equipment I needed to carry for the task ahead. Yes, I could cut down on my picks, since I was familiar with the locks I might be tackling, but I also needed room for the handgun Graziella had so generously loaned me, plus one or two additions from Victoria's spy kit.

So, as I say, I checked my bumbag and verified that there wasn't anything I'd forgotten. Then I removed my torch, popped it into my mouth and clambered onto the trunk.

The way I saw things, and in spite of Graziella's carefree assurances, security could well have been stepped up since the bomb attack. Even if the Count really had banished the police from his property, he might have hired some personal bodyguards in their place. Graziella hadn't said so, which suggested I might be worrying unnecessarily, but I wanted to remain undetected for as long as possible, and it struck me that triggering the security light might be a bad way of achieving that. Stacked upright, the steamer trunk was almost as high as my chin, and by scrambling onto the thing I was able to scale the garden wall without any need to open the gate.

Naturally, I got scratched to hell by whatever variety of prickly shrub had been planted by the Count's ancestors, but I'm pleased to report that there was no barbed wire or broken glass to add to my fun. And, on balance, when I dropped down onto the lawn and stalked through the darkness on my way towards the courtyard, I thought a few cuts and scrapes were a fair bargain in return for remaining wholly undetected.

Since it wasn't raining for once, I was almost sorry that I couldn't linger and enjoy the solitude of the garden. It might have been winter, but there were still plenty of scents and aromas in the air, and as someone who'd been living in Venice for close to a year, I couldn't entirely ignore the novelty of grass. I did, though, have a job to do and a timeframe to do it in, and so I moved onto the cobblestones of the courtyard and crouched behind the old well-head to assess the scene above.

There were lights on in the upper floors again. In fact, I thought they were probably the exact same lights that had been on during my previous visit. The mighty front door was closed just as it had been before, and the external brick staircase leading up to it was temptingly shadowed. I knew the lock was a cinch, and I also knew the layout, but I didn't like the idea of repeating myself. I was inclined to believe that I hadn't left any telltale signs to indicate how I'd got in with the bomb, but since I couldn't be certain, a new route seemed sensible.

After checking the windows one last time, just to be sure nobody was looking out at that particular moment, I bent at the waist and scurried beneath the arched entranceway to the dank-smelling storage area. This time, I left the electricity cupboard undisturbed. If I cut the supply, the Count and anyone who happened to be with him would know I was on my way. That was no good. To have any hope of pulling off my assignment, surprise was vital. So was luck.

I guess there was luck in the form of the stone staircase that led up from the storage area to the *piano nobile*, but I like to think there was an element of skill involved too. After all, if I hadn't studied the plans Graziella had given me, or checked that they were accurate during my previous visit, I wouldn't have known that the option existed. As it was, my approach couldn't have been simpler. There were no locks, let alone any doors. My only challenge was the darkness, but after flashing my torch beam ahead of me for just an instant, I was able to reach out for the rope handrail and edge my way upstairs.

The second flight opened directly onto the impressive reception room I was already familiar with. The terrazzo floor, the ceiling frescoes and the pleated silks were still quite capable of rendering me speechless – which was a good thing, since I was aiming to remain quiet – but second time round, it was a little easier to press on without pausing to carry out a detailed inventory.

I suppose one explanation for my ability to focus on the task at hand was the reluctance I felt to face up to the devastation I'd caused. Care to know what a quick peek revealed? Well all right, it wasn't pretty. At the far end of the room, a stretch of wall had been screened off with thick plastic sheeting. Even so, I could spy bare patches of render where a pricey artwork or two had once been hanging, and several piles of rubble beside a loaded-down wheelbarrow. The doorway into the room containing the vault was charred and splintered, and the beautiful walnut door was now a collection of very desirable matchsticks. A series of metal stilts and braces had been fitted near the windows, stretching upwards from the floor and looking as if they might be necessary to keep the bowed ceiling from collapsing.

Oops-a-daisy.

Then again, this was no time for a fit of guilt. After all, there were worse crimes yet to be visited upon the palazzo and its poor, unfortunate owner, and I was right in the middle of committing one of them.

With that in mind, I progressed to the thin wooden staircase that climbed steeply towards the floor above. No matter where I stepped, or how daintily I moved, the treads creaked and groaned as if they'd been specifically designed to confound me. I paused and composed myself, then realised just what a dumb move it was to loiter on the stairway. I could hear music coming from above, something operatic (which is about as detailed as my knowledge of classical music gets), so there was definitely someone around. Someone who might head downstairs at any moment.

I took a chance and climbed quickly on, hoping the music would conceal the noise I was making. First one flight, then a small landing, followed by a second flight. And then, at last, the floor I was interested in.

The contrast with the fancy interior downstairs was striking. The layout was the same – a long, central space with side rooms leading off from it – but nearly everything else was different. This was somewhere you could actually live. The huge main room was filled with sagging fabric sofas and aged leather arm-chairs, and the floor was covered with a patchwork of rugs in various shades of red – like a giant test card for the walls of a bordello. There were standing lamps and table lamps, two portable fan heaters whirring asthmatically away, a boxy tele-vision in an imposing cabinet, and a large, dated-looking stereo with multiple green lights twinkling on the front of it. Lines of cabling snaked beneath the rugs from the back of the stereo to connect with a series of black-ash speakers. There were no Renaissance artworks – the walls were papered an inoffensive beige colour, and the ceiling featured darkly stained beams. In most other places, the room would have been terribly imposing, but in the context of the statement piece below, it was really quite modest.

Still, I wasn't in the business of appraising interior décor. Ordinarily, I was in the business of clearing it – at least when it was worth my while – but I wouldn't be doing that tonight, either. I have to say, it was more than a shade frustrating. Two clean break-ins to the same richly furnished home, and I hadn't taken a single item on either occasion. Not a record to boast about.

One thing I could be proud of, however, was that my sense of hearing was back on song, as was a gentleman two rooms down on my left. He was singing along in Italian with the rous-ing tune on the stereo, and though I'm no expert, I thought he had a very fine voice.

Flattening myself against the wall and realigning the eyeslits in my balaclava, I stalked as far as the appropriate doorway and peered inside. Turned out the soaring vocals were just one more gift that Count Frederico Borelli had been blessed with.

He was dressed in black tuxedo trousers and a white dress shirt that had obviously been tailored to his exact proportions. A velvet jacket with silk lapels rested on the corner of the large bed beside him, above a pair of pointed black shoes that had been polished to an oily sheen. The man himself was standing in his socks before a full-height mirror, fiddling with his bow tie and entertaining himself with his singing, rising up on his toes and gesticulating with his hand when the tune on the stereo prompted him to give an extra flourish. He grinned at himself, clearly relishing his performance. Good grief. The dope was practically drooling.

His position wasn't ideal. I didn't think he could spot me in the mirror – he only had eyes for himself, after all – but once I began to move from my hiding place there was a good chance he'd notice. I supposed I could wait and see if the set-up improved, but I didn't rate the idea. All things considered, it could have been a lot worse. He appeared to be alone – even men with fine voices and bloated egos don't tend to sing with quite so much gusto in company – and if I could tackle him inside his room, there was less risk of being disturbed by a member of his staff. Speaking of which, I wasn't all that keen to hang around in the open. Better to take my chances and fail, than never to seize my opportunity. Or so I told myself.

Delving inside the bumbag, my fingers touched upon the

hard steel of the gun. With the silencer screwed to the barrel, it had only just fit inside the blue plastic pouch. I'd been very conscious of its weight hanging from my waist as I moved around, but it was still unnerving to look at, especially as I'd discovered that it was most definitely loaded. Twelve bullets, packed inside a magazine that slotted into the butt. I couldn't tell you the calibre, or whether they happened to be hollow-pointed, but I had no doubt that they were quite deadly, particularly if they were fired at close range.

I worked the gun free and felt the heft of it in my palm. I was naturally right-handed but I curled the fingers of my left hand around the dimpled grip, then used my thumb to slide the safety off. If push came to shove – or finger came to trigger – I didn't want my arthritis to get in the way of a clean shot.

My right hand eased back inside my bumbag for one last piece of equipment and then I held the gun before me, swallowed my nerves, and checked his position. He'd slipped on his jacket and was straightening his cuffs and blowing himself a kiss when I made my move.

It was over very fast. The distance from the doorway to my target was no more than ten feet and I couldn't afford to be slow. In three paces I was upon him. One step more and I had an arm wrapped around his neck, yanking him backwards off his feet. His arms circled in the air and he drew a choked breath as if to scream, but before the sound escaped his throat I stabbed him hard in the neck with Victoria's special pen.

I hadn't been prepared for how rapidly the sedative would

work. He went limp almost instantly, head lolling to one side, and it was all I could do to stop myself from dropping him and accidentally firing the gun as his weight crumpled my hand. There was a trickle of blood from where the nib had pierced his neck, and I watched it soak into the fine cotton of his shirt. His sleek hair smelled of pomade with a citrus note, and I remember thinking just what a dumb thing that was to focus on as I sank to my knees with the Count in my lap and the booming opera tune neared a climax that seemed, to my ears at least, to foretell of desperate fates set in motion by hasty actions.

TWENTY-FIVE

The Count was not a large man. Shorter than me, with a trim, athletic build, he was in no need of a diet. Even so, scrambling out from beneath his body and hauling him up by the arm before ducking down and lifting him onto my shoulder took a good deal of strength. There was no way I could stand straight with his weight bearing down on me, and I found myself staggering from side to side in an impromptu jig as I struggled not to collapse in a heap, all while gathering the pistol and stashing it together with the sedative pen inside my bumbag.

After standing still long enough to register the quiver in my thighs and the dull, painful ache that was blooming in my lower back, I swivelled with a grunt and made for the door. I didn't bang the Count's love-struck head on my way out of his bedroom, and I was careful not to tangle his feet in any furniture as I quick-stepped through the living space, but by the time I'd trudged down the first flight of stairs, any scruples I'd had about his welfare had started to desert me. One flight more, and I entered the *piano nobile* as if I was carrying a mannequin on my back. Forget care – I needed speed, and if that meant the Count grazed his knuckles as I skimmed along the wall for balance, or took a few swift ones to the back of the head as I lurched drunkenly down the stone staircase leading to the basement area, then I'm afraid that was a consequence I was prepared to tolerate.

When I reached the basement, my body was in flat-out rebellion, shaking as if I had a peculiar nerve condition, and I would have gladly dumped him onto the mossy flagstones for some respite. The only thing that stopped me was the fear that I'd be unable to lift him a second time around. Better to keep going, I told myself. I told my screaming back and quaking legs the same thing, and then I heaved the Count a touch higher and swore in the darkness as his weight crushed down onto my shoulder. Stuttering on across the cobblestone courtyard, my stance getting steadily lower and my steps coming faster and more desperate, I finally made it as far as the garden and tripped forwards into the black.

The impact was unforgiving, but the Count didn't make a sound. I rolled over onto my side and wheezed and sighed for a time, whining for good measure. I felt so light all of a sudden that I could almost have believed that I was weightless, capable of floating up into the starless sky above. Then I stretched my legs and straightened my back and something twanged painfully near the base of my spine. Christ, I wouldn't be doing that again in a hurry. In fact, I wouldn't have been surprised to discover that I'd never be capable of doing it again. Still, no bother, it wasn't as if I had more heavy lifting to do.

Hmm.

The Count's shoeless foot was beside my head, and I felt my way up his leg and along his body. Gripping him below the armpits and lifting his torso and backside clear of the ground, I squatted and heaved. The Count slid towards me, his heels cutting two furrows into the soggy grass. Truth be told, he didn't move all that far, but I didn't have the strength or the will to raise him onto my shoulder, and the heaving-sliding approach seemed like my best option. Not a great option, true, but better than walking with a stoop for the rest of my life.

I dragged him as far as the gate. Ask me to do it again sometime, and I dare say my response would make you blush. It took far longer than I would have liked, it hurt a damn sight more than I would have cared for, and it did an excellent job of ploughing the lawn. No matter. At last I could dispense with the muscle work and go back to something I was good at – coaxing a lock into submission.

Less than a minute later, I was done, and it was one of the few times in my life when I was sorry it hadn't taken me longer. To get us both through the gate, I had to roll the Count out of the way with my shin, and then drag him back to wedge the gate open with his body. The moment I stepped over him and into the alleyway beyond, I triggered the sensor attached to the security light and damn-near blinded myself.

I left the Count where he lay and felt my way beyond the cone of light to the steamer trunk. I released the bungee cords securing the trunk to the cart, flipped the lid open and tipped the whole thing backwards until the trunk was flat on the floor.

Now that I had the trunk right in front of me and the Count close by, I began to have serious doubts about whether he would fit. If I'd been looking to bury the guy, I could have severed his legs from his torso and packaged him up, no problem. But I wanted him alive and intact and that was a whole different story.

So was hauling him as far as the trunk, not to mention hoisting him and pitching him head-first into the chest. Getting his torso over the lip was the hard part, but I'm pleased to say that his legs followed quite willingly, and I was even able to arrange his arms so that I could bind his wrists together with a pair of Victoria's handcuffs. The problem was his feet. Even by pushing his chin down towards his chest, slamming his shoulders against one end of the trunk and pulling his knees up into a foetal position, they still protruded from the end. One of his mud-caked socks was rolled down as far as his heel, exposing his soft, plump ankle. I stood back and considered the practicalities for a short while, but I figured his feet were kind of important, and he wouldn't be likely to appreciate it if I lopped them off. In the end, I settled for closing the lid as best I could and securing it with the bungee cords before removing my overcoat and draping it over his soggy toes. Then, with an almighty effort and some colourful talk, I managed to lever the handcart up onto its hind wheels and push off along the alley, hastily removing my balaclava and flattening my hair before I emerged onto the busy street beyond.

My journey back to the boat might have been short, but it wasn't easy. While it's true that the tourists I passed seemed mercifully uninterested in my cargo and the way it sported size-eight feet, wheeling the Count along was one of the most physically demanding things I've ever done, surpassed only by the nightmare of lifting the trunk down onto the motor boat without scuttling our craft or pitching a comatose Italian into the murky depths below. Perhaps it's enough to say that somehow we did it, though by the time we were finished, I barely had enough energy left to speak with Victoria.

'What happened?' she asked. 'Why are his feet sticking out?'

'Didn't fit,' I wheezed.

Victoria squinted at me in a way that suggested I'd done a shoddy job. I would have liked to offer her the chance to improve on it, but somehow I suspected that throwing back the lid and allowing her to get to grips with a human jigsaw puzzle in the middle of Venice wasn't the smartest response.

'Did he see you?' she asked.

'Don't think so,' I panted. 'I'm not even sure he knew what was happening. That sedative worked really fast.'

She beamed, obviously pleased with her purchase.

'The chap in the shop said it's good for at least ninety minutes,' she told me.

I checked my watch. 'Better hope he's right. Are you still okay to take him by yourself?'

'Did you cuff him?'

'Like we discussed.'

'Then it should be fine.'

I held her gaze. 'I'll be as quick as I can.'

'Be sure that you are.'

And so I did. Pitching myself upright again, I clambered onto the canal bank and kicked the boat away from the edge. Victoria fired the engine and puttered around in a semi-circle, and I watched until she'd navigated safely back onto the Grand Canal before retracing my steps as far as the alley alongside the palazzo.

It was perhaps as long as fifteen minutes since I'd left, but I didn't think the delay would matter a great deal. Plunging a hand into my bumbag, I removed the pistol and fitted my numbing fingers around the butt before checking over my shoulder to make sure there was nobody close. When I was certain I wasn't being watched, I gingerly reached for the silencer and began to unscrew it from the gun muzzle. It was easier than I'd anticipated, which made me think that perhaps guns weren't as complicated as I'd always imagined. Thumbing the safety off, I pointed the thing high above my head, ducked away as best I could, stuck a finger in my ear, and squeezed off a round.

Damn. It was loud, the noise amplified by the high walls that crowded me on either side. The muzzle flash was brighter than I'd anticipated, as dazzling as sheet lightning. My arm danced with the recoil and I rocked backwards onto my heels, spraying the second bullet up and behind me. The ejected casing glanced off my wrist, singeing my flesh. I swore and clutched my hand to where it stung, then stuffed the hot gun inside my bumbag and ran hard and fast in the direction of Dorsoduro, half-blinded and half-deafened, and very possibly half-deranged, too.

TWENTY-SIX

Later, once I'd made it home and had struggled with Victoria to heave the trunk upstairs to the unoccupied top-floor apartment in my building, then bound and cuffed the dozing Count to a ladder-back chair in the middle of the empty living room, I finally had an opportunity to collapse in a heap and ask myself just what we'd done.

When Victoria had suggested the kidnapping scheme, it had seemed to make sense. The Count might not have known it – drugged and gagged and trussed-up in an unfamiliar location – but the idea had been to protect him. If he couldn't be found, he couldn't be killed, or so our reasoning went. What's more, assuming the gun shots I'd fired off had been reported, there was a chance I could convince Graziella and her mysterious backers that I'd carried out the assassination I'd been tasked with and had disposed of the body.

That was the theory, and when we were at the planning stage, it had struck me as pretty neat. So it was a real shame that the reality now seemed a tad more complicated.

First, the abduction had been arduous – I'm used to vacating the scene of a burglary with a valuable trinket or two in my pocket, not a twelve-stone Italian on my back. Second, it all seemed rather sordid and, well, criminal, right now. The Count didn't appear to be in the rudest of health. Two hours in, and the sedative showed no sign of wearing off. He was still breathing, thank God, but his head was hanging slackly against his chest, pitching the weight of his torso against the ropes that held him. His knuckles were bloodied, his cheeks had swollen quite alarmingly around the makeshift gag we'd tied off at the back of his head, and his tux was crumpled and stained. Then there was the track of dried blood running down his neck from where the pen nib had punctured his skin. He looked like the victim of a vampire bite – only without any of the upsides.

Victoria's main selling point for the plot had been time. Time to keep the Count alive until we worked out exactly what was going on and if there was anything we could do about it. Time to put ourselves in a position where the police might be safely contacted and the real crooks captured. Time, if we were really lucky, to get my book back, and failing that, to flee Venice if it became necessary. Problem was, sitting in the unheated apartment with my balaclava on my head, a bruised and bloodied kidnap victim in front of me and a whole bunch of questions occupying my mind, time felt like the last thing I needed.

I had doubts. Plenty of them. When I'd been in the middle of the action, caught up in the caper, I hadn't had the luxury of contemplating my fears. Now, I couldn't avoid them. We had a stolen boat moored in the canal outside my building that could be found at any moment. We had a prominent citizen tied up and imprisoned against his will less than forty-eight hours after an attempt had been made on his life. It was an attack I'd inadvertently been responsible for, but that given the right evidence, might be proved against me. Not exactly a comfortable position to be in. Hell, far from dodging trouble, I seemed to be actively courting it.

My every instinct was telling me that I'd made a terrible mistake. It was an error I was beginning to think I should correct, but I couldn't see how. I'd set a course of events in action that would be almost impossible to reverse. The Count could wake up at any moment – should, in fact, have already woken up, assuming nothing had gone horribly wrong with the sedative – and although Victoria had another two cartridges of knock-out juice in her weapons case, I didn't rate the idea of giving the guy a booster dose just yet.

And when he did eventually wake up – *please, God, let him wake up* – what then? How long did we plan to hold him for? How could we release him without somehow implicating ourselves? Would he be capable of providing us with useful information, or would he be too terrified to speak? The shock might even give him a heart attack. *A heart attack*. Christ, why hadn't I thought of that before? The man was in fear of his life and here we were abducting the poor sod. What was he meant to think when he came round other than the absolute worst? We were idiots. Utter fools. I really had no idea how we could have been so stupid.

'Good, isn't it?' Victoria said.

'Sorry?'

'Well, I think we've been rather successful, considering.'

'Considering what? That we're nuts? I can't believe I let you talk me into this. Look at what we've done!'

'Oh hush, and stop being such a baby. Everything's under control.'

'*Nothing's* under control.'

'He's alive, isn't he?'

I gawped at her, then gestured at the comatose Count. 'He's meant to have snapped out of it by now. Christ, Vic, are you absolutely sure it was only a sedative in that pen?'

'Stop bellyaching. He's still breathing, isn't he?'

Victoria wafted a hand towards the Count. The room around us was in darkness, but we'd rigged up my desk lamp so that the light was pointing into his eyes. His closed eyes. Now that she mentioned it, I wasn't all that sure he *was* breathing.

'Vic, wasn't his chest moving before?'

'Of course.'

'Well, it isn't moving now.'

Victoria scowled at me, then scowled at the Count. She bit down on her bottom lip.

'Mmm,' she said.

'*Mmm?* That's it? That's all you've got to say?'

'Well, now that you mention it, his breathing does appear to have slowed a touch.'

'Slowed? It's bloody stopped. Look. Listen.' I held up my palm to quieten her. 'There. Nothing. Not a whisper.'

'Mmm.'

'Please tell me we haven't bloody killed him. Who sold you this weapons kit?' I kicked the pigskin case with my toe. 'The bloody KGB?'

'Check for a pulse.'

'*You* check for a pulse.'

'Interesting,' she said. 'I like that idea. But how about, just for a change, *you* check for a pulse.'

'Oh, give me strength.'

Sucking a deep, trembling breath way down into my lungs, I raised my hands above my face in a brief prayer and took a cautious step towards the Count. His head was hanging awkwardly to the left, his tanned skin a sickly greenish colour in the glare of the lamp. It looked unnatural. *Dead* unnatural.

I circled my shoulders, flexed my fingers. Then I sniffed, bent down and pressed firmly against the pulse point on his neck.

Funny thing – the instant I touched his clammy skin, his face

233

snapped upright, his nostrils flared and his eyes opened as wide as they could possibly go. Then he issued a muffled, choked cry from behind his gag, jerked sharply away from me and toppled over the hind legs of his chair.

TWENTY-SEVEN

I clutched my hand to my chest, the way people do when they've had a fright and they're trying to work out exactly where their heart has ended up. There was a tight ball of adrenaline just above my solar plexus and my guts had knitted themselves into a painful knot. I felt dizzy, low on air, and my temples were pounding. And that was just me. Who knew how the Count was faring?

He didn't strike me as altogether relaxed. He was fighting against his constraints, knocking his chair against the floor as he bucked fitfully around. He happened to be screaming too. At least, I *think* he was screaming – it was difficult to tell on account of the gag. Mind you, it would have been a strange moment for him to start singing, and when I factored in the flush of his cheeks and the way his bloodshot eyes were almost crawling out of their sockets, I thought it safe to assume that he'd completely freaked out.

I could understand that. I was freaked out myself, and I wasn't the one being stared at by a guy in a balaclava who happened to have drugged me and whisked me away from the comforts of my home.

I placed a hand on his arm to calm him. It didn't work. He flinched as if an electric charge had passed between us.

'It's okay,' Victoria told him, from over my shoulder. 'We're not going to hurt you.'

Nice try. Her voice had a soothing tone but I had a suspicion that the Venetian plague doctor's mask she was wearing might have compromised the effect somewhat. The mask was blood-red, with a hooked nose and recessed eyeholes, and it covered everything except her mouth and her jaw. It had been the best we could come up with at short notice. We'd taken it down from the wall of my lounge, where it had been hanging since before I'd moved in. I only had one balaclava and we didn't want the Count to see our faces. Even so, I couldn't help think-ing that we might have been better off cutting some holes in a pillow case. The poor sod probably thought he'd woken in some kind of Halloween nightmare.

He recoiled from us. True, it wasn't easy for him to recoil, but he managed it all the same, turning his head away and straining to follow his nose across the floor to a blackened corner of the room. His neck muscles had pulled tight and he wriggled against the ropes we'd wrapped around his chest and thighs. No doubt he was also fighting the handcuffs, thumbcuffs and anklecuffs we'd treated him to, courtesy of Victoria's espionage gear.

'Easy' I said, which, as it goes, was easy for me to say.

It had no effect. The guy still wasn't happy. I turned to Victoria.

'Help me to lift him a moment, will you?'

We did just that, and then I cradled the Count's sweaty face between my hands and looked him straight in the eye. His pupils contracted to pin-pricks of black against the fierce lamp-light and his grey hair was slick beneath my fingertips. He was scared, I could see that, but he was angry, too. Enraged might be a better word for it. It was almost as if he couldn't believe anyone could have the nerve to place a man of his stature in this position.

'Do you speak English?' I asked.

Thoughts darted around behind his lighted eyes. Maybe the thoughts connected back to the masked figure who'd planted a bomb in his home. He sucked air through his nostrils at an irregular pace, as if he was hyperventilating, and snatched his head away from my grip. He tried to yell. I watched the sound build from his chest, funnel up towards his raised mouth and become trapped by the gag. There was no danger of him being heard but it didn't stop him. He summoned more energy and went for a repeat performance. It looked bad for his health. His face had taken on a purplish tinge.

'Calm down.' I reached for his scalp again. 'Just answer the question. Do you speak English?'

He let go of another strangled shout. This one went on longer than the first. I was becoming afraid he might fit if he carried on with it. And I didn't exactly appreciate the way he was ignoring my instructions. Wasn't I meant to be in charge here?

'Hey,' I said. 'Hey!'

Then I slapped him. Hard. I can't say I've ever understood the logic of the move, but it seemed to have the desired effect. He stared dumbly at me for a short moment, eyes watering. Then his beady pupils tippy-toed over and snuck a pensive look at my open palm. He needn't have worried. I wasn't about to repeat myself. It had hurt too much – the impact had jarred my bad fingers in a way I didn't appreciate.

'Now, do you speak English?'

At last, the Count nodded, though he managed to do it with disdain. I hadn't really doubted that the answer would be yes. What had concerned me was whether he'd be sensible enough to deliver it.

I backed off, nudged the lamp with my foot so that the light was pointing just away from his eyes and pulled my cigarettes from my pocket. I took my time over lighting one. Partly it was to calm my nerves, give myself time to think. But it also seemed like the appropriate thing to do. I wasn't a thug, and I didn't plan on beating my man into submission. But I did want to appear in control, as if this was something I'd done many times before. The cigarette struck me as a useful prop, a way of making myself appear more at ease than I felt. More in command, too.

'First thing you should know,' I told him, rolling up the bottom of the balaclava and taking a quick puff, 'is that we don't intend to hurt you.' I exhaled the smoke from the corner of my mouth. 'Truth is, we've brought you here for your own protection. It might not seem that way to you, but it's true, okay?'

He nodded slowly. Contemptuously. I don't suppose it meant a great deal. I dare say I could have got him to agree to just about anything right then.

'Second thing you should know is that this room is in a very discreet location. Nobody is going to find you here, and that includes the people who are a threat to you. It also means you won't be heard if you try to scream or shout. The reason I'm telling you this is that I'd like to remove your gag. I need to ask you some questions. Understand?'

He scowled at me, then at Victoria, and back again. I had a feeling the masks weren't helping, but I wasn't about to suggest that we remove them. Instead, I crouched down in front of him and held his gaze, smoking my cigarette in a leisurely fashion. After a minute or so, I tried again, rolling my hand and tracing figure of eights in the air with the lit embers.

'Understand?'

There was fire in his eyes. A tangible loathing. But he nodded.

'Excellent,' I said, and moved around behind him, balancing my cigarette on my tongue as I tried to loosen his gag. It wasn't easy. The knot we'd used had tightened with his exertions and my dud fingers made the job difficult. I gave up and beckoned at Victoria to put her nails to good use.

Once she'd freed the rag, the Count moved his jaw around cautiously, like a man coming round from a deep and leisurely nap. He licked his lips. They were gummy and dry.

'Would you like some water?' Victoria asked.

'*Si*,' he said, in a gruff voice that sounded as if it needed it.

We waited in silence until Victoria had returned with a mug of tapwater from the unlit kitchen along the hall. She lifted it to his mouth and he swallowed greedily. The water ran down from the corners of his lips over his chin, but he didn't appear to care.

'More,' he panted.

Victoria complied, disappearing into darkness and then re-emerging with a dripping mug. Once he'd polished off a second helping, she used a tea towel to wipe his chin and mop his face. Maybe the plague doctor's mask wasn't so out of place, after all. She was becoming a regular Florence Nightingale.

'Who are you?' His Italian accent was strong, but he spoke at a measured pace and his voice had taken on a soft, coaxing tone, the kind that befits a man with plentiful experience of seducing women.

'That's not important,' I told him, trying to regain the upper hand.

'You are English,' he sneered, as if our nationality was insult enough. 'Both of you.'

'That won't get you very far.' I took a contemplative draw on my cigarette. 'There are plenty of English people in Venice.'

He curled his lip, like he was trying a smirk on for size. It suited him very well. He was the type of man who was used to looking down on others. He'd spent a lifetime enjoying the sensation.

'I know who you work for,' he told me, with a snarl. 'He is a smart man, I am told. A clever opponent. But this I did not expect.'

'You've lost me I'm afraid.'

He grinned drunkenly, eyes lazy and hooded – as if he was calculating what punishment he'd exact the instant this was over. 'You even speak like him.'

'Listen, pal,' I said, jabbing my finger in his direction, 'we don't work for anyone. So you can stop gurning and start telling us who you're talking about. Is he the one who tried to kill you?'

'To kill me?' he frowned, as if he didn't trust the words.

'With the bomb. Don't tell me you've forgotten about that.'

A new expression seeped into his face, scornful and lofty. I didn't like it a great deal. It had all the appeal of slow poison.

'The bomb,' he repeated, as if I was a simpleton. 'To kill me.'

'Yes, the bomb,' Victoria cut in, throwing up her hands. 'The bloody big explosion in your palazzo. You do remember, don't you? It was meant to blow you and your silly little smile into a million tiny pieces.'

He watched Victoria for a moment, mouthing her words back to himself. Then he chuckled. The chuckle turned into a self-satisfied laugh. He slouched in his chair as if he was mighty comfortable all of a sudden. His manner was so relaxed that I had to fight the urge not to walk around and check that his hands and feet were still secured.

'*Allora* ...' He grinned. 'So it's true, you don't work for him.' He tipped his head back and lifted his chin in the air so that the track of blood on his neck was clearly visible, glistening in the electric light like a scald mark that had only recently healed.

I'd just about had my fill of him by now. I flicked my cigarette off into a distant corner of the room and did my best to crowd him, blowing the last of my smoke into his face.

'Who do you mean? You mean a large guy, full beard? Wears a camel-hair coat and a fedora?'

'No,' he said, smiling even wider, not even blinking as the smoke enveloped him. I got the impression that if his hands hadn't been tied behind him, he'd have been airily considering his nails. 'This is not who I mean. And I am beginning to think that you are of little concern to me.'

'We hold you prisoner and you think that, huh?'

He shrugged. Pouted. 'You have already told me you will not hurt me.'

I spun round to face Victoria. 'Where's your stun gun?' I asked.

'*Charlie.*'

'No, I'm serious, I've had enough of this guy. I think maybe we should fry his face.'

'What about Graziella?' Victoria asked him. Just by posing the question, she'd gone further than we'd planned. It had been my intention to keep Graziella's name out of it – at least for the time being – but not any more. 'You know, the girl who accompanied you to the casino the night of the explosion,' Victoria went on. 'Are you aware that she asked us to kill you?'

That seemed to affect him. He frowned, as if confounded by the question, his lips moving soundlessly.

'*Aspetta*,' he muttered, his voice tight all of a sudden. He flexed the muscles of his right arm and lowered his head, as if to consult his watch. When he realised that he couldn't, he gazed up into my eyes. 'You must tell me the time.'

'Excuse me?'

There was a wavering in his pupils – a look of genuine concern. Something told me he was worried about more than a missed dinner date. 'The time,' he pressed. 'I must know it. Tell me. Now.'

'Listen, friend, I really think you might have forgotten the situation you're in. Talk to us about Graziella.'

'Is it later than nine o'clock? Just tell me this. It is a simple question.'

I placed my hands on my hips and glared at him. The glaring didn't seem to affect his attitude. He was used to people doing as he said, and damn if I didn't find myself doing exactly that.

'It's a quarter after ten,' I said, going down on one knee to check my watch in the light from the lamp.

The information caused a small crack in his defence. He swallowed dryly.

'Then you must release me.' His voice was grave, as if the matter was of the utmost importance. 'Immediately.'

'Er, not likely. Not until you answer our questions, in any event.'

'*Immediately*,' he barked, teeth bared, spittle clinging to his lips.

I turned and smiled up at Victoria. Her eyes glimmered from behind her mask.

'And why's that?' she asked, placing a hand on her hip.

The Count curled his lip and stared down at the ropes we'd wrapped around his chest and arms. He flexed his biceps. Then he grunted and tried to kick his feet away from the legs of his chair. It was futile, but he stuck at it. It didn't look all that dignified, or sound it, either.

'Tick tock,' I said, and tapped my watch. 'What's bothering you so much? You have an important appointment?'

He wasn't listening to me as closely as I might have liked. He was fighting his restraints, fidgeting and gnashing his teeth as if we were no longer in the room watching over him. His face was ruddy, speckled with perspiration. I stepped forward and clenched his shoulder. I had to pinch hard before he gave any indication that he was bothered by it.

'Listen, we'll make you a deal,' I said. 'You tell us what's vexing you so much and we'll release you. We'll let you go.'

He growled and tried to bite my hand. I snatched it free just as his teeth scraped my skin.

'Nuh uh,' I said. 'Now, you play nice and I promise you – I give you my word – that if you tell us what the problem is, you'll be a free man.'

His head jerked upright and he considered me with watchful eyes. I could see the rage burning deep within them.

'Time's moving on,' I told him. 'So how about it? Will you trust us?'

He checked on Victoria once more, then glanced down at his lap, concealing his face as if overcome with shame. 'The casino,' he muttered, in a voice that could barely be heard. 'I must be there.'

'See,' I told him, and patted his cheek, 'that wasn't so hard now, was it?'

TWENTY-EIGHT

Never trust a crook. It's a simple lesson, but it's one worth bearing in mind. I might have been an amateur in the art of kidnapping, but I was an experienced thief, and I was used to cheating people. So I had no qualms about lying to the Count. Hell, if I was in the business of keeping my word, I'd have been responsible for shooting the chap by now. Point was, I didn't want him to die. I didn't need his death on my conscience (nor, for that matter, my police record). And if telling a whopper about releasing him would help me to find out who wanted him dead, and why, then I had no hesitation in doing it.

By the same token, I didn't feel all that guilty about delving a hand inside my bumbag to remove Victoria's pen, loading it with a second cartridge of chemical lullabies and sticking him in the neck. He lost consciousness instantly, just as before, and

I wasted no time in removing my balaclava and setting about untying him.

'What are you doing?' Victoria asked, tipping her mask up onto her head and rubbing at her face.

'I want to put him in the bedroom. He'll be more comfortable lying down. And I'm worried about his circulation.'

'So you're not going to release him?'

'Of course not,' I said, grunting as I tackled the ropes behind his back. 'Not yet, anyway.'

'But what about the casino?'

'That's the other reason I want to get him off this chair. I'd say we're about the same size, wouldn't you agree?'

'Eh?'

'His tux,' I said. 'I don't happen to own one myself, and I get the impression this casino is pretty fancy.'

'Wait a minute – are you planning to go there?'

'Absolutely. And you're coming with me. Although, no offence, but I think you may need to glam up just a touch. Oh, and perhaps ditch the mask.'

Now, Victoria has many talents. She's an excellent agent, with an eye for a great story, and she can identify plot holes at a hundred paces. She has nerve and tenacity, she's willing to take a risk when the situation demands it and, if I'm permitted to say as much, she's not a bad kisser. But one skill I hadn't been aware of before, and that I could learn to appreciate, was her ability as a quick-change artist. Seriously. I'd barely had time to free the Count from his bindings, strip him down to his underwear and dump him on the bare mattress in the back bedroom by the time she was standing in the doorway in a long green dress of a stretchy material that clung to her figure the way syrup sticks to a spoon. Her figure looked undeniably good. So did her high-heeled shoes and her tasteful make-up and the way she'd tied her hair to expose her delicate neck and shoulders. If I was the type of character who could pull off an appreciative whistle, I'd have done just that. Unfortunately, I'm more adept at looking startled and awkward.

'Will this do?' she asked, patting her hair.

'Looks good,' I managed.

'How are you getting on? Need a hand?'

'Funnily enough, I do. I'm not in the habit of strapping men down in bed, and I've been trying to work out the best way to set about it.'

I suppose I could have been disturbed by the variety of suggestions that Victoria provided me with, but I chose to focus on the positives and be grateful for her input. After a good deal of discussion, and some experimentation, we decided to dispense with any attempts to secure the Count to the mattress. Instead, we simply bound his wrists, thumbs and ankles with Victoria's cuffs, then tied his feet to his hands with a length of rope. I was fairly pleased with the job we'd done. Flopped on his side on the stained mattress, securely trussed-up, he certainly looked like an authentic kidnap victim.

After placing the keys to the cuffs on a high chest of drawers on the far side of the room, I collected together the Count's dress shirt, tuxedo jacket and trousers, doing my best to brush the dirt from them. Then I kicked off my baseball shoes, unclipped my bumbag and started to unbutton my fly.

'Er, a little privacy?'

Victoria pouted. 'Spoilsport.'

'Go on, scram.'

She rolled her eyes and backed off from the door, and I climbed into my new outfit before moving into the bathroom to wash my face, wet my hair and assess my appearance. The jacket wasn't too bad. A little wide in the shoulders, perhaps, but it was passable, and it was certainly made of a very fine fabric. The trousers were a trifle short, but after I'd used a damp towel to mop away the odd muddy splash, I thought they'd do nicely. The shirt was more crumpled than I would have liked, and I could have done without the fancy pleats over the chest area, but the fit was passable, especially if I didn't attempt to wear a bow tie.

'That won't do,' Victoria said, clucking her tongue as she entered the room. 'Look, you've still got blood on the collar.'

She took the wet towel from me and scrubbed away at the stain.

'It's fine,' I told her, reaching up to steady her hand. 'If anyone asks, I'll tell them I cut myself shaving.'

'That might make more sense if you'd actually shaved today. Don't you have a white shirt downstairs?'

'Not the kind to wear with a suit.'

Victoria sighed, as if I was an errant child, and dabbed at a spot of dirt on the elbow of the jacket. When she was finally satisfied, she plucked a blade of grass from one of the wide lapels and rested her head on my shoulder, considering my reflection in the mirror glass.

'Look at you,' she said, as if I was about to embark on my graduation ceremony. 'You don't scrub up too bad.'

'I could say the same of you.'

'It's funny,' she said. 'This is the first time I've seen you in a dinner suit. Know who you remind me of?'

'James Bond?'

'Nope. The guy in your author photo.'

I could see what she meant. Back when I'd first been published, and I'd been asked to submit a picture of myself, it had struck me as a good idea to send in an image of a catalogue model in a tuxedo. I had a couple of reasons. One, as a burglar, it doesn't pay to be too recognisable. Two, as an author looking to sell some books, I figured it couldn't hurt to be as dashing as possible. Naturally, it had led to one or two complications, not least because it had slipped my mind to come clean with Victoria until some years ago in Paris. I guessed it was a good sign that we could joke about it now, although the subject still made me uncomfortable.

'So, shall we go?' I asked. 'I just need to grab a few things first. Shoes, deodorant, my overcoat, a spectacles case full of burglary tools, your espionage kit. You know, the usual.'

'Pitch ourselves into another puzzle?' She winked at me in the mirror. 'Why the devil not?'

TWENTY-NINE

The Casinò di Venezia was located in the Palazzo Ca'
Vendramin Calergi on the Grand Canal, not more than fifteen
minutes' walk from the Count's home. It was ironic, really,
because I could have saved myself a lot of hassle if I'd known to
go there sooner. Mind you, it would have lacked some of the
drama if I'd simply approached the casino on foot, as opposed
to sailing towards it in a stolen motor boat, gliding along the
misty waters and beneath the lighted windows and restaurants
that lined the canal bank.

The casino had an imposing water entrance. A long wooden
jetty sheltered beneath a burgundy canopy, surrounded by
painted mooring posts hung with glass lanterns that were
ringed in halos of blown fog. Two security guards in burgundy
jackets hollered instructions to us as we drew close, helping to
secure our boat to the landing stage. One of them even offered
Victoria his hand as she hitched up her dress and disembarked

our grubby vessel with all the poise of a minor European royal. A red carpet led the way to the arched entrance doors ahead of us, and Victoria took my arm as we passed through to a generous reception area.

The red carpet snaked across a shiny terrazzo floor towards an Istrian stone staircase that veered off to the left. Beyond the staircase, at the far end of the room, plush burgundy banners were suspended from the ceiling in front of double-height windows. Through the windows I could spy a lighted courtyard where a gleaming Jaguar sports car in racing green was displayed on an angled podium. It was the first car I'd set my eyes on for weeks, and I couldn't help but wonder how it had reached its current location.

A high wooden counter ran along the wall to our right. Behind it, a strikingly tall woman in a tailored grey suit and businesslike spectacles smiled encouragingly at us. I led Victoria towards her and offered up a very English, 'Good evening.'

'Good evening, Sir.' She glanced at my shambolic outfit, the borrowed tuxedo, stained shirt and winter coat that had only recently dried out following my plunge into the Grand Canal, then reassured herself with Victoria's immaculate appearance. 'May I see your passports, please?'

I removed the self-same documents from the inner pocket of the Count's dinner jacket and passed them to her. Normally, I might have tried my luck with a stolen passport, but since there'd been no time to arrange anything for Victoria, I played it straight and provided our genuine papers.

253

The woman opened our passports and peered down from her considerable vantage point to compare our photographs with our faces. After offering up a polite smile, she scanned the barcodes into a computer on her desk. The move made me nervous. This was the first time I'd set foot inside a casino since Victoria and I had vacationed in Las Vegas. We'd only spent a couple of days in Sin City, but we'd managed to become involved in a diverting little scrape. Some troubling allegations had been levelled at us, and the thing that concerned me was whether the details were likely to flash up on the computer screen and bring our evening to an abrupt conclusion.

I studied the woman's reaction. It was a little while coming (not to mention a fair distance away). Her lips puckered up and twisted around one another. Evidently the computer was taking longer than she was used to, and she filled the time by drumming her painted nails on her computer mouse. I was about to say something in an attempt to divert her focus when the computer emitted a discreet *blip* and our leggy gatekeeper inclined her head to one side, as if in mild surprise.

'This is your first visit, *Signor* Howard?'

'For both of us,' I told her.

She tapped a key and a compact printer chattered into life. Two tickets emerged. She slid them across to me, along with our passports and a coupon for a complimentary drink. The tickets contained our names and the date, as well as a barcode. It was impossible to tell whether our presence had triggered an alert.

'You must show this to the man by the stairs,' she said, indicating a portly chap in a beige security guard uniform who was standing beside a velvet rope barrier. 'And here is a plan of the building,' she added, opening a small cardboard folder before us. She circled an area of the map in biro. 'You are standing here. The first floor is closed.' She crossed the relevant area of the floor plan out with two strikes of her biro. 'But the gaming tables on the top floor are open. There is a room for your coats just ahead of you.'

I acknowledged the information with a nod, then gripped Victoria by the elbow and guided her towards the cloakroom. After ditching our overcoats, along with Victoria's zipped weapons case, we presented our tickets to the security guard. He scanned them with an infrared reader, unclipped the velvet rope and ushered us up the carpeted stairs.

'What do you think?' I whispered to Victoria, who was busy lifting the material of her dress clear of her high-heeled shoes. 'Would a warning have come up on her computer?'

'It wouldn't surprise me. My name does tend to have that effect.'

Victoria wasn't simply referring to events in Vegas. Years ago, she'd told me her father was a judge. Later, I'd discovered that was a white lie – or more accurately, a neon falsification. The truth was her dad was a professional casino cheat, last seen touring the Far East with Victoria's mother and a crack team of white-haired accomplices. It wasn't something she was necessarily ashamed about, but it did mean that her parents' reputation had a way of preceding her – at least where gaming houses were concerned.

'They may monitor us, see what we're about,' Victoria told me.

I glanced up. An opaque plastic dome was fitted to the ceiling above the first-floor landing. Behind the brown-tinged Perspex, a lens was pointing its beady eye at us, the camera connected to a flickering bank of monitors somewhere in the recesses of the palazzo.

The gaming floor in front of us was sealed off, just as we'd been warned. A pair of glass doors had been secured to one another with a padlock and chain, and the interior was concealed behind full-length blackout drapes. The ground was coated in dust and plentiful footprints that led towards an open store cupboard overflowing with building equipment. Hard hats and luminous safety bibs, sledgehammers and spades, buckets of dried plaster and paint tins. It was hardly slick but I can't say I was all that surprised. The place was typical of Venice – a prime example of shabby chic – and as if to prove as much, the main gaming floor at the top of the stairs was a statement in faded grandeur. Scuffed terrazzo floors, peeling flocked wallpaper, and a water-stained ceiling with broken cornice work. The space above our heads was dominated by two huge Murano glass chandeliers that were coated in dust and looked fit to drop at any moment, and the windows were dressed with discoloured net curtains.

Three roulette tables were positioned in the middle of the

room, though only two were in use. Each table was staffed by four croupiers, two men and two women, all of them wearing cheap dinner jackets that fitted no better than my own. Business was slow. I counted nine players in all, plus a couple of aged men in tatty lounge suits who were marking off record cards with the sequence of numbers that had cropped up so far.

A doorway to the left took us away from the roulette action and into a small room containing dated slot machines without any players. The machines twittered and blinked to one another in a hopeless fashion, like a bank of forgotten super-computers still running calculations that had been solved decades before.

Beyond the slots was the cashing-out cage, an oddly futuristic space with a sculpted metal counter that looked as if it might have been ripped from a spaceship. Next door was a dingy bar that wouldn't have been out of place in a provincial train station. The counter was faux-marble, with lager on tap and an eye-catching display of breath mints. A glass case contained a selection of drooping sandwiches and panini wrapped in cling film.

The place was staffed by a white-haired chap with a quite remarkable handlebar moustache. Dressed in a bright blue blazer with brass buttons, he appeared old enough to have laid the building's foundations. I ordered a white wine for Victoria and a sparkling water for myself, palming him our coupons along with a modest tip.

I wasn't sure we'd be staying long enough to finish our beverages. The casino struck me as a bust, and I couldn't begin to understand why the Count had been so keen to come here. The table minimums at the roulette wheel were pocket change, and if you happened to win the jackpot on one of the slots, I feared there was a real danger you might be paid in lire rather than euros.

'Spot anything interesting?' I asked Victoria.

'Not even close.'

'I'm starting to suspect the Count might have misled us.'

'Well, suspect away, because I'm inclined to agree with you.'

The barman presented us with our drinks along with a bowl of nuts. I waved the nuts away and led Victoria back through the cashing-out area to the slots.

'What do you think?' I asked, taking a sip of my water. 'Give it another five minutes?'

'I suppose so. The part I'm not sure of is what we do next.' Victoria checked behind her, as if the answer might be creeping up on us. 'We can go back and question the Count again, but that might not get us very far. It looks as if he's already sent us on one wild goose chase. Who knows how many more he has up his sleeve?'

I was about to respond with some suggestions about how we might use her spy tools to encourage the Count to talk openly, when I noticed a doorway I hadn't spotted before. It was located directly ahead, between a pair of twinkling slots and behind a freestanding notice board with a printed sheet tacked to it. The sheet had a bright orange background covered with slanted Italian text and copious explanation marks. In the centre of the page was an image of an open briefcase stuffed with an inordinate amount of cash. Below the case was the one piece of information I could understand. It was only a number, but it was a mighty impressive one all the same.

Euro 500,000!!!

I looked at Victoria. Victoria winked at me. I could hear a burble of voices coming from the room beyond the sign and I inclined my head towards the doorway.

'You know,' Victoria said, 'I think we may just have found our goose.'

What we actually found was a rectangular room about the size of a basketball court. The room was filled with a distinguished-looking crowd in evening wear, drinking chilled *prosecco* from long-stemmed wine glasses and munching on canapés. A harpist over to our left plucked at a pleasing background melody, while two handsome types in burgundy shirts and black ties uncorked bottles of bubbly at a temporary bar.

Beyond the bar was an empty blackjack felt that a group of women in glittering gowns were leaning their hips against. Three more blackjack tables were positioned in the remaining corners of the room. None of them were in play, and all appeared to be functioning as makeshift seats.

Victoria seized me by the hand and dragged me through the well-dressed rabble towards the centre of the room. The wealthy mob became more congested the further we went, and I became aware of a good deal more men. If it hadn't been for

Victoria's polite but firm '*Scusi*'s' and '*Per favores*'s', and her teasingly flirty smile, I dare say I wouldn't have got anywhere close. As it happened, she squeezed us through to the very front, where I peered from over her bare shoulder at the cause of all the excitement.

A blackjack table had been cordoned off at a distance of perhaps five metres away by a circle of velvet ropes attached to brass bollards. The croupier was a thirty-something Italian with a serious, watchful expression, a well-oiled head of thick, black hair and a neatly pressed tux. The sleeves of his jacket were too long for him, stretching over his hands in a way that wouldn't have been tolerated in Vegas.

The table was arranged for six players, but only five were in position – the chair on the inside right was empty. I recognised the player to the left of it. From the way Victoria pinched my hand, I sensed that she did too. He was a big brute of a fellow in a sizeable, threadbare dinner jacket that looked as if it hailed from a charity shop. His beard was full and ragged, and the hair at the nape of his neck was long and curled, like that of a woodsman. The last time we'd seen him he'd looked just as unkempt, although he had sported a fedora. It was a shock to come across him again in the casino, and I half-expected him to pick up on our alarm and turn slowly to offer us a disconcerting grin. Then again, it had to be better than having him watch us kiss. And besides, I could tell that he was focussed on the game, crowding forwards over the table as if it contained a mouth-watering feast he'd been waiting days to consume.

My eyes scanned the other players. Two were of Asian origin – one a hip young man with designer stubble and a preference for playing in wrap-around sunglasses, and the other a prim-looking lady in her late fifties who wore her hair in an immaculate bob and who favoured a Cartier gold watch on her wrist. Beside her was a stiff-looking, white-haired gent in a tuxedo that looked as if it had been shrink-wrapped to fit his wiry frame. If I'd had to guess, I would have said he was British or American. His neatly clipped beard didn't shade it either way, but if I could have seen the bow tie he was wearing, I might have been able to narrow it down. The final contestant couldn't have looked more Italian if she was featured in a pasta advertisement. Middle-aged and pear-shaped, she was dressed in a multicoloured blouse that was just a shade less dazzling than her smile.

Clearly, she was relishing the game, though it was difficult to understand why. Her collection of chips was modest, consisting of perhaps ten markers. The leading player was the Asian lady, who appeared to have enough chips to start a casino of her own. They were arranged in neat rows and columns, like a very large sum on a custom-made abacus. Next came the white-haired gent, and afterwards our friend Brutus the Snooper.

I heard a murmur of conversation between two Americans to my side and managed to catch the eye of one of them. Black-skinned, he was immaculately groomed, with a neat goatee beard and a pair of glittering diamond earrings.

'What's going on here?' I asked.

'Blackjack tournament.' He backed away, as if giving himself more room to marvel at my ignorance. 'Been running all week. Ten thousand euro buy-in. This is the final table.'

Victoria craned her neck towards him. 'They've been playing in a knock-out format?'

'Sure thing. Winner takes the big one.'

'The big one?'

He raised his eyes to the ceiling and Victoria and I followed their path. Suspended on a chain above the blackjack table was a clear glass box. Inside the box was an attaché briefcase that had been opened on an angle to reveal a bundle of neatly stacked notes. Now, I'm not one to make assumptions, or to jump ahead of myself, but I had a funny feeling that owning the case might make someone a cool half-million.

It was mighty impressive. Jaw-dropping, some would say. But the thing that caught my attention wasn't the cash. No, what really caused my eyes to boggle was the case itself. I'd seen it before, you see – or rather, one just like it. I'd carried it in my hands, hidden it under my bed, broken into a palazzo with it. Then I'd prised it open and triggered the bomb it had contained.

Yup, that's right, the reason my spine was tingling and my throat had gone dry was that it looked very much like the case Graziella had handed me.

'What about the spare seat?' I heard Victoria ask.

'Oh that,' said the second of the two Americans, a bloated

Caucasian of about twice his companion's age. 'That's what everyone's talking about. Guy didn't even show. A Duke or some crazy shit like that. Guess five-hundred-thou don't mean jack to him, right?'

I nodded vaguely, then turned to face Victoria. I tried to signal with my eyes that something incredible had happened – that I had vital information to share with her. In truth, my discovery about the briefcase seemed so momentous that if I'd been writing the scene myself, I would have ended it at the precise moment I'd made the connection. Of course, that didn't account for Victoria's input, and the way she always strives to push my writing that little bit further. For her, you see, one revelation just wasn't enough.

Wrapping an arm around my shoulders, she pulled my ear towards her mouth. 'Charlie,' she whispered, 'there's something I need to tell you. See the man with the white hair at the blackjack table?'

I nodded.

'Well, he's my dad.'

THIRTY

I realised the moment Victoria went to speak those words to me that there was something familiar about the chap – a visual echo that jibed with something filed away in my memory banks. I'd only seen his face once before, in a black and white mugshot that had been clipped to a cardboard security file, but I could recall the image quite clearly. He'd shed some weight since the photograph – maybe a little too many pounds, as it happens. His face had taken on a gaunt cast, the cheeks hollowed out above the line of his white beard, and I could have slid a finger down between the wrinkled chicken-skin of his neck and his shirt collar. He reminded me of a turtle sticking its head out of its shell – withered and aged, leaning forward over his betting chips as if he was preparing to crawl slowly across the table-felt. The snowy hair on top of his head was longer than I recalled, as if to compensate for the weight loss, or perhaps he simply hadn't found the time to visit a barber.

I watched his movements for any indication that he'd heard his daughter speak. There was nothing at all. He appeared entirely consumed by the game in front of him, his left hand spread on the green felt, index finger arched and poised to signal the dealer if he required another card. In his right hand he manipulated a stack of casino chips, flipping the top marker up with his thumb and shuffling it down to the bottom in a well-practised gesture. If the move bothered the Italian woman to his left or the young Asian player to his right, they didn't show it. And even if they complained, I doubted he could stop himself. It looked to be a habitual quirk, as natural to him as breathing. This was what he did. This was who he was. Alfred Newbury, professional casino man – card counter, chip switcher, and, if the rumours were to be believed, the brains behind some of the most audacious gambling cons ever devised.

I can't say I'd ever devoted too much thought to the prospect of meeting Victoria's parents. I knew she'd told them about me, because she'd said as much, but I'd hardly expected to be invited round for a Sunday roast. For one thing, we weren't an item, and for another, they spent most of their time travelling – often to new casinos where the security was comparatively lax. Still, if I *had* given it some consideration, I'm sure I would have felt nervous. Yes, I was a writer, but I was also a crook – a lousy house creeper, no less. True, I didn't kill people (at least not intentionally), and more often than not, the folks I stole from were the types who could afford it, but even so, it was hardly the greatest character reference. I wasn't ashamed, exactly, but

I could see how it might look to an outsider. And one thing I would have hated was for Victoria's family to think badly of me.

Now, though, standing in the middle of one of the oldest casinos in Europe, looking towards the blackjack table, the situation had been turned on its head. I wasn't concerned by what Alfred might think of me – I was worried by how I felt about him. My moral compass might have been bent out of shape during my teenage years, but most of the goods I'd stolen in my time were small fry compared to what he appeared to be involved in. If he was cheating the tournament, he stood to win half a million euros – a prize fund that consisted, at least in part, of the entry fees paid by many of the people in the room. Victoria had assured me that he was good at what he did – and I'd heard the same thing from other sources – but was he talented enough to cheat in front of this many people and not get caught?

I didn't rate his odds, no matter the level of his skills. Generally speaking, casino scammers operate in teams, and much of their success relies on the non-playing members distracting casino staff when the key moves are pulled. That goes for switching casino chips in particular – a method that involves a player using sleight of hand to increase his bet *after* a winning card has been played – but it's true of other techniques too. Some of the systems are beyond me. Others Victoria had explained in great detail. But very few could be carried off by a lone operator.

I scanned the crowd. Plenty of the onlookers were older than sixty – at least half the gathering, in fact – but I couldn't spot anyone who looked the least bit suspicious. And anyway, I had no idea what help they might provide. There was just one table, being watched by a large number of people. And this was tournament blackjack, so there was no scope to pull off a single risky move and flee the table with your winnings. It was all about the long play, the strategic accumulation of chips over a number of hours, and that didn't fit the kind of scams I'd heard about.

Except one.

Card counting isn't strictly illegal. You can't be arrested on suspicion of indulging in it. But, at least from a casino's perspective, it goes against the spirit of the game, and it's certainly frowned upon.

In a standard blackjack game, a skilled counter can keep a tally of the high and low cards that emerge from a shoe. Once the count becomes high enough, the player's odds of winning are significantly increased, and he'd be well advised to bet heavy. Of course, the problem with the technique is that betting a big stake all of a sudden can draw attention to what the player is up to. And if they're too obvious about it, they'll be asked to leave – sometimes politely, other times not.

Now, all of that is fine and, dare I say it, dandy too. And I had no doubt that many of the upstanding citizens who'd taken part in the competition had abided by the strict letter of the law. How did I know? Well, it was simple really. They weren't sitting at the final table. Because hell, fair play and noble behaviour was all very commendable, but if you wanted to win a black-jack tournament, you simply *had* to card count.

Now admittedly, the Italian mama sitting on the far left seemed content to play fair, and that explained why she left the competition after going all-in with eighteen, only to find the dealer hit twenty. But I was certain that the remaining contestants were all indulging in the same dark art, something that was confirmed by the way their betting had a curious habit of increasing and decreasing at exactly the same moment. And while that suggested that nobody was likely to cry foul any time soon, I couldn't help but worry that Victoria's father might do something crass and give himself away.

The Americans were still talking beside me. I leaned towards them and interrupted with another question. 'Any idea how long is this likely to go on for?' I asked.

The chubby one pointed to an ornate clock on the wall behind me. 'Tournament ends at midnight.'

'Midnight? That's a bit dramatic, isn't it?'

Apparently, they weren't all that interested in the theatrics of the situation, and they weren't altogether keen to talk to me, either. Before I could ask them anything more, they excused themselves and squeezed off through the crowds to the other side of the table. I gripped Victoria by the arm and dragged her to the bar, exchanging our drinks for two glasses of *prosecco*. Never hurts to blend in, right?

'So,' I said, 'did you know your dad was in Venice?'

'Of course not,' she snapped. 'I'm every bit as surprised as you are.'

I gave her the long stare. God knows why. It wasn't subtle and it didn't get us very far.

'Have you got something in your eye?' she asked.

'This is my interrogation glare.'

'Well, I recommend you get a new one, because it looks as if you're in pain. And once you have it mastered, I'd recommend you don't use it on me, particularly not when I'm telling you the truth.' She took a swig of her wine and folded her other arm across her chest. 'I'm pretty miffed, if you must know. I told Mum that I was visiting you, and she definitely would have told *him*. It's a damn sight easier for us to meet here than for me to travel to the other side of the world. But oh no, telling me his movements would be too much to ask. I'm expected to just bump into him.'

'Being fair,' I said, 'I don't think he expected you to do that. It sounds like he was trying to avoid you altogether.'

Somehow, I didn't end up wearing *eau de prosecco*. It was a close-run thing. I was beginning to think I should be a little more sensitive.

'Perhaps he was aiming to look you up after the tournament,' I suggested.

'Oh, so you're saying that I should be grateful for the consideration he's shown me?'

'No, I, er ...' I shrugged. 'Well, actually, I don't know what I was trying to say. Mostly I was just aiming to make you feel better.'

'Well congratulations.' She gave me a spirited thumbs up. 'You did a swell job.'

'Aw, Vic. Remember what they say about sarcasm, yeah?'

'Uh huh, vaguely.' She formed her right hand into a fist and considered her knuckles. 'Something along the lines of it being preferable to getting punched in the head?'

'Now, now,' I said, backing off a step.

She contemplated her champagne flute. 'Or being glassed, maybe.'

'Easy.' I raised my hands to protect my face, almost as if I was dealing with a caged tiger. Actually, now that I thought of it, a dust-up with a safari cat might have been preferable. 'How about,' I said, 'we discuss something else for a moment? I have an observation that I think you'll be interested to hear.'

'An observation? Oh, goody. That sounds fascinating, Charlie. Why don't you go right ahead and share your *observation* with me?'

'Um, okay.' I hesitated. 'Just so we're clear, do you really mean that, or would you rather I shut up?'

'Speak. Make it quick. I may extend you some mercy.'

Oh boy.

'The briefcase,' I began. 'The one that's suspended from the ceiling in the glass box? Well, I could swear it's identical to the one Graziella gave me. You know, the one with the *explosives* in it.'

Victoria scowled at me. 'You could swear it's identical, or it is identical?'

'Is. I think.'

She nodded. 'Continue.'

'Well, it's curious, don't you think? The Count was meant to be here, playing for the big prize. Meanwhile, the briefcase I delivered to his palazzo is the spitting image of the one containing all the cash.'

'And what do you suppose that means?'

'I don't exactly know. Thought you might have some suggestions.'

Oh, Victoria had some suggestions all right. Fortunately for me, she left them unsaid, and necked her wine instead.

'I need one of your cigarettes,' she told me. 'Come on, follow me.'

I did follow her, tracking her past the slots and through the roulette lounge and down the stairs to the first-floor landing. It was deserted. Victoria lifted the padlock that secured the two glass doors leading to the closed-off gaming area. She rattled the chain.

'Open this, will you?'

'You're kidding me.'

'Do I look like I'm making merry right now?'

No, to be perfectly frank, she didn't. She looked about as pissed off as it's possible to get. Face tight, jaw tense, lips colourless and pressed hard together.

'But the cameras,' I protested.

'Oh for God's sake, Charlie. Take a risk. You're a burglar. It's what you *do*.'

Actually, as a general principle, risks were the one thing I tried to avoid wherever possible. But on this occasion, *not* tackling the padlock seemed like the most perilous option.

Reaching inside my jacket, I removed my spectacles case. I didn't bother with gloves – it wasn't as if we planned on stealing anything (at least so far as I knew) and by angling my back towards the camera at the head of the stairs, I was able to conceal what I was up to. The padlock was very basic and I degraded myself just a touch by using a beginner's technique and shimming it – slipping two thin sheets of metal between the shackles and the body of the lock, and rotating them until the latch was released and the lock popped open. I had it unfastened and the chains freed from the door handles before Victoria even had time to stamp her foot. If we were spotted, we could simply say that we'd found it like that. With the padlock intact, there was nothing to prove otherwise.

I was all for easing the door open and sneaking a look, but Victoria snatched the handle from me and paced brazenly inside.

'Torch,' she barked.

I clicked on my penlight and poked it around. The darkened room was in a hell of a state. Three squat gaming tables were covered in dust sheets, with paint pots, brushes and rollers scattered across them. Bare wires were hanging down from the ceiling space, tangled around paint-spattered stepladders. The floor was covered in a tapestry of thick plastic sheeting that had been roughly taped together. It crinkled as I stepped on it.

'Over here.' Victoria slalomed her way through the decorating equipment to one of the picture windows at the far end of the room. She perched on an old cast-iron radiator and snapped her fingers. 'Cigarette.'

I offered her my packet, then my Zippo, afterwards firing up a cigarette of my own. Victoria sighed a lungful of fumes towards the single-pane window. Outside, the tar-like waters of the Grand Canal glittered in the light from the lanterns on the casino jetty. Our stolen vessel rocked in the tides at the very end, where it was unlikely to attract much attention.

I clicked off my flashlight and turned to check the doors behind us. I could see only shadows amid the shanty town of stepladders and scaffolding.

'Tell me about this briefcase then,' Victoria said, with a heavy sigh.

'I already did.' I inhaled for a moment. 'It would be nice to get a closer look, but I'm pretty sure it's the same. Metal casing. Egg-box interior. Brass combination locks. Rubber handle.'

'Well, did it occur to you that the Count may have won one of these tournaments in the past?' Victoria drew hurriedly on her cigarette, then blew a plume of smoke from the corner of her mouth. 'He must be good, because he'd made it to the final table. If the prize was another case full of money, it would make sense that he kept it in his vault.'

'I suppose that's possible,' I said, casually upping my nicotine intake. 'It's motivation enough for Graziella to steal the case, though it doesn't explain the bomb.'

273

'Perfect getaway. If he's dead, he can't come after the cash, or Graziella.'

'Hmm,' I said, and contemplated the lit end of my cigarette. I wasn't sure exactly what my 'hmm' was meant to signify. I doubt Victoria was either, but she didn't seem eager to pursue the point. 'You spotted our overweight friend at second base, I take it.'

'The one who followed us?' Yes, and watched us kiss, I thought, then felt myself cringe. Awkward subject. I was pretty sure Victoria was trying hard not to think about it too.

'He's definitely tied into this thing,' she said. 'It's too much of a coincidence otherwise.'

'Undoubtedly.'

She crushed her cigarette on the windowsill. The thing was half-smoked, at best.

'Fancy heading back upstairs to watch your dad win all that money?' I asked.

'To be honest, I'd prefer to wait here for a while, if that's okay.'

''Course it is,' I told her. 'I had a word with the owner. We can stay for as long as you need.'

274

THIRTY-ONE

We returned to the tournament room at a quarter to twelve. It was busier than before. The last of the stragglers in the roulette lounge had abandoned their games to watch the conclusion, and everyone had pressed up around the competition table. It took us some time to get to a point where we could see the action, a distant view from off to one side, and even then my line of sight kept being interrupted by the shifting heads in front of us.

There were still four players involved, but the Asian youth with the sunglasses was close to running on empty. I guessed he'd made a big play while we'd been downstairs, and it hadn't worked out. Now his only hope was that his opponents would go all-in to try and secure the win, and that every one of them would crash out. It was highly unlikely, but it was something to cling to, and he appeared to be doing just that.

Chip-leader was Victoria's father, but it was almost too close to call. The Cartier-toting lady with the neat bob and our shaggy, double-width pal were within striking distance, and to the casual observer, it must have seemed really quite exciting.

To me, however, it was more than that. Because while the competitors hadn't altered, a new dealer had been introduced for the final phase. She had a businesslike demeanour and fast, dextrous hands that fluttered around the table-felt like bird wings. Her brown hair was cut short and slicked back behind her ears, but despite the boyish styling and the unflattering tuxedo she was required to wear, it was impossible to ignore her beauty. Her lips were full and lush, her eyes alert and sparkling, and her neck looked entirely suited to being nuzzled. Oh, and in her spare time I happened to know that she had a talent for breaking into people's homes.

Brilliant.

'Er, Vic?' I said, tapping her on the shoulder.

'What is it?'

'I think your dad may have a problem.'

I pressed my mouth to her ear and explained the situation. It didn't take long to give her the headline points. Her reaction was even faster.

'That's the bitch who has your book?' Victoria pointed at Graziella, shaping as if she was about to march through the crowds and start a fight.

'Easy.' I snatched her hand down and fixed a smile to my face. 'Keep it cool.'

'Cool? She's right there, Charlie.'

'I get that. I can even see her real hair for a change. But she hasn't seen *us* yet and I'd like to keep it that way.'

'Well, I'd like to knock her block off.'

I tightened my grip on Victoria's wrist. 'Now's really not the time. Or the place.'

'Why not?' She curled her lip. 'Don't tell me you're scared of her. Charlie, she's nothing to be afraid of.'

'Perhaps not. But what about the people she's connected to?'

'Eh?'

'The bomb, Vic. *Someone* gave it to her.'

As I finished speaking, a smattering of applause rippled through the crowd. Things had changed on the tournament table. Our sizeable friend had enjoyed an equally sizeable win. A huge bet had paid off for him and he'd vaulted way ahead. He knew it, too. Stroking his ragged beard, a look of smug satisfaction on his face, he nodded at his own good fortune, like a gypsy king acknowledging that the fates had finally bent to his will. People slapped him on his wide back, where the fabric of his suit was stretched and shiny.

'Your dad looks kind of bemused,' I said.

'He looks plain angry.'

'Yeah, well, he just lost the lead.' I checked the time on the tournament clock behind us. 'Only ten minutes left.'

'No, it's more than that.' Victoria shook her head. 'See the way he's looking at her?'

The *her* was Graziella. And Vic was right. Alfred was clearly livid. Jaw rotating, as if he was chewing over all manner of indecent thoughts, eyes bulging out of his wrinkled face.

By contrast, our overweight snooper was basking in glee. Reclined comfortably in his chair, he folded his stubby hands across his swollen belly and beamed with delight as Graziella slid a cascade of markers across the table-felt towards him. He reminded me of a glutton who'd just polished off two giant desserts and was being offered a complimentary third. He seemed completely relaxed, as if things were working entirely to plan.

'You reckon it was luck?' I asked Victoria.

'From the way Dad's boiling over, I'd say no.' She went up on her toes for a clearer view. 'A bum card is something he can deal with. This looks much more serious.'

'Are you thinking what I'm thinking?'

'I suspect I'm already there. But why don't you go ahead and fill me in?'

And so I did just that. I explained how I thought there was a good chance that Graziella and the new tournament leader were in cahoots. It struck me that if Graziella was moderately skilled and sufficiently motivated (by a share of half a million euros, say), she had the potential to fix the game any way she pleased. Card counting was all well and good, and I could understand why Vic's dad had placed his faith in the technique, but it was useless if she manipulated the odds. It wouldn't take much, just one or two duds palmed to Alfred, or a sweet card offered to her scruffy partner, and the entire sequence would be out of whack. Not easy, granted, but possible. I'd already seen how talented she was at burglary. What was to say she hadn't mastered another skill?

And there was more. She'd wanted Borelli dead. It seemed obvious now that her motivation had been keeping him away from the tournament table. Just another way of rigging the contest, or something even more sinister? I didn't know, and neither did Victoria. But for once, she didn't take issue with the plot I'd outlined.

'I think Dad's about to blow a gasket,' she told me.

He was about to blow something. As we watched, he pushed all his chips into the betting circle in front of him. A murmur passed through the room. It became chatter. Everyone knew this was a key moment, especially his competitors. The young Asian man pushed his sunglasses up on his nose, then clapped Alfred on the shoulder, clinching him for good measure. He went all-in too. The elegant lady smiled meekly and waved her hand at Graziella, sitting out the round. Our man with the weight issue considered the move with an appreciative nod of his head, then casually pushed roughly a quarter of his markers into play. He sniffed, wiped his nose with the sleeve of his tuxedo, and ran a hand through his long, greasy locks.

I heard the flip and flutter of fresh cards. It was impossible to see what Alfred had scored, and even more difficult to read his reaction. The Asian kid was clearer. He slapped his forehead with his free hand and gestured for a hit. The card was a bust. He threw his arms into the air and smiled glumly as he turned in his chair and acknowledged the sympathetic applause.

Alfred was next. He called on a card. Then another. He opted to stick. The crowd seemed uncertain. Alfred did too.

The bearded lump was content with what he had. He motioned for Graziella to reveal what she was holding with a leisurely twirl of his finger, almost as if he was so sure of winning that the prospect of completing the hand was a tiresome chore.

If Graziella felt emotion, she didn't show it. She simply arranged her cards face up on the felt, then reached for the shoe. One card. Another. One more.

The audience gasped, then groaned, as if the impossible had just happened.

From Alfred's perspective, it had. Lips pursed, he watched stoically as Graziella bent forwards and gathered his chips into her lean arms. Tapping a finger on the felt, he raised his eyebrows in mild surprise, then levered himself up from the table and offered his hand to each of his fellow players. He shook with Beardy last of all, and his hand seemed to be swallowed by the man's bear-like paw. Their eyes locked for just a fraction of a second, long enough for Alfred to try to inject some venom and for the big man to absorb it with a bovine gaze and a drowsy grin, and then Alfred walked stiffly out of the room.

We caught up to him on the stairs sweeping down from the roulette lounge.

'Dad?'

He turned at the sound of Victoria's voice, glancing casually up the stairwell towards us.

'Ah, there you are, darling.' He opened his palms. 'I was wondering when you might come and say hello.'

'You knew we were here?'

'I've trained myself to notice most things, darling, you know that.' He grinned up at me, revealing a set of yellowing dentures amid his snowy beard. 'Charlie Howard, I presume.'

'Yes, Sir.' I moved down the steps and offered him my hand. 'Commiserations on the game.'

'Yes, well. No matter.' His palm was dry and crinkled like tissue paper, but his grip was surprisingly firm. 'I rather got the impression I wasn't destined to win.'

'You mean they rigged it. That last croupier and her cuddly beau.'

'My, my.' He straightened his cuffs, then patted my arm. 'I see my beautiful daughter has taught you a thing or two.'

He glanced at Victoria. She was hovering on the stairs above us, keeping her distance. Her father's flattery wasn't doing a great deal to improve her mood. Her face was stony and her knuckles had whitened where she gripped the brass banister rail. The glamorous green frock she had on was entirely out of keeping with her attitude.

'Dad, why didn't you tell me you'd be in Venice?' she said, her voice tight.

'I intended to, darling. Tomorrow, in fact.'

'She's a touch miffed,' I explained. I'm nothing if not helpful.

'Darling, come here.' Alfred spread his arms and beckoned to Victoria. She tried her best to stay mad, but her resistance was crumbling. 'Don't make a disappointing night any worse, hmm, Sugar Plum?'

Sugar Plum. My, that was going to come in handy.

Victoria shot a look at me, as if she could read my thoughts, then released the banister with a defeated sigh and stomped down the stairs to peck her father on the cheek.

'There now,' he said, and patted her head. 'Friends again?'

'Almost,' she muttered.

'Then where shall I take you? We could all do with a drink, I'd say. My hotel is quite close.'

'Er, actually.' I pulled back my shirt sleeve and drew Victoria's attention to my watch face. 'Time's moving on, Vic. And there was that *thing* we wanted to check back at my apartment.'

'Oh, crumbs. I'd forgotten about that.' She hesitated for a moment, looking between us. 'Listen, Dad, why don't you come along? Charlie has a boat outside. We can chat at his place and drop you back to your hotel later.'

'Splendid,' he said, and grinned famously.

Except it wasn't splendid. Not even close.

THIRTY-TWO

There's a school of thought that says Venice is best experienced from the water. Charting a course away from the casino jetty and puttering along the Grand Canal in the moist, hazy darkness, I couldn't have agreed more. From my position beside the clamorous engine, it was impossible to join in with Alfred and Victoria's conversation, but I was perfectly content all the same. Fog-laced waters, tumbledown buildings, the eerie calm of a drowned city at sleep – it was all so magical that I was almost tempted to turn into one of the crooked side canals and explore for an hour or two. Of course, that would have required me to ignore the small matter of the kidnap victim back at my apartment, which was something I couldn't quite bring myself to do.

Borelli would be awake by now. Alone. Gagged and bound. Dazed by the after-effects of the sedative. Fearing for his life. Sweating into the bare mattress . . .

Hmm. Thinking of the Count like that did detract just a smidgen from my enjoyment of the moment.

Still, it was nothing compared to the ice-cold horror I experienced as I steered into the mouth of the canal I lived on. Flashing blue lights. Shadowy, uniformed figures moving about in the dewy air. The ghostly form of a motor launch with a dark-blue hull. Another vessel in luminous yellow and orange, branded with the words *Venezia Emergenza*.

Powerful fog lights mounted on the boats were pointing towards my apartment building, bleaching the colour from the ramshackle exterior. A blur of police officers and medics had gathered outside the front door, the strobing blue lights giving their movements a jerky, mechanical effect, as if I was watching the scene on the pages of a giant flick-book – a giant *scary* flick-book.

Hell. This hadn't been part of the plan.

Slamming the engine into reverse, I heard a deep churning in the still waters beneath. It wasn't as quiet as I might have liked. A policeman in a heavy blue jacket with luminous patches raised his head to watch me. So did Victoria. She looked stricken – her face bone-white and slack around the jaw, her eyes red-ringed and swimmy.

The boat lurched to the right. I'd turned at too sharp an angle and we were in danger of taking on water. I switched rudder positions, aiming to correct my mistake, and the boat pitched hard to the left. I lost my grip and slammed into the gunwale, jolting my ribs. Momentum carried me on. Saltwater splashed up and wet my face. I felt myself pitching over, but just as I drew a breath and closed my eyes for the impact, I was heaved back. Glancing around, I found Alfred clinging on to the leg of my trousers, a determined glint in his eyes.

I steadied myself, balancing my elbows on the gunwale, then risked a peek at the policeman who'd taken an interest in us. He was still watching, one hand shading his eyes from the swirling vapour, but he hadn't moved any closer or signalled to any of his colleagues. If I was lucky, he might take me for a crabby local – one who knew it was pointless attempting to access a canal in the middle of an emergency response. The last thing I needed was to look like a crook fleeing the scene of a crime. My trusty launch wasn't built for speed, and so far as I knew, it hadn't been fitted with an invisibility cloak.

Wiping the sea spray from my face, I fumbled for the rudder and pointed us back in the direction we'd hailed from.

'Change of plan.' I patted Alfred on the back and guided him down into his seat. 'We'll visit your hotel, after all.'

'Now, would either of you care to tell me what the devil is going on?'

It was a reasonable enough question, I suppose, and no doubt Alfred felt entitled to pose it. Strangely, though, I wasn't all that keen to offer him a response. So far as I could see, there was no good way to explain what had happened.

Ah, well, the truth, Mr Newbury, is that earlier this evening your daughter helped me to abduct a wealthy Venetian resident from his home. We drugged him and we tied him up, and then we left him to doze in his underwear in a strange apartment while we spent time at the casino. What's that? You want to know why we kidnapped him? Oh, that's really quite simple – it was because I'd accidentally been responsible for nearly assassinating the man, and I was eager to make amends.

Somehow, I couldn't see it being terribly well received. In fact, I had more than a vague suspicion that Victoria's father might begin to view me as a bad influence on his *Sugar Plum*.

'It's a little complicated, Dad,' Victoria told him.

No kidding it was complicated. My past few days had been filled with nothing but complications. Never mind *barriers*. I'd had enough hurdles thrown in my way to run a damn steeple-chase.

'Am I to assume the police were outside your home?' he asked me.

And inside it, by the look of things.

'They may have been,' I replied, doing my best to sound carefree.

'And an ambulance too, I think.'

'Was there an ambulance? I hadn't noticed.'

'Listen, Dad,' Victoria said, 'can I get you a whisky?'

She was crouched before the minibar in Alfred's hotel room, wearing her padded winter coat over her evening dress. I didn't know how much booze the minibar contained, but I had a suspicion it wouldn't be enough. Smart thinking, though. Perhaps we could get him sozzled and he'd begin to forget the entire episode.

The hotel was classy and well appointed. Alfred's room featured a wine-red carpet and pink floral wallpaper, plus a good deal of pink fabric around the window. I was resting my backside on a queen-size bed with a doughy mattress. Opposite me were two wing-back chairs. Alfred was sitting in the chair to my left, with his elbows on his knees and his bony fingers pressed together in a steeple. He had the appearance of an elderly professor readying himself to consider a complex theorem. *Good luck, old boy.*

'Charlie, would you like a vodka?' Victoria asked me.

'Anything, so long as it has alcohol in it.'

'There are some nuts here too.'

'Not for me, thanks.'

'How about you, Dad?'

'Oh, for goodness' sake, darling,' he said, in a tone that would have struggled to be any sharper. 'Will you please sit down and talk to me like an adult. I want to know what was happening at Charlie's apartment.'

Victoria passed me a vodka miniature, along with a glum smile. She delayed for a short while longer, fixing herself and Alfred a finger of whisky while I paid careful attention to the corner of the ceiling. Then she armed Alfred with the good stuff and dropped into the chair beside him.

'All right, Dad.' She placed a hand on his knee. 'We're going to tell you what that was about. But you have to remember, we were only trying to do the right thing.'

The right thing. Christ. Next she'd be telling him about my induction into the local monastery. I cracked the seal on my vodka, unscrewed the cap and glugged the foul liquid down. The cheap booze numbed the inside of my mouth and made my sinuses tingle.

Victoria cringed at me, then knocked back a slug of her whisky, pulled an unflattering face, and began.

'The truth is, Dad, we were keeping somebody above Charlie's apartment. And it looks as if the police might have found him ...'

Casting the vodka bottle aside, I pressed my palms against my eyes and zoned out of her explanation. I felt impossibly tired, completely wiped out. It was tempting to lay back on the soft bed and crash out for a time, just to enjoy a little respite. My brain seemed jammed with too much information, too many fears, and I was struggling to think clearly. Some of it was fatigue, but much of it was anxiety. The police were involved now. They'd found the Count in my building. Yes, we'd concealed our faces when we'd spoken to him, but he knew we were English and it wouldn't take long for the authorities to find out about us. They'd speak with Martin and Antea. Perhaps they'd be told about the books that I wrote – the crime angle – and then they'd head to my door and find that we weren't at home. That we were missing. That we could be on the run.

Christ. How on earth had we been so stupid? And how had the Count been found?

My mind drifted back to the way we'd left him. He would have come round some time before we'd left the casino, and quite stupidly, I'd assumed he'd stay put, paralysed with terror. But now that I thought about it, there'd been nothing to stop him from shifting across the bed and dropping down onto the floor. He'd had plenty of motivation, so perhaps he'd shuffled like an earthworm as far as the communal landing, then struggled down the stairs and into my apartment. I couldn't recall locking up in our hurry to leave, and perhaps I hadn't. Finding the place empty, he could have crawled on his knees as far as my living room and knocked the phone from my desk.

All right, his hands and feet were bound, but he could have dialled the police with his nose or his tongue. He could have told them his plight. He didn't know his location, but it would have been a simple matter for them to trace my number and find my address ...

Wait a minute. My mind had snagged on something in the explanation I'd been crafting. A shred of information that jarred, a piece out of place. What was it now?

And then I got it.

Oh crap.

Dialling the police with his tongue. Telling them his plight.

We were morons. Class A idiots. In our rush to get to the casino, there was one trifling detail we'd managed to overlook. Yup, that's right, we'd forgotten to gag him. We'd tied him up. We'd bound him securely. But we hadn't prevented him from yelling for help from the bottom of his lungs. Screw the damn earthworm theory. All he'd needed to do was to scream loudly and there was every chance Martin and Antea would have investigated. They'd heard me stumble home after the bomb blast, for goodness' sake, and Borelli would have been prepared to make a lot more noise.

I lowered my palms from my eyes and looked pitifully at Victoria. She had her father's hands clasped in her own, and she was talking to him in an earnest tone, doing her best to make him understand the incomprehensible.

'But darling,' he said, looking between us with undisguised concern, 'this is simply terrible. What you've been involved in is incredibly dangerous.'

'You're absolutely right, Sir,' I said. 'And it's all my fault. I take complete responsibility.' I placed my hand on my heart. 'No doubt the best thing I can do right now is go straight to the police and confess everything.'

He stared at me, then stared harder. I got the impression he couldn't quite believe that I had the nerve to speak.

'You can forget the ruddy police, Charlie. Goodness, don't you know who this Borelli character is? He's a snake. A viper. One of the nastiest thugs I've ever had the misfortune to cross swords with.' He glanced sideways at Victoria. 'Darling, he's the very reason I came to Venice in the first place.'

THIRTY-THREE

I got the impression that Alfred enjoyed surprising people. You might say that he'd built his life around the sensation. It was there in the improbable triumph of his casino scams – the turn of an unexpected card, the stunning outcome of a risky wager – and I didn't doubt that it had contributed to his success over the years. Educated and well spoken, with a ready smile and an easy charm, not to mention a bus pass, he was hardly your typical crook. I felt sure that any casino that didn't know his reputation would be inclined to underestimate him, along with the crew of pensioners he headed up. That would be a mistake. He was shrewd and enterprising, and from what Victoria had told me, he'd won and lost several fortunes in his lifetime. So he relished a surprise, and judging by the twinkle in his eye, he'd delighted in shocking me, too.

'You didn't know?' he asked.

'About the Count?' I shook my head. 'I don't know much

about him at all, to be honest. Other than that somebody wanted him dead, of course, and that I nearly obliged them in killing him.'

'That would have been no bad thing.'

'*Dad.*'

'Sorry, darling, but it's true.' He patted Victoria's hand. 'He's the very devil of a man.'

Alfred loosened his bow tie and popped the top button on his dress shirt. Standing from his chair, he removed his jacket and hung it in his wardrobe, then unfastened his gold cuf-flinks.

Watching Alfred get comfortable made me realise how much I would have liked to change my own clothes. Wearing another man's duds has never been a favourite hobby of mine – especially when the man in question has sweated under duress. Still, now wasn't an ideal time to ask to borrow one of Alfred's vests. Better just to try and ignore the fusty scent I was experiencing and focus on what he was saying.

Alfred rolled his shirtsleeves up his spindly forearms and gripped the back of a chair. 'Darling, do you remember me telling you about John and Eunice White?'

Victoria nodded. 'Of course. They work with you.'

He grimaced, glancing down at his knuckles. 'A month ago they came to Monte Carlo. We'd enjoyed a rewarding spell in South Korea, you see, and it was time for a break. Never pays to push things too far. John was always a terrific card man, of course. Brain like a computer. Matter of fact,' he said, pointing his chin at me, 'he was quite the crime fiction fan. Enjoyed your work very much.'

There wasn't a lot I could do with the information. Alfred's tone told me this might not be the happiest tale I'd ever heard, so I offered him a neutral smile and waited for him to continue.

'Eunice was a capable player, but where she really scored was awareness. Eyes like a hawk. Can't underestimate that at our age.'

'No, I suppose not,' I said.

'Fantastic couple. Lovely people.' He shot a sideways look at Victoria. 'Your mother and I were very fond of them.'

'I remember Mum talking about them.'

'Even so,' he said, with a tilt of his head, 'John could be a stubborn old mule. Had this blasted obsession with Monte Carlo. I tried to shake him from it, of course – warned him how tight the security can be. But he was always talking with the group about how marvellous it would be to get one over on such a famous casino.' Alfred sighed. 'Your mother and I wouldn't hear of it, naturally, but he was starting to turn heads. Caused a bit of a rumpus, I must say.'

'You fell out?' Victoria asked.

'Hardly. But things were ... difficult for a time. At one stage, it looked like the group might even split. Your mother patched things up, as you might imagine, and it seemed as if the entire issue was forgotten. Then John heard that a blackjack tournament had been scheduled in Monte Carlo during our break. He insisted on participating.'

'Did any of the others go too?'

The fabric of the chair had become pinched around Alfred's bony fingertips. His wrists were shaking. 'The truth is I forbade them. Said it wouldn't do. Had to protect the integrity of the team.'

'Well, that makes sense,' I told him.

'I thought so too – at least at the time. And Eunice could see things from my perspective. That's the only reason I know anything of what happened.'

'Dad, sit down,' Victoria said. 'You're beginning to worry me.'

Alfred did as he was asked, dropping into the chair like he'd been punctured. He took a swig of whisky. The alcohol seemed to help. It didn't calm him, exactly, but when he spoke again, there was a renewed conviction in his voice.

'The tournament went well to begin with. John progressed through the rounds as one might have expected. But Eunice was vigilant, as I say, and something was troubling her. She'd become aware of another player. He was watching John's play whenever he could, and he had a companion with him – a glamorous young woman who monitored John whenever this chap was engaged in a tournament game himself. Eunice became very worried about it. Eventually, she called me.'

Victoria knitted her brow. 'I can see why she might have been concerned, Dad, but it doesn't sound all that sinister.'

'Not to begin with, perhaps.' Alfred held up a finger. 'But as the tournament went on, Eunice became convinced that there was something unsavoury about them. And on one occasion, she felt sure that somebody had been inside her and John's hotel room. Nothing was missing, but some of their belongings had been disturbed.'

'Where were they staying?' I asked.

'A hotel affiliated with the casino, so of course the security was excellent. Eunice reported the incident and the head of security promised to look into the matter. But she heard nothing further.'

'I suppose it's possible that she was imagining it,' Victoria suggested. 'She would have known that you had reservations about Monte Carlo, so perhaps she was being more sensitive than normal.'

'Exactly what I told her,' Alfred said. 'But I also encouraged her to photograph the pair and send their pictures to me. I have a number of European contacts who I thought might recognise the couple, and I promised to pass the images along.'

'And did you?' Victoria asked.

'Of course. By then, Eunice had found out that the man was a titled European of some description – a minor Count from Venice, or so she'd heard. My information confirmed as much. We even had his name. *Borelli.* But neither of us could identify his dazzling companion. The Count was said to be something of a playboy character, so we assumed that she wasn't a permanent fixture.'

Victoria edged forward in her chair. 'So what happened? Was it similar to your experience tonight? Was John tricked in some way?'

'Not in any manner we might have expected.' Alfred tossed back the last of his whisky, his straggly throat bulging and contracting like an intestine. He contemplated the empty glass, turning it in his hands. 'In fact, John went on to win the tournament. The prize was no fortune – winning at Monte Carlo is about prestige as much as anything else – but I understand he was paid close to a quarter of a million euros.'

'Wowzer. Good for John and Eunice.'

Alfred smiled glumly. 'Not so good, I'm afraid. After the tournament, they hired a car to drive down to Cannes. They planned to celebrate, but somewhere along the coast road beyond Nice there was an incident.' He drew a breath. 'They were both killed.'

'My God.' Victoria snatched her hands up to cover her mouth. 'That's awful. I'm so sorry.'

'An incident?' I cut in. 'What does that mean? Were they in a crash?'

'No other vehicle involved.' He shook his head sadly. 'It was only a little Renault. From what I gather, the thing exploded – went up like it had hit a landmine. They never stood a chance.'

I looked across at Victoria. There were questions to be asked but she was a better judge of her father than me. I waited for her lead.

'Dad,' she began, 'are you saying that you think Count Borelli was somehow responsible for what happened?'

'One thing life has taught me, darling, is that there are very few coincidences. I always listened to Eunice's instincts. We walked away from some big wins over the years because she sensed that something was amiss about a given situation. So if she believed there was something fishy about Borelli and his female cohort, then I'm inclined to believe it.'

'That's not exactly proof, Dad.'

Alfred reached across and squeezed Victoria's knee. Offered her a feeble smile. 'You're right. And that's why, when it seemed the police were doing nothing about the situation, your mother and I decided that I should come and see what I could find for myself. I didn't get very far in France – the police and hotel security were next to useless – but then I heard about the blackjack tournament here in Venice and it seemed like the perfect opportunity to assess the Count on his own territory.' He patted Victoria's thigh, then seemed unsure what to do with his hand. He settled for closing it into a fist and propping it on the arm of his chair. 'I hoped I might be able to monitor him and see if he slipped up in some way. Perhaps even gather enough evidence to go to the French police myself and embarrass them into arresting him, or failing that, confront the brute directly. And if not,' he said, unfurling his fist as if releasing something he'd been holding on to, 'I rather fancied the idea of taking the prize money from him. It struck me as a fitting penalty – at least to begin with. And if all that failed, I thought I might return with the rest of our gang and see what other justice we might be able to exact.'

'But meanwhile,' I said, 'somebody tried to kill him with a bomb of their own.'

Alfred frowned, seemingly disappointed by my contribution, as if I'd hit a bum note in the middle of a three-piece instrumental we'd been performing. 'Oh no, Charlie. I don't believe so. I rather think that bomb may have been destined for me.'

I can't say I'm all that familiar with the correct etiquette of how one should respond when a man tells you that he's been the subject of a murder plot. Admittedly, I knew not to guffaw loudly, or to accuse him of being a conspiracy nut, but I was unsure what to say next.

Mind you, it must have been worse for Victoria. This wasn't just a random fantasist – this was her father. And since I'm not completely insensitive, I realised it might be better for me to be the one driving the questioning. After all, nobody enjoys telling their parents that they're talking horse manure.

'You look surprised,' Alfred told me.

'Maybe a little,' I admitted.

'You think I'm mad?'

'Hardly. But if you'll forgive me for saying so, I'm not sure I quite follow your logic.' I pressed my palms together and raised my hands, as if in prayer, so that my fingers were touching my nose and my thumbs were hooked beneath my chin. It was intended to be an educated pose, of the type I'd seen psychologists adopt on television dramas. I wanted Alfred to feel completely at ease. Maybe that way he'd share everything that was going on in his feeble old mind and realise for himself just how much of a loony he sounded. 'Perhaps you could explain why you think the bomb that went off in Count Borelli's palazzo was intended for you.'

He pursed his lips, looking as if he was sucking on something sour. 'Not me, necessarily, though I do believe there was a very good chance of it finding its way to my door.'

'I'm not sure I quite follow you.'

'I might have thought it was pretty obvious to a crime novelist.'

Hmm, now that sounded a little passive-aggressive, didn't it? Still, like any good head doctor, I was willing to weigh all the evidence before I delivered my diagnosis.

'It's not as obvious as it might be, I'm afraid.'

'Well, you do understand that John and Eunice were killed by a bomb.'

'I understand that you believe that to be the case.'

Alfred's lips peeled back, revealing his upper incisors. I got the impression he wasn't the most patient of characters. It was probably best to let him get on with it. I rolled my hand, signalling for him to do just that.

'Well, I rather think the question becomes: *Why?*' Alfred peered at Victoria to make sure she was keeping up. She nodded vaguely and took a sip from her whisky, avoiding his eyes. 'Two reasons occur to me. One is pure spite – the reaction of a bad loser. Perhaps we can't rule that out altogether, but I don't like it a great deal. If someone kills from anger, they're unlikely to use a bomb. A knife or a gun strikes me as much more common. That leaves reason two. The murder must have been designed to conceal something.'

'*Okay.*'

'Now, from what Victoria has told me, the briefcase you were asked to deliver to Count Borelli was very similar to the one the winner of tonight's tournament would have been presented with.'

'It did look that way,' I allowed. 'But the case was pretty high up. I'd need to study it much more closely before I could say for certain.'

Alfred propped his elbow on his knee and pinched his bottom lip between his finger and thumb. 'The Count was meant to be at the final table tonight, agreed?'

I agreed.

'That means he had a one in six chance of taking the main prize. But let's assume he wanted to improve his odds.'

It was a reasonable enough proposition. The Count had certainly been eager to get to the casino, which made me think he'd hoped to win quite badly.

'Well now, what better way to improve his prospects than to ensure that he'd take home the money no matter who won the contest?' Alfred showed me his palm, like a magician aiming to prove that he wasn't concealing anything. 'Let's say I'd won – which, by the way, I was certainly on course to do – I'd have been presented with my briefcase of cash, yes?'

'One would certainly hope so.'

'And meanwhile, the Count had an *identical* case.'

'My God,' Victoria said. 'You think he planned to switch them?'

Alfred clicked his fingers. 'Precisely. He walks away with the money, and I walk away with a case full of Semtex. Then, when I open the thing . . . *SPLAT!*' Alfred slapped his hand against his bony thigh. 'I'm a dead man. No chance of me pursuing my missing half-million.'

He reclined in his chair and studied me for a time, waiting to see the light hit my eyes. The light was a long time coming. I was having trouble with the theory.

'But the Count didn't have the case. It had already exploded by then.'

'Ah, but only because you decided to open it. If your curiosity hadn't got the better of you, he would have had a perfectly primed weapon.'

Hmm. I supposed the theory wasn't completely without merit. But it was a long way from watertight.

'There's still plenty of holes in your explanation,' I told him. 'The girl who gave me the bomb did it because she wanted Borelli dead. So did the people she works for. I was told to go back and shoot him. That has to mean the explosion was originally intended to take him out.'

'This girl,' Alfred said. 'Victoria tells me that you believe she was the dealer at my table tonight?'

I nodded. 'Her name's Graziella. And my understanding is that she rigged the cards in favour of the fellow with the high-calorie diet and the wayward beard.'

'I confess, that did surprise me. I'm not sure how he fits into the picture quite yet.'

I didn't risk looking at Victoria. I wasn't about to explain our connection for fear of sidetracking Alfred. 'He's not someone you'd noticed before?' I asked.

'I was aware of him – been noting his progress during the tournament. French by the sounds of what little he said at the table tonight. Or possibly Belgian. Certainly lacking in manners, not to mention how shoddily he was dressed.'

It was probably best not to concern myself with Alfred's opinion of my own outfit. 'But doesn't the way Graziella helped him to win suggest that Borelli's chances of getting his hands on the case were practically zero?'

Alfred's mouth became a squiggly line. He chewed on the inside of his cheek, then heaved himself up out of his chair and stepped across to a suitcase on a fold-out stand beside his wardrobe. He unzipped a compartment and removed a brown business envelope, offering it across to me.

'What's this?' I asked.

'Take a look.'

I parted the envelope and slipped my hand inside. The envelope contained a set of colour photographs. The images had been printed onto sheets of A4 paper, wrinkled by heavy ink. They looked as if they'd been pulled off a home computer. I shuffled through them, then passed them to Victoria.

'That's Borelli and Graziella,' I said. 'Her hair might be blonde in the photographs, but I happen to know she has a wig just like it.'

'I recognised her myself,' Alfred told me.

'But what does this mean?' Victoria asked, waving the pho-tographs in the air. 'What's the significance of these pictures?'

Alfred rested a hand on her shoulder and bent down to kiss her on the crown of her head. 'These are the photographs Eunice sent me from Monte Carlo. I think we could have assumed it was the same Count. But until I began playing in the tournament, I'd never spotted the girl before. She was dealing every night this week, and our friend Borelli always seemed to rally when she was at his table. I knew why, of course, but now I understand from Charlie that as well as being a card sharp, she also has a facility as a burglar. You'll recall that Eunice believed her hotel room had been broken into. I'd say it's highly likely that our girl here was responsible.'

'You think she helped to switch the briefcases?' I asked.

'I checked with the casino,' he told me. 'John was paid in cash. The notes were packed inside an attaché case – provided *gratis*.'

'An identical scenario.'

Alfred nodded. 'It's beginning to look as if I was fortunate not to win tonight, wouldn't you say?'

THIRTY-FOUR

I'd just about had my fill of talking. There we were, sitting in a hotel room, joining together the dots of what had happened and why, and meanwhile events were moving on without us. It was 1.15 a.m. The blackjack tournament would be over by now, and if things had played out as we suspected, Graziella and her bedraggled companion would be divvying up their winnings. More to the point, the police would have interviewed Count Borelli and there was a good chance they'd be looking for me in connection with his abduction. Now, Venice undoubtedly has its appeals, but one thing I couldn't ignore was how cramped the place happened to be. Once my description and identity were made public, there was no way I could possibly linger. That gave me until morning to move around freely – say ten o'clock at the latest. It was beginning to look as if I wouldn't be enjoying much sleep.

Snatching up the telephone on the side cabinet, I dialled an outside line and punched in Pierre's number. I suppose I should have asked Alfred's permission before hiking his hotel bill with an international call, but given the circumstances, I thought my behaviour might be excused. We had plenty of theories and a good deal of speculation, but what I needed were answers.

The phone buzzed and buzzed again. It repeated the pattern. I checked the time on my watch, then remembered that I already knew how late it was. The phone rang on, without urgency, like a soporific heartbeat.

'Who are you calling?' Victoria asked.

'Hush,' I said, and turned my back on her, covering my free ear for good measure. I don't know why – there was nothing to listen to but the ring tone.

The phone droned on before cutting out without being answered. I knew for a fact that Pierre had an answer machine that he used when he was away from his apartment – mainly because I'd once broken into his place and seen it. I redialled and listened to the droning some more.

'Pick up,' I said. 'Come on. Pick up.'

And then he did. And promptly dropped the phone. There was a crackle and a thud. Some low-level cursing.

'*Allo?*' The voice was drowsy and curt, spiked with resentment.

'Pierre, it's Charlie. I realise it's late, and I'm sorry for calling, but I'm in trouble. I need to know if you've learned anything about the girl.'

'Charlie?' he asked, sounding vague. 'Is this you?'

'Yes, Pierre. Wake up. Please. I need to know if you've spoken to anyone about the woman in Venice – the burglar.'

Pierre mumbled to himself in French. I doubted very much it was complimentary. Then I heard a second voice. A man, calling to him from somewhere far off in his apartment.

'Listen, I'm sorry if you have company,' I told him. 'We can keep this quick.'

'I was sleeping, yes?'

'I got that impression. But the girl – did your contacts know anything?'

He made a noise like a child blowing a raspberry. It was followed by the rustle of paper.

'Pierre?'

'It is here somewhere, yes? Please. Be patient.'

'You don't just remember?'

'I have an address, understand?'

I raised my palm to my face, grinding the heel into my eye. I wondered how long the information had been in Pierre's possession, and why he hadn't called me sooner. Then I reminded myself that I hadn't called him, either. My fault.

'Here, I have it.'

I heard the noise of a scrap of paper being torn from a notepad. I looked to my left and right, then spied a pad and a biro, both of them branded with the name of Alfred's hotel.

'Go ahead.'

And so he did. And halfway through scribbling down the

address I had to refrain from smacking myself upside the head.

'It's okay. I know it,' I said, feeling my body sag.

'My friend tells me it is an old bookshop, yes? This girl, her uncle owns it. They live in the apartment above.'

'I might have guessed.' And really, I suppose I should have done. Living above the bookbinding business would have made it easy for her to set things up with the mobile phone inside the safe. It explained how she'd been able to watch me as I broke in and how she'd spotted the police coming. And there was something else too. The shopkeeper had struck me as nervy when we'd first visited the store. If he was really Graziella's uncle and he had even the vaguest inkling of the kind of things she got up to, then his caginess made sense. 'Anything else?'

While I waited for Pierre to respond, I reached my hand out towards the bed, where I'd dumped my coat. Victoria's pigskin document wallet was there, and I unzipped it and scanned the goodies it contained.

'Only that my contact says that she is good, yes?' Pierre said. 'Maybe the best in Venice. I am thinking, Charlie, perhaps you give her my name? Tell her to call me sometime?'

'You want to hire her?' I asked, stuffing the lipstick-cum-pepper spray into my pocket. 'Christ, Pierre, she stole from me. She's dangerous.'

He yawned. 'She is a thief, no? They are not all nice people like you, Charlie.'

'Tell me about it.'

'Now, I can go?'

'Yes,' I told him, casting my eyes over the equipment that remained, 'you can go. And thanks Pierre. I'll see if I can find a copy of her resumé for you.'

Venice suited black and white. It appeared that way in the postcards I'd nabbed from the news stand in Campo Santo Stefano and had scattered around my desk in the hope of inspiring myself. The cards featured scenes of neglected alleyways and lonesome canals, empty piazzas lit by ornate streetlamps, emaciated cats prowling beneath grand statues of winged lions, and macabre displays of blank *Carnevale* masks. It was the city I found myself in now, hurrying through the small hours of the night, my coat collar up and my footsteps chasing me across rain-slicked flagstones obscured by low, twisted ribbons of mist.

Homes were shuttered, businesses in darkness, there was not a person to be seen. Vaporous rain cloaked the yellow electric light coming from the streetlamps, clinging to my face, and the foggy waters barely glistened beneath the stooped bridges I crossed. In the shadows, rodents skittered among the plastic bags of litter that had been left out for collection, wary of the felines that prowled the streets.

I knew just how they felt.

Thinking helped. It offered me some sense of control. So did smoking. I sparked a cigarette and ran through those things that Alfred had told me, asking myself how much could be true.

Had the bomb really been intended to arm Borelli instead of

killing him? At first, I'd thought the idea made no sense what-soever, but now I wasn't so sure. There was Alfred's story of what had happened in Monte Carlo, for one thing, but my change of heart also had something to do with the Count him-self. Looking back, he hadn't behaved like a man who'd believed his life was in peril. After the explosion, he'd remained in his palazzo, and the following evening, he'd been prepared to spend the night in public at the casino. Hardly the actions of a man aiming to protect himself.

On top of that, kidnapping him had been surprisingly easy. I was a complete beginner but I'd managed to pull it off. More to the point, Graziella had told me that he'd refused the offer of police protection. Was that because he didn't want the author-ities to ask awkward questions?

I didn't know for certain, but I thought it possible. It would certainly explain his attitude after we'd kidnapped him. He'd treated us with contempt, mocking our understanding of the situation, and perhaps now I knew why.

Then something else occurred to me. Borelli had accused us of working for somebody. It was our accents that had made him think as much. What was it he'd said? Something about the man being a clever opponent, and how I sounded just like him.

Could he have been talking about Alfred? If Victoria's father was somebody he'd had on his mind, someone he'd monitored during the tournament as a potential threat, then the fact we were both English might have struck him as an obvious con-nection. Especially if he had some idea of Alfred's background –

his particular expertise with casino games and the likelihood of him making it to the final tournament table. It had been easy enough for Alfred to find out about Borelli from his contacts in the gaming world, so what was to prevent the Count from doing the same thing? And once he knew of Alfred's murkier side, was it really such a stretch for Borelli to think that Alfred might stoop so low as to kidnap him to prevent him from winning?

Of course, if even half of that was really so, and Borelli truly had been planning to use the bomb, then I had no explanation for why Graziella had returned to my apartment and tasked me with killing the poor sod, and I had a feeling that an answer to that particular riddle would be hard to come by. Still, nothing's impossible, right? I had a shot at figuring it out. Granted, it was a long shot, but at least it was something. And besides, if I failed to get to the bottom of what was happening, I hoped there might be some consolation. My copy of *The Maltese Falcon* had to be somewhere, and if there was any justice in the world (or even in Venice for that matter) I didn't think it was too unreasonable to hope that I might find it inside Graziella's home.

My cigarette was almost finished. So was my walk. It would have been pleasant to take a detour through Piazza San Marco, to enjoy the feel of having the entire place to myself. It would have been even nicer to console myself with the idea that I could enjoy the experience another night. That seemed unlikely now. I'd spent more than a year in the city and I still felt like I'd barely scratched the surface. It was somewhere I would have liked to have stayed longer, a place where I'd felt that perhaps I could set down roots for the first time in a long while. All of that was impossible now. Robbed from me despite my attempts to go straight. It didn't strike me as very fair. Nothing did. I was feeling melancholy and bitter. I wanted revenge.

Calle Fiubera was as deserted as every place else. I approached the bookbinding business with slow, careful steps, and glanced inside through the metal shutter. I flicked my cigarette away and reached out a hand. The shutter was bolted, the door locked behind it. I knew I could get in that way, but experience had taught me I could also be seen.

Stepping back, I craned my neck and scanned the building. The wall sloped outwards, leaning over me. There were three windows immediately above the shop, offering a clear view of my position. The one on the right was lit from the inside.

I didn't like it, but there wasn't much I could do. The light might be shining down on somebody who happened to be sitting there waiting for me with a shotgun across their lap. Or it could be illuminating an empty room. Another time, in different circumstances, I would have left and returned the following evening in the hope the light would be gone. Tonight, I didn't have that luxury. I couldn't afford a delay. But I *could* try a different approach.

My memory wasn't as good as I would have liked, and it took ten minutes of searching around to find the alleyway that led to the back entrance of the shop. I wasn't even sure I had the right location until I switched on my penlight and pointed the beam towards the bottom of the door. It was discoloured with damp. I remembered the water that had soaked my feet. Right place.

Stretching a pair of my customised plastic gloves over my hands, I crouched down and assessed the lock. It was nothing special, a piece of cake compared to the security measures at the front. I removed the necessary tools from my spectacles case and picked it open with less trouble than it takes to pick my nose. That should have been it, really – job over – but I was struggling to open the door. The dampness had warped the wood, and I remembered how the door had snagged on the frame the last time I'd used it. There was no handle to hold on to. If I'd had a key, I could have turned it in the lock and pulled hard on the thing, but my pick was too flimsy.

I tried grunting and gurning for a while, but it didn't have the desired effect. Neither did kicking the wall in frustration. I went back to my tools and searched around. I didn't have room for a sledgehammer in my spectacles case, and in my experience, it did give the game away somewhat. Luckily, though, I carried a screwdriver with a blade that was thin enough to squeeze into the slight gap above the top of the door. Leaning on it hurt my bad fingers in a way I could have done without but I couldn't think of an alternative. Pain it was. Considerable pain. I kept the lock open with my pick and levered the door with my screwdriver. There was a good deal of scuffing and squeaking and slipping, and then the door swung outwards with a slurping-sucking noise.

The screwdriver fell to the floor and I buried my screaming fingers beneath my armpit, stomping my feet on the ground. Then I gathered my composure, stepped inside the flooded corridor and had a stab at walking on water.

THIRTY-FIVE

The water had risen since my previous visit. It covered my shoes and soaked into my socks and the hems of my borrowed tuxedo trousers. The cold snaked up my legs, tightening my calf muscles. I waded forward, trying to make as little noise as possible, my movements stiff and constrained, as if I was wearing callipers. The place smelled of damp and mould, like a deep-sea cave.

I flashed my torch. The light danced across the surface of the water, exposing the bare wall ahead. I edged towards it with my gloved hands outstretched, creating small waves in front of me, until my fingers scraped brick. I listened for a moment, and when I was sure I was alone, I tried the beam again. Heavy droplets fell from a pipe above my head, striking the rippled water with a loud *plop*. I touched one of the tarpaulin-covered boxes to my side. The cardboard was soaked through and soft as mulch. It came away in my hand and stuck to my glove like confetti.

Angling my torch inside the box, I saw stacks of paper. I tried another box. Same thing. I didn't think the paper would be any good – it'd be as waterlogged as the cardboard – and I was certain it wasn't worth investigating any further.

I moved on, the water becoming gradually shallower until I was able to see the leather uppers of my shoes again. Stepping to one side, the sodden carpet squelching underfoot, I opened the unmarked door that led into the shop.

A strong aroma of smoke hit me, the scent so pungent that I whirled around, afraid the shopkeeper was sitting there in the dark. I couldn't see him, but his pipe was resting in an ashtray on his desk. I felt the bowl – you don't write a stack of crime fiction without picking up on tricks like that – and found a trace of warmth. That explained the smell.

He must have been working late. My torch revealed a leather-bound volume on his desk, and a needle and thread on top of it. I lifted the cover. Something in Italian. Not my book.

The safe was locked tight, but when I got down on my knees, gripped my penlight between my teeth and tricked it open, I found nothing new. After closing and locking the door, I straightened and walked my fingers along the shelves of books, then rummaged through the desk drawers. No joy. I sighed and gave some thought to stuffing some of the pricier volumes down inside my coat, but I didn't make the move. The bindings were fancy, the workmanship impressive, but I wasn't convinced that they'd hold the same value outside Venice, and I didn't want to risk dropping them as I moved upstairs.

Moving upstairs was just what I had in mind when I happened to glance over towards the paper and stationery on the other side of the shop. There was something out of place, down on the floor behind a display unit. Was it a book? A small box? It seemed about the right size.

I squinted, trying to make out the object in the darkness, then gave up and aimed my torch beam.

Hell. Now why did I have to go and do a stupid thing like that?

The item was a shoe. Tan leather, scuffed around the toe and heel. It was attached to an ankle, sheathed in a fawn-coloured sock. That was all I could see. The rest was concealed behind the display unit, at least until the pale, splayed fingers of a hand emerged from the other side.

I would have liked to have walked away from it. I would have liked it very much. And if I was the ruthless thief I should have been, I would have done just that. But I had character flaws just like the next guy, and one of them was that I was just simple-minded enough to go and take a look.

I chose the end with the foot. Smart choice. The hard terrazzo floor was dry. The area around the head was a different story. Blood. A lot of it. Pooled around his face and shoulders, collecting between the spread fingers of his outstretched hand, getting in under the nails. It looked like someone had emptied a paint tin over him. Maybe two tins. The blood glistened in the light from my torch, shimmering like cranberry juice.

His face was side-on, lips parted and resting in the bloody

316

puddle as if he planned to slurp his way back to life. His right arm was folded beneath his chest, elbow protruding on an awkward angle, with his hand hidden.

I checked the shop window behind me. Nobody watching.

Stepping carefully over his rag-doll legs, water dripping from the soles of my shoes and the bottom of my trousers, I crouched down by his torso and took a closer look. His eye was swollen, bugged out of his head as if he was as shocked to see me as I was to find him. He looked dead – unquestionably so – but I'd made mistakes in the past and I intended to learn from them. I needed to turn the head but I didn't rate the idea of touching him, even through my gloves. A pot of pencils was resting on the stand above me. I plucked one free and poked the end with the rubber eraser inside his mouth, wedging it against his cheek. I tugged. His face turned and turned and then ...

Crap.

I let go of the pencil and fell onto my backside. Pushed myself away across the floor until I bumped hard into a shelf of notepads. I sat there for a while, swearing under my breath as if I was uttering some kind of magic chant that might just be capable of erasing the terrible image that wouldn't go away.

So it had been more than pipe smoke that I'd smelled when I'd entered the room. There'd been gun smoke too – the hot, gassy discharge from a bullet fired at close range. Half the guy's face was missing, and the little that remained really wasn't worth holding onto. It looked as if he'd done it to himself. There was no sign of a disturbance and the shop had been locked when I'd arrived. I had no clear idea what could have driven him to it, but he must have slipped the gun inside his mouth and fired up and out. It was ugly, ragged, messy.

I fumbled around for my torch, hands shaking, and cast it along the shelves at my side. Splatter patterns – covering the walls, the ceiling, the displays of expensive wrapping paper on the angled sliding racks. The paper was marbled more than Graziella's uncle could ever have intended and I very much doubted that he'd be able to sell it any time soon. He wouldn't be smoking his pipe again, either – at least not in this life. He was as dead as it was possible to get.

I glanced around him for the gun he must have used, but I couldn't see it. That was strange but it wasn't capable of troubling me any more than the sight of what he'd done to himself. What did I care, anyway? I certainly didn't want to touch the gun if I found it. Chances were it was beneath him, still gripped in his concealed hand, and he was welcome to keep it.

Using the shelf above me to clamber upright, I patted myself down and checked that I hadn't dropped anything. My spectacles case was still tucked inside my coat, nestled beside my cigarette packet, the pepper spray was safe in my trouser pocket and my torch was in my hand. There was nothing to suggest I'd ever been there, apart from the bloody pencil. I thought about taking it, then changed my mind. Grabbing the pot, I scattered its contents beside the body, hoping it looked as if he'd disturbed the pencils when he fell.

I sucked air through my teeth, squeezed my fists tight shut.

Idiot. I should never have come inside the shop in the first place. The apartment was the better prospect. It was where Graziella lived. If there was anything useful to be found, that was where I'd uncover it. Not here. Especially not now.

I paced stiffly across the room, my drenched socks slurping against my shoes, and through into the soggy corridor, letting the door fall closed behind me. Funny how choices work out. If I hadn't ventured inside the shop, I could have made my way upstairs and set about my search without the shakes that seemed to have taken over my body, or the chill, prickly sensation in the base of my spine. Glancing down, I turned my hands and found that it was like watching somebody else mirror the gesture. My actions felt mechanical, detached from me, as if I was some kind of shabby puppet that didn't work quite right. I jerked on the strings, moved my legs, stumbled forwards into the black until I found a narrow staircase leading up to my left.

Two unmarked doors faced me at the top of the stairs. No locks – just handles. I chose the one directly in front of me and it swung three-quarters open before bumping against something soft. There was light in a room at the end of a short corridor – the light I'd spotted from outside. It was enough to see by, and what I saw was mess and confusion.

The corridor was jammed with boxes, stacked close to the ceiling and leaving only a thin channel to squeeze through. I placed one sodden foot inside, then the other. Checked behind the door. More boxes. The door was resting against them. I pulled it back and closed it behind me.

A box beside my knee was open. It contained blocks of notepaper, the edges printed to look like a map of Venice. Another box held a selection of pens. I abandoned the boxes and shuffled between them in the direction of the light.

The first room I passed was a sparsely furnished bedroom. It contained a single bed, unmade, with a tangle of yellowing sheets and faded blankets. A two-drawer bedside cabinet was loaded down with coffee mugs and dusty water glasses that trapped the light from my torch. In the corner, I spied a small closet, its doors splayed open, with a sorry collection of men's clothing spilling out onto the tatty carpet.

Room two was a bathroom. A cramped space, it greeted me with a dirty toilet, lid up, the rim sticky with urine and curled hairs. Beside the toilet was a cracked sink with a slither of old soap and a disposable safety razor balanced on the shelf above. A hand towel of an indeterminate colour hung from a rusty nail alongside. Tucked behind the door was a freestanding shower with a mildewed curtain that had been fixed to the off-white tiles with gaffer tape.

Next to the bathroom was a kitchen. The sink was loaded with dirty crockery, floating in water that was filmed with a greyish scum. A squat electric oven was positioned on the Formica counter, its underside clogged with crumbs of burned food. Nearby was a two-ring hob, connected to an orange gas canister by a rubber pipe that appeared brittle and permeable enough to spark a decent house fire. Two cupboards had been tacked to the wall. The right-hand cupboard contained a chipped cereal bowl. The shelves on the left held a modest collection of jars and tins. Nothing I was interested in.

That only left the room with the light, and if it was as untidy as the rest of the apartment, I thought I could understand why the shopkeeper had shot himself. Perhaps his sloppy housekeeping was a reaction against the precision his job required of him – or a sign of how much time he devoted to his craft.

Surprising, then, that the room was clean and orderly. A modern flat-screen television filled the corner opposite the doorway and two well-worn lounge chairs were pointed towards it. I craned my neck around the door and found that the centre of the room was dominated by an oval dining table, fashioned from teak, with four mismatched chairs. A three-bulb spotlight was shining down from the middle of the ceiling.

I moved closer. The table was covered in thick plastic sheeting, as if to protect it from a careless decorator, but there was no painting going on. It looked as if the shopkeeper had been engaged in a hobby of some kind. A toolbox was open on the table, the concertina shelves stocked with screwdrivers and pliers, wire trimmers and craft knives, tubes of glue, rolls of sticky tape and a jeweller's loupe. Beside the toolbox were coils of electrical wire (blue, green, red and yellow), wrapped around miniature cardboard drums. Three cheap digital watches had been lined up in a row, laid flat with their wrist straps stretched out.

I sprayed the beam of my torch over the watch faces – God knows why I was still using my torch when there was a main light on in the room – and found that all of them featured the same digital read-out. *00:00:00*.

I'd like to tell you that by the time I'd seen the watches, realisation was dawning on me. I'd love to believe I wasn't *that* slow. But in truth, it wasn't until I'd contemplated the dun-coloured bricks of putty with the strands of brightly coloured wires sticking out of them that I finally understood. This was no ordinary pastime – Graziella's uncle hadn't been in the habit of fitting sailing boats inside glass bottles or fashioning scale models of the Rialto Bridge from spent matchsticks. Far from it. No, it seemed quite obvious to me now that the poor chap I'd lately discovered with one side of his face scattered liberally around his shop floor had applied the dexterity and steady hand he'd developed as a bookbinder to the delicate art of bomb making, and I'd just happened upon his home studio.

THIRTY-SIX

So that was how Graziella had got hold of a bomb. And not just the one I'd had the misfortune to trigger, but also, perhaps, the device that had been used to kill Alfred's friends in Monte Carlo. It was little wonder that the shopkeeper had struck me as suspicious. He was a man with an awful lot to hide.

I backed away from the table and hurried out of the apartment, moving at quite some speed. Yes, that had something to do with the volume of explosives on the table, but there were a couple of other reasons, too. Number one, I wasn't keen to linger in a building with a dead man in it any longer than necessary. And two, I hadn't seen anything to suggest that Graziella shared the apartment with her uncle. There was only one bedroom, and it was something of an understatement to say the place lacked a woman's touch. But there was also the second door at the top of the stairs to investigate, and I'd decided it was high time I did just that.

The door opened onto a flight of wooden steps that curled steeply to the right. I followed them and they kept turning, spiralling around like the staircase in the tower Graziella had led me to. It was every bit as dizzying, and I kept scraping my kneecap on the treads above, but just before I lost my bearings and my patience altogether, the steps unwound and opened into a charming entrance hall.

The first thing I noticed was the hat stand, weighed down with a selection of hats and coats, not to mention an extensive collection of wigs. Some I recognised – the glamorous blonde sweep, the harsh black bob and, of course, the vivid red number – but there were many others that were new to me. I have to confess I was glad I hadn't been exposed to Graziella's entire repertoire, because it was hard to imagine how much chaos that many encounters would have involved.

The hallway floor was wooden, laid in a herringbone pattern, buffed to an oily sheen and smelling strongly of cleaning fluid. Either side of the hat stand were two copper planters with plastic lilies poking out of them, and a short distance further along was a porcelain cat figurine. The cat was jet-black in colour, with green ceramic eyes that flashed like gems in the light from my torch. It was arranged in a sitting position, licking a paw, with a long tail curling above it, a closed door positioned just behind and two open doorways on either side.

One doorway led into the bathroom, which was small but neatly kept. The dated brown suite was spotlessly clean and decorated with scented candles and stylish toiletries. The towels stacked beside the sink were pale green and fluffy, and the white plastic shower curtain looked shop-fresh.

There was nothing for me in the bathroom aside from a pleasant fragrance, so I crossed the hallway and found myself in a bedroom. The bed was a futon – probably the only thing that could be transported up the narrow staircase, and then only just. It was neatly made with a pink embroidered duvet and a generous collection of pillows and cushions. Off to the side was a metal hanging rail, crammed with clothes, and a small alcove in the wall where a pile of shoes had been stashed. The bedside cabinet was an upturned wooden crate with a carton of cigarettes on top of it. On the floor beside the crate were a stack of paperback novels.

I lifted the top novel and a leather bookmark fell out. She was about a third of the way through. There were four books underneath, their spines all thoroughly cracked, and I could see that a number of pages had been turned down at the corner. I checked some of the flagged pages and found that she'd drawn on them in biro – underscoring certain passages, jotting down a question mark or a little smiley face beside others.

I fanned the pages, feeling the breeze against my face. Small world. I'd read the same books myself. Many times, in fact. Because it just so happened that I was the author.

The five titles formed a complete collection of the mass-market editions of my Michael Faulks burglar novels. Each one had a jacket in a different lurid colour and each featured my name on the front, printed in a modest black font along the bottom, and a deceptive author photo at the back. The most recent edition had been published some years ago now. It was called *The Thief and I* and it was dedicated to one Victoria Newbury, *My Fabulous Agent*.

Hmm, what to do? There was a biro on the floor and I snatched it up and pulled off the lid with my teeth. Turning to the first page, I flexed my arm and started to write.

Dear Friend. As a fan of mystery fiction, you might appreciate this twist. Your pal the Count isn't dead – he's safe in police custody. Sincerely, Charles E. Howard.

I jabbed my pen into the page, laying down a mighty full stop. I was quite pleased with the way I'd structured the message. The reference to 'police custody' had just the right degree of ambiguity. It covered me if the Count was being cared for by the authorities following his kidnap ordeal, but Graziella might also interpret it as meaning that Borelli had been arrested, perhaps in connection with the murders in Monte Carlo. That could plant a timely seed of doubt in her mind – maybe even cause her to experience some of the angst I imagined her uncle had undergone before taking his life. Granted, she hadn't struck me as the type to show a great deal of remorse for her actions, but it didn't take a psychologist to speculate that her uncle's death might change all that.

I tossed the book down onto her bed and set my mind to

considering my next move. My next move was to conduct a quick search. I started with the hollow in the wall and it didn't take me long to conclude that all the alcove contained was shoes, and all the shoes contained was stale air and the occasional shred of sock fluff. I moved across to the hanging rail and patted down her clothes. There was nothing that felt like a hardback book or an incriminating piece of evidence. The same was almost true of the packing crate beside the bed. I lifted it clear from the ground and checked underneath. A clear plastic bag had been taped to the inside of the crate. It was filled with a modest stash of casino chips. I reached for a blue chip and saw that it was branded with the words *Casinò di Venezia*. I thought it likely she'd been palming the odd chip to herself while dealing, but my suspicion wouldn't get me very far.

Normally, I'd have swiped the bag, but since I couldn't imagine I'd have an opportunity to return to the casino, I popped the chip back, dropped the crate and tackled the bed. Pillows, then duvet, then mattress. It was only as I rolled up the lower half of the mattress to peek beneath that I spotted something on the floor through the wooden slats of the futon frame. A small, glossy pamphlet, the pages stapled together along the spine.

I let go of the mattress and fell to my knees, hooking the pamphlet out from under the frame with the end of my penlight. Then I pointed the beam at the pamphlet and released a pitiful groan.

'So that's how you knew about my book,' I said, to no one in particular.

Printed on the page I was looking at was an article all about me. What was it – seven, eight months ago now? I'd been at a dinner party that Martin and Antea had invited me to, where I'd got stuck chatting to some ex-pat windbag who ran a freebie English-language arts journal in the city. He'd convinced me to answer some questions on my burglar novels – even though I very much doubted that the chattering classes would be inclined to sully their hands reading anything of the sort. Oh, and my picture had been featured, too – a shot of me sitting at the desk in my apartment with my laptop behind me, a cigarette on the go, and, of course, my signed copy of *The Maltese Falcon* hanging in its frame on the wall above my shoulder.

I'd answered some questions about the book – explaining how important it was to me, how I viewed it as a lucky charm that helped me to write, and claiming that I'd bought it with an inheritance I'd received from one of my grandparents not long before my first novel was published. The twit who'd interviewed me had even made some foolish remark about how Sam Spade might have fared on the mean streets of the City of Bridges.

Good grief.

I'd let myself be persuaded into thinking the piece might be good publicity, but all it had really been was a full-colour advertisement for someone with the appropriate knowledge and skills to come and burgle me. Graziella's uncle knew about books – maybe she did too – so it wouldn't have been hard for her to find out how much my Hammett novel was worth, and I'd made its personal value to me blindingly clear. Worse still, I'd had some fun in the piece by implying that I had a more practical appreciation of how to burgle a place than I might care to let on. And sure, that was nothing new, considering I'd composed a moderately successful memoir some years ago, but it seemed clear to me now that my charming little routine had been sufficient to pique Graziella's interest – enough, at least, for her to resolve to test my abilities by tricking me into breaking into the bookshop.

Vanity and ego. I'd be the first to admit that I had plenty of both, and not for the first time, they'd combined to land me in a steaming pile of doo-doo.

I raised my middle finger in salute to the grinning imbecile in the glossy pamphlet – the past version of me who'd so witlessly sown the seeds of my recent troubles. I tell you, if I ever caught up with that guy, he was in for a pummelling.

For the time being, though, the pamphlet went back beneath the bed and I went back to the hallway. The cat figurine was still grooming itself in front of the closed door, and I thought I could detect something new in its glinting eyes – a kind of haughty superiority, as if it was aware of a devious secret I hadn't the first clue about. I was sorely tempted to have an unfortunate accident, to lash out and kick the little bugger into a gazillion pieces. I didn't, though. It would be cruel and unnecessary, and it would make an awful lot of noise. And besides, knowing my luck the remains of its beady green eyes would still be visible among the shards of broken china, staring smugly up like the final biting remark in a lost argument.

I curled my lip and did my best to appear unruffled, then aimed my torch in front of me and pushed open the door the cat was guarding. There was another futon, this time arranged like a chair, and it was furnished with a collection of plush fabric cushions. A beanbag was positioned nearby, close to a portable radio. There was a large canvas print on the wall – a mass-produced likeness of Audrey Hepburn. Audrey was smoking a cigarette in a long-stemmed holder, and if she wasn't careful she was in danger of dropping ash into the fronds of the spider plant that was wilting on the console unit beneath her.

I turned and discovered a series of fitted kitchen units at the end of the room, beyond a circular table that was covered in a jaunty gingham tablecloth. A collection of playing cards were spread across the table, some face up, others face down, and alongside them was a black plastic dealer's shoe. There were two wine glasses, a half-finished bottle of red Bordeaux wine, and a number of spent cigarettes in an ashtray. Seemed like this was where Graziella had practised with her hairy stooge before shaking down the casino.

I was just reaching for a card when a sense of movement caught my eye and I glanced up at a lopsided sash window positioned above the kitchen sink. I could see the reflection of my torch beam in the glass, along with a translucent outline of myself. There was something about my opaque double that didn't quite add up – a second form behind the first, like the ghost on a badly tuned television. Then, quite suddenly, it made sense in the most abrupt and grievous way I could have imagined, and I experienced a hard, sharp jolt to the back of my head.

My legs gave out and I slumped to my knees, my torch falling from my slackened hands. I cried out in shock, then in pain, and was aiming to twist around when the blur of an arm came down a second time. There was a crunching noise I didn't appreciate, and my head pitched sideways until my chin played kissy-kissy with the wooden floor. The impact seemed to have dislodged something inside me – something that was too big to be contained. It swelled and pressed up against my skull, then trickled out in a warm dribble from my ear. I was still conscious, but only just. I'd been struck twice, and neither blow had been quite on the money, but I wasn't dumb enough to invite another attempt. I stayed down and closed my eyes, jaw gaping open as I performed my best impression of an Englishman beaten utterly senseless.

A shoe was planted beside my nose, smelling of rubber, and my head was yanked up by the hair, close to where I'd been hit. It hurt just fine, but I was determined not to whimper. I was pretty good at it, even if I do say so myself, and I must have lasted a clear half-second before the sound of footfall and voices became audible from the spiral stairs at the end of the hall.

My attacker let go of my hair, giving my nose a fair stab at breaking itself on the floor. Then a pair of hands were hooked beneath my armpits and I was heaved back behind the door.

THIRTY-SEVEN

The voices belonged to a woman and a man. Even with a dashed skull I recognised Graziella. She was talking with her companion in rapid-fire French, which gave me a pretty good idea of who to expect.

My shadowy friend with the speedy arm had forgotten to snatch up my torch. It was shining in a diagonal slant across the floor, casting the spider plant and the picture of Audrey Hepburn in a weak spotlight. If things had been going my way, it might have been enough to alert Graziella to the danger that was lurking behind her door, but it wasn't to be. An overhead light *snicked* on and she bustled inside, followed by the oversize blackjack champ with the pronounced limp and out-of-control beard. His fedora was missing – perhaps he'd tossed it onto the hat stand – but he did have on his XXL camel-hair coat, his black suit trousers and white sports socks. Graziella was wearing her tuxedo, minus the bow tie, with her pearl-white blouse open at the collar.

They approached the kitchen table, chatting at a quick tempo. It sounded as if they were in high spirits, which suggested that she hadn't popped her head inside the bookshop on the way upstairs to see what had become of her uncle.

Beardy was carrying a metal attaché briefcase of a design I couldn't fail to recognise. He swung it freely in his huge fist and slapped it down on top of the playing cards on the chequered tablecloth, then twirled it around so that the combination dials were pointing towards Graziella. He spread his arms wide, grinning toothily, like a game-show host flaunting a star prize. Graziella smirked, then hung her tongue out of the corner of her mouth and was just in the process of entering the combination when she happened to glance sideways and fix directly on me.

The colour left her face. So did the animation.

I heard a click, followed by a ratchet sound, and then my mysterious companion stepped out from behind me and shouted, 'Peek-a-boo!'

Well all right, he didn't do *that*, but he did straighten his arm and point a finger. Scratch that – a *gun*. I might have been slumped on the ground, peering out from half-lidded eyes as I performed my man-in-a-coma routine, but I could see the pistol quite clearly. It was a big, clumsy thing, fitted with a screw-on suppressor. And hell, it looked an awful lot like the weapon Graziella had provided me with.

I'd last seen the pistol when I'd ditched my bumbag on the floor of the bedroom in which we'd restrained Borelli. Since that was also the last time I'd seen the Count, I suppose it was only fitting that he was the chap toting the gun.

Borelli's face was flushed and he was perspiring heavily. His forehead and upper lip were coated in an oily sheen and his wavy grey hair was flattened on top of his head, as if he'd been smoothing his wet palm over it. His greasy fingers seemed to be slipping on the dimpled pistol grip, but not enough to make life any more comfortable for Graziella and Beardy.

The clothes he had on didn't exactly suit him, but that shouldn't have surprised me, considering they were mine. A hooded sweatshirt and faded jeans, plus a pair of smelly baseball shoes. The jeans were too long for him, caught up around the heels of the trainers, and the hoodie made him look like he was in the grip of a mid-life crisis. He was woefully underdressed, considering the rest of us were in dinner wear, and if only the circumstances had been different, I might have suggested swapping outfits again. Somehow, though, I imagined he'd be reluctant to go the whole way and return my gun-shaped accessory.

He must have discovered the pistol when he'd been climbing into my duds, but that still left questions unanswered. Questions like: Why wasn't he being interviewed by the police right now? If he'd been found by the officers I'd seen outside my building, wouldn't they have insisted on keeping my clothes as evidence of the abduction? And fine, Borelli might have powerful contacts, but could the police really turn a blind eye while he skulked around Venice with a weapon taken from a crime scene?

I didn't know, and I wasn't about to find out any time soon. He raised his chin in the air, peered down his nose, and barked something to Graziella in Italian. She held up her palms and backed off from the table. He repeated the command to Beardy and the hairy slob didn't require a translation to comply. He did take his time over it, though. I got the impression there wasn't much he did in a hurry and his grudging reaction suggested this wasn't the first time he'd been confronted with a gun.

Borelli waited until he was satisfied with their positioning, then stepped forwards and snatched up the case as if it had been delivered to the room expressly for his convenience. He felt the weight in his hand, bobbing his head from side to side like a set of scales, and snarled more Italian at Graziella. She answered with a sullen nod. I wasn't entirely clear what he'd asked, but I could hazard an educated guess. If I was him, I'd want to be certain it was all there – the entire 500,000 euros – and judging by the nasty grin that curled his lip and split his face in two, that's precisely what he'd been told.

He shuffled backwards, covering Graziella and Beardy with the gun. I didn't know if he was a good shot but I rated his chances of hitting them as pretty high, and evidently they did too. I could see the anger and frustration bubbling away in Graziella. Her eyes were narrowed, chin jutting forwards, but she didn't make a move. Beardy sighed loudly and leaned to one side, favouring his good leg.

Borelli was close to me by now. From where I was lying prone on the floor, it would have been a simple matter to grab his ankle and yank him off his feet, and if this was your typical Hollywood movie, I dare say that's just what I would have been expected to do. Problem being, like any actor working a scene, I needed to know what my motivation was supposed to be, and quite frankly, I couldn't think of one. Based on what Alfred had told me, not to mention my recent pistol whipping, I had good reason to suspect that the Count was what one might call a *baddie*. Then again, Graziella and Beardy were no saints, and if I managed to disarm the Count, there was no guarantee that my situation would improve a whole lot. It didn't help that my head was pounding in a quite sickening way, or that I'd broken out in a heavy sweat. And then there was the small matter of the bloody big gun the Count had in his hand – a weapon that was liable to go off in a struggle and that might very well be pointed towards some vital part of my anatomy when it did.

Hmm. Decisions, decisions. Stay still and avoid being shot, or go down in history as a have-a-go hero with a gory hole where his pulmonary artery used to be?

Shockingly, I chose option A.

And I hazard to say, I could have lived quite comfortably with my decision. But then Borelli decided to give his parting speech. All baddies have them, I suppose, and it seemed that he was no exception. Of course, it would have helped if he'd slipped into heavily accented English, or if some snappy subtitles had magically appeared so that I was able to understand his words, but the truth is the vast majority of what he said was a complete mystery to me. Except for one thing. He spat a short sentence and gestured flamboyantly with the gun, pointing down through the floor to the bookshop far below, and fixed a nasty snarl on his face.

Graziella crumpled. Her knees went from under her and she fell into Beardy, clutching at his camel-hair overcoat and wailing quite disturbingly. She buried her head behind his wide back, as if trying to shield herself from the Count's words.

It didn't work. If anything, it just seemed to encourage him. He kept up his talk, seeming to revel in the pain he was administering, and meanwhile he mimed something. The mime was quite clear. Picture the briefcase as a man's head. Picture the gun as, well, a gun. Now watch him press the gun against the briefcase – see him dry-fire the pistol. The bastard even made a plosive noise with his lips.

Language barrier aside, it was perfectly clear to me that Graziella's uncle hadn't shot himself. Borelli had done it for him. And judging by the perverse delight he seemed to take in sharing the news, he wasn't the least bit sorry about it, either.

Now, on reflection, I can't say that I was conscious of my motivation having changed. But something definitely shifted inside me, especially when I looked at Graziella and saw the snivelling mess she'd become. She was curled into a ball, gripping hold of Beardy's trouser leg, banging her head against the cupboard door beneath the sink. And yes, I might have been coward enough to dither over the role I should have been playing, but right at that moment, my emotions took over and I watched with some amazement as I dug a hand inside my pocket, flicked off the lid of the pepper spray with my thumbnail and surged up from the floor.

The surprise helped, and I had plenty of time to depress the aerosol. Sadly, what I lacked was an opportunity to check my aim. No, the outlet wasn't pointing towards me, but it wasn't pointing towards Borelli, either. I blitzed the wall between us, coating it with a dirty brown smear, and before I was able to correct my mistake, Borelli's face twisted in anger and distaste, and he swiped down fast with the gun, knocking the canister from my fingers.

On instinct, I grabbed for his wrist with both hands. He tried to tear himself free, cursing me in extravagant, full-blooded Italian, but I knew what letting go would mean and I held on for all I was worth. I felt the muscles of his hand flex. His trigger finger curled. *Pfft.* There was a flash of light and a bullet went high, *thunking* into the ceiling with a shower of plaster dust. Beardy ducked for cover, his bad leg giving way like the rotten foundations of a collapsing warehouse.

The Count's hand jerked backwards with the recoil. He was fighting to bring his arm down while I strained to force it up. It would have helped if I could have snatched a hand free and punched him in the face, but I didn't have the strength. It was a different story for him, and he seemed to have a similar idea. Bumping me with his hip, he swung with his free arm and the briefcase came around in a fast arc, heading for my kidney. I raised my leg and took the blow on my thigh. He cursed me some more and swung back for a second go, and meanwhile I stamped down on his toe. Bad idea. The move worked, but he keeled sideways. *Pfft*. The second bullet went lower, *pinging* off a kitchen tile. If Beardy hadn't been crouching already, it would have punctured his abdomen.

I wrenched Borelli's arm up, forcing the gun towards the ceiling, and we lost our footing and toppled over onto the floor. The Count was on top of me, rolling around fitfully, using his elbows and his weight to crush the air from my lungs and the hooded sweater to smother my face. It was beginning to work. I couldn't inhale. I felt my grip loosen a fraction, and he was just seconds from having the gun all to himself when Beardy pushed himself up with a mighty groan and came lumbering across the room, kicking the Count in the temple and tearing the weapon from us with all the ease of an adult confiscating a toy from a pair of brawling kids.

I skittered clear of Borelli, who was clutching his head and moaning groggily, and rested on my back, panting for a moment. The moment was short. Before I could do anything more, Beardy stomped around me, aimed down at the Count and squirted two carefree rounds into his bucking chest.

Borelli didn't cry and clutch at his wounds. He didn't yell out in pain. He lay prone. Unmoving. Dead.

Beardy swivelled, lungs heaving, and kicked the pepper spray away into a distant corner of the room with a twitch of his bad leg. Then he aligned the gun with my forehead, stifled a yawn, and presented me with the opportunity for a brief spell of introspection.

When I'm writing about Michael Faulks, I like to exploit what I think of as his *key moments of awareness*. Every now and again, I move the action inside his head so that my readers can listen to him think, hear him tick. And if I do this often enough, and at the right instances, then when Faulks faces a major test, he'll experience a *key moment of awareness* where he begins to understand something fundamentally important about himself.

Now, I don't like to crow, but I believe that having a gun turned on me, especially a gun that had been nonchalantly discharged to kill a man lying a few feet away, could be said to qualify as just such a challenge. And what was I aware of? Absolutely nothing. My mind was a complete blank. I didn't see my life pass before me. I didn't ask forgiveness for my sins. All I did was squint through the ache in my head and stare into the gaping hole at the end of the gun muzzle, unsure if it was the last thing I'd ever see.

I did, though, still retain my sense of hearing, and it was this precious gift that enabled me to listen as Graziella said something in French from a voice that was hoarse and scratchy, but which carried an unmistakable note of urgency. My French might have been limited, but it was better than my Italian, and I got the impression she was telling Beardy not to shoot.

I saw his meaty hand shift around the butt as he adjusted his grip. I wet my lip and risked glancing up. His eyes didn't lock with my own – they were focussed on the area of my chest where my heart was beating a jaunty melody I like to call flat out fear.

'Remi,' Graziella said. At last, I had his name. I can't say I took much consolation from it. *'Pose ton arme.'* Put the gun down. Funny how my French was improving. Who knew, maybe if he ever got round to shooting me, I'd die fluent? *'Pose ton arme,'* she repeated, and to my everlasting relief, he shrugged, scratched his beard, and did just that.

The gun hung limply at his side, looking like a miniature replica inside his large fist, and I allowed myself the luxury of drawing a breath. I even went so far as to prop myself up on my elbows and blow a gust of air towards my brow. Talk about a *key moment of awareness*. I was beginning to wonder if there was a chance I might live.

THIRTY-EIGHT

Despite his bulk, Remi was no slouch. I'd barely had time to appreciate my good fortune before he'd manhandled Graziella onto a folding kitchen chair, fitted her limp hand around the gun and arranged her arm so that her elbow was resting on the table and she was pointing the pistol at me. Once he was satisfied with her aim, he nodded to himself and hobbled through to the bathroom, returning moments later with a bundle of towels and the white shower curtain that he'd torn from the rail. By now, he was whistling a carefree tune, and it seemed to occupy him while he used the towels to pack the Count's chest wounds, then rolled him in the shower curtain until he was thoroughly cocooned. If he was fazed by the nature of the housekeeping task he'd set himself, he didn't show it. I knew people who found vacuuming more stressful.

Graziella appeared to be somewhere else entirely. She didn't pay attention to what Remi was doing, and she didn't react

343

when he gathered up the attaché briefcase and set it down on the floor between her feet. He stopped whistling for a moment to watch her, as if uncertain if she could be relied upon, and then he squinted along the barrel of the gun towards me again. Finally content, he murmured a quick instruction into her ear, rustled her hair, then heaved the shrink-wrapped corpse up onto his capacious shoulder like a man lifting a giant vacuum-packed fish fillet, and staggered blithely out of the room to the accompaniment of his own breezy theme tune.

His uneven footsteps on the spiral stairs gradually faded to nothing, leaving us in silence. I glanced at the dark stain on the floor where Borelli's body had been, then at a discharged shell from one of the bullets that had killed him, then at Graziella. Her eyes were black swirls, the corners very pink against her colourless skin, her lips forming a perfect circle almost as inert as the gun muzzle.

I counted off two minutes on the kitchen clock behind her shoulder. Then three.

'Mind if I sit down with you?' I asked.

There was a twinge in the muscles of her cheek. Not the surest sign of consent, but I got the impression it was all I was going to get.

'I'll move slowly,' I told her. 'If you want me to stop at any point, you just say.' No response. 'Okay, here I come.'

I'd seen plants grow quicker. It seemed to take forever until I was upright, followed by an eternity until I was close to the chair. I'd left my penlight resting on the floor. Didn't want her to think I might try to use it as a weapon. 'I'm sitting down now,' I told her.

Blankly, she watched me do just that. If she was impressed by my commentary or my athleticism, she didn't say. She did, though, lower her arm and rest the gun sideways on the table, close to the glass ashtray and on top of a clutch of playing cards, her finger hooked lightly around the trigger.

'Cigarette?' I asked.

I parted the jacket I had on, revealing the lining, and used my gloved fingers to very delicately remove my cigarettes from the inside pocket. I tapped one out, eased it into the corner of my mouth and sparked it with my lighter. I took a swift draw, then offered it across to her.

Her pupils flickered, snagged by the lit end, and she reached out mechanically with her left hand, keeping her right free for the gun.

'Where's he going?' I asked, lighting a cigarette of my own. 'Remi, I mean.'

She shrugged and took an unsteady drag. Her hand was shaking, much like my own. So much for the pair of hardened criminals.

'I'm guessing he's disposing of the body,' I said. 'Strikes me as the type of character who's done this kind of thing before.'

She exhaled fumes through her crinkled lips, fogging her face.

'Where's he taking Borelli? A canal? The lagoon?'

'Yes, I think so.' Her voice sounded distant and feeble, like a whisper from deep inside an underground bunker. I didn't mind. I was just glad to hear it.

'Huh,' I said. 'What if someone sees him?'

She shrugged. 'It is late.'

I nodded as if that made complete sense, then raised my cigarette to my mouth. She was right about the time. The clock behind her said that it was close to three o'clock. I couldn't remember passing anyone on my way to the bookshop. Perhaps Remi would be just as fortunate.

'I'm sorry about your uncle,' I said, sighing smoke towards the ceiling.

She pinched her cigarette between her finger and thumb and made a jerky stabbing motion with the lit end, squinting at me like a darts player lining up a throw. 'You did not kill him,' she said.

'Your uncle?'

She peered hard at me and shook her head, as if clearing her mind of the numbness that had gripped her. 'Borelli. I told you he must die. That he was dangerous.'

'You don't say.' I raised my palm to the back of my skull and tested the spot that was aching the most. My glove came away sticky with blood. The wound felt ragged and worryingly deep. I had visions of brain matter clotting my hair. Sometimes, a writer's imagination can be a real burden.

Graziella hadn't asked me how I'd ended up in her apartment along with Borelli. Perhaps she assumed he'd got the better of me and had marched me here after I'd confessed everything to him. That would make sense, I supposed, but the truth wasn't nearly so kind. We'd given him Graziella's name. We'd told him she'd wanted him dead. And once he'd escaped from my building, he'd come here to claim his revenge, first by killing her uncle and then by waiting for her to return from the casino.

The explanation seemed to fit. True, I could be missing a few steps, but Borelli was no longer around to tell me where I'd gone wrong. My attempt to save his life by kidnapping him had backfired spectacularly, and I couldn't ignore that I was culpable for at least some of what had followed.

'I'm no assassin,' I told Graziella, wiping my glove on my trousers. 'Not like Remi.'

That seemed to amuse her. A half-smile tugged at one corner of her mouth. I waited for more, but she wasn't about to offer an explanation.

'*Okay*,' I said, tamping the ash on the end of my cigarette. 'So I don't know as much as I might like. But how about this? I'd say there's a fair chance Remi comes from Monte Carlo.'

All right, it was a guess, but it was an educated one. The guy spoke French. It looked as if Graziella had teamed up with him against Borelli. They'd worked together to scam the casino of the money in the briefcase down by her feet. It was practically the same routine she'd run with the Count against Alfred's friends. Only this time the target had been different.

Graziella's head pivoted to one side. Her pupils contracted. I had her interest. Now all that remained was to slot all the puzzle pieces into the appropriate holes. Hmm. If only Victoria was with me.

'I know about Monte Carlo,' I told her. 'The bomb. The English couple you killed.'

She bit down on her lip. Hard to tell what it meant, or what I should say next.

'I have photographs. Evidence. You and Borelli.' I gestured at her with my cigarette. 'But you were the one who planted the bomb. The one who switched the case.'

She released her lip from between her teeth. It was flat and bloodless. 'I did not know it,' she replied, her voice scratchy.

'*Please*. Your uncle made the device. I saw his equipment downstairs.'

'I know this now,' she said, 'but not then.'

'You expect me to believe that?'

She twisted her lips in thought and reached out with her hand, taking her fingers for a leisurely stroll along the length of the pistol. Then, without warning, she grunted and snatched up the gun and moved across to the sink, extinguishing her cigarette in a puddle of water on the draining board.

'I did not know there was a bomb.' The skin of her face had pulled taut. It had a shiny, translucent texture. 'I was to take the money. Replace it with another case. That is all.'

'You'll understand why that's difficult for me to believe. You wanted me to kill the Count for you. You had me take a bomb to his home.'

She shook her head. Smiled sadly. 'You were returning it.'

'Care to tell me why?'

Apparently, she did. I could see from the resigned way she lifted her shoulders that she was inclined to share. Hard to know her reasons. It could be she was easing a guilty conscience. Or perhaps the likelihood of Remi killing me when he returned was so high that it simply didn't matter. I chose to tell myself it was the guilt.

'Only last week I heard about the English couple,' she said. 'The way they died.'

'But it happened over a month ago.'

'I did not know it. Why would I? I did not know I had given them a bomb.'

'So how'd you find out?'

'Remi.' She spoke in a fading whisper, as if she feared that by saying his name any louder she risked summoning him from the netherworld. 'He came to Venice. He found me. He had photographs, from the hotel. Like you say.'

'And what's his angle?' She appeared confused. 'What's his connection to this?'

'He worked for the hotel. In Monte Carlo.'

'He did? How?'

'He was in the security team.' She folded her arms across her chest and hugged herself, the pistol tucked down beneath her armpit. 'He told me about the car. The explosion. He said he had a recording from a camera in the hotel – the only copy. It showed me breaking into their room.'

Huh. It sounded as if Remi had known a lot more than

Alfred had been able to find out. And as if he'd decided to use the information for his own purposes.

'So he came to question you?' I asked.

She hesitated. 'At first, yes.'

'But I'm guessing that changed. When you told him about the tournament here in Venice, maybe?'

She nodded, cagily. 'I have worked at the casino for many years.'

'Useful to Borelli, I imagine.'

'I helped him,' she said, grimacing.

'To win?'

'Of course to win.' She threw up a hand. 'But this tournament, it was not easy. There were many good players. One in particular. An Englishman. He was at the final table tonight.'

Ah, yes. I thought I could just about recall the fellow.

'If anyone other than Borelli won,' she went on, 'I was to switch the briefcase.'

'Just like Monte Carlo.'

'*Si*. But when Remi told me about the bomb ...'

She let the information hang in the air between us. My cigarette was finished. I crushed it out on the leg of my chair, smoke weaving around my fingers.

'Let me get this straight,' I said. 'You had a change of heart when Remi told you about the explosives?'

She nodded. 'It is when I stole the case from Borelli.'

'From his vault, to be exact. How'd you know the combination?'

She paused, and I could see from the flickering of her pupils that she was debating whether to continue. It might not change things for me, but I wanted to know all the same. She'd involved me in this mess. People had been killed. I felt like I deserved an explanation.

'The combination,' I pressed. 'All the information about his palazzo. How did you know it?'

She swallowed. 'Because I used it too.'

'Used it?'

'I am like you. A burglar, yes?'

To be fair, she was quite out of my league, but I wasn't about to say as much. I waited for her to continue.

'It is as I tell you, Borelli has many connections. He heard about me.'

'About your abilities?'

She nodded. 'He spoke with my uncle. Told him what he wanted.'

'And what was that exactly?'

'He had many women.'

'Wait – he planned to date you?'

She scowled, as if I was way off. 'These women, they were rich. Their husbands too. They had nice things – jewellery, paintings, money. When he saw them, he told me. The things I stole, we kept in the vault. Soon, he planned to sell them. He needed the money. A palazzo in Venice, it is expensive, *capito*? There is maintenance. Renovation. And the heating! This is why he lives on one floor only.'

I raised my eyebrows. This was news I hadn't expected. Judging from the riches inside the vault, she'd been working with the Count very closely, for longer than I might have liked to believe. But what she said appeared to add up. It also explained her reaction when I'd told her that the bomb had destroyed the contents of the strongroom.

'He paid you?' I asked.

She shook her head.

'What then?'

'My uncle.' She gazed down through the floor and her smile was a broken, sorry thing. 'Borelli owned this building. My uncle's business has been here many years. Since he was a boy. His father opened it before him. But it has been difficult.' I wasn't surprised, given the prices he'd been trying to charge. Graziella glanced up, her eyes swollen and moist. 'Borelli said he would increase the rent many times unless I did as he wanted.'

'The stealing?'

She hitched her shoulders. 'I worked for myself, and for him.'

'And the casino?'

'I work there since before I meet him. It is a cover, yes? Like your writing. But when Borelli found out ...'

'He liked you even better.'

She nodded, then used her arms to lift herself up until she was sitting on the kitchen counter. She kicked at a cupboard door with her heels.

'Go back to the bomb,' I said. 'To Remi. If I understand

what you've been saying, once you found out about what really happened in Monte Carlo, you took the briefcase from the Count so that he couldn't kill anyone else.'

'*Si.*'

'Then why have me return it?'

She exhaled heavily and pressed a hand to her forehead. 'It was Remi's idea,' she said, as if the logic of it now escaped her. 'He told me if I put the bomb back, he could watch Borelli. He already had evidence for what we had done in Monte Carlo. The bomb was more proof.'

'But that would implicate you too. If Remi told the police, you'd be in serious trouble.'

Her face took on a crooked slant – a wry smile. It seemed I'd misread the situation.

'Oh, I get it,' I said. 'You weren't looking to involve the police. You figured you could bribe him. For what? The tournament win?'

'For Remi, yes.' She pouted. 'But for me, the things I stole. In the vault.' She jabbed her thumb towards her chest. 'They were mine.'

'*Okay*,' I said. I imagined a lawyer might query her interpretation, but I could appreciate where she was coming from. 'But why involve me? Why not return the bomb yourself?'

'It was like I told you,' she replied, becoming impatient. 'I did not know if he had seen that the case was missing, but it was a risk. It had to be returned when I was at the casino. So he could not suspect me.'

'You don't think he would have suspected you anyway? That you had a contact involved?'

'But this is why I chose you. I did not know you. There was no way I could.'

Boy, how I wished that were really so.

'But then you did not follow my instructions,' she said, her face darkening, as if she was repulsed by my behaviour. 'The bomb exploded.'

'Yeah, I remember that part.' *Distinctly.*

'And that is when Remi and me decide. Maybe it looks like somebody tried to kill the Count. Maybe he *should* be killed. By the same person.'

'I see. So you get rid of the Count and he can no longer make you steal things for him. Life is better for your uncle. Everything's dandy, in fact. Only, your motives weren't quite so pure as you're making out.' I passed a hand over the playing cards scattered across the table. 'Because you and Remi also fixed the blackjack tournament.'

She paused for a beat. 'Remi is a good player.'

'No. You worked the cards. I watched you do it. Looks like you practised here first. Did you rig his entry fee, too? I don't reckon a guy working hotel security in Monte Carlo has 10,000 euros just lying around. And he doesn't exactly look the type who's used to wearing a tuxedo in the company of high-stakes players.'

'So I find him a suit, at the casino. In lost property, yes? But I pay for him myself. From other work.'

'Other stealing work?'

Her eyes narrowed. 'Remi had to be in the tournament. He had to watch Borelli.'

'Oh, you can dress it like that if you like. But if you ask me, your pal Remi is pulling your strings just as much as Borelli ever did. You ever consider that?'

She glanced to the space on the floor where Borelli had been shot. 'Of course. Just now especially.'

'And? What's the solution?'

A smile seeped across her lips and into her eyes, as if the answer had suddenly presented itself to her. She lifted the pistol and twirled it before her face, like it was the golden key to a cherished future. One outside of Venice, perhaps. With a new name and a new lifestyle funded by half a million in printed notes. And if Remi's fate seemed clear to me now, there could be little doubt about my own. Maybe there was some way she could arrange our bodies and the gun to make it look as if we were involved in the death of her uncle. Perhaps the police would interpret it as a disagreement over the explosives in his flat downstairs. The possibilities seemed endless. And all too real.

Even as the thoughts were running through my mind, I watched her reach for a dishcloth beside the sink and set about carefully wiping the gun down, smearing or removing every latent print. Ready to be pressed into a dead hand, perhaps. Or maybe she'd arrange it so that I looked like the shooter. I still had my gloves on, after all.

I reached clumsily for my cigarette packet and fumbled with the lid. My hands were shaking worse than before, and it made lighting up a regular game of chance. I took a ragged hit. It didn't help.

Would she shoot me before Remi, I wondered? Or would she wait for his return? If she waited, she could catch him while his guard was down. That was how I saw her doing it. Cold and deliberate, leaving no room for error.

It may sound strange, but I've never really viewed myself as a serious criminal. Yes, I've been known to break the law, and granted, I've stolen plenty of things, but I've always operated by a set of rules that are important to me. Hell, I'll admit it, I even take a certain pride in what I do. I don't ransack homes. I don't rob personal mementoes. Wherever possible, I set about my business while a place is empty, because I don't enjoy scaring people. I believe these are signs of what's commonly known as a conscience. My sense of right and wrong might be bent out of shape, but when it comes to major crimes – like murder, say – I know there are lines I simply won't cross. And, perhaps naively, I'd assumed there were other thieves just like me. Not your average chump with a crowbar, maybe, but educated types who adhered to a certain code, who enjoyed the sport in what they did but who rarely stepped beyond the realms of what I would have seen as acceptable.

Now, I was beginning to wonder just how wrong I'd been. Graziella didn't seem like me at all. I sensed that her morals were more flexible than my own, and that she was prepared to adapt to any situation – no matter how extreme – so long as she came out on top. Isn't that how it had been with Borelli? With Remi? Like a darker shadow, she represented something I might have become if only I'd allowed myself to slip that far. I can't say the revelation gave me a great deal of comfort.

My tongue was dry, sticking to the end of my cigarette. When I went to speak again, there was gravel in my throat.

'Just out of interest, what happened to my book?' I asked, exhaling. 'The one you stole? I came here looking for it tonight, but I couldn't find it. Is it in this room? It's the only place I haven't had a chance to search.'

I patted my bleeding skull. Hard to tell if there was more blood than before. I waited for her answer. It wasn't long in coming.

'I put your book with all the things that I stole.'

Oh, crap.

'Please tell me you don't mean Borelli's vault,' I said.

She shrugged, meanwhile wrapping the butt of the gun in the dishcloth.

'But I looked,' I told her. 'Before the bomb went off. I didn't see it.'

She quit binding the gun for a moment, and frowned up at the ceiling, as if dredging her memory. 'It was in a metal box,' she said, in a thoughtful voice. 'I did not want it to be damaged, yes? At the time, I hoped I would return it to you. This was my plan. To keep my word.'

'And now?'

357

'Things change, no? I think so.'

I thought so too. Things had certainly changed for me. Throughout this entire mess, I'd been clinging to the hope that I might somehow get my book back, and now I realised that couldn't possibly happen. It was gone, and I was the fool who'd destroyed it. Just a few hours ago I'd been planning my escape from Venice. Now, I was beginning to fear I might never leave.

Thank heavens for cigarettes. I wasn't sure I could have coped without one, and I thought the same might be true of Graziella.

Freeing a cigarette from the carton, I placed it on the opposite side of the table from me, along with my lighter. 'Your hand is trembling,' I said, struggling to kill the quaver in my voice as I drew on my own cigarette. 'And if you're planning to shoot me, I'd rather you get it right first time. I'd prefer not to know too much about it.'

I watched her weigh my words, along with the pistol. She eyed the cigarette, twisting her lips in contemplation, before considering the smoke escaping my nostrils. Finally, after checking that I wasn't about to pounce from the other side of the table, she stepped across and popped the cigarette into her mouth, gathering up the lighter. The flame sparked and she raised it towards the end of the cigarette, inhaling instinctively. And that's when everything shifted.

Her eyes contracted, then widened with alarm, searching me for an explanation. A whiff of vapour escaped her open mouth. The unlit cigarette fell from her lips, bringing a cascade of white powder with it, as if she'd sucked on a bag of icing sugar. She dropped the gun to the floor and raised her hand to her throat, clawing at her skin and making a dreadful croaking noise. Stumbling backwards, she crashed into a kitchen unit, then groped at the taps above the sink, turning the water on fast and cupping it greedily to her mouth.

Now seemed like an opportune moment to stand up and claim the gun for myself, so I did just that, grinding my cigarette into the floor.

Graziella turned at the sink, her face a plummy colour, a powder-and-water paste running down her chin. She heaved air desperately, her legs giving way from beneath her, her eyes imploring me for some kind of explanation.

'Take it easy,' I said. 'Breathe through your nose. It's a temporary thing. A muscle spasm, triggered by a chemical reaction. The sooner you relax, the quicker it'll pass.'

She didn't look as if she believed me and I don't suppose I could blame her for that. After all, I didn't know if what I'd said was true. The cigarette I'd provided her with was one of the trick gaspers from Victoria's weapons case, a last-second selection I'd made back in Alfred's hotel room. It could be it was deadly, but I seriously doubted it. The rest of Victoria's equipment had been designed to incapacitate an assailant, not kill them, and I'd been willing to bet it was the same with the cigarettes.

Mind you, I had no idea how long the effects would last, and now didn't strike me as the time to hang around and find out.

Seizing her slackened arm, I pressed the gun into her palm, making sure the contact was good and firm. I curled her index finger around the trigger, jerked her arm sideways and pointed it towards the far end of the room. Compressing her finger with the gloved digits of my left hand, I pumped two rounds into the futon cushions, the muzzle flashes throwing everything into bright relief as a plume of feathers rose up towards the ceiling. Then I yanked the gun free and wrapped it in the tea towel, aware of the heat coming through the cloth as she flopped down onto the floor.

Another time, I might have knelt and stroked her hair until the fear passed, offering words of comfort and consolation. Not tonight. I gathered up the briefcase from beneath the table and paced away without a backwards glance, the soggy gargling of her fraught breaths chasing me away along the hall.

THIRTY-NINE

My route back to the Dorsoduro was second nature to me by now, and I seemed to have crossed the Accademia Bridge in no time at all. The Fondamenta Venier was suspended in a dim, pre-dawn stillness. The pavement was empty, the canal water a hard green enamel, and the neighbourhood I'd called home muffled in silence and gauzy fog. I hadn't wanted to go back. I knew it was a risk. But I also knew I might not get another chance.

Borelli was dead, and regardless of whether his body was found or he remained missing, I had to be a prime suspect for the crime. The police could be inside my apartment searching for clues linking me to his abduction, or they might have my building under surveillance. More to the point, it was the first place Graziella and Remi would come looking for me. I knew Graziella could get in without arousing suspicion, and I didn't want to leave anything behind that might help them to track me down.

It wasn't much consolation that I had no need to pick open the lock on the front door. My key still worked just fine, but right at that moment, it didn't feel a great deal more legal than breaking in. I checked behind me as I eased the door open, but I couldn't see anything suspicious. Maybe it would have felt less sinister if I'd spotted someone. Then again, perhaps not.

Switching on the hallway lights wasn't an option I was willing to entertain, and I was familiar enough with the layout to be able to reach the door to my apartment without using my torch. I was a little surprised to find that my apartment was locked, but I wasn't about to complain, especially when I stepped inside and found my holdall and my suitcase just where I'd left them.

I carried the holdall into Victoria's room and emptied it onto the bed, then set about filling it with her things. Most of my belongings could be replaced, but I didn't know what Victoria would consider important, so I did my best to take everything I could before adding the bound pistol as a final item. The gun was my insurance. If Borelli's body was found before I got away, then having Graziella's prints on the murder weapon could prove useful.

As for myself, I was only concerned to make sure that I had a change of clothes, my passports (real and stolen), my burglary tools and my laptop and writing notes. After a final skim through the apartment to make sure there was nothing I'd missed, I slung the holdall over my shoulder, lifted the briefcase in one hand and my suitcase in the other, and made for the exit.

I was at the bottom of the stairs and close to freedom when the spring lock clunked back and the front door swung open into the hall. There was no time to turn and hide, and with my hands full, I didn't have a prayer of shoving my way past who-ever was coming in. So I just stood there, loaded down with my bags, in my heavy overcoat and Borelli's dusty, ill-fitting suit, and watched as Martin stepped into the hallway and switched on the overhead light.

He barely jumped when he saw me, his door keys jangling loosely in his hand. The skin beneath his eyes was swollen and heavily pouched, his normally immaculate hair was tangled and there was a crust of dried saliva at the corners of his mouth. The check-shirt he had on was snarled up beneath his V-neck jumper, one side of his collar raised and the other folded down, as if he'd slept in his clothes.

He cast a forlorn look from my face, to the luggage I was holding, to my stained clothing. Then he leaned to one side and took in the glazing of blood that had trickled down through my hair, behind my ear and along the back of my neck.

'Going somewhere?' he asked.

I gulped by way of response. There wasn't a lot else I could do.

'Time for a drink before you go?' He brushed past me and fitted his key in the door to his apartment. 'I could do with a scotch. Looks like you could, too.'

Even now, I'm not quite sure why I followed him, or why I stood in his living room holding my baggage in such a clueless fashion. Perhaps it was the after-effects of a concussion. From the moment Martin had peered at my head wound, it appeared to be throbbing much worse than before.

He emerged from his kitchen carrying two chipped mugs and a long-necked bottle. It could have been my imagination but he appeared sickly thin. His cheeks were scooped out, as if he hadn't eaten a square meal in days.

'Put your things down,' he said. 'And help me with this, will you?'

I looked around me for a moment, then dumped my bags beside an overstuffed armchair and clutched the mugs as he poured two generous measures.

'Your health,' he told me, raising his drink.

The spirit was about as welcome as the blow I'd taken to the back of my head. The last thing I needed was for my thinking to become even more muddled. I hesitated, then knocked it back. The burning at the back of my throat made me croak – an ill-timed reminder of Graziella.

'Ah, I needed that,' Martin said, smacking his gummy lips. 'Been an eventful night.'

I wiped my hand across my mouth, wondering what on earth I could say. I wanted more than anything to get out of there, to leave the house and the area as soon as possible. I settled for contemplating the depths of my mug instead.

'Just got back from the hospital,' Martin told me. 'Three hours of waiting. A woman Antea's age – it's just not civilised, is it?'

My head snapped up. 'Is she okay?'

'In a fashion.' He pursed his lips. 'She's in pain, of course. That's to be expected. It's the healing process that concerns me. Venice is a damn inconvenient city for a lower limb fracture. And the collarbone can be tricky.' His eyes bored into me. 'Washing and dressing oneself rather goes out the window, wouldn't you say?'

'I don't understand,' I said, shaking my head. 'How did Antea get hurt?'

He snorted. 'You truly care?'

'Of course.'

'Wouldn't rather run than hear it?'

Well, being honest, I was quite keen to take my exit. But right now didn't seem like the time to say as much.

'Martin, I know this doesn't look good.' I nudged my bags with my foot. 'And the truth is, I can't really explain my situation just now. But one thing I never intended was for you or Antea to come to any harm.'

Another snort. 'You realise Antea's very fond of you?'

No, that wasn't something I'd devoted too much time to thinking about before now. It seemed best not to faint at the revelation.

'Never had a child,' he grunted. 'Not the man for it, see? Wasn't a decision that rested easily with Antea.' His voice trailed off as he glanced away to the corner of the ceiling. It took him a moment to compose himself. 'Point is,' he said, clearing his throat, 'if it was up to me I'd have called the police while I was in the kitchen fetching the scotch.'

Christ. 'You didn't, did you?'

He shook his head. 'Didn't tell them much at the hospital, either. Antea's idea. Made me promise. Damn silly if you ask me.'

I watched Martin unscrew the bottle of scotch and splash more liquid into our mugs. He tossed his back as if he was planning to gargle mouthwash. I nursed mine, swilling the liquid around.

'If you don't mind my asking, Martin, what exactly *didn't* you tell the police?'

He swallowed, tapping a nail on the side of his mug. 'Well, let's see,' he said, his voice a touch hoarse. 'I *didn't* say we heard a man yelling in distress over my recording of Brahms' Waltz in A Flat – I simply mentioned that we'd heard a noise from what we knew to be an empty apartment, and that Antea had insisted that I go upstairs to investigate while she called the police. I *didn't* say how I found that the man doing the screaming was handcuffed and bound in his underwear, and that I recognised him to be Count Frederico Borelli. I *didn't* explain that when I released him with a set of keys I found, he yelled a whole lot of nonsense about my having kidnapped him, or that during our argument he kicked at a bag on the floor, from which a gun fell out – a gun that he then held on me as he dressed in clothes that obviously didn't belong to him.'

He exhaled wearily and gazed down at his shoes until his long grey fringe covered his eyes, then shook his head in apparent wonder at his own behaviour. 'I *did* say that I came across a strange man in the upstairs corridor, and that upon seeing me, the fellow ran, barging his way past my poor wife as she came upstairs with such force that she fell and fractured her ankle and her collarbone. I *did* say that I hadn't got a good look at him, but that I thought it likely that he was a burglar. Oh, and I *didn't* say how, as I held my wife's hand while we waited for the emergency services to arrive, she made me agree against my better judgement to hide the salient facts from the police simply because of her damn maternal instincts and some misplaced faith in our reprobate tenant – who, I might add, had returned to his apartment late at night just a few days previously, with a set of injuries entirely consistent with those I might expect to see sustained during an explosion, of the type that had occurred at Palazzo Borelli at broadly the same time.'

I winced. 'Martin, I don't know what to say.'

'Well, then.' He made a growling noise deep in his throat and avoided my eyes. Apparently he didn't know what to say, either.

'Do you mind my asking if the police accepted your version of events?'

'Didn't have any reason to doubt it,' he mumbled. 'And once they heard it was a burglary ...' He shrugged. 'Hardly exerted themselves investigating the matter.'

I released a long breath. 'I can't tell you how grateful I am. Really. I don't know how I can ever repay you.'

But right then, just as I said those very words, it occurred to me that perhaps I did. Kneeling on the floor, I rested the briefcase on my thigh and set about working the dials, feeling for the telltale stiffness of the correct combination. I had it in under a minute, and was poised to open the lid when a flicker of doubt took hold of me.

Could there have been a switch? Had I been duped?

No, I didn't think so, but just to be certain I held up a finger and hurried outside to the dark and misted canal bank before popping the clasps. My heart switched to standby and I turned my face away as I raised the lid. There was no beeping noise and no sudden burst of flames. I looked down and cracked my eyes open.

Row after row of neatly stacked banknotes were laid out before me. Lilac in colour, with the number 500 imprinted on them in deep purple, they were held together with neat paper bands bearing the legend: *Casinò di Venezia*. I grabbed a hand-ful, closed the briefcase and made my way back to Martin.

He nodded his chin at a console unit as I entered his living room. My mug of scotch had been moved there. Beside it was a small bottle made of brown tinted glass and a cardboard carton.

'Antiseptic solution and a box of butterfly stitches,' he told me. 'Have your ladyfriend clear you up. You may still need sutures in a day or two, but you don't want an infection in the meantime.'

I tried passing the money to him, but his hands remained tucked beneath his armpits, his face stern. Feeling a burn creep-ing into my cheeks, I hooked the strap of my holdall over my shoulder and lifted my suitcase and the briefcase from the floor.

Then I stepped awkwardly across the room and traded the first-aid equipment for the bank notes.

'I owe you rent, anyway,' I said. 'In lieu of notice. And it sounds as if Antea may need some care. Hopefully this can go towards paying for it. Tell her I'm sorry, will you? And tell her I appreciate everything she's done for me – from the moment I arrived until now. All of it.'

He tossed back his head, clearing his fringe from his piercing eyes. I looked down sheepishly and made for the door, then turned as I bundled my way through.

'Listen,' I told him, 'for what it's worth, I'm really not the monster you might take me for.'

He glowered back, jaw clenched. 'Whatever it is you need to tell yourself when you look in the mirror, young man, is no concern of mine.'

FORTY

I checked myself into a one-star hotel in Cannaregio, close to the train station. The place rated itself too highly. My single bed sagged in the middle, the sheets were stiffened with age and the lock on the door to my room wasn't worth the name. Still, I didn't believe it was somewhere Graziella and Remi would be inclined to look for me, and even if they did, I'd taken the precaution of registering with one of my stolen passports. I needed rest, and plenty of it, and after tucking the attaché briefcase under my arm, I eased my head down against the lumpy pillow and fell into a deep, zombie sleep.

Hours later, feeling groggy and smelling worse, I stumbled outside in my borrowed tux as far as a shabby internet café. Once I had the information I needed, I called Victoria on her mobile to tell her my plan and then I frequented a couple of tourist outlets until I'd acquired a bottle of water, a pizza of questionable origin and a red Ferrari baseball cap to take back to my foul-smelling suite.

Time dragged. After I'd amused myself by watching the bugs crawling across the ceiling of my room, and disgusted myself by consuming two-thirds of the soggy pizza, I popped the clasps on the briefcase and counted the cash inside. I'd given Martin more than I'd realised – fifty thousand euros, to be exact – but it still left me with plenty. Four hundred and fifty thousand euros was far from shabby, I admit, though I'd gladly have traded it for the chance to go back to the life I'd been leading before Graziella showed up.

I smoked the last of my cigarettes and waited until evening before sampling the delights of the communal bathroom, where I showered beneath a dribble of cold water without soap or shampoo. There was no towel to dry myself on, so I turned the tux inside out and used that instead. Then I climbed into clean clothes, eased my new baseball hat on over the weeping sore at the back of my head, gathered together my belongings and headed out into the grey winter light.

The concrete steps outside the Santa Lucia station were clogged with backpackers and day trippers. I weaved between them, feeling conspicuous. The shiny metal briefcase didn't exactly complement the blue sweatshirt and jeans, worn baseball shoes and bright-red Ferrari hat I had on, and I guess if I'd been sporting a three-piece suit, I might have blended in a little better. Unfortunately, there wasn't much I could do about that, and so I settled for keeping my head down and using the peak of the cap to cover my eyes. True, it risked making me appear even more suspicious, but the alternative was probably worse.

An electronic departure board was suspended high above the station concourse and I craned my neck to scan it. I could smell diesel fumes and brake dust, mingled with the aromas of a fast-food buffet. My train was the next to depart, in less than five minutes, and I swerved around a young couple with Canadian flags embroidered on their rucksacks and broke into a lurching shuffle.

The Stendhal – destination Padua, Vicenza, Verona, Brescia and Paris – was made up of a long chain of white-on-blue carriages, some of them laid out with sleeping compartments and others with rows of reclining seats. I was nearing the last of the sleepers and beginning to fear the worst when I finally spied Alfred and Victoria watching for me from a half-open window.

Checking over my shoulder, it looked as if I was in the clear. A man in a green jumpsuit was emptying bags of rubbish into a litter cart and a woman with a cashmere shawl and sunglasses was carrying a Chihuahua towards the next carriage along. Up ahead, a stringy guard in a blue Trenitalia uniform waved me aboard and I clambered up the steps and bundled inside our three-bed compartment to be greeted by a crushing hug.

'Steady, Vic.' I eased her away, choosing to ignore the way her eyes had misted over. It seemed she'd invested in a new outfit. Gone was the green evening dress, replaced by a pair of tan cotton trousers and a pink sweater over a lemon blouse.

'Were you followed?' she asked.

'Of course not,' I told her. 'There's nothing to worry about.'

I threw my luggage onto the bench beside Alfred, then lifted the briefcase for them both to see.

'My goodness,' Alfred said. 'Is that what I think it is?' He found his feet in a hurry and slapped me hard on the back, the brass buttons rattling on his navy-blue blazer. 'How on earth did you get it?'

'Long story,' I told him. 'But take a seat. It'd be a relief to share it.'

We were rolling out of Padua a half-hour later, passing grimy freight carriages, a double-decker commuter train and an unlit football stadium, when I completed my account. An attendant had interrupted us shortly after we'd left Venice to claim our passports and find out which dinner sitting we wished to attend. Other than that, we'd enjoyed complete privacy by keeping the door to our compartment closed and trusting the rumble of wheels on track to mask anything an eavesdropper might hear.

Part-way through my story, Victoria had donned a pair of my plastic disposable gloves and had taken to kneeling on the bench seat beside me while she tended to the gash on the back of my head. She'd used cotton pads from her make-up bag to apply the antiseptic solution Martin had given me, then done her best to stick me back together with the butterfly plasters. She didn't seem entirely satisfied with her work, but I'd already had close to my fill of being prodded and jabbed when the carriage rocked unexpectedly and she damn near tickled my frontal lobe.

'Bloody hell, Vic.' I ducked away and pressed my palm to where it hurt. 'That's it, you're finished.'

'But I think you may need a few more stitches.'

'I'd rather bleed. Now, sit.'

She made a huffing noise and arranged her lips into a sulky pout, then collapsed next to me and peeled off her gloves. 'It's not easy, you know.'

I did know. Believe me. But after carefully slipping my baseball cap back onto my head, I reached across and gave her hand a squeeze.

'You're an angel.'

'And you're a moron.' She snatched her hand free, stuffing the used gloves into the metal litterbin fitted beneath our compartment window. 'I can't believe you didn't get the hell away from that bookshop when you found Graziella's uncle had been shot.'

'I thought he'd done it to himself, Vic.'

'Well, you should have checked for the gun.'

I was about to respond when a high-speed train flew by in the opposite direction, sucking us towards it and then blowing us aside. A two-tone horn blared out, too late to offer any kind of warning, and I waited for the noise and the juddering to subside before continuing.

'Point taken,' I said. 'But hindsight is a wonderful thing.'

'And you definitely should have left when you saw the bomb-making equipment.'

I glanced across at Alfred for help. He seemed delighted to provide it.

'Darling, why don't we just focus on the positives, hmm? I'd say it's all worked out rather well, wouldn't you?'

'Charlie could have been killed, Dad.'

'Yes, but he wasn't. That rat Borelli was. And I can't think of a more fitting way for him to go. Shot by a fellow who only tracked him down because of what he did to poor John and Eunice in Monte Carlo.'

'I'm not sure Remi's motives were quite that noble, Dad. And anyway, wouldn't you have preferred to see Borelli stand trial for what he did?'

Alfred smoothed his fingers across the plush fabric of his seat. 'Darling, I think the likelihood of that happening was rather slim, don't you? And if you canvassed the members of my team, your mother included, I'd wager they'd be quite satisfied with his fate.'

'And we'll share the money,' I put in. 'A three-way split. Not so bad, considering.'

'Considering what?' Victoria snapped. 'Has it occurred to you that the police might still link you to the Count's death?'

'I don't see how. Martin and Antea won't say anything.

And Graziella and Remi are hardly going to want to advertise their involvement in all this.'

'You're assuming Remi is still alive. Didn't you say that Graziella was planning to kill him?'

There was a sudden clatter and *whoosh* as we plunged into a tunnel. The vacuum was fierce, popping my ears, and it wasn't until we emerged from the other side that I was able to continue.

'It did seem to be on the cards at the time,' I admitted. 'Though it's possible I jumped to the wrong conclusion.'

'Doesn't that bother you?'

'Not unduly. And I'm not sure why it should concern you, either. He had evidence linking Borelli and Graziella to the murder of your father's friends, but he chose to use it for his own profit. Hardly the behaviour of a saint.' I paused, and absorbed the look of horror on Victoria's face. 'But, if you care for my opinion, I don't think Graziella was in a fit state to kill anyone when I left. Your trick cigarettes made sure of that, not to mention that I'd swiped her gun. And besides, Remi has already proved himself adept at tracking people down. I imagine she could find that appealing.'

'You mean they might come after you?'

'They might.' I nodded, studiously avoiding my own reflection in the darkened glass of our carriage window. 'But they'd have to find me first. And I'm really not sure they'll bother. For all they know, I might have spent the money by the time they catch up with me. And what's to prevent me from going to the police? True, none of this paints me in an appealing light, but it'd be an awful lot worse for them.'

'You really believe they'll just let it go?'

'I didn't see them at the train station, did you?'

She thumped a fist into her thigh. 'But I'm worried, Charlie.'

'Don't be. It's not good for your blood pressure. Although, if it makes you feel any brighter, I do have one more trick up my sleeve.'

Actually, it wasn't up my sleeve – it was inside the rear pocket of my jeans. I plucked the item free and held it between my forefinger and thumb for Victoria to see.

'Holy cow! That's my data recorder.'

'It is indeed.' I clicked the *rewind* button, followed by *pause* and *play*. Graziella's voice could be heard. It was a little tinny, I confess, but her words were audible all the same. I thumbed the *stop* button. 'I had it with me when I returned to the bookbinding shop,' I explained. 'The transmitter in the lid of your pepper spray was powerful enough to record everything Graziella said. Every incriminating word.'

Victoria reached out for the recorder and I pressed it into her hands before inclining my head towards Alfred and patting him on the knee. 'Hungry?' I asked.

'Ravenous,' he replied.

The meal was surprisingly good. The dining car was a light, airy space, cocooned against the shimmering blackness outside our window. We indulged ourselves with a three-course meal, followed by a selection of cheeses, all of it accompanied by a passable white wine from the Veneto region. True, it wasn't quite the Orient Express, but I could feel the tension and stresses of the past few days begin to fade away as the train rattled onwards through the low-lying countryside beyond Vicenza, passing the occasional glow of a minor station and tracking the odd stretch of motorway.

It was while I was letting some of the cheese settle in my belly and watching the hypnotic rise and dip of the electricity cables running alongside us that Alfred reclined in the chair opposite me, laced his hands behind his head and asked, through an indulgent yawn, where I planned to go next.

'I'm not altogether sure,' I told him, and to be honest, I wasn't very comforted by my answer. Yes, I'm a wandering soul, but I usually like to have some idea of where I intend to wander *to*. 'I won't stay in Paris for long – the consequence of a promise I made some years ago – but I'd like to see Pierre and ask his advice on what to do with my share of the money. You'll know yourself how difficult it can be to open a bank account with cash these days, but he's likely to have some suggestions. And after that, who knows?'

'Well, have you considered Asia? My team could use a man like you.'

I smiled. 'I'm flattered, Alfred, but I suspect my destination lies elsewhere.'

Victoria was sitting next to me with an earphone in her ear, connected by a wire to the data recorder. I plucked the earbud free, keen to have her complete attention.

'I hope you'll forgive me for this, Vic, but I also want to see if Pierre has any work for me. I gave clean living a shot, but I don't think I'm cut out to be just a writer. I miss my other life too much. This past week has been hellish, no question, but I can't pretend there weren't times when it felt good to be out on the scam again. It's reprehensible, I know, but it's who I am.'

'Oh, relax,' she said, winding her earphones around the recorder and then reaching for her wine. 'I was telling Dad the same thing last night.'

'You were?'

She rolled her eyes. 'I know you better than you think, Charlie. And to be perfectly honest, I happen to believe it's a good idea.'

'You do?' I placed my palm against her forehead. 'Are you feeling okay? Got a temperature at all?'

'I'm no idiot, Charlie.' She batted my hand away. 'Any fool could see how twitchy you've been. And it was quite obvious from your manuscript how much you've missed it. If you ask me, that's why your book was so over the top.'

'Oh.'

'Well, don't give me that hang-dog look. You already had some idea how I felt about the script.'

'That bad, huh?'

'Depends.' She rested her wine glass on the table and twisted it by the stem. 'I have a plan that might work.'

'Uh-oh. Major rewrite alert.'

I glanced across at Alfred. He flashed his dentures at me as he helped himself to a triangle of soft cheese. 'Victoria told me her idea last night,' he said, popping the cheese into his mouth. 'I think it's rather good.'

'It would have to be,' I told him, 'seeing as I don't have my copy of *The Maltese Falcon* to rely on any more.'

'It's really quite simple,' Victoria said, ignoring my woe-is-me routine. 'It just took me a little while to work out. The fact is, you haven't written a Michael Faulks novel. You may *think* you have, but it's far too different – the change from the rest of the series would be too marked. But I think you can keep the core of your book, with the odd tweak here and there, provided you make one major change.'

'And what's that?'

'Alter your lead character.' She reached up and patted my cheek. 'Ditch Faulks and replace him with a glamorous female cat burglar.'

'You're kidding.'

'Not remotely.' She shook her head, as if to prove it to me. 'The book becomes a stand-alone, maybe even the start of a new series. Obviously you'll need to come up with a better name for her than Graziella, but otherwise, I'd say you have a pretty good model to base your character on, wouldn't you?'

I pursed my lips, then raised my wine glass to them, tasting around the idea. 'You think it could work?'

'I already made some notes with Dad last night.' She bundled up her napkin and placed it on the tabletop. 'Want me to fetch them?'

'Hell,' I said, 'might as well, I suppose.'

Victoria squirmed out of our seating booth and moved away down the carriage towards the sliding automatic door. I signalled our waiter and ordered three espressos. There was a judder and hiss as the brakes engaged, slowing us for our arrival into Verona. Outside our window, a lighted Agip petrol station eased by, followed by a concrete water tower and a frothing river.

'You know,' Alfred said, 'my daughter is very selective with her affections.'

I'd turned to face him before I'd quite heard what he'd said. I was beginning to think that may have been a mistake.

'Oh don't look so horrified,' he told me. 'I'm not about to give you some heavy-handed warning, Charlie. I like you. My point is, so does Victoria. She might not say anything directly, but I could tell from how agitated she became last night.' He paused, and studied me wolfishly. 'Don't tell me you didn't know.'

I made like a goldfish, opening and closing my mouth.

'Not one to discuss affairs of the heart with an old-timer like me, eh? Well, fair enough. Just thought you should be aware of what you're dealing with.' He cleared his throat, then spoke in a hasty whisper. 'Be awfully decent if you could do your best not to break her heart.' He glanced up and fixed a blazing smile onto his face. 'Sugar Plum, you're back.'

He was right. *Sugar Plum* was approaching our table, and from her tight expression, I was afraid she'd overheard her father. She looked every bit as panicked as I felt. I searched her eyes for some indication of whether there was any truth to what Alfred had said. But there was nothing there for me. At least, nothing I could decipher. I wasn't sure how I felt about that.

'Something's happened,' she said, then stumbled and gripped the table as the train came to a screeching halt. 'Someone's been in our compartment. Look, I found this.' She lifted a brown paper package for me to see. My name had been printed on the package with a magic marker. As she spoke, I could hear a series of train doors being thrown back with a thud. 'And the briefcase is gone,' she added.

'*What?*'

I heaved myself out from beneath the table, shoving Victoria aside and racing to the end of the dining car. The corridor ahead of me was blocked by passengers struggling aboard with heavy luggage.

'*Scusi!*' I waded in, forcing my way through. '*Scusi, per favore!*' My bad Italian and bad manners weren't endearing me to anyone. I didn't care. I muscled my way past a series of couchette compartments, then tackled a gaggle of passengers at the other end. But when I reached our compartment, I discovered that Victoria was right.

The briefcase was no longer on the metal rack above the door beside my holdall, and it hadn't been moved to the rack above the window. The bench seats had been converted into bunks, but there were only blankets and pillows on top of them, and no sign of the briefcase underneath.

'Charlie, look.' Victoria was standing in the doorway. She'd ripped open the brown paper of the package and I could glimpse bright yellow beneath. She plucked the object from its wrapping and passed it to me, and the moment I saw it, I had an undeniable urge to kiss her again. It might have been charred and discoloured, half the jacket burned away and the bottom edge of the pages reduced to little more than ash, but it was unquestionably mine. *The Maltese Falcon*, a first edition, signed by one Dashiell Hammett. No longer in mint condition – far from it, in fact – but very possibly still capable of weaving its particular magic from above my writing desk.

I heard the slamming of doors, the squeal of a conductor's whistle and the clunk of released brakes. I was nudged sideways by the lurch of sudden movement. The carriage shunted forwards and I rushed to the window, flattening my palms against the glass.

We slid by a lighted waiting room, an Armani advertising hoarding, a soft-drink vending machine. We glided past a station clock and a yellow departure timetable.

Then I finally saw them. Graziella was standing beneath the blue platform number in her platinum blonde wig, clutching the attaché briefcase in front of her waist. Remi was loitering beside her, leaning his weight on his good leg, hands deep inside the pockets of his camel-hair coat, the brim of his fedora slashing his eyes.

I didn't watch him for long. Graziella was the one who had my attention. I thought perhaps she'd chosen the blonde wig for some kind of symmetry. Then she did something that made me feel sure of it. Lifting one hand, she raised a gloved finger to her pursed lips and winked. Unwittingly, my palm against the glass became a wordless farewell as the train drifted on, leaving Graziella to slide smoothly out of my life along the vanishing platform.

I banged my forehead against the window and marvelled at the book in my hand, telling myself it really wasn't such a shabby deal. And perhaps, on balance, it wasn't such a terrible ending, either. Any worthwhile mystery novel needs a twist in the tale, and no doubt, if it were up to me, I'd say this just about cut it.

Victoria, though, likes to finesse things, as you know. And if I was to allow her to contribute a final paragraph, I dare say she'd let you into a little secret about the briefcase Graziella was holding so primly. She might, for instance, tell you that I have a tendency to prepare for certain eventualities. She could just speculate that during my time in that grubby backstreet hotel, I'd had a sneaking suspicion that I hadn't seen the last of my Venetian *bella donna*. She might even go so far as to say that before leaving for the station, I took the liberty of transferring all but a single bundle of notes from the briefcase to my holdall, replacing the bulk of the cash with a ruined tuxedo, an unwanted pistol and the sorry bedding from my room. But then, what do I know? I'm just the author.

ACKNOWLEDGEMENTS

Grateful thanks to Lucy Hanington, Tom Jackson, Patrizia Apollonio and covert operative Katrina Hands; to Mum, Dad, and my sister, Allison; to Maxine Hitchcock, Emma Lowth, Hope Dellon, Laura Bourgeois and all at Simon and Schuster and St Martin's Press; and to Vivien Green, Gaia Banks and the team at Sheil Land Associates. Special thanks, as always, to my wife, Jo.

Chris Ewan
The Good Thief's Guide to Vegas

Charlie Howard – mystery writer and incorrigible
thief – is in for a tough vacation in Las Vegas.
Losing heavily at poker is one thing, but to find his
literary agent, Victoria, being charmed by the
Fifty-Fifty casino resort's star magician,
Josh Masters, is another thing entirely.

Still, Charlie's not one to hold a grudge, least of all
when he could be holding Masters' wallet. With access
to the magician's deluxe suite now tantalizingly at hand,
a spot of burglary seems to be in order and Charlie's
only too happy to oblige. Problem is, everything's
bigger in Sin City – including the fall-out from petty
crimes – and it isn't long before Charlie and Victoria
find themselves threatened with a one-way trip into the
Nevada desert unless they can conjure up a small
fortune in twenty-four hours.

For Charlie, there's only one viable course of action:
break into as many hotel rooms as he can, steal as much
as possible, and just hope that Victoria can summon
Lady Luck to the gaming table of her choice.

Mind you, it would all be a lot easier if Charlie hadn't
stumbled upon a dead woman, and if Josh Masters
hadn't vanished in the middle of his act . . .

ISBN 978-1-84739-956-4

Chris Ewan
The Good Thief's Guide to Paris

Flush with the success of his Paris book reading (not to mention a few glasses of French wine), Charlie Howard – mystery writer and professional thief – agrees to show a novice how to break into an apartment on the Marais. Twenty-four hours later, Charlie's fence hires him to steal an ordinary-looking oil painting – from the same address.

Mere coincidence? Charlie reckons there's no harm in finding out – until a dead body shows up in his living room.

Nobody ever said being a burglar was easy but things are getting way out of control. And that's before Charlie's agent, Victoria, finally decides they should meet face to face . . .

ISBN 978-1-84739-359-3

Chris Ewan
The Good Thief's Guide
to Amsterdam

In Amsterdam working on his latest novel,
Charlie is approached by a mysterious American
who asks him to steal two apparently worthless monkey
figurines from two separate addresses on the same
night. At first he says no. Then he changes his mind.
Only later, kidnapped and bound to a chair, the
American very dead, and a spell in police custody
behind him, does Charlie begin to realise how
costly a mistake he might have made.

The police think he killed the American.
Others think he knows the whereabouts of the
elusive third monkey. But for Charlie only three
things matter. Can he clear his name? Can he
get away with the haul of a lifetime? And can he
solve the gaping plot-hole in his latest novel?

'Intelligent and witty, with a lightness of
tone more P. G. Wodehouse than James Ellroy'
Sydney Morning Herald

ISBN 978-1-84739-127-8

Megan Abbott
Queenpin

Her legs were the legs of a 20-year-old
Vegas showgirl, a hundred feet long and with
just enough curve and give and promise ... Two
decades her junior, my skinny matchsticks
were no competition. She was legend.

A young woman hired to keep the books at
a down-at-heel nightclub is taken under the wing
of the infamous Gloria Denton, a mob luminary who
reigned during the Golden Era of Bugsy Siegel and
Lucky Luciano. The moll to end all molls, Gloria is
notoriously cunning and ruthless. She shows her
eager young protégée the ropes, ushering her into a
glittering whirl of late-night casinos, racetracks,
betting parlours, inside heists and big, big
money. Suddenly, the world is at her fee –
as long as she doesn't take any chances,
like falling for the wrong guy.

It all falls to pieces with a few turns of the
roulette wheel, as both mentor and protégée
scramble to stay one step ahead of their
bosses and each other.

ISBN: 978-1-84739-440-8

Megan Abbott
Bury Me Deep

In October 1931, a station agent found two large trunks abandoned in L.A.'s Union Station. What he found inside ignited one of the most scandalous tabloid sensations of the decade.

Inspired by this notorious true crime, *Bury Me Deep* is the story of Marion Seeley, a young woman abandoned in Phoenix by her husband. At the medical clinic where she finds a job, Marion becomes fast friends with Louise, a vivacious nurse, and her roommate, Ginny. Before long, the demure Marion is swept up in the exuberant life of the girls, who supplement their scant income by entertaining the town's most powerful men with wild parties. At one of these events, Marion meets – and falls hard for – the charming Joe Lanigan, a local rogue and politician on the rise, whose ties to all three women bring events to a dramatic and deadly collision.

A story born of Depression-era desperation and Jazz Age nostalgia, *Bury Me Deep*-with its hothouse of jealousy, illicit sex, and shifting loyalties-is a timeless portrait of the dark side of desire.

ISBN: 978-1-84739-633-4

These titles are all available from your local bookshop
or can be ordered direct from the publisher.

978-1-84739-956-4	The Good Thief's Guide to Vegas	£7.99
978-1-84739-359-3	The Good Thief's Guide to Paris	£6.99
978-1-84739-127-8	The Good Thief's Guide to Amsterdam	£6.99
978-1-84739-440-8	Queenpin	£6.99
978-1-84739-633-4	Bury Me Deep	£6.99
978-1-84739-345-6	The Song Is You	£6.99